Thank You
Tyler
&
Best Wishes
[signature] 2019

Shaman
THE DAWN'S PEOPLE

VR MCCOY

VANDABRY-LIT

Copyright

This work is copy written and licensed
under VanDaBry Entertainment Media LLC 2018

7637 Northington Court
Gainesville, Va. 20155
USA

Published by
VanDaBry Lit, LLC
VanDaBry.com

Edited by
Jacqueline Trescott
trescottj@gmail.com

Cover Art by
The Cover Collection
http://www.thecovercollection.com

Creative Advisor
Evander Banks
Ebanks0530@yahoo.com

Print ISBN: 978-1-54393-112-9

TABLE OF CONTENTS

PROLOGUE   IX

CHAPTER ONE
THE SPIRIT WARRIOR   1

CHAPTER TWO
THE TSILA   15

CHAPTER THREE
CALL OF DUTY   23

CHAPTER FOUR
THE SOKOKI TRIBAL COUNCIL/ UNWANTED GUESTS   47

CHAPTER FIVE
THE BLACK FOREST   72

CHAPTER SIX
CHIBAISKWEDA   79

CHAPTER SEVEN
SCORCHED EARTH   97

CHAPTER EIGHT
MIDEWIWIN   115

CHAPTER NINE
THE LINE-UP   131

CHAPTER TEN
PADOGIYIK   138

CHAPTER ELEVEN
MSKAGWEDEMOOS   157

CHAPTER TWELVE
BLACK ROSES   176

CHAPTER THIRTEEN
THE VALKYRIES   186

CHAPTER FOURTEEN
POSSESSION   193

CHAPTER FIFTEEN
GICI AWAS (THE BEAST)   207

CHAPTER SIXTEEN
NIXKAMICH   226

CHAPTER SEVENTEEN
THE MALSUM   241

CHAPTER EIGHTEEN
THE HANGING TREE   254

CHAPTER NINETEEN
THE RAVEN MOCKER   269

CHAPTER TWENTY
THE AZTEC TEMPLE   292

ACKNOWLEDGEMENTS   317

DEDICATION   319

NOTE FROM THE AUTHOR   320

PROLOGUE

It was a quiet night in this small New England town. The night sky was filled with millions of stars and the moon was bright. They appeared so close that you could pick them right out of the sky. It seemed like you were on top of the world in New England or close to it. There was 4 inches of snow on the ground and it had just begun to snow again. This was nothing unusual for New England. In fact, they welcomed the snow. The ski season brought in more tourism revenue than any other industry in New England which had more ski resorts in the United States followed by its neighboring states of New York and Pennsylvania. This was just another ordinary night. Most of the townies were asleep and awaiting another day to begin. There was no activity out on the streets as the snow continued to fall.

Tom Hancock, the town's mayor, had worked later than he wanted in his home office. The office used to be a den that they converted several years ago, while he was running for mayor. It hadn't started out to be the office, but unsuspectingly became the harbor for his campaign. It was the resting place of campaign posters, buttons, memorabilia, speeches, newspapers and whatever else contributed to the campaign. The room was involuntarily elected due to its availability and location in the house. Also, the garage was already swamped with vehicles and other assorted storage items.

Mayor Hancock was ready to call it a night. He put down his pen, took off his glasses, and rubbed his weary blood shot eyes while yawning. He looked at the picture of his family on his desk and smiled. He was ready to join his wife in the upstairs bedroom, but first he had to do what most fathers do before retiring. It was time for him to act as a sentry and check the security of the house. He checked the alarm system first, and then the doors and windows on the first floor. He looked outside the living room window which faced the front of the house to check the perimeter. He discovered the snow falling once again.

After conducting his check of the first floor he went upstairs and checked in on his two school age children, Marcy and Charles. Their ages were eight and ten, Marcy being the oldest. He checked the windows in their rooms, and then kissed them. He ruminates in the hallway for a second or two. He can't believe how lucky he is or what he had to do to get this far. He turns off the light in the hallway, and tells himself it was worth it. Now he could rest knowing that all was safe and secure, but this was far from an ordinary night in this small New England town. There was something maleficent lurking in the streets on this presumably quiet night. It moved quickly and quietly throughout the town without opposition, like a thief in the night, not a peep or sound.

When morning came, you could hear the frightening screams echoing throughout the small town, as they woke; one house after another, to a horrific discovery. Distraught and terrified parents emptied into the snow-covered streets crying, and clueless, as to what had occurred. Some of them lay flat out upon the snow, some of them on their knees, weeping in their pajamas, housecoats and robes, while others held each other in anguish and disbelief. The emergency telephones lines at the sheriff's office were inundated with calls about the inexplicable phenomena that occurred overnight. It was like one of the plagues of Egypt; their children had disappeared in one single night without a trace.

None of the houses showed signs of a breaking and entering. Their houses were locked shut and secured. There were no footsteps in the snow-covered ground outside the homes or fingerprints to be found anywhere inside or around the house. It is as if they all vanished.

For the next weeks to months the entire country converged on the small town of Swanton, Vermont. Federal Investigators from multifarious agencies under the umbrella of homeland security, and media from all over the world came to witness, report and investigate the mysterious occurrence.

There were various rumors behind the actual cause of the event. Some said that the parents conspired and killed the children, others said it was a sacrificial ritual, and then there were the rumors of alien abductions. Another popular rumor was that it was a biblical occurrence leading to the apocalypse. Everyone with an opinion and avarice for publicity homed in on the tragedy; from politicians to psychologists, end of the world fanatics to conspiracy theorists, but no one knew for sure or had a clue.

CHAPTER ONE

THE SPIRIT WARRIOR

The gut-shattering scent of ammonia from days old urine, laced with fecal matter and vomit consumed the air of the teen aged decorated room that Jamila once occupied in her parent's home. They never redecorated it when she left home for college, like most nesters with only one child. It was a reminder of the days of past, spent with their child, who was now a woman. It was also left that way to welcome her back, if she ever needed to come back home or returned for visits, which she often did, but they never expected her to return to them in this manner.

The room was dark with the windows shut and the curtains drawn. Several crucifixes were turned upside down on the walls of her room, which were splattered with human waste; fluids and debris. It looked like someone finally reached the conclusion that whatever was wrong with Jamila wasn't psychological or physical. Perhaps a priest visited at one point, but wasn't up for the challenge. Catholic priests are very capable of exorcising demons, in fact they are some of the most renowned exorcist in the world, but even they must be trained in this skill set.

Askuwheteau and I were always the last-ditch effort, the last ray of hope, when all else failed! Unfortunately for the host or possessed because most times we can save them, if we get to them early enough.

When you exorcise a demon, you pull it from out of a host, but it still lives on to infect or possess another. Experienced exorcist can send them back to Hell, but still they live on. I go inside the Soul and kill the demon from within, unlike most exorcists that perform their rituals from the outside. That is why Asku gave me the name, Cheveyo; the Spirit Warrior. He had already seen what I was capable of doing in the spiritual realm, with his all-seeing eye, through visions.

The Spirit Realm is where the soul resides, yet it is a major part of the world of the living. The demon possesses the person's soul or Axis Mundi and feeds off their energy; sucking the life out of them, like a virus' blackening rot, infecting them from the inside and manifesting its way to their outer appearance. Sometimes you can manage to save the host, if you can exorcise it before the damage is too severe or before the soul has been completely drained of energy and dies. Someone once asked me; how do you fight demons in a soul? You do it with faith, will and strength. Also, a little bit of cunning can carry you a long way against these creatures of deception.

The beautiful person that I observed in the pictures hanging on the walls, throughout the house, while I was attempting to connect with her spirit, was no longer present. This thing squatting in the corner of the room speaking to me in different tongues was something else. It faintly resembled the beautiful woman that once occupied that soul, but the beast had a firm grip on her and it showed in her unsightly outer appearance.

She no longer looked like the healthy debutante and beauty pageant queen. She had lost an undesirable amount of weight. Her hair was scraggly, dirty and unkempt. She had lesions and sores covering her skin, and smelled ungodly. She probably hadn't eaten or bathed in weeks. The only thing keeping her alive was her will to survive and this evil within her. It spoke to me in the ancient dialect of Mesopotamia first, then Babylonian, Arabic, Hebrew and Latin, saying the same thing repeatedly,

"Tlazolteotl"

I didn't give pause to think about what it was saying. I'm aware of the mind games and deceptions that these things rely upon. I continued to draw my concealment glyphs on the filth covered four walls of the room;

a pentagram within a circle and the containment symbols and writings surrounding it.

The demon screamed and yelled louder and louder with each pentagram drawn, cursing me in several languages, moving back and forth erratically like a cornered animal, feeling the concealment of its fate!

When I completed the last pentagram, I no longer heard its cries, and looked over to the where it was positioned, but it was no longer there. I quickly perused the room and didn't see it. I felt its warm urine upon my brow. The demon was on the ceiling with one leg cocked like a dog urinating on me. I quickly maneuvered to prevent a further showering from the disgusting beast. I made a circle on the floor with satchel dust, sat in the lotus position, and began my chants.

The demon quickly fell from the ceiling to the floor, hearing the chants, and ran around the room in a desperate attempt to escape, but the pentagrams prevented it! Then suddenly the room began to shake violently, as in a tremor or quake, and the thick black smoldering ooze associated with these demons and possessions began to blanket the walls of the room, like lava. The temperature rose exponentially, as smoke filled the room. Then the floor began to shift and move from the tremors, and when Jamila fell unconscious, the floor erupted, and I fell downwards, sucked into its void like a vacuum.

It seemed like I would never stop falling, but when I finally landed, I was seated in several inches of the hot black slime. It was pitch black, and the only thing left visible were the jaundice yellow eyes of the demon; that quickly faded into the distance.

When the nauseous sulfur-like smoke finally cleared, I found myself in an extremely arid wasteland, standing in the black slime which rose to my ankles. I was now inside Jamila's Axis Mundi; the center of her spiritual and life's energy, her soul!

The first couple of times I performed these exorcisms, I was sick for days, vomiting from the foul, pungent odor of the sulfur, but now I was used to it. I was immune to the sulfur, but the super-heated black lava-like slime slowed me down. It was thick as mud, but it was much more than that. I wasn't as quick as I usually am in the spiritual realms when confronted with the black slime. It was a weakness that has been unobserved by my adversaries, thus far, and I hope to keep it that way.

There was a tempest wind blowing from the west, striking my face with dirt and debris associated with deserted wastelands. I viewed old abandoned homes and apartments where she used to live through her lifetime, including her parent's homes in the background. I observed abandoned vehicles that she once owned or spent most of her time driving or being a passenger, including public transportation.

I viewed dark intimate secrets that she hadn't shared with anyone; secrets of personal lust, envy, greed, pride, wrath, gluttony, and sloth. All the seven deadly sins that she had committed through her life were displayed like slides in a projector upon the grayish sky used as a screen. I saw abandoned and deserted dreams of hers quickly moving by.

These were the stages of her life that she regretted; the melancholy that we all harbor in one way or another. It was these regrets and sympathetic pity that demons feed upon; self-loathing was like a smorgasbord for these, guilt eating, leaches. It was to the west where I'd find the source of her energy or whatever was left of it, but judging by the looks of things, I believe it might be too late.

Then the thick black slime began to rain from the grayish sky, covering me and slowing me down even further. I could barely see when suddenly I fell inside a pit of the black slime which resembled a tar pit. There was nothing for me to brace myself with, as I struggled to prevent myself from sinking into the heavy goo. The pressure from the thick tar-like substance began to squeeze the life energy out of me, as I panicked! This was the first time one of these things got the drop on me. They're usually surprised by my presence, but not this one! I guess the word is getting around.

This was a middle hierarchy demon trying to make a name for itself and move up the ladder. They are usually the ones that partake in singular possessions. The lower hierarchy demons and soldier demons can't possess human souls; they are merely puppets and pawns to do the bidding of more power demons. Demons can turn any mortals into a lower hierarchy or soldier demon. Demons above the middle hierarchy rarely involve themselves in such possessions unless it is mass carnage, death and destruction!

The pressure from the drowning felt like I was being buried alive with hundreds of pounds of dirt being thrown upon me. I needed to calm down and center myself. I concentrated on my energy crystal and used the stored energy from it to cocoon myself in a blanket of energy which rose above the tar pit and shattered the hardening slime from around me. I floated back down to the ground afterwards.

My energy crystal was my life line. It protected me from receiving too much energy in the world of the living by storing the consumption, and it is a weapon against the demons in the spiritual world. It is transcendent and can cross through the different realms, like celestial stones, which it very well may be, but I'm not certain how Asku acquired it. When I first put it on, I knew it was something passed down from a greater power, I could feel it like any symbiotic attaching itself to the host. I never asked Asku of its origins, but I know for certain that it's not just some family heirloom of Asku's. The energy crystal is opaque, clear and hard as a diamond, yet the only time it shows its brilliance is when it is storing and emitting energy.

When I finally freed myself from the black slime, I could hear the faint sounds of people gathered in the background. As the ambient sounds grew, I could discern the voices of children; playing of some sort, and like a movie fading into focus, I found myself no longer in the wasteland, but inside of a school's cafeteria with children jubilantly running around, shouting and doing what school aged children do during lunch.

Wait! I know this place. This is my old grade school in Washington, D.C. I quickly panned the area to the corner where I always sat and ate my lunch alone, and there I was, little Christian Sands or Reds, as the children called me.

He was sitting alone in the cafeteria, like I did every day, staring into oblivion with a stoic expression upon his face. He was thinking about the monsters last night, and how they'd revisit him tonight! As if my childhood nightmares weren't enough, the bullying he faced during the day was all a part of a continuous nightmare that he prayed would end.

I was singled out, as the weird kid, because of my psychological issues and my appearance. It wasn't just the teasing about being a half-breed, but consecutive nights with limited to no sleep had me looking like a zombie with dark rings under my eyes, a pale complexion and unkempt hair. My overall looks were the least of my worries then, as I spent my nights with visions of demons.

Then the bully who ritualistically visited my table, Donald Lewis, arrived. He had repeated the 8th grade so many times; they passed him because he was too old to be in grade school any longer. He was the only kid with a mustache in our class, and that's no exaggeration! He was bigger, stronger and older than the rest of the class, and never let us forget it! He was there to collect his daily bounty from me, and to dish out his brand of harassment and torture. Bullying was different back then. You accepted it and didn't tell anyone, because you were ashamed to let anyone know it was happening to you.

"Hey, Redskin, what's for lunch today?" He yelled, so all the children in the cafeteria could hear and take notice, as he strutted towards me.

I could feel the emptiness inside of me, as if I were reliving it all over again, yet anxious and angered by what was about to ensue! I was caught up in the moment, as I moved in quickly to intervene, before the bully could begin his torture, and just as he cocked his arm and hand upward to strike my younger self, I interrupted his swing, and held his arm with a firm grip!

"I wouldn't do that if I were you," I insisted with a commanding voice, and sharp stare.

He was surprised by my intrusion, and a little scared, but then his temperament changed suddenly. His eyebrows appear to shrink upon his brow, as his eyes squinted, and his mouth protruded in anger. Then he gave me the most insolent and arrogant look that I've ever seen from a child. This kid was just mean, even to adults! Then, he tried to jerk his arm away with the force of a little man, but I held on, and squeezed tighter, as he winced under the pressure of my grip! I let go of his arm at that point, as Donald Lewis, the bully, went running off.

My younger self never turned around during the whole episode, still thinking about last night. I was amazing that I did so well in class with all the chaos, but it was all I had to distract me from the pandemonium.

Everything inside of me told me not to disturb my younger self, as I looked upon him from behind. I just wanted to give him a great big hug, which he so desperately needed, and to tell him that it's going to be alright in the years to come. What the hell, how can it hurt? I couldn't resist my urge to show myself some compassion and love. As I approached from behind, and extended my hand to touch him on the shoulder, he swung around with lightning speed, and slashed at my midsection with a dagger! I barely escaped being completely gutted by the perversion of myself. My face was twisted and distorted with the yellow eyes and fangs of the demon!

It continued to lunge at me with the dagger, swinging wildly, as I back peddled in shock, still slower than usual. It was the black slime, and I was still standing in it. Although, I couldn't see it because of the illusion, I was still in the wasteland. Therefore, I used the slime to my advantage, and kicked it into his eyes! This gave me enough time to attack the demon and disarm him. I quickly took the dagger from him, and embracing the demon, I used all my strength to shove it into him. This was a dagger from Hell, and whatever weapons Hell uses can be turned against them. My demon look-a-like turned into black ash and fell slowly to the floor.

The once vibrant and jovial cafeteria now became silent and filled with an assortment of gray in color hues from the black and white movies of the past. It looked like an old dilapidated structure; crumbling and just barely standing by a matrix of dirt, cobwebs, and decay which held it together.

The children stood still in their tracks, motionless and silent; paused in still life with their heads hanging down. Every one of them was brandishing the same kind of hand blade of my doppelganger. Then, they slowly and meticulously raised their heads, concertedly displaying the amber colored eyes of the demon, glaring at me from the distorted faces of the children, I once knew. And without further hesitation, the horde of child sized demons attacked!

I slashed my way through the horde using the demonic blade I acquired, but sustained some injuries due to my slower reaction time. It seemed like I'd been fighting forever when I slashed the last of them, and sent it back to hell with the others. I could have sent them to the Evoid, but I wasn't going to give up my Ace in the hole, not yet. These things are just manifestations of the thing I needed to kill. I had to get closer to the source of this evil to terminate it. My school cafeteria faded with the ashes of the demons, and once again, I was in the in the wasteland, chasing the westward wind.

I could finally feel the energy getting stronger as I came upon a series of blood red, jagged cliffs. As morbid as this evil being was, this sight was truly phenomenal. It made you wonder how something so wicked could produce something so beautiful or perhaps I've just spent a little too much time in the company of demons.

I followed the energy trail up the red rock cliffs, and found Jamila. She was on her knees, drooped over, with her arms chained and spread out, as if she was on a crucifix. She was wearing the white sleeping gown that I had originally seen her in, while in her room. I couldn't see her face with her head hanging down and her hair covering it, as I slowly approached her. She was lifeless and still, and I wondered if I had reached her too late.

My first reaction was to release her from the bondage, the thick and heavy black ironclad chains which held her. The chains were hot as fire, to my surprise, but showed no indication of it, as I tried pulling it from the red rocks where they were anchored. Then from out of nowhere, I heard something cutting through the air, but before I could react, it crashed into my head, and sending me several feet on to the ground.

While I collected myself, and attempted to unscramble my marbles from the intense blow, I observed Jamila, no longer drooped over and bonded. She was standing tall with her hair blowing in different directions, and the same amber colored eyes of the demon that I'd observe since I began this exorcism. The singe-ing, black ironclad chains were still connected to her wrists, but unattached from the red rock cliffs. They were wavering in the air above her, moving like slithering snakes with no regards to gravity, and as though they were alive!

Before I could take another breath, she whipped another chain in my direction. I jumped out of its path, and managed to dodge it, but the other one came swiftly, and wrapped around my left leg. It was draining my life energy. Then, the other chain came with even more force, and knocked me down. As I attempted to free myself from the demonic bondage, a barrage of blows ensued from the other chain, one after another; pummeling me until I was left weakened on the ground, and drained of most of my life's energy. Then I observed the true form of the demon. I was no longer a threat to it.

The chained manifestation of Jamila backed away from me, and integrated with the evil perversion that I witnessed in the background. It sighed and grinned at the completion of the integration, as if it just completed a sexual act. It was blood red like the cliffs. Its head bore the horns of a ram, and stood on the hoofs of ram. It was about 7 feet tall, and its skin was leathery and without hair.

It was embracing Jamila in some sort of perverse sexual way. She was naked with her legs and arms wrapped around him, yet the rest of her body seemed to be fused with the demon's, except for her head. She appeared to be enjoying what was taking place, as I heard passionate sighs and moans from her. I can only imagine what she's probably seeing; some handsome prince charming of her dreams or someone from the past. This is how they get inside you, and make you succumb to their whims and wishes. This is how they get you to stop fighting and resisting their desires, but it's all a charade, an elaborate deception to inhabit your soul and drain your life's energy. Perhaps at one point she resisted, but it was a lost cause now.

It walked towards me with Jamila in tow. It wanted to gloat or boasts in its victory, before finishing me off. Why else didn't it completely drain me, if not for its hubris? It would also be the thing that causes its undoing, as it gives me all I needed.

It stood over me, slumped on the ground, and my energy crystal dull and opaque. It probably didn't even notice it around my neck.

"I've heard the whispers of you, Shaman. Look at you, but a mere maggot, squirming at my feet. The Darkness has consumed you, there's nothing else you can do now, accept it and give into it!"

"By darkness you mean Hell? Well, you're correct about the energy consumption. You've drained just about all of it, besides it would be futile to attempt to separate the both of you at this point." I confirmed, as it grinned, thinking I was in submission. I paused for a bit to allow him to soak in his pride, and savor his victory before continuing.

"Therefore, I guess I'll have to take it from you! The same way you raped her and drained many others." I interjected, and his face went blank.

"And how do you expect to do that? Only higher demons and angels can do such a thing," he nervously spewed.

"Yeah, that's what your kind keeps telling me," I replied standing up.

"Impossible!" It shrieked.

"I guess you didn't know all there was to know about me after all."

He was close enough now, and this wasn't a manifestation, but the real deal! I extended my hands in his direction and began draining the energy from him!

What the demon didn't know is that he'd drained my life energy, but the energy crystal still had more than enough energy to sustain me. It's like a celestial stone, a symbiotic, and no demon can tap into its energy. I had turned the table of deception upon him. As I stated previously, you fight these things with faith, will and strength, but a little bit of cunning can carry you a long way against these creatures of deception.

Now the demon had fallen to its knees below me, as I continued to drain its energy. Then it attempted trickery again, and turning into Jamila, as she kneeled in front of me pleading.

"Please, stop it Christian, please, it hurts too much, you're killing me, please!"

This wasn't far from the truth, except there wasn't enough of Jamila's soul left inside her to save, only the demon, who had taken it all, and now I will take all that he took from her and more! She continued to beg and plead for me to stop, as I continued, listening to her screams and cries. It caused me to hesitate for a second or two wondering if I could possibly separate them, now that the demon was weak, but just as I was prepared to begin my chants, Jamila appeared.

She had mustered just enough strength to show herself, and not the demon in disguise. She didn't have enough energy to speak, but her eyes said it all. They were filled with pain and remorse, but she nodded her head in a desperate plea for me to continue, and I did just that.

When the pleading stopped and the beast knew it was to no resolve, like any desperate cornered animal, it lunged at me, in its final attempt to survive. It was still in the form of Jamila, as I caught it in mid-air by the neck, and kept it there, feet dangling above the black tar surface. It kicked, clawed and screeched furiously, as I watched without remorse as its energy drained.

First the screeching stopped, as it desperately continued to swing and kick, languidly without any force, until it drooped over motionless, depleted of all its energy. My energy crystal glowed bright as a star. This thing had been possessing souls for quite some time, but now it has come to its end! I set it on fire and sent it where it will never return, the Evoid.

The temperature had dropped and everything associated with the demon had disappeared around me, and once again I found myself back in the dark, malodourous laden room where I began. Jamila was lying on the floor dead, with her eyes open, and the black slime trickling from her nose. I picked her up, laid her in her bed, and closed her eyes. Maybe she'll find peace in the afterlife, but victims of these exorcists rarely do, unless they survive and repent. I've even seen the ones that survive, not accept that Heaven and Hell exist after all that they've experienced. It truly boggles the mind.

Now came the ugly side of our business; I had to tell Jamila's parents that their daughter is dead. How do you tell someone their daughter was going to die anyway from this evil within, and I only sped up the process by killing the demon that was living off her like a virus? She was already too far gone, and past the point of redemption.

How do I tell them that there wasn't enough of a soul to save, and her life's energy had been completely depleted, but I could prevent this from happening to another? I could prevent it from spreading by preventing the demon from possessing another by killing it, and sending it to the Eternal Void or Evoid! The place beyond the spiritual realms, beyond Heaven and Hell; a place where energy ceases to exist, a black hole.

It all sounds good and noble, but it isn't what they wanted to hear. I was their last hope of getting their daughter back, yet all I was bringing back to them was death. I didn't kill her, but I didn't save her either in their eyes. I managed to kill another demon, but I didn't feel any better for it. It was only half a win, if I can't save the host; the possessed.

If killing your younger self and wrestling with a demon wasn't enough mind-fuck to deal with, now I had to carry around the guilt and sorrow I experienced in Jamila's parents' eyes. I wanted to just drown myself in a good bottle of whiskey, but I had guests arriving for the Labor Day holiday, therefore I had to put on my happy face, the façade and demeanor that everything was right in the world, but he'd know I was lying, Dr. Banks is one of the most notable and gifted psychologists of his generation. I was lucky to have him on my side. There's no telling where my train wreck of a life would be without him.

Dr. Banks was coming down with one of his sons, a gifted artist who wanted to explore and do some paintings of the breath-taking scenery the Smokey Mountains had to offer. I promised he wouldn't leave uninspired. Carlyle, my tech geek friend from the FBI, was coming down, also. He assisted me greatly on the Coyote Case. It will do him some good to get away from that dungeon he calls work for a change. It was a much-needed respite from the dark side for me, as well.

It was daylight outside; I had been working all night. The sun was shining bright, as the intensity of its rays struck my eyes with a sharp blinding pain, causing me to close them immediately! I had been in the dark too long, and had to adjust to its brilliance. I smelled like Hell! I had been up all night battling this thing, but it seemed like days in the spiritual realm. I was beat, and in desperate need of sleep, and a long hot soak in the tub. I paused on Jamila's parent's porch, took in a deep breath and exhaled, as if sighing. I stood there for several minutes ruminating over the past night's events.

"You did all you could do, Chris," Kelle whispered softly, and gently held my hand, seeing the guilt written across my face.

"I know Ke, but it doesn't make it any easier," I replied with a heavy voice

"Were you able to contact her before she passed on?"

"Yes, she was at peace with it all, and knew what needed to be done," I informed her, sadly.

"Then your peace should lie within that solace," she replied.

"Thanks, Kelle, I appreciate that."

"Anytime, Bro. Are you coming over for dinner, tonight?"

"I think I'll rest in tonight, Dr. Banks, his son, and Carlyle are coming down for the holiday weekend."

"Oh, that's right; you're going to bring them over for Sunday dinner, aren't you?"

"Yes, I wouldn't deprive them of that. Besides, mother would kill me if I didn't."

"You got that right," she replied, laughing.

"Can you drive us back? I want to get a little shut eye on the way," I asked her.

"Sure thing, relax and enjoy the ride." She retorted, smiling.

I was tired from spending several endless days exorcising demons that had crossed over to the realm of the living. Although my travels were vast in the Spirit Realm, I only physically traveled within the vicinity of the Smokey Mountain Range of North Carolina, Tennessee and West Virginia.

Recently, I had been taking Kelle, Asku's daughter, with me on my excursions. She had finally received the calling, and was interested in becoming a shaman. She was already dream walking, but hasn't had her awakening yet. She was a late bloomer, like me. If it was up to Asku, she would never receive it. He understood the risks of being a shaman, and tried to delay the inevitable for as long as he could. I needed someone to watch over me, because my physical body was vulnerable when my spirit traveled.

While I rested in the car, I gazed upon Kelle before closing my eyes and reminisced about my shamanic training, which she would be undergoing soon enough.

CHAPTER TWO

THE TSILA

It has been almost two years since I was released from the psychiatric ward and forced into retirement by the FBI in lieu of the Coyote case, as they were referring to it. It's been eighteen months, seven days and counting to be exact. I would be lying if I said I didn't miss some aspects of the FBI. I enjoyed assisting in the apprehension of serial killers and the camaraderie of being with a team. I had been a recluse for much of my life and being with the team gave me an extended family as well as a social outlet.

Life has a way of making us change and adjust to its nuances. Some call it survival and others call it adaptation. A lot has changed in my life since then. I had a new extended family in Cherokee, North Carolina. Nina and Askuwheteau accepted me into the Blackwater clan and I became an unofficial member of the Eastern Band of Cherokee Indians.

Nina and I were still going strong even though she was strongly against long distance relationships. I guess having the ability to dreamscape made it easier to accept. Every night I would dreamscape with her and she would come down every other weekend and holidays to visit. I was staying in her cabin while she was in D.C. She insisted on it. It was vacant except for when she was able to come down. I gave her monies to cover the utilities and lease payments that she reluctantly accepted. I also kept my Foggy Bottom condo in Georgetown, D.C. The pension release provided by the FBI was very lucrative. It was their way of saying thanks for all you've done, but you're a liability, and no longer wanted. I thought of it as guilt money, but I wasn't complaining.

I loved the serenity of living in the Oconaluftee River Valley amongst the Smokey Mountain Range. I fished, swam in the river and hiked the mountains as I became closer to nature and its magic. I had become one with Mother Earth, its animals and elements. I communicated with her on a spiritual level. I also had the time to get back into my true love, music. I received immense pleasure out of playing the cello in the forest, as certain animals would come and listen to me playing, like I was the Pied Piper. I couldn't help, but smile, and wonder what John Coltrane would think of this. He once said,

"All a musician can do is to get closer to the sources of nature, and so feel that he is in communion with the natural laws." He was a pioneer that was beyond his time.

It was a spectacular sight to witness. I would be surrounded by butterflies, dragonflies, birds, deer, rabbits and other non-predatory animals. They didn't fear me at all and readily came up to me and listened to me playing. Nina would plan special picnics just to witness it. This was nothing new to Askuwheteau or his daughter, Kele, who was learning the ways of shamanism also.

This was my Garden of Eden. I sometimes wish I could take a picture of this and share it with others, but this would be a considered an invasion. Cameras extract the essence and spirit of natural things and make them weaker. Shamanism can't be explained to the layman. They confuse what they don't understand or comprehend with a different purpose. They fear what they can't deduce, label it as evil, and consider its acts for evil purposes. Witches, Warlocks, Wiccans, Wizards and Sorcerers have been persecuted for centuries, and up to this day for practicing natural magic, although, some do participate in the Black Magic Arts and Satanic Magic. Shamanism is strictly natural in its essence. It doesn't participate in black magic, satanic magic or necromancy. There are some who break this natural order of shamanism.

My abilities had grown tremendously since Askuwheteau and I began my vision quest. My panther imprinting, shadowing, and ability to dreamscape were just a foot inside the door of shamanism. While Asku was guiding me in the ways of shamanism, my spirit guide was teaching the ways of traversing the realms. Before I could only dreamscape with the living in the spiritual realm, where dreams lie, but now I could communicate with the dead in the spiritual world.

I was learning the secret customs and traditions passed down from over four thousand years. I was called Tsila amongst the tribes. In the Tsalagi language; Tsila means apprentice. It was a title of endearment and recognition because one doesn't set out or chooses to become a shaman. It is something that is gifted to you and passed down through your family, but even then, you must be chosen by Nvyunuwi (Stone Clad), the ancient Aniyvwiya Spirit, to be able to utilize these gifts.

My shamanic training consisted of seven fundamentals; Herbal Medicine, Physical Medicine, Tradition, Languages, Spirit Medicine, Natural Law and Conjuring. Herbal Medicine consisted of learning botany and about numerous plants like Mugwort in the application of healing. Physical Medicine consisted of learning the minor applications and practices of a field medic. A Shaman's medicine bag was a quick and accessible way for healing a myriad of maladies. The study of tradition was the study of the history of the Tsalagi people and the shaman's role to the people.

The study of languages was in acceptance of tongues. This was something that came natural to me, as well. Asku stated that he has never seen anyone able to perform what I could do, in reference to speaking in tongues. Most Shamans go into trances to speak in tongues. They acquire it from the spiritual realm, but I could speak in tongues readily, without the assistance of the spiritual realm or at least not in a transcendental way.

Spirit Medicine dealt with the use of dreams and utilizing the spirit realm in healing. I was already adept in the mastery of the spiritual realm. I had been crossing back and forth in my dreams since I was a child, but I was unaware of what I was doing. There was no further training Asku could offer me in the spiritual realm. Whatever training I received in the spiritual realm had to come from experiences, and my spirit guide, Ebony, the black panther. I did require assistance in the field of interpreting dreams which I found extremely difficult. Learning how to read the signs and symbols that appear in everyday life from the spiritual realm was something that would take time.

A shaman's Axis Mundi is more than just a noumena or spiritual energy source. The Axis Mundi for a shaman is a spiritual place that we traverse between the realms. It exists outside of the realms and is our connection to them. It's sort of like a wayward train station in which the shaman travels to the other realms. Although we have sacred places existing in the world of the living where we go to get closer to nature and communicate with the other realms, it is only a backdrop to assist us in getting in touch with our inner Axis Mundi.

This connecting station, higher level of spirituality or heightened consciousness is different for all shamans and other supernaturals that traverse the realms. My Axis Mundi is a rainforest, like the ones you see in the Amazon. My spirit guide, Ebony, is the guardian and protector of my Axis Mundi. She is one with me. We share each other's thoughts, soul and energy. She is sort of like my alter ego, yet more intense!

Shamanism has opened my compassion, and understanding of those who are ridiculed and hospitalized for schizophrenia, and other mental ailments. These patients could have a stronger connection to the spiritual realm, and cognitively more in touch with their conscience. Seeing ghosts and talking to people that the average person can't see is considered mentally ill, instead of gifted, yet shamans and others with abilities do it consistently.

I have also retained the physical abilities of my panther spirit guide through imprinting. I have all the strength and abilities of a panther while I'm in the world of the living or phenomenal world. Besides my increased vision during the day and extraordinary night vision; my hearing, sense of smell, speed, agility and strength increased exponentially to mimic or immolate that of a panther. All shamans have animal spirit guides and are gifted with imprinting abilities. For some shamans like Asku, connection with their spirit guide surpasses mere imprinting, and they can achieve the ability of shape shifting into their spirit guide. I hadn't learned to shape-shift yet, but I'm sure it was in the cards for me.

The one imprinting gift that I wasn't fond of was the sexual promiscuity of the panther or lust for multiple partners. Asku warned me of this, and I was trying to keep it in check, to remain with Nina. I was determined to be monogamous, and not let this thing come between me and the woman I love.

Natural Law dealt with the understandings of Nature and everything outside of the spiritual realm. It is about the relationship of man with animals, the elements, the earth, everything within it and how we are connected. We are all connected through energy. Everything on earth has energy, including inanimate objects.

Natural or Elemental Magic is the manipulation or practical use of the Shamanic Pentacle of Spirit, Water, Air, Fire and Earth. It is used for healing, defensive purposes or offensive. This is the area of my training that most intrigued me.

I was so excited about learning how to manipulate, influence and channel the elements to do my bidding. All the legends and folklore about Native American Medicine Men performing rain dances and making it rain, as well as, controlling the wind, and crops; all stemmed from shaman's manipulation of the elements or elemental energy.

Shamans manipulate elements through particle energy, charged leptons to be precise. At the core of all atoms are protons, neutrons and electrons that are composed of charged subatomic particles called leptons. Leptons are at the core of all energy: cosmic, earthly and supernatural. Spirits, ghosts, apparitions, poltergeists or whatever your choice of terminology are comprised of energy. Shamans can manipulate the wind, water, fire and earth through elemental energy.

Asku stated that there has never been a shaman able to manipulate all the elements of the pentacle; air, water, fire, earth and the spirit realm, which I had the potential to achieve. He also stated that I could possibly be able to manipulate celestial energy. This was the purest of energies which was also called Angelic energy because it was wielded by the Angels. I've never seen an angel, so I disregarded that notion and concentrated on the elemental energies.

Manipulating the wind and fire came naturally to me. I didn't concentrate on the other elements which didn't come as natural as the wind, which I made my priority. Although fire appeared to be the strongest and most powerful of my elemental manipulations, I couldn't control its destructive nature. I kept burning down things and causing unexplainable accidents in the mountains. Then there was this thing that I couldn't explain whenever I used it. The use of fire brought out a dark side of me. It made me feel good, invigorating and powerful, but in the wrong way. It confused me with a plethora of emotions, but mostly intensive rage that I couldn't control. It was like I was another person when I wielded it; therefore, I minimized my practice of it.

I was taught to push, pull, throw, extract and aim, and that was only for air. Although I could manipulate all the elements, I wasn't skillful with them yet. Mastering all the elements with the same precision and skill level would take some time, even at my advanced learning.

Asku's element was the earth. He was also a master healer, and had the ability to shift change into the likeness of his spirit guide, the bear. It took him years to master shift changing as well. There are several distinct types of magic and the base of Shamanism comes from the magic or energy of Nature and its elements. There are also several types of shift changers that derive their abilities from dissimilar sources.

After my awakening was achieved, and I was set on my vision quest with my spirit guide, my abilities, and spiritual awareness were wakened. The greatest of my abilities that was awakened was also my weakness. I had the ability to absorb the energy of other supernaturals. I was like a magnet, as the Great Mother foretold, but it was more so like a battery or storage cell. I had no control over the absorption, and like any fuse or battery that is overcharged, it will blow or explode. That was the reason why Asku had me wearing the Crystal. He felt the pull from the moment he met me, but it wasn't fully developed until I was awakened, and in touch with my spirit guide. The Crystal acts like a surge protector, and protects me against such overpowering. I'm also able to redirect the transference of energy from my Crystal while in the spiritual realm, and use it as weapon.

The basis of my energy absorption is the transference of energy. In physics, the law of conservation states that the total energy of an isolated system remains constant or conserved over time. Energy can neither be created nor destroyed, but transferred or transformed from one form to another. From Huygens to Leibniz, Newton to Einstein this law has been proven. In fact, Empedocles (490-430 BC) stated that the universe is composed of four roots; earth, air, water and fire. He stated that nothing comes to be or perishes, but these elements suffer continual rearrangements. The law of energy conservation holds true to this realm as well as the other realms.

A greater portion of my training consisted of learning the healing or Nvwoti in Tsalagi which means medicine. Asku and I traveled throughout the tribes of Cherokee County and Swain County treating the ill. Asku never asked for anything in exchange for his healing services, but crops and other goods were often given. Asku stated that being a healer was the greatest gift a shaman could offer his people. He thought healing was more powerful than any of the elemental energies because it brings them all together. Although my future was foretold as the Spirit Warrior, and thus my Tsalagi name Cheveyo was given, he thought being a healer would give me balance. *Balance was the key to life, and the universe*, Asku would often say.

I enjoyed helping others, so healing people brought me a greater pleasure than hunting down serial killers. I didn't have to deal with the horrors of entering their maleficent dreams or the side effects that came with it. Asku's Earth Healing Store and everything came together and made sense to me now. What I once thought to be a lot of mumbo jumbo was a way of life for me now.

It takes decades to master shamanism, but I was growing and learning at an incredible rate. My supernatural speed and strength was growing amazingly. All supernaturals, as well as shamans, didn't move at the same rate of speed or have the same strengths. Some were faster and stronger than others. It doesn't depend on the particular species of supernatural it just depended upon the individual's ability. I was faster and stronger than Asku, but he would defeat me with his elemental ability which he's mastered over time.

It was no longer a requirement for me to fall asleep to dreamscape. I could do it just by meditating now. I was still in a trance like state and incapacitated when I performed it, so for all practical purposes I was still asleep. My spirit guide, Ebony, also taught me how to channel myself, and speak to the other side now. I used to only be able to dreamscape with the living, but now I could speak with those who have passed away as well.

I spent nearly two years in the mountains learning and perfecting the manipulation of air and fire in accordance with nature. Asku wasn't teaching me to take over for him. This was left to his daughter, Kelle. She had the ability, but it was nothing compared to what I could perform. At times Asku referred to me as the Shaman Prince, when he wasn't calling me Cheveyo, the Spirit Warrior.

CHAPTER THREE

CALL OF DUTY

It was Memorial Day weekend, the unofficial beginning of summer. Nina couldn't make it down for the holidays because she was busy in D.C. with some big investigation that was going on up North. I was elated that that was no longer a part of my life, especially on beautiful weekends like this one. Days and weeks just ran by without any factual knowledge of their difference. They were all the same during an investigation, and the only thing that mattered was solving it.

Dr. Gregory Banks, his son, Ecko and my former FBI colleague, Carlyle, came down for the weekend. We spent some male bonding time together in the mountains, fishing, canoeing and sightseeing on the river. We drank beers and watched the basketball playoffs. I hadn't been much of a basketball fan until Max, my ex-team mate from the ViCAP force, fed it to me whenever he visited my condo in D.C. and while I was in the hospital. The Washington Wizards had made it to the Conference finals against LeBron James and the Cleveland Cavaliers. It had been decades since the Wizards made it to the Conference finals. In fact, they weren't even called the Wizards when they made their last appearance; they were called the Washington Bullets.

It was a great weekend spent with the guys. They were introduced to Asku and my extended Cherokee family. Just seeing Dr. Banks and Asku holding an intense conversation on dreams was priceless. I'm certain it was a Nobel worthy discussion. I just knew the two were going to include me at one point or another, but they were too immersed in their repartee.

My guests were invited to observe an exclusive celebratory ritual performed by one of the local tribes, but the three-day weekend went by too quickly. It was time for Dr. Banks and the others to head back to the hustle and bustle of life as they knew it. It was great bringing my two extended families together.

The next morning Asku and I went to the sacred place (Wakhan Waki), where the Earth meets the Water and the Sky (Mahkah-Odahingum-Mahpee), high in the Smokey Mountain Range to dreamscape. We performed our usual ritual before entering the sacred grounds; we took off our shoes and gave blessings to the Four Winds, turning north, south, east and west, and then asking the Mother Earth to purify us before entering sacred ground.

We entered the Wakhan Waki, and lit a fire in the ceremonial pit. It was south of the stone altar and the Great Ancestral Tree which contained generations of names and ritualistic symbols carved into it. Everything was placed in a single line on the slope of the mountain which created a vertical angle leading upward towards the sky, as did the great tree, as did the mountain top behind it. We gave blessing to the Great Spirit, Massauu, and to the One God, who presides over all. We returned to the ceremonial pit and shared a peyote pipe before dreamscaping. Besides being a gifted healer, Asku was also blessed with sight. I was lucky to have such a gifted Shaman teach me the ways of Shamanism.

"You have chosen your element wisely, Cheveyo. Although you will become versed in them all, eventually. You are gifted like no other shaman that I've witnessed, but first, you must learn to wield one or two of them to perfection, before mastering them all. The panther walks the path of water, earth and air. They are the pre-existing elements in nature. Light is also pre-existing in nature, but this is not the path of the panther; neither is fire. Fire is not pre-existing in nature. It is a causative reaction. It is created in nature by the sun's heat; the Light or it is created by lightening from the air and clouds. Therefore, it is a natural reaction that must be manifested and

not pre-existing, therefore I must warn you to be careful with it. Sometimes within the greatest power comes the greatest destruction."

"You favor the shadows and rely heavily on your shadow skills which are created by the dark, and the light. Once again, Cheveyo, you witness the duality of your skills, but the weighing factor here is that shadows exist in the air as well. The air moves in the light and in the dark, like the panther. You will be magnificent with this element…"

"You will be called upon again, to take another quest, Spirit Warrior. Although you are reluctant to do so, you must leave here now and fulfill your destiny. Your journey will be perilous; filled with storms and lots of thunder. It is a path which you must travel alone, but remember that you're not alone. For one should never measure a man by his strength alone, for he carries the will and the strength of his family, friends and people. You will learn much from those you meet during this vision quest; some good, and some bad, but don't be too quick to judge, for it will be hard to distinguish friend from enemy."

Asku spoke in riddles, as usual, during our dreamscape. I'm sure it made perfect sense to him, but it all sounded a little contradictory and confusing to me. If I didn't know any better, I would say his visions extended from the fact that my friends were visiting over the holiday weekend, but he hasn't been wrong yet. Perhaps, it's just a spiritual journey that I would be taking, because I was through with the FBI and didn't have any intentions on going back.

A week had passed since my friends visited Cherokee and Asku's vision. I was out enjoying nature in the mountains and doing my favorite exercise, tree jumping. It was something that I had picked up while exploring my panther imprinting. I only did it late at night or just before the dawn. I didn't get a chance to go out last night, so I did it in wake of the sunrise. It was a perfect morning for it. The temperature was cool and the fog was low to the ground which gave me excellent visibility from above. I didn't have to shadow myself or anything due to the fog below.

It was relaxing and invigorating, scaling and jumping from tree to tree. The Smokey Mountains have some of the tallest trees in the nation and the view was heavenly. It felt like I was above the clouds with a blanket of fog covering the ground so thick you could cut it with a knife. While exercising, I received a phone call from Nina. I usually call her after working out, it had become a ritual. We would discuss our dreamscaping from last night and tease each other about its contents. Then I wouldn't hear from her again until lunch, if she wasn't too busy or later in the evening. I knew something was wrong for her to call me this early in morning, so I immediately paused while high in a tree and answered the phone.

"Hello, baby, is everything alright?" I asked, anxiously with heavy breaths.

"I'm fine, but things just became more complicated on the case I'm overseeing in Vermont." She answered with a level of concern in her voice.

"What's going on?"

"Well, I told you there were several missing children in Swanton and two reported deaths near the forest of the Abenaki Village. Now the two Bureau of Indian Affairs agents that I sent up to investigate the matter are missing. There have been reports of escalated civil unrest as well. I wanted to know if you were up to going there and investigating the matter. I've cleared it with the BIA and have you cleared as a special agent with us. The place is crawling with FBI and your reputation is at legendary status within the bureau," she asked with a nervous tremble in her voice.

"I appreciate the compliment Nina, but I don't know how exemplary my reputation is with them, they did let me go." I reminded her with a hint of poignancy.

"Come on, you know how they play politics in D.C. with their bureaucratic bullshit. It's just a matter of time before they call you back. They had to let the smoke clear first," she replied.

"Yeah, but that's just it, Nina, I don't want to go back," I retorted with certainty.

There was a moment of silence on the phone afterwards. It was a time out to allow us both to think over the situation. I could tell by her voice that she was desperate and needed me. I would have jumped immediately to her rescue, but I had turned the page on that chapter in my life, and wasn't looking forward to going back, regardless of what Asku told me.

"Well, if you change your mind, let me know. I really could use you on this one," she interjected with despair.

"Who will I be working with?" I inquired just out of curiosity, before she hung up the phone.

"I know how you like to operate, baby. It will just be you, unless you want some additional agents," she sighed.

"No, that will be fine," I quickly blurted, *"I'll do it for you, but I'm not making any promises."*

"Excellent! How quickly can you fly to D.C. to pick up your credentials and an official briefing?" she anxiously asked.

"Well, I'm doing my morning exercise right now. I'll have to return to the cabin, pack, and then I can fly out today."

"Ok, call me when you return home, so we can work out the timing to schedule your flight. Thanks again baby, I love you," she retorted joyfully before hanging up.

Asku's vision was right on the money, again. I *am* apprehensive about jumping back into the field so quickly. It's like taking a dive into the deep end of a cold-water lake, but I could never say no to Nina, not even when I first met her. I couldn't resist her then, and this was no exception. I discontinued my workout and hurried back to the cabin. I was nervous and thought about being reactivated in field during the entire way back. I was so deep in thought; I was unaware how I reached the cabin so quickly. I must admit, although I missed the action involved in being in the field; I had grown to love the life that I was building here in Cherokee.

While I was packing my luggage, I noticed that my clothing drawers were in an orderly manner like I knew this day would eventually come. Everything was already neatly folded and ready to be transferred to the suitcase. Perhaps it was just my FBI conditioning. It really didn't matter, but I was ready to leave in under thirty minutes.

I flew non-stop from Ashville to D.C. on Southwest Airlines. We were late arriving in D.C. and circled the busy skies around the Potomac and Reagan National Airport before landing. Out of all the multifarious and phenomenal feelings that I've experience getting in touch with my abilities, the one that really touched me the most was seeing the Potomac again. I grew up around it. I boated on it, fished in it, and sat on its shores with family, friends and lovers. I snuck in the East Potomac Pool with friends and lovers and used Haynes Point as a lover's lane. I've watched the Fourth of July Fireworks, seen Presidential inaugurations and many other wondrous things while nestled in its rich history. It was the warm feeling of being home. No matter where life takes me, D.C. will always be my home.

Nina met me at the Arrivals Terminal. It always seemed to be extremely busy at Reagan National even with Baltimore-Washington International Airport and Dulles International within driving distance. I guess people wanted the convenience of being directly in the city. Even within the crowded terminal I found Nina without a problem. I felt her energy signature as soon as I entered the terminal and followed it.

She was looking beautiful as ever and made me wonder what the hell I was doing in North Carolina while she was in D.C. I hadn't physically seen her in weeks, but it seemed like an eternity. Her new position as Assistant Deputy Director gave her more responsibilities as a bureaucrat instead of a field investigator, which I often teased her about.

She was wearing a blue pinstriped skirtsuit with sheer stockings that showed her well-developed legs in high heels. The suit jacket couldn't contain the hour glass figure that her skirt portrayed. The top two buttons on her white blouse were unbuttoned and showed a little cleavage; just enough to remain professional, yet still entice the imagination. She knew how to finagle that demarcation line between business attire and sexy as hell wear and she did it well.

She flashed that great big smile of hers at me and I immediately picked up my pace. Like a school boy in love, rushing to see his new-found love, I quickly closed in for a kiss. I squeezed her gently, but tight enough to let her know how much I missed her. It seemed like everyone and everything around us disappeared for that brief moment in time as we kissed. We remained locked in each other's arms for a couple of minutes reacquainting ourselves.

She felt soft and smelled fresh with a slight hint of coco butter. She had cleaned herself up before picking me up. I could have remained in her arms forever, but our moment was interrupted by the ringing and vibrations of her cell phone, nestled between us, inside her suit jacket. We both laughed at the interruption because the vibrations were intense and felt by us both. AND IT WAS BACK TO THE RAT RACE OF THE BELTWAY, as were submerged into the ambient sounds and sights of the crowded terminal again.

We parted our embrace still smiling at each other as she answered her phone. She was a big wheel now and had to attend to every call. Although we were no longer within each other's arms, our eyes remained fixed and never left each other's stare. I gazed at the magnificence of her beauty as she spoke to the caller. She enjoyed the way I watched her, fixated like a surgeon, and examining every detail with delight until she hung up the phone.

"Wow, I can really get used to a reception like that," she said grinning from ear to ear.

"I've missed you, so much" I replied, and we kissed again, but this time it wasn't extended. It was her job on the telephone and they were waiting for me.

I was taken directly to the Indian Affairs Bureau on 18th and C Street N.W. and adjacent to the National Mall. I was sworn in and briefed on the case. The one thing you must remember about Washingtonians is that we often turn around the lettering of our Federal Departments. The Indian Affairs Bureau is called the Bureau of Indian Affairs, the Department of

State is called the State Department, and the Department of Interior is called the Interior Department and so on.

It was supposed to be an express initiation, but it took all day. I was given credentials, a badge, and a Glock 9mm handgun with two clips. It was a part of the initiation package. Nina knew I didn't need the weapon and placed it in her desk drawer for me. It was the first time I had seen her office. It was huge with a window view of the National Mall. She had done well for herself and I was elated for her. The Coyote case paid off well for her and the others associated with it. I was the only one that felt the adverse effects from it, but I was never one for playing the bureaucracy games of the Beltway.

It was late in the evening when we finally left the Bureau of Indian Affairs. Nina still had some work to do in the office due to the gravity of the case, so I decided to take this time to visit the House of our Lord, since I was back in DC. It's been a while since I've stepped into a traditional church, although I was more spiritual than I had ever been when I was attending church regularly. I went back to the Basilica of the National Shrine of the Immaculate Conception, where my high school graduation was held.

I graduated from Archbishop Carroll H.S. and attended church on a regular basis back then. It was my sanctuary during high school. I used to hide out in the school's chapel to escape the ridicule and confrontation from the other kids due to my scrawny physique and lack of sleep appearance. No one bothered me there. It's as if it wasn't a part of the school. In my four years, there, I was never disturbed in the chapel with another visitor, besides the Jesuits that occasionally checked in on me.

The shrine brought back all those old memories, most of which weren't good. Guess you can call me a late bloomer. Man, I miss the smell of incense burning. It always had a calming effect on me, and still does after all these years. It felt like I could float away on a cloud with the ease that it puts me in.

There weren't a lot of people in attendance due to no mass being held today, but there were enough to take notice. They were waiting for the confessionals that were being held. I sat in the middle pews, behind the parishioners waiting for absolution, and began praying.

Then the strangest feeling came over me which caused me to open my eyes, and interrupting my tranquility. A person wearing an overcoat with a large hood that came all the way down over his head was walking down the aisles. I couldn't see the face of the person due to the huge extended hood, as he moved effortlessly towards the front of the church, as if gliding on air.

I'm not certain what it is about him, but I've experience similar feelings when my energy crystal illuminates around other immortals or supernatural entities, except it was different this time, and not a glimmer from my crystal. I stared at the individual until he disappeared behind a door in the corner of the altar area. No one else seemed bothered by this spectacle, but me, as I canvassed my surroundings. I knew this couldn't be a demon because we were in the House of the Lord. I was still learning to read and control these gifts of mine, perhaps the eccentric looking man was one of the priests? It wouldn't be the first time I've come across one with oddities, but I couldn't shake this strange feeling.

I waited around for a few minutes after praying, as confessional came to an end. I was hoping it wasn't something ominous that I was feeling. I didn't see the stranger leave from the area behind the altar, but I observed the priests enter and leave the area unharmed, so I decided to curb my paranoid concerns and depart. Then I observed the stranger in black turning around from the balcony, as I turned to leave. It felt as if he was there all this time observing me, so I hurried towards the balcony stairs to confront him, but didn't see him. I walked up the stairs and searched the balcony, but there were no signs of the black garmented stranger.

I was annoyed by the quickness of the stranger and how he eluded me. What hope did I have in finding these missing children if I couldn't even locate a man in the same building? I had to let go of those thoughts, it was only the jitters that had me thinking this way, besides the man in black hadn't done anything wrong that I could see, so I let it go and departed, but only to find him at the bottom of the outside steps about to turn the corner.

I quickly scanned the area for witnesses, and then used my supernatural speed to hurtle down the steps, but when I turned the corner once again he was nowhere in sight. The stranger had completely vanished. The only thing present was a huge black raven perched on a telephone pole, looking down upon me with black beady eyes. An omen for sure!

This had to be another immortal and most likely one that was just as fast as me. But why was he here and what did he want? Also, why didn't my energy crystal illuminate at his presence? At least I know now to trust my instincts, no matter how indifferent they may be, because this was someone with supernatural energy. Yet, I didn't pick up its energy signature? I don't know if it was evil or good, but how could he enter such a sacred place if he was evil? I could feel a quaint cold creep up my spine, as I involuntarily jerked to shake it off. The thought of anything evil being that powerful made me shiver.

I met Nina back at my condo in Foggy Bottom. She had taken loving care of the place in my absence, but when I looked upon my old condo, it seemed like someone else's life. I was moving slowly, but surely, away from the life that I once knew. I was elated when Asku awakened my abilities, and gave me an anchor into whom and what I am, but it was only a peep hole in my journey. I was on a vision quest with more questions than answers, in search of my identity. The real question is how long or how far will this quest take me, and will I even be recognizable afterwards when I get where I'm going? It's the gift and the curse, infinitely.

When I entered inside, everything was just as I had left it. She brought over carryout from my favorite Japanese restaurant, and after eating we spent the rest of the night together making love. I got up from bed around 3:00 in the morning. I was nervous and couldn't sleep. There was just too much on my mind. All of this was happening so suddenly. I don't know if I was experiencing culture shock or what. The environment and pace of D.C. and Cherokee County were like night and day.

I went down to the garage and checked my '64 Volvo. It was covered in dust and in need of detailing. I tried to start it up, but the battery was dead. Nina was already doing too much by watching the loft for me. I couldn't ask her to occasionally start my vehicle. I kept a battery charger in the garage that I hooked up to the vehicle and went back upstairs. The rest of the house was immaculate. All my instruments were still in place and with no signs of dust, except the Cello which I took to Cherokee with me.

I stayed up for the rest of the morning and prepared breakfast for Nina. We made love together in the shower, and then it was off to the Bureau of Indian Affairs again for a final briefing. These briefings were really a meet and greet session before I departed for Vermont. I had lunch with her superiors who wanted to meet me and present me with an award for my involvement in the Coyote case. Nina was correct when she said they thought highly of me in the Bureau of Indian Affairs, but I wasn't certain how my FBI reception would go in Vermont.

I was touched by their gratitude for my services to the Southwestern Indian Nations. They were honoring me, while the FBI didn't know what to do with me. I had toppled most of their beliefs and techniques. Their resolve was to just sweep me under the rug and forget about me and the case, but there was just too much national publicity behind it.

Afterwards, Nina took me directly to Reagan National Airport. She stayed with me until I boarded the plane. We kissed and I left her with tears in her eyes as I departed. There just wasn't enough time, but we have our dreamscapes to hold us until we meet again.

I boarded a Jet Blue flight from Reagan National Airport to JFK International in New York for a connecting flight to Burlington, Vermont. Nina teased me about flying commercial as opposed to the ViCAP's private jet with an espresso machine on board. I must admit I had grown accustomed to flying around the country like a VIP and became a little spoiled. At least they booked me with business class seating.

While awaiting transfer at JFK, I ventured to the Friday's Restaurant for a beer to past the time. There was a fair crowd in the restaurant. I sat at the bar and I ordered a Corona while watching CNN on the television. I would have expected some sports program to be playing, but the missing children were still the focus of the media headlines. It has been over two months now since their disappearance. The media had no knowledge of the missing Federal agents.

I rather enjoyed my anonymity while listening to the bartender discuss the incident with others at the bar. The usual plethora of theories was floating back and forth about what happened, from serial killers to sacrificial Indian Cults, and of course, aliens. The townspeople of Swanton fueled the Native American rumors from what Nina told me. Some people, especially the *'End of the World'* fanatics, believed that the missing children were an act of God, like the Hebrew Passover in Egypt, but they were all just rumors. I learned a long time ago to investigate and profile with an open mind to all possibilities, but never jump to any conclusions. I followed the evidence with the assistance of my unique gifts, natural or supernatural.

The Bureau of Indian Affairs briefed me on the hostility between the townspeople and the Abenaki Native Americans, who they were blaming for the missing children, and thus the reasons for the missing BIA agents' involvement. They were sent there on a diplomatic mission to usher in a peaceful accord between the Abenaki and the citizens of Swanton.

Once I finally landed in Burlington, I rented a vehicle and drove for about 50 minutes towards Swanton. Just before I reached the city limits, my energy crystal unexpectedly lit up like a Christmas tree while I was driving. The flash was so bright it blinded me, and almost caused me to skid off the road. I just barely missed crashing into another vehicle judging by its resounding horn. I pulled over to the side of the road to catch my breath and take assessment of what just occurred.

How in the hell could something emit energy so extensively? I could feel its abundance, but it wasn't very strong. I was on the cusp of its source. It was nothing like any energy signature I'd come across. It's even different than the stranger's signature at the Shrine. Duh, I guess that's why they are called signatures. Yet, I can tell the difference between malevolent and good signatures. Except this one and the stranger's signature didn't register in either.

I attempted to pinpoint its direction by walking in the four cardinal directions. It appeared to be coming from the direction in which I was traveling, the town.

"Now isn't that special?" I said aloud to myself, and smiled.

If I didn't know any better, I'd think Asku and Nina already knew this, and hence my return from retirement. It didn't matter; it was time for me to get back into the world, and fulfill my destiny, as Asku stated, but first I had to fix the flat tire I noticed on my vehicle while walking.

My energy crystal remained illuminated. Therefore, I took it from around my neck, and tied it around my arm to conceal it with my sleeve. It was less likely to blind me that way, and less conspicuous. I could always tell someone it was the LED light from my watch.

I returned to the vehicle, and continued towards the town of Swanton. I could feel the omnipotent energy getting stronger and stronger as I drove, except I couldn't pinpoint it. It appeared to be all around me, as if it was blanketing the town. This was peculiar, indeed. How in the hell do you fight such a thing, if it is causing these abductions?

It seemed like I'd been driving for an eternity through the winding roads and hills of Vermont when I observed a guide sign on the highway indicating that Swanton was 10 miles away. I enjoyed the scenery, but it was becoming one big repetitious blur, as I struggled to avoid the lullaby of highway tunnel vision.

Then, from out of nowhere, the windshield of the vehicle exploded, and sent a blizzard of glass shards ripping through the interior, as a huge black mass quickly encompassed the vehicle, absorbing the light, and turning the day into night. It felt like I was in a meat grinder, the way I was sliced and diced, but I couldn't tell if it was the shards of glass cutting me or the black mass bombarding me, and hitting me with the intensity of a ton of bricks!

My first instinctive reaction was to cover my face from the propulsive shards of glass, jetting through the vehicle, and thus taking my hands off the steering wheel. I couldn't see a thing due to dense black mass, and shards, as I lost control of the vehicle. It swerved to the left and to the right, before flipping on the last tumultuous turn, and taking flight! The vehicle tumbled for several yards on the highway. It appeared as if time had slowed down, and gravity was suspended while I was tumbling in a freefall off the road.

I woke up groggy, lying on the cool moist ground with damp leaves plastered to my face, and ravens circling in the night's sky above me. They didn't make a sound like other birds do, but I could feel their desire. They waited for death, and the carrion buffet that it provided, except this time they were misled, and probably just as confused as me. The vehicle was twisted and folded in ways that no one should have survived, yet here I was lying on the ground without a scratch, except for a headache. I have no idea how I became separated from the car. I recall having my seatbelt on before the crash, I never drive without strapping up first. It's just a habit.

Have no idea how long I was unconscious, but it was dark outside now, and the fog was thick as pea soup. I couldn't see 5 feet ahead of me. I hear this is a normal occurrence at night the further up north you travel, but this was ridiculous. Then I heard a wolf howl in the near distance. The ravens weren't the only opportunistic predators out tonight. The wind must have carried my scent by now, and it won't be long before the pack is upon me, therefore I'd better make haste, and start moving, headache or not.

Even with my night vision it was difficult to see in this fog. It also slowed down the wolves, which could only rely upon scent at this point, so I had to keep distance between us. I managed to make my way back to the road without incident. This place was already proving to be an uncannily special excursion. A normal person would have thought he was losing his mind at this point, and high tailed it back home, but this part of the job is the reason why they sent me here, and thus far it is proving to be for a just cause.

I hitched a ride into town with a trucker, who was making a delivery to Canada, and stopping in Swanton for a rest stop. While in route to the town, I thought about the flock of ravens, silently circling the crash site, and the one that appeared outside of the National Shrine. It truly was an omen. Although, I'm uncertain if something was trying to kill me or save me, and then I ironically observed the city limit sign, *Welcome to Swanton.*

It was already dark outside when I arrived. I didn't expect to see so many people still out on the streets. This wasn't the big city urban metropolis, where people remained out in the streets day and night. This was a somewhat small town with a population of about 6,200 people. I suspect their visitor ratio has spiked since the disappearance of the children with all the media attention the town has been receiving.

The trucker, who was kind enough to give me a ride, drove slowly through the town with the windows open, as we absorbed the sounds and sights of the community. There were no ambient sounds of merriment whatsoever. It has been at least two months now since the disappearance of the children, but it still had a grip on the town. It seemed to blanket the town like a black cloud. I observed several of the citizens walking with their heads down as if in a daze or something. No one looked up, as I passed by or gave me any eye contact. They were lethargic-like lifeless zombies. It was as if the mysterious enigma had affected them deep down and had taken more than just their children, but their souls.

There wasn't much to see here unless you like visiting graveyards or funerals. That was the mood of Swanton, grave and depressed. There were three hotels in the town of Swanton, the Swanton Motel, the Tabor House Inn and where I was staying at the Europa Motel & Restaurant, 49 Spring Street.

When I arrived at the hotel the receptionist at the front desk was unlike any that I've encountered at a hotel. She was cold and unfriendly instead of the warm and welcoming like reception that usually accompanies the check in process.

"The rooms are one- twenty-five for a double and one-ten for a single per night." She stoically stated with her eyes glued to the magazine she was reading, and chewing gum.

I wasn't expecting a king's welcoming, but there was no hello, how are you, good evening or welcome to the hotel greeting. I didn't mind that so much as the smirk she had on her face when she was saying it. She made me feel like I wasn't wanted there. She didn't even inquire if I had a reservation or anything. I ignored her rudeness, as if she had greeted me properly.

"Good evening miss. I have a reservation under the name Christian Sands."

She rolled her eyes upward towards me, as if I cursed her, because I was upbeat after her discourtesy. She rolled her eyes down at the computer screen and made several hits on the keyboard then rolled her eyes back up at me.

"Will it be cash or card?" she asked, smacking gum while chewing it. They say New Yorkers were rude, but to the contrary, I received better treatment in a busy New York airport than I received here.

"Credit card, thank you," I replied with a smile and handed her the GSA credit card the BIA issued me.

I guess with all the fresh faces and strangers in town coupled with the tragedy of the children disappearing in one night made the citizens of Swanton a little apprehensive and distant of strangers. I guess I would be as well. I don't think the citizens were prepared for the massive incursion upon their town. The demeanor of large city dwellers is very different from that of small rural town's people, differing pleasantries and etiquette could be misinterpreted so quickly.

Tragedy has a way of affecting people differently. Some people pull back into themselves and become very reserve and isolated. Others strike out and become angry which results in rudeness and sometimes violence. I believe the desk clerk was experiencing the later.

There was always the slight chance that she could be a racist and I was feeling the fallout of some pent-up hostility, either way it was par for the course for me. I had been treated indifferently all my life, by Whites, Blacks, and Native Americans being of mixed race. She handed me the transaction sheet to sign and then supplied me with my copy, the cardkey and returned my credit card. I was hungry and wanted to inquire about something to eat, but it was clear that she didn't want to be bothered, so I departed without any further discourtesy.

After settling in my room, I went back down to the lobby and discovered that the bar was still open for business. There was nothing fancy about the bar, like the rest of the hotel. There were no booths, stain glass, mahogany, or brass accenting the contour like you see at established franchise restaurants and bars. They had several red oak tables scattered about and surrounded by their matching chairs. There were different ceiling fans with light fixtures that weeded the ceiling with their blades slowly swirling around and immolating the mood of the town and the bar.

There were several reporters at the bar drinking and making merriment while listening to Top Pop being played over the speakers. I sat as far away from them as I possibly could. I didn't have anything against reporters, but they often get in the way of what you're trying to accomplish. There was a tall, lanky, young man with red hair and freckles attending the bar. He reminded me of Richie Cunningham from the old Happy Days television show or a good representative of the character from the MAD comic books. He looked as though he was just out of high school or first years of college.

He was wearing jeans, basketball shoes, and an old Milwaukee Bucks Jersey with (Lew) Alcindor's name on the back. If it was authentic, it should be enclosed under glass somewhere because it was a collector's item and worth at least 200,000 dollars. Then again, if it was authentic he wouldn't be working for the summer. An authentic Lew Alcindor (Kareem Abdul Jabbar) jersey could pay for his college tuition. He looked as if he could have been a basketball player himself standing at about 6 feet 5 inches. Most likely he was going to college and working during the summer break.

I found it odd that he would wear a Bucks jersey in New England, the backyard of the Celtics. New Englanders are fanatics when it comes to their sports teams, but it wasn't the only thing I found peculiar here thus far. He was a friendly fellow, a lot friendlier than the front desk clerk and greeted me as a customer service professional should.

"Good evening, sir, my name's Jock, how can I help you?" He asked with a smile and a New England accent.

"I was wondering if the kitchen was still open for service." I replied.

"Yes, it is. Let me get you a menu."

He flung the towel in his hands over his shoulders and reached beneath the counter top of the bar and produced a paper menu. It wasn't enclosed in any fancy embroidery or special paper encased in plastic or a bi-folder. It appeared as if they made it themselves on a laptop and printer.

"Thank you, Jock" I replied, as I quickly browsed the menu.

"Can I get you something to drink while you're deciding?"

"Yes, I'll take whatever you have on tap." Then he started calling out all these different beers favored by New Englanders. I was surprised at the selection and didn't expect there to be so many. I guess they drink a lot of beer here.

"I'll have the Sam Adams, and a cheese burger with fries," I instructed him. It's hard to mess up something as simple as a cheese burger and fries. I liked to keep it simple when uncertain.

"You here for the freak show?" He asked, as he served my draft.

"What do you mean?" I replied, curiously with a raised eyebrow, because it was a term that's often been used to describe me and others with abilities at the FBI's ViCAP Unit.

"Are you a reporter here covering the disappearances?" He further asked, examining me more carefully now.

He was checking out my countenance and looking to see if he saw any signs of a news media person; cameras, or whatever they carry around with them. I'm sure he had their composure and identity memorized by now, but couldn't figure out where I fit into the equation, like the desk sergeant. He never figured me for one of the many FBI agents that were in the motel with their off the rack suits that looked like each other.

"No, I'm not, a reporter or with the media groups." I responded with a slight grin and sipped on my beer. It was refreshing not to be categorized for a change.

"We've had a lot of them here lately," he said, and looked over at the men on the other side of the bar. He didn't care much for reporters or perhaps just those reporters, judging by the way he cut his eyes towards them. They were a little rowdy, even for a bar.

"We've had several people go missing in the forest recently, and with the missing children; this place has been crawling with reporters. Most of them prefer to stay in the expensive hotels outside of town, like the Tabor Inn, but these fellas came in yesterday and have been drinking like fraternity guys since they arrived. I don't know how they get anything done," he said, and then the rambunctious men called him for another round.

Jock sparked my interest, and I wanted to ask him about the other missing people, but they called him away. The Bureau of Indian Affairs didn't brief me on any citizens missing and I wasn't up to date on current affairs in the news. The Bureau was probably more concerned about their missing agents since the local law enforcement and FBI would be handling everything else.

While Jock was servicing the obstreperous group of men, I took a better look at them and noticed some peculiar features about the men. I observed scar tissue on their faces, and other observable areas where fighters and brawlers have noticeable scar tissue. Jock was right about one thing, they weren't the usual reporters that you run across, if they were reporters at all. He might have profiled them incorrectly. He was used to seeing the massive influx of reporters and agents, and just dumped these gentlemen in with the media since they clearly weren't with the FBI.

It didn't take long to prepare my simple meal, as I suspected. I wasn't really interested in hearing any further stories about vociferous reporters or the 'freak show' as the bartender put it. I've heard more than enough stories about being a freak myself. I asked the bartender to pack my food to go and departed. I left him a very sizeable tip because I've seen men like the raucous reporters. They asked for the world, in reference to service, but give so little in return. It's probably what the bartender dislikes about them.

"Mister, you don't want your change?" He asked surprisingly, as I got up from my seat. It was a sure giveaway that he was used to dealing with some real non-tippers.

"No, keep the change," I replied and continued out.

"Thank you very much," he shouted elatedly, *"My name is Jock; if you need anything just let me know."*

"Oh, there is one thing. My luggage was misplaced at the airport. Where can I purchase some clothes, and toiletries around here?"

"Well, we don't have a haberdashery or anything like that, but we do have a Dollar General for toiletries and such things, and if you go about 8 miles up the road to St. Albans, they have a Walmart, JC Penney, and other big chain department stores there," he replied with a smile. He was happy that he could accommodate me, unlike the receptionist, who could take a few pointers from him in customer service.

"Thanks, Jock. Have a nice night." I told him, and waved goodbye, as I exited.

I had to restrain myself from laughing at his apropos name. It couldn't have been any simpler, but I liked simple. I just made a new friend and a reliable source of information if I needed it. Bartenders knew all there was about the town and its residents. They were the sounding board of the town. I left with my meal in hand and went to my room.

As I walked down the hallway of the hotel, I sensed the energy of another supernatural. My energy crystal began to light up inside my shirt, as I approached the door to my suite. Whatever was inside was powerful. I curiously opened the door and entered the room cautiously, as my adrenalin began to kick in. I was ready to meet whoever or whatever was waiting. I didn't see anyone, as I looked around the room, but I could feel their energy. What exactly did it want?

It must have no idea that I can sense it, so I walked casually over to the small oval shaped table in the corner of the room and placed my meal on it. Then I went about my normal routine, and spotted it in my periphery. It was hiding in the mirror. I pretended not to see it, so I can get a better understanding of what it wanted. It was a transpicuous silhouette of a figure, but I could see it shifting in the mirror and displaying only its outer contour, like observing the refractive waves of light that appear to be rising from the ground on a sweltering summer day.

After several minutes, I realized that it just wanted to watch me, but why? I just arrived in Swanton, and already I had a fan club. Something that picked up on my energy signature and was now spying on me. I couldn't tell if it was friend or foe, but I'll play along with it for now, or at least until I can see its true intent. It's probably just a lost soul trying to find its way, like the others that I've assisted.

I took a shower after eating to relax and wash off the day before hitting the sack. I needed to get a fresh start in the morning. After showering I opened the bathroom door and discovered all the furniture in the room stacked in one corner of the room. I didn't think for a second that someone entered the room and did this. The door was still locked from the inside with the chain in place. This entity was clearly trying to send me a message, but it will take a lot more than that to scare me off.

While I was rearranging the furniture the chest drawer with the mirror began shaking, and then its drawers began opening and slamming violently back and forth. I waited and watched the spectacle until its conclusion, and when it was over the mirror became cold as a meat locker freezer. The frigid air flowed from the icy depths of the frost ridden anomaly like smoke emitted after extinguishing a blaze. I could feel the temperature drop in the room, as I watched the smoky exhale of my breath fuse with the chilled air surrounding the mirror. I could no longer see inside the mirror due to the ice and frost covering it.

I placed my hand on the mirror to initiate contact with the entity and it tried to pull me inside the mirror, but I held on to the outer frame of the mirror and only my head went inside. I witnessed a wasteland of dead uninhabited cities and ghost towns inside the mirror. The winds were blowing so hard you could hear it whistling and kicking up dirt, like in a sandstorm. Then I saw the graves of thousands of people, and the tiny glassy glowing eyes of thousands of apparitions appeared and began screaming with a deafening resound. I quickly used all my strength to pull myself back to the other side of the mirror to escape the pain.

I'm not certain what I was looking at Was it a vision from this timeframe and realm or the spiritual realm? What type of message was the apparition trying to tell me and why did it want me to leave? At least now I had its energy signature committed to memory. I spent the rest of the night dreamscaping with Nina in peaceful bliss.

I woke up several hours before dawn. It was going to be a busy day. It was like your first day at work and thinking you must prove yourself and your worth. I went over the files Nina gave me, which weren't much. They were depending on me to give them some resolve to the missing agents. The FBI Task force here in Swanton is supposed to brief me further on the case. I'm sure their hands are full, so my investigation of the missing BIA agents would be a welcome relief for them.

I heard several ravens and an owl outside my window, as I looked over the deficient case file. Owls are the most prolific nocturnal raptors in the sky at night. Their vision and hearing is impeccably suited for hunting in the dark, and their wings don't make a sound as they stealthily swoop down upon their prey. Its characteristics were very similar to my panther imprinting. The ravens were probably watching the owl and waiting for scraps.

Unlike the raptors, who hunt for their prey, ravens are scavengers, like the buzzards and vultures; they wait for the leftovers from another's kill. The ravens were opportunistic in every sense of the word. They are scavengers and didn't care if it was day or night, but they wouldn't dare approach the mighty owl. It would tear them apart and make them the next meal, because smaller birds were on the menu, and if provoked even larger ones.

I went to the window and opened it, to feel the cool breeze of the night's air against my face, and to satisfy my nocturnal instincts as well. The night's sky was painted with grey and dark blue water color hues, as ominous clouds veiled the light from the moon and stars, which mimicked the gloom that had encapsulated the small town. It was a lowly melancholy feeling that I've known all too well over the years, uprooted from solipsism, caustic and viral.

I closed my eyes and took in a deep breath; catching as much of this untainted night's air as I could pull into my lungs, and then releasing it slowly. I kept my eyes closed and listened to the primeval echoes of the wild sing its sweet and harmonious song, as the nocturnal creatures performed on the grandest of stages. It was life in its simplistic form; unfettered and untarnished by civilization. I was calm and at peace within it. I was one with nature, as my panther instincts took over.

I listened to the crickets and grasshoppers singing loudly, like the sound of a continuous and annoying ringer from an old telephone attempting to drown out the ambient sounds around them. I had learned back in the mountains of Cherokee how to filter their deafening sounds. To an average person, they were loud, but to my ears they were amplified and drum shattering. I heard an alpha male wolf, miles away, howling into the night, and gathering his pack, as their night's hunt was about to come to an end.

I could hear every creature outside with the ears of a panther, and when I opened my eyes I could see them as well with the night vision of a panther. I saw the owl in the distant tree with a rabbit that it had captured with its razor-sharp talons. The prey was already dead from its talons and now it was just picking at its prey with his sharp beak. I looked deep inside the glassy wonderful eyes of the owl, which appeared to look right back at me. It uncannily shared the same green eyes as me and the panther, but far larger and superior in depth, range and accuracy. They seemed to glow or reflect the light that shined upon them from the hotel when it looked in my direction. It was a magnificent and beautiful creature.

The eyes of most nocturnal predators looked this way in the dark, including the panther. I wondered if my eyes shined when looked upon in the darkness. The beady little black eyes of the ravens did no such thing, as they stared at me. They soaked up all the light and reflected nothing in return, pretty much like their lives. They say the eyes are the windows of the soul, and this seemed to be a good analogy of the raven. I spotted several deer in the distant forest, as the wolf pack gathered for an early morning hunt. My adrenaline began to spike, like the exhilarating rush you feel when you're on a rollercoaster ride!

It is times like these that it felt good to be different. For years, I shunned being different, and being looked upon as an outcast or a freak, but now it has empowered me beyond belief. I was at peace with myself for a change; spiritually, mentally and socially.

Swanton wasn't that different than the Smokey Mountains of Cherokee when it came to its wildlife and natural resources. Swanton was nestled between Lake Champlain and the Missisquoi River, and home of the Missisquoi National Wildlife Refuge. It was surrounded with forest lands and the Green Mountain Range to the north. I would have felt right at home in Swanton, if it wasn't for the dark tragedy looming over the town. My solace was disrupted as usual, this time by a hotel guest coming outside to smoke a cigarette. Man, and his unnatural ways. I closed the window to my suite and meditated until it was time to get ready for my first actual day back to work.

CHAPTER FOUR

THE SOKOKI TRIBAL COUNCIL/ UNWANTED GUESTS

Nina had scheduled a meeting for me with the FBI SAC (Special Agent in Charge) for 10:00 am at the police headquarters. Ten and eleven seemed to be the usual hours for the D.C. Beltway movers and shakers. Most of them didn't arrive to work until 9:00, and from nine to ten, they did coffee, looked over the work they were supposed to be doing for the day, and then B.S.

The clouds from last night remained into the morning, and produced a gloomy overcast sky which covered Swanton today. I haven't seen the sun since I'd been here. The weather seemed to have immolated the temperament of the town's people. Rain was definitely coming, but I was the only one who seemed concerned about weather. None of the pedestrians walking on the street had umbrellas or any rain gear in preparation for it. I guess they had more important things to think about in a town on the verge of erupting violence and chaos.

It was busier in Swanton during the daylight hours. The streets were filled with people and traffic. It was the overflow of visitors coming from all corners of the nation due to the mystery surrounding the missing children. The streets were also swamped with law enforcement officers and patrols from the city, county and state to combat the civil disobedience.

There had been several attacks on innocent Native Americans and some altercations with Native Americans fighting back.

The Swanton Sheriff's Department was located on Main Street with the other Government Municipalities. I drove smack dab into chaos when I arrived. It was like a scene from the Civil Rights Movement, but in reverse. There was a mob of reporters in front of the building and protestors rallying across the street with a wall of law enforcement officers in riot gear preventing them from rallying in the street. The protestors were shouting and yelling at the top of their lungs, some using obscenities to get their point across.

Their assorted signs asked for justice, the arrest of those responsible, and to find the missing children. There were hate signs of bigotry and racism that read: *Indian Murderers, Stop Indian Sacrifices,* and signs with *Native Americans* written on them and a red circle with a diagonal line covering the print. This was clearly a volatile situation. The unpleasant welcome of the hotel's desk clerk was a prelude to what I was witnessing. I couldn't stop thinking of how it reminded me of the black and white videos I observed of the Civil Rights Movement, but this was taking place in Bizarre World.

There was no unambiguous evidence that the Abenaki were involved in any of the abductions. The Abenaki were victims of proximity. There were several recent disappearances of citizens in the forest between the Abenaki Village and the town of Swanton; therefore, the Abenaki became the focal point of their hostility. They needed someone to blame for the mysterious disappearances, so it might as well be the minorities of the town.

I decided it would probably be best to park somewhere unnoticed and away from the station to avoid any backlash from vandals seeing me go inside the sheriff's station. It was chaos on the streets and the sidewalk was crowded with people as I walked towards the station. Even through the crowd I couldn't help but notice the attractive young woman wearing a red dress approaching me. She was turning the heads of men and women, as she walked by. We made eye contact, as she smiled and spoke to me or more like whispered something, as she passed by. I couldn't make out what it was, so I paused and looked back.

"Excuse me?" I said, aloud and hoping to get her attention, but the beautiful woman in red never looked back.

Before I could fully turn around to proceed, a man bumped into me, almost knocking me over, and said in a very low whisper, *"Turn around."*

"Pardon me," I replied, sharply, and quickly turning around, but he continued walking, like the woman in red, as if he didn't hear me.

I hurried in the direction of the man, but then a teen aged boy coming from the same direction of the man whispered, *"Leave this place."*

I grabbed the teenager firmly by the arm before he walked away and asked, *"What was that?"*

"Excuse me?" He said, startled, and with a shocked look on his face.

I could tell by his expression that he was scared and oblivious as to what I was talking about. He thought I was a crazy man, as he pulled back his arm and rushed away. But no sooner as he departed an elderly woman in passing said, *"Before it's too late."*

Then another woman passing by whispered, *"You're not wanted here."*

I grabbed her sternly by the arm, before she could continue.

"What did you say," I asked, hearing fully what she said.

"Get off me," she snapped anxiously, as she vigorously snatched her arm from my clutches.

"What was that you said to me?" I inquired again, tempestuously, and with a stern look.

"Look, I don't know what your problem is, but if you touch me again I'm calling the cops," she angrily roared with her face squinched tight

and giving me the evil eye cross-over before departing, as the passersby took notice.

I remained there, stuck in a period of stasis, in the middle of the crowded sidewalk, as I watched her continue walking away without turning back around. Then a dizzying barrage of people passing me on the street, one by one, repeated the same thing in succession, as the previous pedestrians. I thought my head was going to explode, as I walked towards the sheriff' station. Then I closed my eyes to center myself for a couple of seconds. I was caught off guard by something playing with my head, and using innocent people to do it.

This is definitely one freaked out, creep show. Whatever it is, it's extremely powerful. I've never encountered such a quick and temporary possession of a mass of random people before. I must admit, it was quite impressive. I can't wait to tell Asku about it.

I paused for a few more seconds on the sidewalk to wait for the next succession of possessions, but nothing presented itself, except for the occasional odd look from pedestrians passing by. The strange thing is I didn't feel its presence, and my energy crystal was still on full blast from whatever was looming over the town. Perhaps they're the same entity. Nonetheless, this anomaly was affecting me in the strangest ways.

This was the second time my energy crystal has failed me; the first time was in D.C. with the stranger in black, and now. I was beginning to think the damn thing was broken. One thing is for sure, it's obvious that something didn't want me here.

Before I reached the entrance of the sheriff's office, I spotted something peculiar in the mob across the street. The four men from the hotel's bar were front and center in the crowd, and inciting the mob into a riot. These men weren't reporters, as I expected, they were boosters; hired to create chaos and ignite the crowd. That would explain all the scar tissue I observed on their faces. It appears that someone or party has a vested interest in seeing the town divided or at least going after the Abenaki.

Swanton was already proving to be one interesting small town. I dodged through the blockade of media personnel stationed outside of the police headquarters in order to get inside. All I needed was someone from the media to recognize me from the Coyote case and compound the difficulties of this case even further. It been a little outside two years since the Coyote case. The media has short term memories, and what is news today is forgotten tomorrow, as they constantly search for the next big story. I couldn't afford to take any chances of being recognized. This is one of those times when having long hair that covered your face provided the perfect disguise. I walked quickly through the media horde with my head down and face covered by my hair. They stared and examined me, as I passed, but no one could get a good description.

I straightened out my hair in the vestibule, once I entered the building, and then I went directly to the desk sergeant. He scrutinized me, as I approached, given me the up and down. I could see his mind working trying to determine the reasons why I was here. It was probably a game that he played daily with himself, and might have been good at it until the invasion of out-of-towners. I could see the puzzlement on the sergeant's face. He couldn't tell what profession I was in or what category to place me in, so I made it easy on him and his game. I began pulling out my credentials before I gave it to him and had it in my hand. He recognized the standard bi-fold Government Wallet. I could see his eyes enlarge with surprise at the discovery that I was law enforcement, but he took recompense in directing me to the conference room before I could state the nature of my visit.

"They're all in there, join the party," he said with a look of satisfaction and relief on his face, even though I assisted him in his game.

The meeting was already well on its way when I entered the conference room. It appeared to have started at least an hour before I arrived. Nina got her information from Washington Bureau in reference to the start of the briefing. Someone must have passed the information to her incorrectly because she was a stickler for accuracy. There were various agencies present in the conference room with the FBI Task Force heading the investigation. I didn't want to interrupt the SAC during his briefing, but others in the audience turned and watched, as I took a seat in the rear. The room became a bit louder, as some recognized me in the audience and the gossip spread like a wild fire.

"Ok, people, that's enough, quiet down; I need your attention up here." The SAC called the room to order, as he sharply glanced at me with cold and disapproving stare.

The SAC with his New England accent outlined what each agency's responsibility would be during the investigation. The Canadian Secret Intelligence Service (CSIS) was present and represented by an Inspector Antoine Rubidoux, who also spoke briefly for the CSIS and the Royal Canadian Mounties. The National Forest and Wildlife Rangers, the Border Patrol, Vermont State Police, the County Police and Swanton Police were in attendance. Then there was little ole me, the party crasher, who came late and sat in the back.

The FBI SAC was Agent Whyte. He was about 5 feet 7 inches in height, a short man, relatively in his mid-thirties and beginning to bald on the top already. Law enforcement can do that to certain people if you let it. It's an extremely demanding and stressful career if not managed properly. He was husky, but didn't appear to be fat. He was wearing an off the rack suit with shirt and tie. His team consisted of five men and one woman. They were the ones in the blue and gray bureaucratic suits that immolated his outfit, including the female agent, as she attempted to fit in with the boys.

She is an African American female, and probably has it just as hard as me, except she's trying to assimilate, instead of trailblazing, as I did. She blended right in with her male counterparts. She wore a pants suit, oxford shirt; buttoned almost to the top and low-heeled shoes, all in the standard black, grey and blue. The only thing that separated her attire from the other cronies is that she didn't wear a tie, which was a good thing. In law enforcement work, a tie can be used as a weapon against you and could cost you, your life, if not a clip-on. It's like having a ready-made noose around your neck.

She has a pretty face, even without make up. Her body was perfectly sculpted, like an athlete. I'm not certain if she played sports or if she acquired her figure from attempting to keep up with the boys in a male dominated profession, but it would prove its worth in the field. She didn't want to attract the attention of male counterparts or be singled out for anything, except for her work ethics. Therefore, she tried to conceal her figure in loosely fitted clothing. Although, if you looked careful enough, you could see the contours of her well-built body, as she moved.

She reminded me of the tennis star Serena Williams. If she put on a bathing suit or more appealing, tight fitting clothing, then all bets would be off. She would grab more attention than Serena in a Cat Suit at the U.S. Open! Except, she would never want to be seen that way. She wanted to make it on an equal playing field, as if there was such a thing. Like I've always said, *"Within the chaos, there's always rhythm. You just have to listen a bit more arduously."*

Inspector Rubidoux of the CSIS was dressed differently from the FBI Agents. He had on a tailored suit and looked like a Swiss banker. I had on jeans, cowboy boots, a white oxford shirt and a tan colored blazer. Tan went with every color combination; besides it was the only sports coat that fit me at the local JC Penny's. As soon as the meeting is adjourned it was coming off.

I had missed most of the meeting, but I got the gist of it. The Forest and Wildlife Rangers along with the Mounties were tasked with tracking down a bear that was believed to be a man killer. The Border Patrol and CSIS would conduct investigations along the Canadian border and the CSIS would continue within Canada. The locals would assist the FBI with their interior investigations on the missing children, which was going nowhere. They were no closer to bringing in a suspect than they were months ago, hence the civil unrest.

I wasn't included in any of the teams paired. I don't know if it was intentional or because I arrived late, but Nina ensured me that all jurisdictions would be notified of my involvement in the case. I guess someone didn't get the memo. I was sent to bridge the gap between the Bureau of Indian Affairs and the FBI and thus far I was getting off to a bad start. Most people would feel isolated or ostracized by this, but I had grown accustomed to such things. I didn't mind not being paired, I preferred working alone, but I was a bit curious about his theory on the search for bears.

I was a little perplexed on which way to approach with my question because I was used to just randomly blurting out answers or scenarios while working with the ViCAP Unit. Agent Whyte was conducting a more regimental and controlled briefing. I immediately thought about Agent Gracie Mullins, and how this must have been what it was like when she raised her hand during the Coyote case, eons ago. It seemed a strange thing to me back then; to see a grown person raise their hand like in grade school, so I just blurted out.

"Excuse me Agent Whyte, so you think a bear or bears broke into the homes of several families in one night and took their children without making a sound or signs of forced entry? And what type of bear devours several people without leaving any tracks behind?"

There were soft giggles and faint laughter in the conference room after my soliloquy which only lit the flames of discontent in Special Agent Whyte that were somewhat masked until now or at least tolerable.

"Oh, excuse me everyone, but this is the celebrated ex-FBI Profiler Agent Christian Sands. He is here on behalf of the Indian Affairs Bureau. I'm sorry, but perhaps you can rub two sticks together, cut the head off a rooster and show us who or what the killer is. I heard all about that hoodoo voodoo crap you pulled in the Southwest. I tell you what, why don't you leave the analytic police work to us, and you can go round-up some frog legs and chicken heads. We're doing real investigative work here." He sarcastically replied.

"Last I checked Quantico is teaching procedures based upon that case that you are so nonchalantly dismissing. I was told that the FBI had to rewrite most of the standard procedures on investigating and profiling serial killers based upon my findings."

"I guess they left out the chickens, huh?" He quipped with a smile, and redirected the laughter in his favor.

"I'm sorry if I offended you in anyway Special Agent Whyte, but I was merely trying to say we need to broaden our approach and examine the evidence a little closer before we jump to the conclusion that we are only looking for a bear."

"Look, I understand the diplomacy of D.C. getting the tribal investigators involved in this, but you're a day late and a dollar short arriving to the party. I'll ask you this only once, please don't hinder this investigation with any of your mumbo jumbo methods, there are enough real investigators here. If you are here as a liaison for the Native Americans, then that's fine with me, but this is an FBI led case. I don't think I'll be requiring your type of expertise." He remarked.

"But you still haven't answered my question." I riposted, before he could continue.

He balled up his fist, breathed in deeply, and puckered his lips inwardly in a display of displaced self-control. The room became quiet after Special Agent Whyte displayed his contempt for me, but it wasn't anything new to me. I was used to being despised and looked upon as a freak since I agreed to work with the ViCAP Unit.

"To answer your question Mr. Sands, no we don't believe that bears are responsible for the abduction of children of course. Yesterday we found the body parts of your missing agents in the forest. They were mangled body parts displaying signs that they were attacked by a rather large animal and portions of their remains had been eaten. We also have several other citizens reported missing last seen in the forest where we discovered the body parts of the agents." He callously stated with no regards for the missing agents.

"Does Indian Affairs know about this?" I asked, morosely.

"No one knows about this. That's why we're having this meeting that started an hour and a half before you arrived," he coarsely replied.

"So, these body parts have been verified belonging to the agents?" I continued.

"Yes, we handed out folders containing everything we have on the case at the beginning of the meeting. Please feel free to take one," he said annoyed, and attempted to turn his attention back to the general assembly, but I wasn't finished with him.

"And the hotel where the agents were staying, were their rooms preserved as crime scenes?" I abruptly blurted out.

"Yes, they were for about 48 hours, and then we had to relinquish the rooms to the hotel. They have a business to run with the heavy flow of traffic coming here now. We searched the area top and bottom and it didn't find any information vital to the case," he annoyingly huffed.

"And where are their personal items?" I asked.

"We shipped them back to D.C." he sternly retorted.

"To the FBI?" I inquired.

"No to the Indian Affairs Bureau, now if you would just read the folder I'll provide to you I'm sure all your questions will be answered," he replied with a flustered and bothersome voice.

I didn't give my opinion for the duration of the meeting, and waited to the end to retrieve my folder for the case. They at least had to provide me with that. The FBI just took away my crypt notes, literally. Any contact I wanted to do with the dead was through dreamscape as well. I need to be in contact with some personal items of the dead like the living. I couldn't even go to their rooms and feel around to make a connection because there would have been countless guests in there by now.

I knew this wasn't going to be an open and shut case, but I didn't expect it to be complicated by incompetency. I could care less about the hotel wanting the rooms back. My concerns were about the two dead agents. I would have sat on the rooms till next year if need be. After about thirty more minutes of briefing, the SAC ended the meeting with a precautionary statement for all regarding the case.

"Once again I urge you to treat this case and the information as sensitive. We don't want the media scaring the local citizens any more than they *already are. We have a powder keg waiting to explode between the locals, and the Native Americans, so let's not add media fuel to the investigation."*

I didn't wait to raise my hand and be called on by the SAC after his closing statements because I knew I'd be reaching for the ceiling for an eternity. I also knew this would bury any chances I had to win any brownie points with the SAC, but then again, it seems I was already on his shit list from the start. Therefore, I quickly blurted out my closing statements before the meeting was adjourned.

"Excuse me, Agent Whyte, but you didn't mention anything about quarantining the forest until we can get a better idea of what we are dealing with here. Is that also included in your folder briefing?"

"I'm sorry, Mr. Sands, but we're not the CDC, and we can't just go around quarantining areas as we feel," he smugly responded.

"Perhaps I'm using the wrong vernacular, did you close off or blockade the forest from the public?" I inserted.

"No, do you understand what that would entail? There is no way to implement such a suggestion. We don't have the funding or the personnel to perform such a large-scale deployment. The size of the forest makes it an impossible task, but what we have done is inform the public to stay out of the park for safety purposes." He said, and began packing his things, as if the conversation was over, but neither his audience nor I moved a muscle. They were enjoying the verbal jousting between us.

"So how did you accomplish informing the public of the safety concerns?" I returned.

"We had Park Services place pamphlets up around the forest," he uttered, impatiently.

"You're talking about an impossible task, the likelihood of a tourist or sightseer seeing such a thing is farfetched, and looking at the assembly in this room, I'd say we have more than enough cooperating agencies to accomplish what you consider impossible." I retorted.

"Mr. Sands this meeting is adjourned. If you have any further questions I suggest we meet afterwards, since you arrived an hour late and didn't have the courtesy or decency to get here when the rest of us arrived for the meeting." He blustered, and closed his briefcase.

"No, I'm finished," I responded, and everyone got up from their seats.

My first day back didn't go anything like I expected it. I understood the concerns of the SAC, but he was thinking like a bureaucrat and concerned about numbers and money, when I was concerned about saving lives. I was against holding back information from the public and giving them as much information as required to keep them safe. My philosophy is that the more knowledge and awareness they have, meant the better prepared they'd be. Besides the media frenzy was already here. It was like an obstacle course just to get inside the building. It will be difficult enough keeping them out of the forest without a proper plan.

After the meeting, I was bombarded by the other members of the conference room. Apparently, I wasn't forgotten by the law enforcement community, as everyone greeted me, introduced themselves, shook my hand and questioned me on the case. The FBI SAC and four of his cronies held back and remained by his side, as the other two agents approached me with the rest of the crowd.

I felt like a celebrity and must admit, it did feel a little gratifying. I politely explained to everyone that I was just getting in on the case and didn't have anything to offer. Afterwards everyone handed me their business cards and extended their assistance if I needed it.

I was most impressed with Inspector Rubidoux. He was thorough and professional. He asked if I would be interested in visiting their headquarters and speaking to their agents and if I was interested in teaching at their academy. I explained to him that I was only a music teacher, but he stated that he already knew. He said my knowledge in the field and the fact that I was a former teacher made me the perfect candidate. I told him that I would think about it and he insisted that I at least visit and speak after the case. I agreed to it, but things have a way of changing quickly on these types of cases, and I didn't really want to commit, but he seemed like a nice enough gent.

When the fanfare was over I went over to the SAC to get a case file. I didn't need to be a Shaman to tell that neither he nor his bookend cronies liked me for whatever reason. Everyone in the conference room could feel the negative energy and the tone in which he spoke with me. Another dead giveaway was the scowl on his face when he spoke to me. He looked as if he had just tasted a very tart lemon when addressing me.

"Look Mr. Sands, I don't care who let you out of the loony bin and gave you credentials, but this is an FBI investigation. I don't need an ex-profiler released on a Psych Eval screwing this up. I remember you from the Freak Show at Quantico. Now you're supposed to be some sort of legend; the man who saved the agency and re-wrote the books on investigating. Well we do things by the letter in this Task Force, so please just stay out of the way." He flung a case folder onto the table for me to take that just barely missed falling to the floor.

"I assure you that I'm not here to cause you or the bureau any problems, but since the two Indian Affairs Agents were discovered dead, I'll be sticking around for a little while. You don't have to worry though, I won't be getting in your way, and please stay out of mine." I riposted, picked up the case file and departed without another word.

The SAC made his intentions clear enough; I was an unwanted guest here. Agent Whyte telling me that I had to go at it alone without the assistance or the resources of the FBI was nothing new to me. It was a song that I heard before and knew all the lyrics. My head was still spinning from the possession merry-go-round that I experienced just before entering this circus, now I must deal with this. What in the hell have I gotten myself into? I must be a glutton for punishment! I'll just play it cool for now. I don't need to be rocking the boat any further.

I was beyond being an unwanted guest. Nothing and no one wanted me here in Swanton, from the residents to the FBI, and the supernatural. I had half a mind to say to hell with it, turn around and retreat to the solace of the Smoky Mountains and Cherokee County, but I kept hearing Asku's voice telling me to persevere. Then there was my spirit guide on the other shoulder telling me to stay the course for the sake of the vision quest, and what I might find. Also, there were missing children involved and several unsolved murders.

If I leave now, this case would never be solved, especially if I left it up to the FBI and their bear theory. The concept of a supernatural entity behind any of this would only discredit my already shaky status with Special Agent Whyte, and most of the law enforcement personnel present, even though I experienced it right outside their door.

Lucky for me, I don't have to answer to the FBI and those sycophant bureaucrats any longer. I have a BIA special agent badge to prove it. Although I didn't feel special nor did it grant me any special privileges; except get me in the game, and grant me access to information, which was already filtering down to me in a hand-me-down fashion.

I departed through the rear door of the police headquarters and made my way down the backstreet avoiding the crowd to get to my rental vehicle. I sat in the car with the engine off and quickly perused the case file. The pictures of the mangled body parts were gruesome. My first question was why they were in the forest or were they taken there and slaughtered? I spent enough time with the bears in the Smokies to know that this wasn't the work of bears. There would be more parts of the agents still around and intact. Human consumption wasn't a part of a bear's diet. They will kill with one blow, but only if threatened and never for food.

The last place the BIA agents were seen according to the files was at the Sokoki Abenaki Tribal Council. That will be my next visit. I'll let the FBI concentrate on the missing children and I'll do what I came here to do. I won't be surprised if they are related incidents. I don't think for a second that a bear ate a total of four people and only left a few selective body parts behind.

I must have driven for about a block when I noticed that someone was following me. It couldn't be anyone but the FBI, no one else knows I'm here. They weren't even trying to hide the fact that they were tailing me or at least I don't think so, because if they are, they're the worst surveillance team I've ever seen. Agent Whyte decided it was in his best interest to monitor me. I thought we had laid out our ground rules. I guess he was covering all the angles. I didn't mind them following me, if they stay out of the way.

The Missisquoi/ Sokoki Abenaki Tribal Council was located near the north side of town, 100 Grand Avenue, Swanton, Vermont. It's housed in an old brownstone building with three floors. The steps to the entrance went directly to the second floor. There is an abundance of buildings in this part of the country with similar construction because of the inclement weather. There is snow on the ground for 6 months out of the year in Vermont with an average 81.2 inches over the course of that period.

There were several small shops and businesses closed in this part of Swanton. Most of the business was south of here, on or near Main Street where the government municipals where located. It appeared as if they started developing this area, but over the course of whatever, discontinued. The businesses that remained were the essentials; a corner store, laundromat, gas station and a couple of other small low-end stores.

I didn't know what to expect from the Abenaki. Will they welcome me or refute? There was a sheriff's cruiser parked near the Tribal Council building, 100 Grand Avenue, and about four protestors across the street. Most of the protestors were at the police headquarters soaking up the media attention today. I'm sure they met at various places daily. These stragglers were like me in that regards, they didn't get the memo on the change of time or venue. Once again, I parked further down the street from the protestors to avoid the vehicle from being vandalized by an unruly demonstrator. I don't think the FBI would stop them from defacing the vehicle or flattening the tires, it would make their job easier by slowing me down.

It was hard not being seen going inside the council building. There wasn't any traffic or congestion like on Main Street. The protestors watched me as I walked towards the steps of Tribal Council and yelled even louder, now that they had an audience. The sheriff had his head buried deep in some sort of magazine until the protestors caught his attention with the elevation of their voices. I would have easily slipped by him if it wasn't for their quick roar. He lifted his head and examined me, as I climbed the steps leading to the entrance. He had been here all morning and didn't know my identity.

The lobby of the Tribal Council was gorgeous. The walls and floors were comprised of Polished Cappuccino marble and what appeared to be very expensive artifacts and artwork from the Sokoki/Abenaki history. There were four items, large than life, etched on the four walls of the lobby which professed the Sokoki beliefs. The north wall has their traditional name etched on it *"The Sokoki Band of the Abenaki Nation of Missisquoi."*

The east wall contained the Constitution of the Sokoki Band with the preamble etched into the wall, *"The Abenaki people of the Sokoki Band of the Abenaki Nation of Missisquoi and our descendants, recognize the need to preserve the heritage of our Ancestors, our culture, our history, our language, our ancestral naïve lands, and our sovereign right to live free and commune with the spirits of the natural world, do hereby establish this constitution as the Great Law."* Underneath the preamble were the articles of the constitution, encased in glass frames under soft lights.

The west wall contained the Three Truths etched on it; *"1. Peace: Is it preserved? 2. Righteousness: Is it moral, and 3. Power: Does it preserve the integrity of the people."* I found the Three Truths to be simplistic, yet pure in the most Machiavellian way. Etched in the marble wall of the south wall, above the entrance/exit door, was the phrase *"Remembering the Past, while heading into the Future."* It was an excellent parting message.

There was an elderly Abenaki woman seated at the receptionist desk, and typing on a laptop that I approached for assistance. She immediately stopped what she was doing; and swayed her attention towards me with a smile.

"Good morning sir, can I help you?"

"Yes, my name is Christian Sands; I'm from the Bureau of Indian Affairs, and I would like to speak to a council member. It's a matter of grave importance."

"They're in a meeting right now Mr. Sands, but I will inform them that you are here. Will you have a seat please?" she asked, politely.

"Thank you very much, Mam."

She waved her hand towards the chairs that were lined up in a row to the right of her, as a conductor would do. She smiled again, and then she proceeded down the hallway to the door that had conference room written above it. She looked back at me before opening the door; smiled, and then proceeded inside. After about 5 minutes the elderly woman returned to the desk and informed me that one of the council members would be joining me soon, so I waited patiently.

There was no one else in the huge lobby area except for me and the elderly receptionist, and she resumed what she was doing on the laptop, only looking at me randomly and smiling. She one fingered the keypad of the laptop like a burly construction worker hitting a thumbtack with a sledge hammer, hard and forcefully. She was treating the keys as if it was an old typewriter that required a little pressure to force the hammered mechanism to move. Each smack of the keys resounded through the vacant lobby. Although she wasn't struggling to find the keys, she had become fast and proficient using two fingers.

I took a small tour of the lobby area while I waited for a council member. All the artwork and artifacts were exquisite, but I took considerable interest in the beautiful paintings that surrounded the lobby walls. There was one that really stood out to me; it was a painting containing a chieftain or shaman speaking to his tribe around a campfire. It just seemed to capture life in its fullest. The artist didn't leave out one detail, as if he or she took a picture with a camera, but it was better because of the color schemes used.

I later attempted to amuse myself with some outdated magazines, and several of those crosswords puzzle books that I haven't seen since my childhood. I thought the puzzle publications were extinct with the emergence of the internet. I flipped through an old John Deere tractor magazine; they had a few of them. I guess that was a popular item in this part of the country. When I got to the end of the second magazine an elderly distinguished gentleman exited the conference room and approached me.

"Good afternoon, Agent Sands, I'm Joseph Fox, chairmen of the Sokoki Tribal Council, and how can I help you?" he said and extended his hand. I was relieved that he greeted me kindly.

"I'm here investigating the deaths of Agents Stone and Wankaego," I replied, dolefully and shook his hand.

"Yes, Agent (Nina) Blackwater telephoned us and stated that you would probably be visiting, but we were under the impression that the agents were only missing. I'm saddened by this news Agent Sands, they were good men," he said, solemnly.

"Can we go somewhere, so I can ask you a few questions about the agents?" I inquired.

"Sure, I'll take you in to see the council. We will help you in any way possible. All of us knew Agents Stone and Wankaego."

Chairmen Fox, who is considered the chief in tribal law, took me inside and introduced me to the council members. The council was composed of nine members including the chief. Most of the members were elders except for Kateri Ichtyol and Mat Youngblood, who quickly corrected the chief and demanded that I call him by his full Abenaki name, Matunaagd Youngblood. The other members of the council were Sam Youngblood, Steve Nighthorse, Tihkoosue (Ty) Echohawk, Brian Eaglewing, Moose St. Francis, and Huritt Tenskwatawa. This was the usual number of council members I've noticed.

Kateri was young and beautiful. She reminded me of an exotic model that could ornament any of the top fashion magazines or run ways. She was tall with knock out curves, a gorgeous face and long jet-black hair that went down to the middle of her back. Her smile was intoxicating, and made you crave for more. Her eyes were beautifully brown, and spoke to you of a deep passion and affection. Then there was her soft toffee colored skin that was unblemished by the hands of man. She wore no make-up, because it would only tarnish the natural beauty that God has created. She reminded me of Nina in every way.

By having Kateri and Youngblood on the council it was in accordance with the writing etched into the stone wall of the lobby, *"Remembering the Past, while heading into the Future."* The elders composed their past while Kateri and Youngblood were their future.

I shook everyone's hand, as I introduced myself. Since my days of working with the FBI, I made it a habit of touching everyone, and items in their possession during an investigation. This allowed me to weed out potential suspects during dreamscape, now it just came naturally to me. I would be a Mysophobe's worst nightmare.

Everyone shook my hand, except for Councilman Matunaagd Youngblood. He was about my age, and height. His hair was just a little bit longer than mine, and he wore it in a ponytail. We could have easily been mistaken for brothers, but by the frosty reception and the estranged look he gave me, I don't think we'll be exchanging family history. He was very physically fit, all muscle, and would be a formidable adversary for anyone, at least anyone without supernatural abilities. He was fierce looking and had a commanding presence with a tomahawk strapped to his side.

The wearing of tomahawks isn't unusual in Native American cultures; they are an all-purpose tool, like a Swiss Army Knife. It's used for cutting, chopping, piercing, digging, smashing, scrapping, hammering and hunting. In the right hands, it can also be used as a deadly weapon; that you can wield, throw, and use offensively or defensively.

I could tell that Matunaagd and I weren't going to be friends any time soon, and his cooperation would be scarce, as he spoke to the council in Algonquian, the language of the Abenaki.

"So, the wobi zanoba (white man) sent another unwanted Mekwi (Red) wannabe to speak to us, thinking this would change anything. How many will they send us? This one is probably just Mkazawi (Black)," he said with disdain.

"Mat, please, this is not the time or place for this," Sam Youngblood, Matunaagd's father, advised him.

I understood every word they said. Then again, Youngblood probably knows I speak the language, and doesn't care. Why else would they send me here? I smiled and didn't comment, as if I didn't understand, to see how much further he would take this.

"Why should we cow down to this disrespect. It is an insult. He's not wanted here, at least send us someone who is First Nations people, instead they send us sucki (half-breeds) ..."

"We've heard enough Mat," Kateri briskly interrupted him.

My patience was running a bit thin today, because of the meeting at the police headquarters, so I quickly ended Matunaagd's rants by addressing the council in Algonquian.

"I'm not here as an enemy of the Abenaki, nor am I here on behalf of the wobi zanobi. Chief Fox said that the Indian Affairs Bureau has been a friend of the Abenaki; is it customary for the Sokoki to insult those who you consider friends or do the Sokoki speak with two tongues? I believed Chief Fox's words to be true, but then I hear the insults from another council member." I looked directly at Matunaagd.

"Councilman Matunaagd Youngblood doesn't speak for the council majority, he is just one voice, and a minority voice at that. Council Youngblood should apologize for his rudeness. It is disrespectful to you and the council." Chief Fox replied, and looked sternly at Matunaagd.

"Where is the apology when they exploit our lands, and keep us from what is rightfully ours? Why doesn't the Government send someone to investigate that? When Boss Winchester pollutes our waters, and desecrate the lands with his factories, where are the investigators? We're the ones who should be receiving the apologies," Youngblood bellowed, and then angrily got up from his chair, and flung it to the floor in an outburst of rage, before storming out of the room.

Matunaagd Youngblood was a hot head, who wore his emotions on his sleeves, like cheap cufflinks that stood out while wearing an expensive suit, tasteless. He was full of pride and had a rebellious streak in him a mile long. This was an explosive combination during volatile times between the Abenaki village and the people of Swanton. I'll have to keep an eye on him for sure. The rest of the council was speechless, and embarrassed, after his outburst, so I broke the silence with a question to bridge the gap.

"Who is Boss Winchester, and what is he speaking about?"

"Mr. Winchester is the most powerful person in Swanton, and perhaps in Northern Vermont. His factory was built on the edge of the town near the Missisquoi River. The factory is believed to have been polluting the waters and the lands surrounding it with waste byproducts. We protested to the Mayor, but it did no good, and then we notified Congress about it, but with no resolve. The Indian Affairs Bureau became involved and finally EPA Agents were sent to investigate, but they stated they couldn't find any pollutants, yet the fish were dying as were other animals living off the river. Our people became sick shortly afterwards, but the EPA's investigation was determined to be negative for pollutants," Chief Fox paused with a tearful look before clearing his throat, as Kateri continued for the elder who was becoming emotional.

"Most of us lost loved ones during that period. Chief Fox lost his son to the illness. After our people became sick, the factory workers became ill also, and one by one, they quit their jobs at the factory, and it closed. They couldn't find the cause of the illness, but whenever someone was hired on, they became ill for days and when they returned to work they just became sick again. Boss Winchester blames us for the factory closing; he says we placed a curse on the factory. He has been an enemy of the Sokoki ever since, and has rallied the town's people behind him." Then she paused for a brief period, as if reflecting upon something solemnly with concern, and then she snapped out of it and continued with an angrier tone.

"Now he (Winchester) blames us for everything bad that happens in Swanton, including the missing children and the recent deaths. Youngblood was just acting out of frustration because of all the allegations and mistreatment of the Sokoki. He can't see past his hatred presently,"

Councilman Yellowbear stated, as the other elders nodded their heads in agreement.

"Hatred of the Abenaki stretches back as far as the French and Indian Wars. We just recently became recognized as a people by the State of Vermont in 2006, after being here hundreds of years before the colonist. On May 7, 2012, we (the Abenaki Sokoki People of Missisiquoi) were recognized as a tribe by the State. We are now known as the Abenaki Nation at Missisquoi. Now we fight to have what is left of our lands to be recognized as a reservation, and the right to vote, but the State is reluctant to do so," Kateri inserted with a worried look across her face.

"And what about the Mayor, how does he factor into all of this?" I asked.

"He represents the interest of the town, but mainly Boss Winchester's interest. Mayor Hancock is Boss Winchester's brother-in-law, and he is also a victim of the missing children tragedy," Kateri replied.

"So, you see Agent Sands, you've stepped into a war zone," Chief Fox went on to say with a burdened look.

We went back to speaking in English, as the council continued cooperating and answering my questions about the town, and about the murdered agents. I was satisfied with their answers, but I'll be keeping an eye on Councilman Youngblood and his temper. Nothing good can result from his behavior. I said good bye to the council, and Kateri handed me a tee-shirt before leaving.

"Here, Agent Sands, this is something for you to wear, and remember us when you get back to D.C."

It was a red tee-shirt that had the letters NARF in large bold white letters and underneath it was smaller print describing the acronym: Native Americans Right Fund. It was a fund established to achieve civil rights for the First Nations People. It's still hard to believe that in this day and age the First Nations People are still struggling just to get voting rights. Then I remembered the struggles of my ancestors, the Cherokee Freedmen, and the other tribal freedmen with their unending fight just to be recognized by the tribes, yet alone voting rights.

"Thank you very much, Ms. Ichtyol. I will most definitely wear it," I replied, as she walked me back to the exit.

I didn't have the heart to tell her that I've been a resident of North Carolina for the past several years, and that I rarely get the chance to visit my hometown, D.C. I was only working this case as a favor, and God willing; I'll be back in North Carolina, as soon as it's over. She had been overly kind and helpful to me throughout the meeting. She cleared up and bridged some grey areas to give me a full scope of what is going on between the town's people and the Abenaki.

Kateri is young, beautiful, and intelligent. She reminded me of Nina. It was just one of the perks that came with traveling on assignment; meeting gorgeous women from various parts of the country. I could see her one day being the council chairman which I'm certain Youngblood had his sights on. The elderly woman was still pounding away at the laptop in the lobby as I departed.

"Travel safely Mr. Sands," the elderly woman said, looking up from the laptop.

I paused for a moment because it kind of startled me. This was the same thing Mrs. Jerrells and the Great Mother said to me when I departed their company. I thought it was strange then, and find it even stranger now, because I've never heard it said quite that way.

"Thank you... you too," I stammered after pausing for about a half of a minute.

"Is everything alright?" Kateri asked when she saw the flustered look on my face.

"Yes, everything is fine, thank you." I informed her, and created a smile to hide my bewilderment.

"Once again, Agent Sands, please excuse Youngblood's rudeness. It's been a little turbulent around here lately," she said, staring endlessly out the door at the protestors.

"I can understand that, but only calmer heads will prevail under these circumstances," I reassured her.

"Are you going to the forest now?" She inquired, now looking back at me.

"Yes…I am, but how did you know?" I asked curiously with raised eye brows, but she didn't answer and further asked.

"Do you have a guide or someone to show you around up there?"

"Not really, but I'm a pretty good scout," I answered, colorfully.

"People have been getting lost up there for years, but not until recently have actual bodies and remnants of bodies been found. Whenever the Abenaki are missing it goes unnoticed and without any actions taking by the police, but now that townies are missing, they want to riot and lynch us. Damned if we do, damned if we don't," she fumed in a disturbed voice and her face squinched into a mad expression.

"I'm sorry to hear about the injustices projected upon the Abenaki. Hopefully I can solve this and put an end to it." I attempted to console her.

"As I told you, this has been going on way before the missing town's children and the killings," she replied.

"Well at least they'll have one less thing to blame on you. I'll see you later," I said and touched her on the side of her arm.

"Please allow me to escort you up there. The last thing we need is another missing agent. I know the forest and surroundings well," she urged me.

"I couldn't ask you to do that, it's too dangerous in the forest right now."

"Yes, it is for those who don't know it, besides it's no more dangerous than it is in here," she replied, again, looking out the door at the demonstrators.

"They'll behave themselves, as long as the sheriff is parked there," I replied. I could tell that she had some reserved concerns about the protestors. "Besides, like I said, I have pretty good tracking instincts."

"You mean like an Indian," she quipped with a smile.

"No, I rely on the GPS tracker," I retorted, and laughed with her. "And if that doesn't work I always have those guys to show me the way." I pointed to the FBI Agents in the vehicle parked down the street from the protestors. She didn't understand who they were and looked at me curiously.

"Well here's my number, call me if you need anything," she said, as her face lit up with a grin, and she handed me a business card.

"Thanks, I'll do that, and have a wonderful day, Ms. Ichtyol or should I say Doctor Ichtyol," I replied after reading the card, and returned the smile.

It seemed like I was collecting business cards on this trip. Everyone and their grandmother had one of the damn things; except me, and I was beginning to feel a little inadequate about it. I bet the boosters even had business cards, I thought to myself and smiling at what it might say.

I returned to the unharmed rental vehicle and headed for the forest with my FBI escort behind me. The only thought that kept resonating in my head was Youngblood's reaction. It's always the negative things that you remember the most. He was just another straw in the haystack of people and things that didn't want me here. I didn't particularly want to be here, as well. I had enough of this bureaucratic bullshit when I worked for the FBI and wasn't particularly fond about rehashing it. Therefore, the quicker I get to the bottom of this, the better for everyone.

CHAPTER FIVE

THE BLACK FOREST

The scenic drive was breathtaking, as I drove up Route 89 to what the town's people are now calling the Black Forest. The forest is considered to be sacred grounds of the Abenaki, especially the area near the springs. The question that continues to haunt me is why the agents in the forest were there in the first place. There's no need to stop there in route to the Abenaki Village, so why even go there? As I came closer to the forest I began to feel the odd supernatural energy that encapsulated the town even more. It felt like what a normal person would feel when being slightly shocked by static electricity, as the hairs on my body began to slightly stand up. The closer I came within proximity of the forest the stronger the energy became. It moved through me and tingled, as it traveled to my energy crystal which began to glow even more from the massive surge of energy.

When I was knee deep within the forest my energy crystal was glowing, as bright as a flood light under my sleeve. There was no way of hiding its luster. My gift was for seeing in the dark and I suffered from the bright light just like anyone else. I've never seen it glow like this before, as I pulled over on the side of the highway to contain its luster. The agents behind me were following at a good distance and slowed down, as I pulled to the side of the road. When I came to a complete stop, they continued, passing me at a very slow rate, and looked in on me. I'm certain they saw the light also, but couldn't make out what they were observing.

I put my blazer back on to help conceal the brilliance emitted from the crystal. I had tailored my blazers and jackets for such the occasion. They were insulated with a black wool cloth to shield any light from escaping. Nothing beats the preparedness I learned working with the FBI ViCAP Unit. They taught me to think proactively, and work out possible scenarios before they occurred; preparedness is the key to success was our motto.

The agents slowed down to a crawl and were about to pull over to the side of the road when they saw me pulling off. At least they were sticking to the agreement that Whyte and I had established; that they would stay out of my way. It made me wonder if I got in trouble would they do anything to assist me.

I detoured off the highway and onto a dirt road with a sign that said Spring Road. I wasn't using any GPS at this point and relying only on my instincts to take me where I needed to go. I drove several miles deep into the forest and parked the vehicle on the side of the dirt road. My FBI escort was still behind me at a good distance.

When I got out of the vehicle I could feel the supernatural energy surging all around me like a blanket covering the forest. My energy crystal was working overtime absorbing the energy and shining bright as stadium lights on a Monday Night Football game, but I could still feel its energy. It was a euphoric feeling, like floating on cloud nine or being high off some opiate stimulant.

I don't know the origin of this ubiquitous, omnipotent energy, but whom or whatever was behind it was extremely powerful to blanket such a large area. I've never seen or even heard of such a thing so powerful with its energy signature during my training. Thus far, it hasn't tried to harm me or the agents following me, so that's a good sign.

I'm not certain if this is the cause behind the killings, but it's a damn good place to start looking. The only problem is tracing its origin. How do you trace something to its core when it's everywhere? Usually you can find the source of energy by tracing it back to its strongest point, but there was no wavering in the supernatural energy. It was as thick as pea soup and homogenous. All I can do at this juncture is search for any remnants of clues under the mysterious energy shroud.

This supernatural energy is the creepy feeling that normal people, who are very sensitive, feel in the presence of the supernatural. Their body hairs stand up from the kinetic energy, and cause goose bumps to appear from the hairs being slightly pulled and releasing body heat. Some people confuse this reaction, and believe that the temperature around them is getting colder when nothing could further from the truth. Your body temperature drops slightly only because of the heat you release from within. This energy has no temperature and exists regardless of Fahrenheit or Celsius. The energy surrounding this place would surely creep them the bleep out!

It appeared to be an average day in the forest to an unsuspecting bystander without natural gifts or abilities. Although the sky was steel grey with low hanging granite gray clouds, the sun would variably peep through the overcast, in an attempt to bring you a sunny day. The wilderness was functioning and going about its natural business as usual; regardless of the peek-a-boo sunlight, playing in the sky above. The agents didn't seem to feel the slightest disturbance. They were too engaged in following me.

The two agents assigned to follow me were two thirds of the trio that was glued to Agent Whyte's hip along with the female agent. I guess she was given something more important to do than to tail me around. They didn't like me due to protocol; the SAC didn't like me, so they fell in line with him.

I closed my eyes to awaken my panther instincts. I calmed my nerves and listened to the wilderness around me. I heard everything within the forest, including the FBI agents talking in the vehicle. They were laughing at me, and calling me a kook, amongst other things. I quickly drowned them out, and let the nose of the panther take over, as I sniffed for blood. I smelled lots of blood being exchanged in the wild, but nothing human. Then I opened my eyes after several minutes and just stood there, listening and smelling. I didn't pick up anything even with my heightened senses, so I did it the old fashion way with human technology and entered the coordinates into the GPS tracker I brought with me.

The agents weren't prepared for this excursion. They had on business attire; suits and hard heeled dress shoes. It wouldn't be hard to lose them in the forest even without my abilities. I allowed them to follow me to the crime scene. I was a late arrival to the party, but this was far from being fashionably late. Just like all the evidence was removed from Agents Stone and Wankaego's rooms, finding any intact or legitimate evidence preserved in the wilderness would be like wishing on angels.

As a child, my mother and granny used to have me include certain guardian angels in my nightly prayers. They said these angels looked after all human souls while on earth, thus the term guardian angels. They even assigned names to the guardian angels that protected me; Uriel, Ester and Kara. They thought it would help me to sleep better; help with the nightmares. I guess they didn't hear me, but that was a lifetime ago. Now I'm in control of my dreams. As I said before, I've never seen an angel, yet alone receive assistance from one, and at this point I don't really need it. What I need is tangible evidence, not a bedtime story.

When I arrived at the crime scene I was greeted by those damn ravens again. They must be the state bird or something, because they were everywhere in Swanton. They were all over the crime scene as well. Any remnants or crumbs of evidence that I hoped to stumble upon were a meal within their collective bellies. I could still see the remnants of the dried blood on the foliage in the forest, but even that was tainted with bird feces. They were opportunistic scavengers, the lot of them. I had the mindset to just vanquish them, here and now, but it wouldn't be in balance with nature. They were doing what they were placed here to do.

I looked around and examined the area for any other oddities that I could find, but it was too late. Most of the crime scene had been destroyed by the wilderness. I did receive the most peculiar and uncanny feeling though. I felt as if someone or something was watching me, and it wasn't the FBI agents. This was an ordinary quiet day in the forest to them. They didn't feel the supernatural energy or experience any of the sensations that I was experiencing. I felt a myriad of emotions going through me as I walked through the forest. My emotions wavered greatly here. I can't really explain it, but I felt undulations of great depression to euphoric elation. I did everything I could to hide my emotions from the FBI Agents observing me.

I spent several hours searching through the forest for clues, but there was nothing in sight, except the regular activities of life in the forest. The agents began laughing in the distance and calling me names again. It would have been alright if I didn't hear so well, but it was becoming distracting, so I decided to finally lose them in the forest. While they were laughing hardily, in the blink of an eye, I used my supernatural speed to mysteriously disappear from their sights within the shadows of the forest. Their gut busting laughter was halted immediately by my disappearance, as they frantically searched for their assignment, me.

I waited around and laughed at them for a little while before heading back towards the vehicle. That's when I came across the strangest thing, even in my travels. It was a very old and distinctively creepy tree. There was no other way of putting it. This thing was straight out of a "Creep show" movie. It boldly stood alone, separated from the other trees, and flaunted a certain insidious demeanor. I know trees are officially alive, but this one was more than animated. I didn't have to feel its potent sinister energy signature to know that this thing was bad news, and it let everyone know with its bold and obtrusive appearance.

It was twisted and mangled in ways I never thought a tree could grow. Its bark was coiled so tightly around itself, that it appeared as if there were several barks fused together and twisting in an attempt to strangle each other. It could have been mistaken for dead and rotting, but it was grandiose, and seemed to bask in tis macabre appearance, yet showing no physical signs of decay. It curved and swirled, decrepitly towards the sky, like a contortionist. Its roots grew out from the ground, tangled and twisted in a matrix that was waiting to trap you inside.

The limbs of the tree radiated outward like the snakes of medusa; oscillating, and slithering, as if wavering in the wind, but still like rigor mortis. There were no leaves or any other signs of life growing on the tree. It was barren as the desert, except for the crows that fittingly rested upon it, and even they didn't nest in it. Nothing grew on it or around it. The grass around it was dead and only black soil surrounded it.

There was a huge hole at the base of the tree, where the roots had separated to give way to the trunk's growth. The aperture looked like the opening of a mouth, wailing in agony. It was large enough for a 5ft.-8in. man to walk inside without stooping. Most people would've avoided this thing based on its looks alone. You don't need to be a shaman to feel that something was extremely wrong here, but I had to enter. I had to find the source of this malevolence.

As I approached the tree, the crows began squawking, like some sort of natural alarm system. All their beady little eyes were focused on me. They were acting like sentries guarding the entrance. I just knew they were going to attack me. I couldn't shadow myself because it was daylight and there was no shade or anything to assist around the isolated tree. I continued slowly and with trepidation. For all I know, it could have been some large predator's den, even the bear that Agent Whyte was trying to catch. Just the thought of a being attacked by a bear caused me to smile, because all I could see was Whyte's smug face glowing with satisfaction. I don't think my escorts will try to follow me inside.

The winged sentries didn't attack me, hell; they were probably thinking I'd make an excellent feast. There had to be a reason why they were resting here. They usually follow carrion. I could feel a slight breeze being emitted from inside the hole, like when you come to the entrance of a cave. It was dark inside the hollowed tree, but I could see perfectly clear with my panther abilities. I could have just rolled up my sleeve and allowed my energy crystal to illuminate area, but I didn't want to alert anyone or anything that the crows already haven't.

I ventured several feet down the dark narrow passage, and into the precarious depths of the tree. It led me to an enormously large underground cave. There were torches that lined the wall, but they were unlit and I kept it that way. There didn't seem to be anyone here and I didn't want anyone to know I was here. There were several archaic symbols, writings and drawings encompassing the wall and floor. There was also a huge pentagram on the floor with several archaic symbols surrounding it. Shamans aren't the only ones to utilize the symbol. Who knows what type of evil black magic perversion they're using the symbol for?

There was also an altar and fire pit in the middle of the cave similar to the sacred place built by the Nvyunuwi in the Smokey Mountains of Cherokee County. It sickened me to see this debasement. I could feel the fire starting to burn inside of me, ignited by my rage. I wanted to bring the entire place down around me, but I took a second to calm down and curb my feelings. I needed to keep this place intact, just like they left it. Destroying it won't do any good if the perpetrators weren't here. I needed to monitor this place and find out who the inhabitants are.

I quickly ascended from the cave and discovered that the sky had finally burst open from the gloomy overcast and allowed the rain to fall. It was pouring down outside with the roar of thunder echoing throughout the charcoal grey sky. My escorts were nowhere in sight, as I anticipated, but the crows remained, perched upon the insidious tree, and enduring the rain like the Queen's Guards outside of Buckingham Palace, loyal, obedient and still. I walked gingerly back to my vehicle. I was in no hurry, as I enjoyed the rain, and watched it wash my footprints away.

I drove back to Swanton to see Kateri. I had some further questions for her about the Abenaki and this supernatural energy that is blanketing the forest. I know she wouldn't have the slightest idea of what I'm talking about, but it was only a matter of wording the questions properly to receive the answers that I'm looking for regarding the supernatural.

CHAPTER SIX

CHIBAISKWEDA

It was dark when I arrived back at the Tribal Council. The demonstrators and sheriff had departed for the night. The streets seemed deserted and most of the lights were out in the council building. Then I noticed several young Abenaki men leaving together from the building. They were dressed in black Keikogis and had just finished training. There's nothing more zealous than a group of martial arts practitioners after a good training session. Therefore, I waited in my vehicle for them to leave, to avoid any confrontation. The door was still open, so I went inside. The receptionist had departed, and all I heard were two voices emanating from an office on the left side of the receptionist desk with the lights on.

It was Kateri and Youngblood arguing, but not in a confrontational form. He was making advances to have dinner with her and she was rejecting his advances. I'll give him one thing, he was persistent. I cleared my voice in the lobby for them to hear me and not think I was ease dropping, which is exactly what I was doing.

"My God, get a life will you," Youngblood ululated, dressed in a black Keikogi, and frustrated at my unwelcomed appearance.

"I'm sorry, but is this a bad time?" I inquired with an innocent tone.

"Yes, this is a bad time, you're being here altogether is bad timing," he blustered with an angry look upon his face.

"No, Agent Sands, this isn't an inconvenient time. How can I assist you?" Kateri asked in a relieved and up-tempo voice, annoyingly looking at Youngblood.

"I had a few questions about the Black Forest that I wanted to ask you."

"Damn it Sands, we're closed for the evening!" Youngblood barked.

"Please Agent Sands come in. I'll be happy to answer any of your questions," she interjected, and walked around Youngblood who appeared to have her cornered in the room.

"So, it's like that, huh." Youngblood glared at Kateri and me.

"Yes, it's like that," she retorted, and once again, Youngblood went storming out of the council building fuming.

"Thanks for saving me, Agent Sands, now how can I assist you?" She sighed, smiling and relieved that Youngblood had departed.

"You stated that you knew the forest very well, so I wanted to ask you a little about its history, if you don't mind."

"Sure thing, where do I start?" She gestured for me to have a seat with her hand, and grinning as if she'd remembered fond memories of it; better times I'm sure, before the murders.

Kateri and I talked for about thirty to forty minutes, but there was nothing relevant or noteworthy to the investigation. It was getting late, so I decided not to keep her any longer.

Just as we were about to depart I could hear several men in the street. It was unusual for anyone, especially a large group of men to be congregating in this part of the town. There was nothing open at this hour, from what was left of the few businesses that the factory's closing didn't wipe out. Kateri couldn't hear the men, but from what I heard they weren't the welcoming committee for me or the uninvited escorts to see her home.

I walked quickly in front of Kateri, and rudely proceeded out the door ahead of her. She looked at me strangely because of the action. She thought I was rushing to open the door for her, but I wanted to make sure she wasn't the first to be attacked, these men could be armed.

There were six of them standing in the middle of the street holding baseball bats, tire irons, and other assorted street gang weapons, but no guns. It was the boosters from the protest, the same rowdy group from the hotel's bar moonlighting as thugs. Now I see the cause of the scar tissue. I had really stepped into a domestic cesspool with this case. They were standing nonchalantly in plain sight, and didn't care who saw them. They acted as if they owned the town or had the town's permission to conduct such acts of violence and terrorism. The sheriff that was parked in front previously was gone, so perhaps they did have permission.

Someone had a deep hatred for the Sokoki Abenaki. I'm not certain who hired these men, but someone's agenda of antagonizing a protest crowd into a hostile mob coincided with physically harming the Abenaki as well. Kateri was terrified as she looked out into the street and grabbed my hand. The men saw me and began yelling obscenities at us.

"Hey, Cochise, come over here, we'd like to talk to you," one of them yelled out.

"Yeah, and bring the squaw with you, we like red meat," another added, as they began laughing.

"I don't know about this one, I think his chicken ass might be dark meat," someone said, as they continued laughing.

"How can you tell? He looks like he might be coon meat to me," another one shouted from the mob.

"More like road kill," someone else quipped.

"You need to go back inside, lock the door, and call the sheriff," I instructed Kateri.

"Why send her away? She's the bell of the ball," one of them laughed.

Kateri was too afraid to move and squeezed my hand, staring at the men as if in a daze. I could feel her trembling, as she squeezed my hand even tighter. I grabbed her by the shoulders and slightly shook her to snap her out of it.

"Listen, I need you to go back inside, lock the door behind you, and telephone the sheriff's department, can you do that for me?" I asked her, and looking intensely into her eyes to distract her from staring at the rambunctious men. She finally went back inside and locked the door, as I instructed.

"Ok, half-breed, I guess you'll have to provide us with that pleasure," one of the thugs hollered.

"Yeah sunshine come out and play with us. I promise we'll have you back at the hotel before sunrise," another inserted.

They remembered me from the hotel. I need to really put a beat down on these men, and hurt them enough to make them want to leave Swanton. I couldn't display any supernatural abilities with Kateri probably still watching from inside, but I will remain slightly above average in speed and strength.

"It really takes a special type of cowardice for six men to use baseball bats on a defenseless woman," I said to the goons.

"After we beat you silly we'll ram them up your ass."

"Is that what the boys use to tell you in prison?" I quipped with a grin.

These men were foul and vulgar, just as Jock stated. I was going to take pleasure in beating them. I would have preferred to just shadow myself and blend into the night to avoid an altercation with these men all together, but they would only try it again on some other occasion. I didn't need to be looking over my shoulder for the next attack, so it was best to nip it in the bud. Besides, I had Kateri inside the building, and they weren't about to let either of us just walk away from this one. I needed to make an example of them. They needed to see me put the beat down on them, so they wouldn't even think about trying it again.

I allowed them to proceed with their callous bantering, as I walked towards them. I dodged one baseball bat after another swung in my direction. I didn't want to have to kill these men. I caught one of the bats swung in mid-air, and with lighting fast speed I took the bat from him, and knocked him unconscious with a quick tap of the bat to his forehead. Now I was ready to go to work.

They attacked all at once. It was ridiculous how much faster and stronger I was compared to them, even without using my supernatural speed. I had the speed, agility and strength of a panther, as I dodged their blows, one after another. I weaved through them with fluidity, as they attempted to hit me, and putting them down one by one.

I went low on one assailant and delivered a powerful blow with the bat to his stomach, ripping the air completely out of him. He immediately went down to the ground gasping for air. I blocked a blow from a second attacker while I was low, as our bats hit together in one loud bang, and then I quickly shattered his knee with one clean swing and crippled him. He went down screaming and in tears.

The next one approached and threw his bat at me, and then tried to run away. He was frightened from what he had seen, but I threw my bat, squarely into the center of his back, and knocking him off his feet from the power that I possessed. He was also rendered unconscious.

The third attacker was larger than the others and though he could overpower me with his strength and attacked me like a berserker. I quickly side stepped his attack and delivered a good old fashion clothes line chop to his throat. When he bent over I delivered a knee to his head, as he fell backwards and out cold.

The fourth attacker came at me with a knife. I kicked him at center mass, in the chest, using my full speed and strength. He met my foot like running into a brick wall at full speed, as he dropped the knife and fell backwards to the ground. His injuries were the worst of all. I had crushed his sternum and he laid on the ground wheezing for air. He had escalated the assault level with the knife, so I returned the favor. He would survive, but he needed medical attention. I walked away slowly, leaving the men on the ground, and back towards the building.

I was only kidding when I said that even the boosters had business cards, but there it was lying on the ground. One of them had dropped his business card on the ground during the fight. I was curious to read what was on, so I picked it up. I wasn't surprised when I read the name on the business card; it was Winchester's business card. I didn't have time to ruminate about it; I'll deal with him later. I needed to go check on Kateri, and see why the police haven't arrived.

When I went inside, I didn't see Kateri anywhere. I had to calm down the adrenaline rush from the fight and concentrate on my heightened listening. I heard her crying in a room near the rear of the building. She was hiding in a closet inside the room. I didn't want to scare her even further, so I called out to her before entering the room. She opened the door swiftly, and then ran into my arms. She held me as tight as she could with her head nestled on my chest, as the tears continued to flow from her beautiful brown eyes.

"I thought they were going to kill you," she whimpered, hugging me as if her life depended on it.

"It takes a little more than that to kill me. Everything's alright. You're safe now, Kateri," I informed her, but she didn't let go. The goons partially accomplished what they set out to do; they terrorized her.

We stood in the middle of the room for several minutes locked in each other's arms. I was attempting to calm her from the traumatic event that she just witnessed. She really was a pacifist and abhorred violence. Anyone would have been terrified of the scene she witnessed. The men were clearly here to do grave physical harm to her and whoever else was inside the council building. I decided to escort Kateri back to the Abenaki village just in case.

I looked outside the door first to see if the men were still there, but they managed to round up their wounded and departed. Kateri still had tears welling in her eyes, as she stood frightened and shaking at the door. She was afraid to go outside. I had to assure her that it was safe, as I held her in my arms and escorted her out the door. I don't know what happened to the police that were supposed to be outside of the tribal council building or where Mat Youngblood was located. Hopefully he left early enough to escape the wrath of these men. If he isn't seen by tomorrow, I'll notify the sheriff's department of the incident and file a missing person's report.

I drove through the Black Forest, and once again, I felt the strong supernatural energy being emitted from within. This time I already had my energy crystal covered within the sleeve of my jacket. I'm sure it seemed a little strange to Kateri, as it did to the FBI agents that followed me into the forest earlier. The weather was warm enough for short sleeves and shorts, but I was wearing a sport coat. The Black Forest separated the Abenaki Village from the town of Swanton going north.

It was beautiful in the Abenaki Village. It was nestled between the mountains and Lake Champlain on the Missisquoi River. This wasn't a modern village like most reservations were becoming with new development and housing. They stuck to their traditions like the Hopi's of the Southwest that I spent some time with during the Coyote Investigation. They still lived in log cabins and there were a few wigwams still erected near the river, but they were used mostly for the quick storing of game, salted fish, and other storage purposes.

Kateri invited me in for tea and I accepted. She had her own place near the river. It was quaint, but perfect in every way. I've become accustomed to living frugally and enjoying the gifts of the land from my days spent living in the Oconaluftee River Valley amongst the Smokey Mountain Range. They weren't without electricity or running water, but everything else was reminiscence of the way their ancestors lived. It was like going back in time.

We sat in two lounge chairs that she had on her wooden porch in the front of the cabin and drank our tea under the stars. We discussed the beauty of nature and listened to the wolves howling, and other animals of the wilderness. The wolves were very near and seemed to surround the village, but their song was beautiful amongst the setting of the pale full moon. Not even the overcast night sky could hide its brilliance tonight. There were several stars that manage to glimmer through the cloudy night sky, as the dark clouds appeared like a slow-moving river in the sky. It was an excellent respite from the violence and turbulence that surrounded us.

"They say the wolves are the spirit protectors of Abenaki people," she informed me looking up at the sky and listening to them singing.

"I know, I've heard this before. It is a belief throughout several First Nations culture," I replied.

"And what nation do you belong Agent Sands?" she inquired, gazing at me with moonlit eyes.

"Please, call me Christian. I'm a descendent of the Cherokee Freedmen of North Carolina."

"Is that why they sent you?"

"Amongst other reasons," I uttered lowly.

Then our conversation went off into another direction. I don't know if it was the moon on this beautiful night or the encounter that we just endured. Sometimes crisis can bring people closer together.

"You have the strangest eyes, Christian," she said staring into them.

"You mean their color (green)? I asked.

"Not just that, but they do remind me of cat eyes; the eyes of a predator," she asserted, and touched the side of my face.

I immediately returned the comment with a smile and was amazed by her keen intuition. She was gazing into the eyes of my panther spirit. The awareness of normal humans never ceases to amaze me, even when they don't know the actuality of what they're observing, it is quite clear to them that they are observing something different.

"I don't know if that's a compliment or not." I chuckled.

"I find it hard to believe that a man like yourself doesn't know a compliment when you hear it." She grinned.

"I receive them less frequently than you may think, but enough about me, what's your story?"

"Well, there's really not much to tell. When my parents died during the Factory Incident, Chief Fox, the Council Chief, was kind enough to take me in with his family. I didn't have any other family, no brothers or sisters. I went to the University of Minnesota on scholarship. Pretty boring stuff," she said, sighing.

"Wait a minute," I quickly interjected, "There's more to this story than that. You could have gone anywhere and practiced medicine, what made you come back here?"

"My people needed me. Don't get me wrong, I thought about it, and received several offers of residency in numerous large cities, but Dr. Vance happily offered me residency here. He's getting older, and ready to retire soon. We both thought it would be good for both our people, if I practiced here. I could assist with bridging the gap, as a doctor treating those in town, and on the reservation." She said, and ruminated for a second.

"I received a chilly reception at first, and then they began to come around, but when the children went missing, they reverted to their resentment and hatred. Dr. Vance and I thought it would be best if I spent a limited amount of time in the town's clinic due to threats I received. My vehicle and the clinic were vandalized several times with hate graffiti. It's been a real volatile situation since the children disappeared," she said, solemnly.

"So, what do you think happen to them?"

"I don't know. No one knows for certain. The Abenaki are saying that the monsters have returned," she replied.

"Monsters?" I inquired with curiously raised eye brows.

"Yeah, some are saying it's the Spirit of the Lake. The factory was poisoning the water, and killing the fish and wildlife that depended on the lake, including the Abenaki. They say it was the Spirit of the Lake that cursed the factory for its transgressions against nature, and eventually shut it down. The Abenaki say the Spirit of the Lake has returned and sent the Wendigo to take their children, if you believe in that sort of thing," she said, sarcastically.

"*And you don't?*" I asked her.

"*There could have been in number of reasons for the people working in the factory to become sick. It could have been mold, asbestos, even the water, who knows? Boss Winchester closed it so suddenly after his wife died that no one had a chance to go in and inspect it.*"

"*But why return now?*" I inquired.

"*It's speculated that Boss Winchester was looking for a way to reopen the Factory, and the Spirits of the Lake didn't like it,*" she replied, and turned and looked at me with a jokingly scary face which made us both laugh.

I wanted badly to dreamscape with her. I don't know why, but I had this inalienable attraction towards her. I know she wasn't hiding anything; she's been the most honest and kindest person that I met since I got off the plane. It didn't hurt that she was pleasing to the eyes in every way, face and body wise, so I found a clever way to skip the subject to something less personal. The supernatural entity that was hovering over the village and the forest was something worth inquiring about in an indirect way.

"*Do you have a medicine man or healer in the village?*" I inquired, as she looked at me dumbfoundedly at me with her beautiful brown eyes opened wider.

"*No, as I stated, besides my duties on the council, I'm also the physician for the village working for Dr. Vance at the town's clinic,*" she reinstated.

"*Wow, where do you find the time to do all that?*" I asked.

"*Sometimes I wonder myself,*" she laughed.

"*But is there a spiritual healer or guide?*" I further questioned.

"*Oh, you mean like a medicine man or shaman,*" she said, grinning, "*No, we prefer modern medicables and treatment. We may appear primitive, Christian, but I assure you, and we are very up to speed with modern technologies. We chose not to forget who we are or our past,"* she said in a stringent voice.

"I didn't mean to offend you in any way," I apologized.

"No offense taken. Why do you ask, do you believe in such things?"

"I believe that nothing is out of the realm of reality, once you've acquired the knowledge to perceive it," I answered.

"We do have an old wise man that lives in the mountains. People say that he used to belong to the Midewiwin, the Secret Grand Medicine Society. They say he was a powerful Midewinini or medicine man, but he is senile now. His niece takes care of him. He doesn't speak due to a stroke and is confined to a wheelchair. His cabin is right on the edge of the Green Mountain range. Some say he is one of the original people that time has forgotten. I can show you were it is in the morning, but as I said, he's right outside of being catatonic," she informed me.

"No, that's alright, but thanks, perhaps later." I replied, took a sip of tea, and reclined in my chair to gaze at the stars.

"You know people say that the forest is cursed and haunted by ghosts. They say you can see visions of the people of the past. The whisper of the trees and the ground sometimes come alive. They say you can see the leaves of the trees change colors right before your eyes. If you believe in that sort of thing," Kateri said with an ambiguous grin, and then let out a ghost sound that a kid would do and laughed.

She was joking with me, and I returned the laugh, but her tales reminded me of the feeling that I had when I was in the forest. It felt like someone or something was watching me. Most fables and myths masquerade themselves in the truth. If only she knew the things that I have witnessed and am able to do. None of this would seem surreal to her. I've seen Asku move and manipulate the ground, and perform other things she has described.

I heard Matunaagd Youngblood approaching from the east in the dark, and then I saw him with two brown bags in his hands. I could smell the food within them. He was under the impression that he was sneaking up on us. I played it off and acted as if I didn't know he was out there. He moved in closer and hid in order to listen in on our conversation. Our conversation had taken another turn and we were discussing Mr. Winchester again when he came out of hiding.

"Damn it, Matt, what the hell are you doing sneaking up on us like that?" Kateri barked, excitedly. She was the only one he allowed to call him Matt, as she caught her breath from the surprise. Her nerves were just calming down from the scare in town. Now here this jack-ass comes, just like a prick, to place her back on the edge.

"Some townies visited the Tribal Council tonight and tried to assault me, but Agent Sands scared them off. Where were you?" She snapped, fistedly.

"I picked up some dinner and came here. I was going to surprise you with it." He lifted the two brown bags in his hands.

"I'm fine by the way," she said, sarcastically, because Youngblood didn't inquire.

"I'm sorry, I'm just a little startled by what you said. Are you, all right?" He inquired looking dumbfounded.

"Yes, I was just scared to death by the violence, I'm lucky Christian was there or who knows what they would have done to me," she sighed, and flashed a grin in my direction.

"Thanks Agent Sands, but you're no longer needed here," he rudely inserted.

"Agent Sands is my guest and I invited him here. Last, I checked this was my house. Now if you will excuse us, we were enjoying a civil conversation until you scurried this way," she fumed.

I learned a long time ago that a man can never win in an argument with a woman. They have more command over the skills of conversing.

Youngblood departed, angry and dejected. I could tell that Kateri knew for sure that she had him wrapped around her fingers. I felt sorry for him because there was nothing he could do. He was in love with a woman that didn't love him in return. That was a position that I've never been in before, partially due to not being able to communicate with the opposite sex when I was younger. I was considered a freak and an outsider, and when I became a young man I relied upon dreamscape for sexual lasciviousness. I could still feel his pain, regardless. It sunk in like the loss of a best friend. I had second thoughts about asking her the obvious, but I've never been coy when it comes to clarity.

"So, what is the deal with you and Matt, if you don't mind me asking?"

"He will make someone very happy one day," she retorted, unimpassioned, and looked down into her cup before taking a sip.

"But not you, I'm sensing." I stated.

"No, not me," she replied, with a quaint smile.

"And why not, may I ask?"

"I had changed when I returned home from college. Matt was expecting me to come back and be one thing, but I was another. I was no longer a girl with girlish ideas of marriage like when I left. We dated for a couple of years, but it just didn't work. Besides, he's a very proud man, and his pride often clouds his judgment, as you've witnessed. His temperament can be erratic and unfocused to the point of being destructive." Her face immediately went blank, as if she was miles away.

"You no longer want marriage?

"Perhaps one day I'll find that unique person," she replied, gazing at me with star lit eyes.

We continued star gazing and enjoying this brilliant full moon out tonight and everything beneath it. It was gorgeous. The further north you traveled it seemed like the closer the moon appeared and it was no different tonight. It was so huge and close that you could see the indentations, and varying colors of the craters. I felt like I could reach out and touch it.

I took a moment to perlustrate her veneer. She had a stoic look upon her face, as she gazed endlessly into the darkness, stopping time and encapsulating me in a still life moment. I could have sworn that all sounds and movements around us had temporarily ceased, and I was trapped in a spell. Then I heard her voice, speaking to me from a distance, and pulling me back from wherever I had momentarily traveled. It was like someone waking me from a dream.

"Christian, Christian, are you ok?" She inquired, now focusing her intense, beautiful brown eyed stare upon me.

"Ah, yeah, I'm fine, why?" I replied with trepidation in my voice.

"For a minute, you had spaced out, like you were somewhere else," she replied with concern.

"Yeah, I'm just a little tired, that's all.

Truth is, I didn't know what the hell that was about, but it was getting late, and staring into the eyes of a beautiful and intoxicating woman was something that I couldn't afford to do. I had to remain focused on my assignment, and my commitments, but I needed some answers and she's the only one willing to talk to me at this point.

"Would you like some more tea? I have some bagels, also, if you care for any?" She asked, getting up from her chair.

I continued questioning her on the relationship of the Abenaki and the townspeople when she returned. Then from out of nowhere the fog began to set in. This was my cue to depart and start heading back down the road, before it became unbearable. My panther vision did nothing for me during heavy fog. I was blind just as everyone else. It was also a good excuse to leave before I got myself into something that I would regret in the morning.

"Well, I think it's time for me to depart," I said, getting up from my chair and stretching.

"Are you sure you want to drive in this fog? The Abenaki call this the Chibaiskweda; the marsh gas of the ancient ghosts," she cautioned, *"It*

comes down from the mountains around this time and last until the dawn. The elders believe it is our ancestors coming down from the mountains."

"*And what do you believe?*" I curiously asked.

"*I believe people should hold on to their past, it is a connection to who you are, your identity, yet keep in mind the future, and move forward to evolve and survive.*" She candidly explained.

Then she smiled and her eyes grew larger, as she approached me, hunched down with her hands in the air and fingers twiddling while making the sound of a cartoon ghost.

"*Wooooo.*" She laughed aloud, and quickly placed her arms around me.

Then, before I could say anything or react, she kissed me with her soft and inviting lips. My mind was telling me to pull back, but the rest of me wanted more. She finally broke the connection and smiled. My heightened senses exploded like fireworks. I could feel her heart racing and the rush of her blood pulsating through her body, as her temperature rose. She closed her eyes and gently sighed, like she had taken in a breath of fresh air. That was all it took to get me excited. She had awakened the panther inside, as I felt myself slipping away.

My neurons were having a rave party inside and firing up my senses until the hairs on my skin were standing up from the electrical energy charge. My temperature was rising also, as well as another part of my anatomy. I breathed in deeply and accepted whatever would come next. My will power was standing on the edge of a cliff and ready to take the plunge into the unknown. I was utterly helpless in her hands, like putty waiting to be molded. That's when she broke the connection, and our lips parted much to my chagrin. I didn't realize that my eyes were closed the entire time until I opened them and found her, once again, gazing into my eyes and smiling.

"*Are you certain, you won't stay?*" She inquired, now grinning amorously.

I was lucky she didn't continue. She allowed me one last chance to decide on my own how the rest of this evening would unfold. It was the break that I needed to place me back on the fidelity track.

"No, I'm afraid I might have overstepped already. I appreciate the offer, but I need to go now before I do something without thinking it through. I have a plethora of things and other commitments that require my attention in the morning, and it's getting late. Thanks for a lovely evening, Kateri."

"Hey, I have a spare bedroom, and I promise not to attack you, at least not tonight," she grinned standing within a breath's space of me and gazing into my eyes.

"Thank you, but I'll be fine," I replied, watching her smile fade in disappointment.

"Ok, but if it gets bad and you want to turn around, the invitation is still open," she inserted, continuing to gaze into my eyes. I couldn't let this happen again. I was weak to her charms, but determined to beat the odds, and the prophecy about my monogamy.

She placed her hand on the side of my face again, smiled, and backed away. Whew, what a close damn call. I just knew she was going to give me another kiss to persuade me. She was a gorgeous woman and the offer was tempting, but I was in a committed relationship with a woman that I was fully in love with. I shouldn't have let it go this far, but I was already there and within her spell. It infuriated me to think how close I came to ruining the best thing that has ever happened to me... Nina.

While walking back to my vehicle, I spotted several Abenaki men in the distance with my panther's vision. They were hiding in the surrounding woods between me and my vehicle, preparing to ambush me. It had been a long day, and this was something that I just didn't want to be bothered with, so I decided to just shadow myself, and walk right pass them.

Then the dense fog rolled in quickly! This would only assist my cover or so I thought. Then I heard something quickly slashing through the air, like the sound of a sword swung exuberantly, and it was racing my way! I couldn't see what it was in the thick fog, but I ducked just in time, barely escaping the path of a twirling tomahawk lodged into a tree next to me. How in the hell? I was still shadowed!

Then another one and another came swishing from out of the mist, as I ducked, weaved and spun from their lethal trajectory. It was as if they could see me while I was shadowed and through the dense fog. They clearly had the advantage here. The tables were completely turned. The mist didn't provide me with additional cover; it provided my assailants with cover. The only thing that was keeping me alive this night was my supernatural speed and my panther instincts. I couldn't sense if these men were supernatural due to the ominous energy field that covered the village and the forest.

I made my way to a tree that provided temporary cover from the flying tomahawks, and then I summoned and manipulated the wind for assistance.

"Ayv wiwadvhv nvgi ganolvvsgv, hnadvga gadousdi Ayv adanetsedi"

I created a turbulent gust of wind that moved at the speeds of a hurricane and directed them towards the men. The wind had cleared out the fog and knocked down several trees in its path. I saw one of the men in the distance knocked out cold or dead, I couldn't tell. I didn't see the others in the path of the destruction, even with my night vision.

The rented car was pushed some distance away and turned on its side. This was such a waste. I hated seeing the toppled trees and the destruction that I had caused, as I walked towards the vehicle. I could live with whatever happened to the men, they were trying to kill me, but the destruction of nature weighed heavy on me. One of the biggest doctrines of being a shaman is to be one with nature and constantly move towards creating a balance with her. This type of destruction went totally against that.

As I walked towards the vehicle I heard something peculiar in the nearby tree line, as I made my way back towards my vehicle. It wasn't the usual chaotic rumblings of the forest, but something meticulous, as it tarringly paralleled my movements. I stopped to take assessment of the situation, and when I did, it did the same. It paused its motion. After living in the mountains of North Carolina for the past several years I knew exactly what was happening. Something was hunting me, and it wasn't the Abenaki men.

I continued towards my vehicle with a bit more haste in my step, as my predator mirrored my gait, except now the faint meticulous rumblings became louder, like the under breath whining of a disgruntled crowd becoming a mob. It was quite clear that there was more than one now; they were hunting in a pack!

When I arrived at the vehicle, I quickly pushed it back over onto four wheels, and then I heard the howls of a pack of wolves, as they called out to each other. I saw them in the tree lines, watching me, or at least I saw their eyes in the dense woods.

They had surrounded me, as wolves do, but remained hidden in the woods. There were at least ten or more, growling and snarling in anger. I would have thought they'd go after the Abenaki men that were injured in the woods, but they focused their attention on me. Perhaps they looked at me as a threat after the destruction that I just caused. I had really gotten to know the habits of wolves by becoming friends with a few in the Smokey Mountains, but these weren't here to make friends. It was strange seeing them this close to the dwellings of men, but I have seen stranger things.

I wasn't prepared to cause any more destruction here, so I stepped into the vehicle. It took several tries before the car started, as the wolves looked on. They followed me for a good amount of time through the woods, howling and communicating with each other, as if they were escorting me out. This was strange indeed, the whole ordeal.

CHAPTER SEVEN
SCORCHED EARTH

Early, the next morning, I was awakened by a sound outside of my window. I discovered the green eyed, horn owl perched on the window sill with its prey. I could sense that it was a female. She had one of the many ravens that were in abundance around here in her clutches. I'm certain she would have preferred something more delectable like the rabbit she captured the nights before. The ravens were probably secondary on the menu after a non-productive night's hunt.

She remained on the sill and didn't seem to mind me watching her. In fact, it seemed as if she wanted me to see her, like a cat bringing its master the mouse it caught. She was a fearless apex-predator with a brief list of natural enemies.

I opened the window of the hotel suite and she turned her head completely around, as owls are able to do and watched me, regal and calm. I slowly reached out my hand and gently caressed her soft contour feathers and smiled. She closed her eyes several times, as her ear tufts relaxed, indicating that she was pleased with the show of affection. I had similar experiences with the wildlife in the Smokey Mountains of North Carolina. I was truly one with nature now as Shamans strive to be.

Now I could call upon her whenever I wanted after bonding with her. It was one of the gifts of being a Shaman that I enjoyed the most. The dawn was fading quickly and giving way to the morning sun, so I let her go, as she flew off with her prey. I couldn't have asked for a better way of waking or starting the day. I needed that momentary respite from the chaos. It was as if the owl knew; perhaps Mother Earth sent her to ground me. I was still horrible at reading the signs and symbols of Mother Earth, it is my greatest flaw. Some shamans are gifted with what we call 'sight'. They can predict future events by reading the signs and symbols of Mother Earth. I was having a challenging time just reading present indicators.

I closed the window, pulled the curtains shut, and laid back down to continue enjoying the tranquility of the morning. I was about to meditate when someone began banging on the door. I tried ignoring them, but they wouldn't go away. I got up from a very serene state and journeyed towards the door as they knocked again. What in the hell could be so urgent? I looked out the peep hole and it was Sheriff Meehan. I didn't have enough personal time with him to recognize his energy signature. It must be something important for him to be knocking at my door, this time in the morning, I thought to myself, so I hurried to let him in.

"Good morning, Sheriff, how can I help you?" I grumbled, looking out the slit of the barely opened door.

"Can I come in?" He replied, seriously in a deep New England accent with his hands nestled on his gun belt.

"Yes, I'm sorry, come in" I apologized for my rudeness, and opened the door further, and allowing him to enter past me.

Sheriff Meehan is a tall, husky built man with curly salt and pepper hair that he kept close cropped, clean shaven, and cold steel blue eyes. He carried himself as if he was the king of Swanton and everyone else was his subjects.

He paused after taking a couple of steps inside, and observed the dark and untidy room. He wondered if he wanted to come in at all. The shades were drawn shut, just the way I like it, dark. He immediately helped himself with turning on the lights, as he entered, and moved towards the window and pulled the curtains open. I thought this was rude of him, but I'd seen it before working with law enforcement. They sometimes forget their manners when dealing with the public, and take liberties that aren't theirs to take. It was conditioning from dealing with undesirables on the job. Things only looked worst when he illuminated the room.

"My god man, you do know they have room service here, right?" He complained with his lips curled in disgust.

It's not that I was an untidy person because I kept my house neat and clean, down to my closets and drawers. I hadn't had the time to clean up since I'd been in Swanton. I had a problem with people rummaging through my stuff and personal space, so I kept the "Do Not Disturb" sign on the door. It was another oddity of mine from the panther imprinting, I was intrinsically very territorial now. I removed some clothes I had from a chair and offered the Sheriff a seat, but he declined with a disturbed look on his face; appalled by the mess.

"This won't take long," he quickly replied, and moved from the window to the middle of the room to engage me. *"We do things differently around here in Swanton than they do in the bigger cities. I spoke to Agent Whyte about you. He said you were some nut case released from the FBI before you came here on assignment for the Indian Bureau of Affairs. In fact, he didn't have anything nice to say about you at all. He stated that you had a very high opinion of yourself and that you were a little flighty and reckless at times. He said you are someone who likes bending the rules as you see fit."*

"Where's this going Sheriff?" I quickly interrupted.

"Someone filed a complaint about you. They said you were disturbing the peace, a public nuisance and abusing your authority as an officer of the law." He advised me, with a smug haughty look upon his face. I looked him square in the eyes, as he moved towards the window to avoid eye contact.

"In what way, might I ask?" I inquired with eyebrows raised.

"It was reported that you were assaulting several men near the Tribal Council Building," he answered standing in the middle of the window and creating a silhouette of himself.

"These men were armed with baseball bats and knives, and were going to assault Ms. Ichtyol and whoever else they could. I have a witness," I retorted, angered by the false allegations.

"Yet, you chose not to notify us?" he quipped with sarcasm.

"I was going to today," I snapped, still heated by the exchange.

"So, you decided to beat up those men in a show for Ms. Ichtyol, and not make one arrest. Is that how you've been taught to handle assault cases where you're from or are you just playing by your own set of rules, as Agent Whyte stated?" He questioned, approaching me.

"I notified Ms. Ichtyol to call you from inside the building, but the men tampered with the telephone lines."

"That's very convenient, and you don't have a cell phone like most people do?" He smugly quipped.

"I do, but when I learned the lines were down it was too late, the men had already fled." I explained.

"And Ms. Ichtyol didn't have a cell phone?"

"Yes, she does, but she was too shaken up to think straight. I found her balled up in the fetal position, hiding in a closet. And yes, my main concern was the safety of Ms. Ichtyol, and not the apprehension of some thugs."

"Typical," he retorted with a smirk on his face, looking down upon me.

"By the way who did notify you of this incident?" I asked, and got up from the chair I was seated in.

"It was an anonymous caller." He replied.

"Now that's convenient and typical," I replied, sarcastically.

"What are you trying to say, Agent Sands?" he grumbled.

"I'm not trying to say anything except where I'm from it is respect and common courtesy to give a fellow officer the benefit of the doubt, especially when there are no presentable witnesses. It was convenient that the caller didn't give his or her name," I replied sharply.

"It was a concerned citizen who didn't want to get involved. It happens all the time," he slyly remarked, and discarded my comment.

"That's an oxymoron if I ever heard of one, the word 'concern' doesn't go with 'not get involved'," I quipped, "By the way what happened to the patrol car that was parked out front of the council building?" I asked, and folded my arms sitting on the table with my legs crossed.

"It was shift change, besides we're only there if protestors show up. We don't have the manpower to remain at every door step in town." He responded, sourly.

"Sure," I retorted, with sarcasm, and a grin.

"Are we going to have an obstruction of justice problem with you Agent Sands?" he then asked.

"Not at all sheriff, but the next time you bring up accusations of misconduct, and abuse of authority make sure you present my accusers or I'll have to inform your State DA about professional defamation of character, wrongful accusations leading to the interference of a Federal Investigation, harassment, and a shit load of other violations I don't think you want presented in court," I cautioned him, "Oh, and by the way, tell Mr. Winchester the next time he wants to talk to me, do it himself." I pulled out the business card that one of the thugs dropped at that point and presented it to the sheriff.

"One of those thugs dropped his business card, as he was running from the scene. Can you return it to him? I don't think I'll need it." I reached out to give it to him.

"Do I look like a messenger to you?" he bellowed. Now he was on the defensive, as I walked towards him.

"Well, if the shoe fits," I grinned.

"*Fuck you, Sands, give it to him yourself,*" he replied, and stormed out of the room without another word.

I laughed for several minutes after he departed. I guess that's one more enemy to add to the growing list of people who don't want me here. Perhaps it's time I paid Boss Winchester a visit. Whatever else I had planned for today will have to take a back seat, since Mr. Winchester reached out to me so early, I'll return the favor.

I quickly showered, dressed and departed. I picked up the egg, cheese and bacon sandwich I ordered in advance from the hotel, and ate it on the way to the sheriff's office. Meehan was right about one thing, as much as I hate filling out paperwork, I need to file my account of what occurred last night at the Tribal Council to cover my ass. Everyone was gunning for me here, so why give them the ammunition.

When I arrived at Winchester's mansion, I drove passed it to get a layout of the perimeter. It was surrounded by a tall, black, cast iron security fence, and men patrolling the inner perimeter. The bodyguards had the look of hired killers. They were dressed in suits, and carried expensive submachine guns. Boss Winchester was one of the most powerful men in the state from what the Abenaki Council informed me, no one would dare attempt to attack such a powerful man, yet he was still paranoid due to the missing children tragedy and the recent deaths.

I parked down the street unnoticed by any spectators, and walked to a secluded area of the fence. I shadowed myself, so I wouldn't be detected, and leaped over the security fence with the speed and agility of a cat, my panther imprinting. It was early in the afternoon and the sun was still high in the sky. Therefore, I ran quickly, with supernatural speed, through the guards, because during the daylight my shadowing could be seen. It appeared as a distortion or fragmenting of visible light, but still noticeable. I made it to the front entrance of the house without being noticed.

This was just too easy, and to top it all off, I discovered that the door was unlocked when I turned the doorknob. I guess he figured with all the security guards why even bother; besides they would have to respond inside the house if something occurred. I turned and looked around to see if there were any guards watching before I opened the door. I wouldn't want to arouse the suspicion of a patrol seeing the anomaly of the front door opening without seeing anyone. They were busy looking outward towards the fence which I had already scaled. I smiled at how easy this was, as I let myself in, undetected.

After taking few steps, they sprang from out of nowhere, surprising me. They were lurking in stealth mode with amber colored eyes that appeared to glow in the darkness. I could see them very well in the dark with my vision, but they did take me by surprise. I didn't detect them due to all the ambient human energy signatures, and the omnipotent energy source that was hoovering throughout the town. These two wolves were far from being supernatural, although they were huge and ferocious. They began to growl in a very low tone, as their mouths began to tremble in anger.

They couldn't see me while I was shadowed, but they could sense my presence through their smelling and hearing abilities. I took down my shadow ability, and appeared in front of the wolves, so they could see what they were sensing, and to settle them. These were domesticated wolves or they wouldn't be living in the house and among humans.

Once I was visible to the wolves, I got down on one knee, so I could be within eye contact of them instead of hovering above them in a threatening manner. I kept my arms and hands down close to my body and allowed them to use their senses to smell the history of the wilderness on me. I had come across several wolves while in the Smoky Mountains and they accepted me as a friend. Hopefully these wolves would smell that as well.

After walking slowly around me, growling, and smelling me, they came in closer. It took some time, but they finally let their guard down and moved in even closer. I began petting them like the other wolves I've come across, and they seemed to enjoy it. Being one with nature felt good. They continued to walk with me, as I heard voices coming from down the hall; I also smelled the warm food they were serving. They were in the dining room having a meeting over lunch.

I surprised Mr. Winchester, and the other four men at the dining table. They paused in the middle of their conversation, and dropped their knives and folks upon their plates. It wasn't just that I had quietly snuck up on them amidst all the guards, but it was the sight of seeing me accompanied by the two wolves who escorted me inside.

"What the hell are you doing here?" Mr. Winchester barked angrily.

"I thought it was time you and I had a conversation," I politely smiled.

"Look, I don't know where you're from, but we have laws against trespassing, and breaking and entering," he bellowed.

"Oh, the front door was open and the guards didn't seem to mind. Didn't the sheriff give you my response to your earlier invitation? I thought you would be expecting a visit from me. He asked me to deliver you this," I gazed directly at the sheriff, and threw Mr. Winchester's business card on the table.

"Who the hell is this?" one of the surprised and enraged men inquired, and stood up from the table.

"Forgive me, but this is Special Agent Christian Sands of the Bureau of Indian Affairs," Winchester said grinning.

"What is the meaning of this intrusion Agent Sands? I'm Mayor Hancock, and I will speak to your superiors about this."

"What have I done, Mayor Hancock?" I coyishly asked.

"For starters, this is private property, regardless of the way in which you got inside, you are uninvited, and therefore you are breaking the law. I'm sure the sheriff will take it from here." He blustered.

The sheriff got up from his seat reluctantly. He didn't want any parts of arresting a federal agent. He understood the ramifications that would come from it. There would be an inquiry into the arrest and it would only bring more Feds to the small town of Swanton.

"*Wait!*" Boss Winchester said to the sheriff, as he approached me, "*I did extend Agent Sands an invitation. He isn't trespassing.*" The Mayor was dumbfounded and gave Winchester an astonished look.

"*Yes, Tom, I forgot I extended him an open invitation. I think we can finish this tomorrow*" he said to the others in the dining room, still smiling, as if he had a secret that no one else knew. "*Oh, and make sure you tell Addison that we're finish here, so he can have the help come in here,*" he said aloud to the three men exiting.

It was clear who was in charge here, as he dismissed Mayor Hancock, Sheriff Meehan, and the other gentleman, whom I didn't know. It seemed no one was in a hurry to introduce the stranger to me, as well. Then Winchester reprimanded his pet wolves, and commanded that they come over to him and sit.

"*Please accompany me to the parlor, Agent Sands, we can talk in there,*" Winchester suggested, as I followed him, accompanied by the wolves.

His library was unique. It was a grand room, like something out of the Victorian era, yet it was a hybrid of a library and a sports room. Three of the walls had shelves of books that towered towards the soaring ceilings with two ladders to reach the books on the top shelves. The fourth wall contained the spoils and trophies of his hunting expeditions. It sickened me to see the heads of the animals displayed in such a manner. It made me want to rip his head off. I wonder how he would do against such magnificent creatures if he didn't have a powerful long-range rifle, but I endured not allowing him to see my emotions. It would be perceived as a sign of weakness with such a man.

I observed a large and distinguishing painting of Winchester with a beautiful woman in the library which he also used as a smoking room. I could smell the stale left over aroma of cigar and pipe tobacco in the air. It seemed like a shame to dilute books with the smell of burnt tobacco. The woman was his wife no doubt. She would explain the Victorian style décor that was diminished by the big game trophies and rifles.

I'm certain she no longer lived with him because no woman with the impeccable taste to furnish three-fourths of a room would allow him to destroy it with the other third. It just didn't make sense. It had the look of an emotional reaction that a single man would carry out to boast of his newly found independence, and to rebel against his past. My mother would have called it the reaction of a little boy acting out. You could also tell that the break up was something that he didn't want or he wouldn't have held on to what she created.

Boss Winchester was also big man, around 6 feet - 5 inches and weighed about 240 lbs. He kept his head clean shaven and had a mustache connected to his goatee, which was thick, bushy and black with strands of grey fused within. His thick busy eyebrows matched his mustache and goatee. He was wide and thick, not overly muscular, but solid like a lumber jack, which are his main enterprises- lumber and maple syrup. Then he tried getting into plastic bottling until the factory closed due to the strange illnesses of the workers. The place was deemed cursed by the Abenaki which exacerbated the bad blood between them. When the children went missing things only became volatile.

He directed me to have a seat in one of the huge throne like leather chairs near the mahogany bar in the room and offered me a cigar and a drink, which I denied. He sat down in the adjacent throne chair, which were separated by a mahogany round table that was already outfitted with a large ivory ash tray and a golden cigar lighter. It was obvious that this was a part of his routine after a meal, as he sat his cordial down on the table.

The unknown gentleman who accompanied him for lunch returned at that point. He visually perused the library, and waited by the entrance for Mr. Winchester to give him a signal or command. Winchester smiled, and nodded his head to assure the man that everything was alright. He slightly moved his unlit cigar towards the door, directing the man to leave, as he posted outside the entrance. Now I knew who he was, he's Boss Winchester's personal body guard, the head goon in charge of security, and other clandestine operations, like overseeing thug activities.

"So, what brings you here today, Agent Sands?" he asked, as he lit up his cigar.

"Oh, I thought it was about time we discussed how you're running things here." I bluntly responded.

He smiled at my response, but never broke focus on his cigar. He twirled it around the lighter while puffing on it, slowly taking his time, and creating a smoke cloud until he got just the right burn started. He didn't fear me at all and was acting like a boss of a town would, in control.

"Well now, Agent Sands, I'm a man who is used to getting what he wants, as you can see, and right now I want you, and all the rest of your kind out of my town," he riposted, looking me directly in the eyes.

"By my kind, you mean Federal Agents?" I asked.

"Take it any way you like, but sooner or later I get what I want," he boasted, and took another puff from the cigar.

I knew exactly what he was talking about. He was talking about the Abenaki. Mr. Winchester had his rubber stamp on the whole town. There was nothing that didn't cross his purview. He had the mayor, the sheriff and everyone else in the town basically working for him. I wouldn't put it pass him to try and get rid of Indian Affairs Agents, but he didn't cause the mangling those bodies endured.

"Well, Mr. Winchester, I hate to disappoint you, but you're going to have to get use to rejection, because I'm not going anywhere until I get to the bottom of what I came here to do. If I find out that any Abenaki have been injured during my investigation, I'll be paying you another visit, but this time I won't be so hospitable. I've shown you today that I can get pass your guards and get to you whenever needed." I threatened, and got up from the chair, as the wolves stood at attention.

He remained seated and took another slow drag from his cigar, held the smoke in his lungs for a half a minute while examining the cigar then exhaled, releasing the smoke.

"You know, if I didn't know better Agent Sands, I'd think that sounded like a threat," he grinned.

"Take it any way you like," I quipped, repeating his statement.

"You know, reaching out and touching someone goes both ways, Agent Sands," he said, and picked up the tulip glass resting on the table, and raised it in a toast like manner.

"I can show myself out Mr. Winchester, I think I know the way," I replied, as the wolves escorted me to the parlor entrance before he commanded them to come back to him.

The bodyguard escorted me to the front door, as I casually walked through a gang of angry armed men waiting inside the house now. I smiled at them, and made my way to the front door, as they walked behind me. The unknown gentleman sitting at the dining table was leading the pack to the entrance. He had chiseled facial features with what appeared to be a permanent scowl. His hair was blonde and cut short to his scalp like they do in the military which he probably served, Black Ops probably or mercenary. He was a massive man that stood 6ft-6in., muscular wide build, and weighed close to 280lbs. He had a crooked hook nose like a fighter, and deep embedded scar tissue around the eyes, and check bones like a fighter. He was a brut in every way.

"If you come here again, it'll be your last visit," he warned me with a deep Germanic accent, and opened the door.

He would have frightened most men, but then, I wasn't most men. I continued to smile and exited the house, as the guards continue escorting me to the front gate. One of them tried to push me out the gate, but I dodged his advances with my speed, tripped him, and sent him stumbling to the ground in front of me.

"Quit while you're ahead," I warned him, and departed without further incident.

Afterwards, I drove to the Tribal Council, to check on Kateri, and see how she was adjusting after the attempted abduction. There was an AT&T telephone truck parked outside the building when I arrived. They were here to reconnect the telephone lines that were cut by those thugs last night. It was just my luck that Youngblood would be the first one I see as I enter the building. He was standing at the secretary's desk with some papers and instructing her on them.

"Good afternoon, Ma'am," I greeted the elderly secretary at the desk. She greeted me in return and then I spoke to Youngblood who was standing beside her.

"Good afternoon, Councilman Youngblood, how are you?" We weren't on first name bases, so I kept it strictly professional. He frowned while slightly tilting his head away from me, rolled his eyes, and took in a quick deep breath and released it; paused for a second, then continued talking to the receptionist, as if I wasn't there.

"Can you tell me if Kateri is in today?" I asked him, unswayed by his rudeness.

"No, Metis (Half-breed), she's not here, and we don't need you lurking around here acting as if you're Sokoki." He snapped.

"You do realize I'm only here to help. I'm not here to cause you or the Abenaki any trouble," I solemnly replied.

"We don't need your assistance, Metis," he retorted angrily, not even giving me the courtesy of looking at me before continuing with the secretary.

"Well can you tell me where I can find her?"

He ignored me, and the secretary spoke up to bridge his rudeness.

"She should be making her morning rounds at the village today. She doesn't usually check in here until after that."

"Thank you very much, and have a wonderful day." I replied, and departed.

His persistent rudeness and calling me a half- breed was no longer annoying to me, because I knew where the hatred was stemming from. He was threatened by my presence and Kateri's continuous rejections. Her actions last night only exacerbated the situation, so I'll just get used to him calling me that, because nothing is going to change her mind, and I plan on being around until I solve this case.

I drove out to the Abenaki Village to find Kateri. I had some further questions to ask her. I drove for about 10 minutes before noticing that I was being followed. It could have been the FBI, but I doubt it. These men were driving a black in color, Range Rover, and the FBI doesn't use high-end vehicles. They were Winchester's men. I've always believed in not taking trouble to someone else's door, so I drove into the Black Forest, off the highway, to lose my tail and to check out their intent.

The ominous supernatural energy was still present, covering the forest and thick as ever. I parked my vehicle and walked into the midst of thick foliage. I shadowed myself within the shade of the forest and observed five men pouring out of the SUV, armed with submachine guns. Now I was certain that they were Winchester's men. He had sent them to kill me. I hadn't been on the case for a week and already someone was out to kill me. This thing between us had escalated after I intruded on his property. He had to be powerful or insane to go after a Federal Officer.

I led them deep into the forest. I thought the rumors of the Forest Monster would scare them off or they would grow tired of the chase, but they were determined. I was having fun with the goons, as I utilized my speed and shadow abilities. I had them walking in circles in the forest trying to kill me. Then I felt this uncanny feeling like something was watching me again. I learned a long time ago to adhere to my instincts, even more so now with my panther imprinting.

I didn't feel any other energy signatures due to the omnipresent energy that hovered over the forest and the town. It was the same thing I experienced when the wolves were hunting me. This thing was watching me or hunting me, as the goons were attempting to do? It was time to end this game of cat and mouse and head out of the forest, where I would have a better chance of seeing my pursuers.

As I journeyed from the forest, I heard the screams of the goons behind me, one by one, as they fired their weapons for the last time. Whoever or whatever was covering a lot of ground quickly, because I left the goons with a good amount of distance between them, as they searched for me. I stopped my progression and waited motionless for a moment. There were no more screams or the firing of weapons echoing in the distance. My instincts were telling me to keep walking and not turn around, but my duty and curiosity got the best of me. I wasn't turning around to save these men, who were trying to kill me; they were probably all dead by the sound of things. These men deserved whatever happened to them, but this could be my break in the case.

I retraced my steps back to the area of the screams and discovered blood everywhere among the forest flora. There were assorted pieces of body parts and the inner guts of men, still warm, and scattered on the ground. Some were ripped clean in half with one whole portion missing. It was just like the horrific pictures that I viewed in the FBI case files, except their images didn't have the crows present. They were already pecking through the carnage, pulling out flesh and devouring it. It's as if they were already waiting or perhaps they knew the scent of the beast and followed it here. How in the hell did it do this so quickly and leave? I've seen a lot of horrific deaths working with the FBI ViCAP, but I wouldn't wish this on anyone. Being eaten alive is no way for a man to die, not even this scum.

This thing had vanished without a trace, as quickly as it had emerged, swiftly killing the men with ease. I now knew for a fact that it was a supernatural being and not a bear, but what kind of creature could have done such a thing? Whatever this thing is, I'm sure it won't be long before our paths cross again, but until then I'll just stay out of the FBI's way, as Agent Whyte requested. No one will be filing a missing person's reports on these men and they surely won't be missed, as I watched the ravens continue feasting on their corpses.

I got back inside my rented vehicle and pulled off. I shouldn't feel any remorse for these men, but I did. Although, if I notify the FBI of this, I'll be tied up in paperwork and interrogations for days attempting to explain what occurred. I'll leave them for the task force to discover and attempt to figure out. Lucky for me, I didn't drive my vehicle near here. The bureau can identify tire markings and easily connect me.

The evening sky was toying with night. It had already been an eventful day for me. I should have just turned around and head back into town, but I still hadn't checked on Kateri yet. I was still full of life; everything seemed to come alive at night to me, including my energy level.

I've been a nocturnal creature since I can remember. From sleep walking to nightmares and dreamscaping, most of my life centered on the night, so I continued driving to the Abenaki Village, hopefully this time without distraction.

There were no street lights high in the mountains where the Sokoki Abenaki Village was located. There was only the head lights of the vehicle and the light of the moon illuminating the road, but I could have turned the headlights completely off. My vision was just as adept at seeing in the dark, as any other nocturnal predator. It was an imprinting gift amongst many from my spirit guide, the Black Panther. I only left the lights on to steer the deer and other pedestrian animals away from the road. I already knew no other vehicles would be traveling this way.

When I arrived at Kateri's cabin, I had second thoughts about knocking on the door. It was getting late, and I didn't want to disturb her, so I ventured to the Medicine Man's cabin alone. Kateri had already given me the directions, so I continued driving through the quiet village of the Sokoki without an incident. The Midewinini cabin was isolated from the rest of the villagers on the Missisquoi River; he lived further up into the mountains.

I drove 7 miles pass the village before the rural road ended about a quarter mile from the base of the mountains. If I had a four-wheel drive vehicle, or an ATV, I could keep driving, but that wasn't the case. I had to walk from here. I wouldn't have dreamed of walking in the dark wilderness like this a couple of years ago, but things had changed drastically since then. I was now a resident of the Great Smoky Mountains. I was one with nature and had all the senses and abilities of a panther in the dark, and that wasn't all.

This part of the trail was basically open field, so all-terrain vehicles could maneuver up the mountain. I could hear the night predators out hunting in the forest ridge. Some even silenced themselves and took notice of me. It was a beautiful night with a three-quarter moon illuminating the sky. It's remarkable how bright it all seemed to me. It was like walking in the daylight with sunshades.

I thought the ominous supernatural blanket was the thickest in the Black Forest, but it was ridiculously thick here near the mountains. This only made me more suspicious of the Medicine Man and his involvement in all this.

I continued walking in the direction Kateri gave me until suddenly, the forest became abnormally quiet. It didn't take a rocket scientist or a Shaman to know that this was the warning or alarm sound of the wilderness. Then I heard thunder in what appeared to be a calm, cloudless sky. Then I saw an enormous black mass in the night sky heading my way. It was moving too fast to be a storm cloud, and then I realized it was the thunderous sounds of hundreds of wings belonging to a swarm of ravens. They masked the moonlit night sky and rendering it pitch black, as they approached.

I had seen these blackbirds everywhere, in and around town, but never in this capacity. This was more than just an anomaly; this had supernatural forces behind it, seeing a swarm this massive wasn't a natural occurrence. I hoped that the mass of birds was just migrating north, but I was only kidding myself, this wasn't the migrating season, if anything they would be going south. Now they began to squawk in a deafening roar as they circled above me. The sound alone was detrimental, as I covered my ears to shield them from the piercing noise. Then they attacked me, swooping down in a massive wave and knocking me to the ground!

I suffered tremendous blows from their speed and sheer numbers. It was like being stoned by bricks. I tried to cover up while on the ground to protect myself, but this did no good, as they began swiftly cutting me with their beaks and claws. It felt like hundreds of razor blades lacerating me, as they shredded my clothes. They weren't going to stop until they killed me, and judging by my previous encounters with them, it wouldn't stop there either. These flesh eaters would pick my body to the bone after killing me. I noticed something different about these birds than previously. They had scarlet red eyes, every one of them.

The main Shamanic principle is to be one with nature or in balance with it. That meant we didn't indiscriminately or actively kill the creatures of Mother Earth, but I think it's sufficient to say that this incident was outside of the balance and far from normal. Therefore, I summoned the wind to assist me. I created a small concentrated funnel cloud that swept the birds inside and killing them. I also destroyed a couple of trees with the funnel, but luckily, I was in an open field with minimal damage to the surrounding forest.

There were hundreds of dead ravens covering the ground. It was like something from out of an apocalyptic prophecy, just what those '*End of the World*' fanatics in town would rave over. I didn't know what to do with them, but I knew this massive carnage would only do further harm to nature by becoming a diseased open graveyard. As much as I hated conjuring fire, I didn't see any other way of containing this, so I burnt them, and once again, I felt good doing it. I should feel despair having killed these creatures, as I did before using fire, but I felt no remorse. I hate the emotional ambivalence it created whenever I summoned its uncontrollable power. Lucky for me I was in an open field which assisted me in controlling the flames.

After coming down from the high of using the fire, I looked over the scorched earth and it sickened me. All the carnage and destruction, yet there was another side of me, something deep inside that still felt good. I hated those pesky birds, but they were innocent creatures being manipulated by some malevolent entity. I had enough for one day, at least mentally; physically I could have continued. Whatever wanted to deter me from continuing up the mountain had accomplished its goal. Perhaps it was the Midewinini behind it. This was something that I would have to investigate later. They won this round in the battle, but the war was far from over. I'll resume tomorrow, for sure.

CHAPTER EIGHT

MIDEWIWIN

When I woke this morning, I felt rejuvenated, and with a sense of clarity. The owl was on my mind as soon as I woke. I wanted to thank her for her wisdom in trying to warn me of the dangers that I would encounter. Mother Earth was giving me signs and symbols through her since the moment we met. The dead rabbit which indicates death in certain cultures and then she appeared with the dead crow on my window sill to warn me of the raven's attack. As I stated, the gift of reading signs and symbols wasn't a strong suit for me, like with Shaman seers.

I opened the hotel window and called upon her. It didn't take long before I saw her quietly flying from the nearby tree line where she lived. Mother Nature gifted her with the ability of silent flight like no other raptors. Her long wings where particularly designed for stealth attacks. I caressed her as soon as she landed on the window sill. It would not be natural to offer such a gifted Apex hunter with prey as a reward, so I took several minutes to caress her, and share a few minutes of bonding before I let her go.

I departed the hotel with the rising sun. I wanted to catch Kateri before both our day became hectic, and without someone tailing me for a change. I managed to catch her just before she was about to make her medical rounds in the nearby village. She told me that she had a very busy schedule, so I volunteered to lend a hand, if she would assist me later, which she agreed.

I didn't have my medicine bag with me that contained certain powders, roots, plants, and seeds and crushed leaves which Asku instructed me on how to use in the healing arts. At first, I was reluctant about learning such a laborious task, but later found it to be rewarding and soothing to the soul. Going out with Asku to cure the tribal members became one of my favorite excursions.

I assisted Kateri with minor settings and administering medication. Some of her patients required the care of a hospital, but refused "the White Man's medicine" and preferred to let nature take its course. It is considered the cycle of life to them. The Abenaki People have a strong connection with the spirit realm, like the Cherokee. They knew that even in death that their spirit would live on; therefore, they weren't afraid of death. It is called *'the passing'* when a soul moves on to the next realm.

The Chief of the tribe was an elderly woman name Malgelit. She became very interested in me, and wanted to meet me. After being introduced, she grasped my hands between hers, just as Asku had done when I first met him. I guest some customs are transcended. I knew exactly what she was doing, but Kateri didn't inform me that she was a Shaman. She was reading my energy and perhaps my past and future depending on her skill set.

After our meeting, she asked if I would visit the sick that were beyond the scope of Kateri's medical help. I was puzzled because I didn't know what I could do to assist them, but I adhered to her wishes. We had been speaking in Algonquian the whole time until we visited the first patient, who was waiting to die, and then the elderly chief spoke to me in Tsalagi. Now I was certain that she was a Shaman, because she had the gift of speaking in tongues.

"I know who you are; you are Cheveyo, the Spirit Warrior from the Mountain People's Clan. You are the chosen one of the prophecy. You have powers beyond your comprehension. The medicine bag that you seek, you already have. All you have to do is have faith and it will be done by

a mere touch of your hand." She pointed to the elderly man lying on his buckskin rug.

I didn't have the slightest idea what this elderly man was suffering from, but she was asking me to perform a miracle. I only knew of one man who could heal the sick as such, and he was the Son of God. She saw the hesitation in me and added.

"This isn't anything new to your kind. They have been performing this since the beginning of time. Even some men have been gifted with this ability. Holy Men of the Bible that you've read about, and others throughout history that isn't so common." She stated with certainty.

Her words made sense. There were lots of men throughout history and within several holy books from the Torah to the Holy Christian Bible, the Quran and the Shruti. I looked down into the elderly man's eyes. They were covered with a shadowy film of despair. I've seen it on many occasions now. It is the color of deep sickness which was usually followed by death. The old man struggled to reach out to me with the little strength remaining within him.

"He has faith in you," Malgelit inserted.

I grabbed the old man's hand, and Malgelit grabbed mine and told me to repeat after her, as she chanted. It was a healing chant that I'd never heard before. Then the strangest thing began to occur. I began to feel ill holding on to the elderly man's hand. I felt like I wanted to vomit, and ran from the wigwam. I threw up as soon as I exited. Kateri hurried out after me.

"Are you alright?" She asked rubbing my back with the look of concern on her face.

"Yeah, I could use a…" Then she offered me a towel before I could complete my sentence.

"Is there anything else I can get for you?"

"Yes, I could use a bottle of water." She produced that as well, as if prepared for what I was going to be experiencing.

"You'll have to forgive the old woman. She used to belong to the Midewiwin until they made her the chief and she relinquished those duties over to the old wise man in the mountains, which no longer perform the duties. He came down with a debilitating illness and has been in a wheel chair ever since."

I got up from my crouching position and wondered where the spew even came from. I hadn't eaten any breakfast this morning and skipped dinner last night. Neither one of us has ever seen vomit like this before, it was grayish in color, like the old man's eyes. When we reentered the wigwam, the old man was sitting up on the buckskin rug to our surprise.

"How in the hell!" Kateri blurted with her eyes opened wide and jaw dropped. I was just as surprised, as she ran over to the elderly man, and immediately took out her stethoscope, and began checking his vitals.

"Amazing!" She exclaimed, while her ears were plugged with the stethoscope, and examining the elderly man, *"His heart is beating like that of a middle- aged man, as if he discovered the fountain of youth!"*

The elderly woman smiled and took my hands into hers, again, and said, *"I'm glad you are here. They told us that you would be coming."*

"Who told you that?" I solemnly inquired, still a little weak.

"The effects will wear off in a little while. The illness was discharged from your system with the vomit," she replied without answering my question.

She let go of my hands staring into my eyes, and said, "It was our ancestors. Now I must go and attend to other business of the tribe. Remember what I taught you, Cheveyo, and we'll talk later."

It was a full day of work assisting Kateri and treating the Abenaki. It reminded me of my travels with Asku and treating the Cherokee. Afterwards the tribe prepared a late lunch for us. They often did this for Kateri to take with her while she did her rounds. This time they prepared enough for two.

I got the opportunity to question the elderly chief about the supernatural entity surrounding the Forest and the villages before we departed. She informed me that it was the Chibasikweda, the fog that they referred to their ancestors. I wasn't the least bit satisfied with her explanation, but I didn't let it show, and left it at that. This thing I felt was always present, even when the Chibaiskweda or fog wasn't out. The elderly chief's parting words were just as confusing.

"Thank you again, Cheveyo, and you're welcome here anytime. Remember what I taught you, and beware of the crows, the Atsolowas comes in many forms. Safe travels to you."

"Thank you, I appreciate the hospitality," I replied, and departed with Kateri.

The elderly chief was a little late in warning me about the crows. I could have used that news yesterday when the owl was attempting to warn me, but I couldn't read the sign. I'm totally confused about her comment concerning the Atsolowas. She reminded me so much of Asku and his riddles.

Kateri and I ate lunch in a spot where the Missisiquoi River met Lake Champlain. It was like a small paradise here. The sun was shining with a cool breeze coming down from Canada and the mountains. I would have loved to just waste the entire day here, on the lake with a beautiful woman and a picnic lunch provided by the Abenaki of Missisquoi tribe for services rendered.

Kateri had on a tan linen summer dress that accented her beautiful brown eyes. Her thick, black wavy hair was one long braided pony tail that came down from the back and draped over her right shoulder landing on her breast, and ending just above her waist. Her smile was intoxicating and with flawlessly bright teeth that made her face light up whenever she displayed them.

It was a beautiful and serene here with only the sound of nature providing music in the background. There was a chorus of different birds singing with an assortment of colorful butterflies and dragon flies playing among us. Several stopped in and greeted us.

"I've been here on several occasions, but never have they come down like this to greet me. Is it one of your abilities? Can you communicate with nature as well? Why didn't you tell me you were a Shaman?" Kateri hastily inquired with a smile, and curious eyes.

"It isn't something that comes up in conversation, especially in my professional circle," I informed her.

"You could have told me," she responded in Algonquian, and reached out and held my hand.

"I'm not here in the capacity of a visiting Shaman, but that of a Federal Agent investigating the murder of several agents, and to see if there is a connection between them and the missing children." I affirmed, looking at her with a stoic stare.

"You may find that your skills as a Shaman are more valuable in finding the truth than your investigative skills. Isn't that the real reason why they sent you? I have a feeling that you've done this before with similar cases." She said, and tilted her head with a fixed stare on my lips in anticipation for my next response.

"Yes, there have been others when I worked with the FBI, but I no longer work for them. I'm only investigating this as a favor."

"What made you stop working for them?"

"The last case I worked on went a little deeper than I nor they anticipated and it was just best for all to part ways," I replied, in a low tone.

"It doesn't sound like you wanted to stop. I don't think you'd be here if that was the case, but I'm glad that you are." She smiled and squeezed my hand.

"Can we eat now, I'm famished!" I chuckled.

"Yes, we can stop talking about it and eat," she giggled, and released my hand.

After lunch, we continued conversing about Swanton, and the Abenaki People. It was information that could be helpful later in my investigation. I also wanted to know more about the elderly chief.

"So, what can you tell me about this Atsolowas?" I inquired.

"Oh, so now you want to talk after being fed, I see, so I'll feed you from now on," she laughed, and nudged me with her shoulder. She enjoys slight physical contact, I've noticed.

"Well in Abenaki lore, Atsolowas is the trickster. It appears in different forms to entice, and trick her victims into doing her bidding. They say it appears in the form of a fox, a weasel, and other animals, even crows, it just depends on who's telling the story." She informed me.

We shared pleasantries, jokes and stories as people do when they're on a date and getting to know one another, but I made my intentions clear, that I was involved with someone. She had already told me that she wasn't in a relationship, so I left it at that. It baffled me why someone as gorgeous and smart as she wasn't in a relationship. It surely wasn't due to a lack of suitors, because I've seen the way Youngblood and several other men look at her. Perhaps she was finicky. Then I spotted several crows above us in the sky disturbingly circling around.

"What's wrong," Kateri inquired looking at the concerned look on my face.

"Those crows up there are acting erratic." I cautioned her.

"What do you mean?" She asked, nervously.

"Well, why are they circling overhead, there's no carrion that I can smell in the vicinity?"

"You can smell carrion within the immediate surroundings?" She asked with a high pitch astonished voice, and raised eye brows.

"Well, I mean we would have smelled it on the way up here," I retorted. I didn't want to get back on the subject of what I was capable of doing.

"It's probably just our lunch that has attracted them, lots of people picnic out here and leave behind refuse," she laughed and nudged me on the shoulder, again, *"the old mother has you paranoid, and afraid of black birds now?"*

Yes, I was weary of the crows now, especially ones with scarlet red eyes, that travel in masses, I thought to myself. Then she got up and took off her dress and shoes. She was wearing a sports bra and undies that resembled something that you'd see professional volleyball players wearing, and she had the body of one as well. She gazed at me the whole time she was undressing, smiling from ear-to-ear. She was gauging my expressions, and watching my eyes take in the full of her body. She wasn't the shy type or bashful about her body. She had nothing to be shy about; her body was perfect in every way.

"What are you doing?" I inquired, and thought about how stupid that sounded after it rolled off my lips.

"What does it look like? I'm going for a swim. The water is wonderful here," she replied, running towards the water and diving in.

Here I go again; I recall this is how I got in trouble when Nina and I kissed in a swimming pool in Arizona. I was currently with someone else, and now déjà vu all over again. Although things were a bit different, since Nina and I already had a connection through dreamscape. I wasn't about to go down that road of infidelity. I was determined to prove Asku wrong about me and my panther infidelity.

She waded in the water alone coaxing me to come inside, but I refused, and just watched the beauty as she swam. She was a graceful swimmer like I, but nothing was going to get me in that water, I already know what would happen if I did.

She exited the water appearing even sexier with wet jet-black hair hanging down to her back. Her bra and panties clung to her body like a transparent outer skin due to its wetness. Her hips were round and her waist was small. She had a flat stomach, voluptuous thighs, and an apple bottom butt that looked soft and inviting. Her hips seemed to move from side to side, in a rhythmic seductive dance, as she moved towards me.

Then she flashed one of the prettiest smiles I've ever seen, it was radiant with sparkling white teeth.

She continued glaring straight into my eyes with those big beautiful brown eyes of hers, and enjoyed the way my eyes took in the contour of her full figure. I lowered my eyes to the ground because it was just too obvious, and embarrassing; the way I was gawking at her. She knew exactly what she was doing. She flopped right down beside me, still wet from her swim and gently grabbed my arm.

"What is it, Christian, did I do something wrong?"

She placed her face right in front of mine, so I couldn't avoid looking at her, as tiny water droplets fell from her face and body upon mine. It felt inviting cool to the touch, and sunk deep within my skin, as it began slowly melting away my resolve.

"No, Kateri, it's not you. It's just that I'm with someone that I care about," I quickly glanced up at her and then back down.

"I understand, but it was just a swim," she laughed, and nudged me again. *"You really need to lighten up, Chris."* Then she got up from the blanket and dried herself off.

I continued looking away, so I didn't give the wrong impression. She had a body that screamed attention, and my carnal desires were beginning to weaken me. Women never cease to confuse me with their emotions. I thought Kateri would feel differently after the swim, but she was totally alright with it. That's when I saw something strange in the waterfalls. It looked like the silhouette of something large, like a bear, perhaps bigger, but I couldn't make it out. I quickly jumped to my feet, and looked more diligently in its direction, but I didn't see anything. It could have been my eyes playing tricks on me with the water and the sun gleaming on it.

I looked back at Kateri to see if she had noticed it, but she had her back towards me, pulling down her dress. If there were something in the water it would have attacked her a long time ago or it was waiting for her to return. Man, I was paranoid like Kateri said, but the mother's warnings were just half of the story.

We made a couple of more rounds that lasted into the early evening, and then Kateri took me up the mountains to see the old medicine man or Midewinini, whose name was Chogan (Blackbird), but the Abenaki referred to him as the Nixkamich or Great Father. It was a term of endearment among the Abenaki like the Great Mother was to the Hopi People. I wondered if his real name is a sign about the attack I experienced last night by the blackbirds.

When we arrived at the cabin, I could feel the supernatural energy emitted from inside of the house. It was remarkably different from the massive energy smothering the surroundings that I had been experiencing since I arrived. It was probably the energy signature emitted by Chogan.

Kateri introduced me to Chogan and his niece, Tahki, who was attending to him, which I thought was very noble and considerate of her. She was a very attractive young woman in her early twenties. She was an artist, and had several paintings around the cabin, and up on the walls. There was one unfinished one on the easel of wolves running under a full moon. She was an impressionistic artist like Van Gogh.

Although all the paintings were exquisite, some of them had darkness to them, just like Van Gogh's. There was a painting of a graveyard with angels, her rendition of the phoenix, some Abenaki women playing in the forest and kicking up black leaves; of all things, but the darkest of them all were the two paintings that laid on the floor. One of them was a haunted looking building and the other resembled "Starry Night" except it looked like a cave with stars in it.

There was one that I really enjoyed; it was a painting of a bear, a wolf and a leopard on a mountain side with a Native American Warrior. Then there was the unmistakable painting of the Black Forest with the luminescent mist-like fog or Chibaiskweda swirling through the trees and throughout the forest. It looked like a scene she snatched from one of my experiences there. She was highly gifted.

"Wow, these paintings are magnificent!" I said, perusing the ones on the wall.

"Yes, they are. Tahki has paintings hanging up at the tribal council, all around the town, and throughout the state. I keep trying to get her to open a store online, but she's traditional," Kateri spoke up, while Tahki shyly grinned.

"So, those were your paintings I was admiring at the council building. I really enjoyed the one with the Abenaki men around the fireside. It was so detailed, and the hues were extraordinary," I informed her.

"Thank you," she reservedly replied.

"How long have you been painting, Tahki?" I asked, just to converse with the shy young lady.

"Since I can remember, I've always wanted to recreate the world," she answered.

What a strange way of putting it, I thought, but she was like most artists, a bit different than the rest of us. Then again, who am I to call someone different; the pot calling the kettle black?

"Even Mr. Winchester purchased a few of her paintings at her last showing. This was before the factory closed," Kateri informed me.

"Are the ones on the wall for sale?" I inquired, and then the shy young lady lit up.

"Which one do you like?" She asked, excitedly.

"I think they are all wonderful, but this one really speaks to me. How much?" I said, pointing to the painting of the Abenaki Warrior with the leopard, wolf, and bear.

"Consider it a gift," she replied, elated and smiling from ear-to-ear.

"Oh, I couldn't do that, please let me pay for it."

"I would consider it an honor, if you would accept this as a gift. This way my work can travel beyond Swanton," she riposted.

"No, the honor is mine, and thanks you very much. I will treasure it."

Tahki and Kateri could have been sisters. Almost exact same shape, eye color, hair, except Tahki was a bit more reserved, and shy, especially around strangers. She looked down at the floor most of the time, and avoided eye contact with me the whole time, except for the few times she caught me staring at her. Then she would turn away, blush, and start playing with her hair. She wore it in a long pony tail that was plaited going down her back, but she swung it forward across her right shoulder. It looked nice that way, but it seemed like she only did it, so she could play with it when she became nervous or fidgety. She played with it a lot while I was there.

Chogan was an elderly man confined to a wheel chair and incoherent. He was small in stature from being in the wheel chair, but his legs had suffered the most which were significantly small. There was no way he was faking being confined to the chair judging by the muscular atrophy. I attempted to speak to him, but received nothing in return. His energy was still shinning bright, but there was no one home. I'm certain that I can reach him in dreamscape, but why bother; he clearly isn't the one I'm looking for. The excursion wasn't a complete lost though, now I can delete Chogan's name from the list of supernatural suspects.

"You seem almost disappointed," Kateri, said examining my face.

"No, not at all, it's just a process of narrowing down potential suspects. It's part of the job," I replied, smiling in return.

"You thought Nixkamich was a suspect in the disappearance of the children?" she asked, astonished by the allegation.

"I'm just following a few hunches that I have," I replied.

She laughed hardily at the possibility that I thought Chogan was involved. I didn't blame her after seeing the condition that he was in, but I didn't feel any different about checking it out. It helped me cross him off the list, and now I could move on to finding others. Kateri invited me to dinner at her place after we left the mountains. I was hungry and accepted whole heartedly.

The meal was superb. She prepared a traditional Abenaki meal for me. We ate venison with a casserole consisting of the three sisters' crop of corn, beans, and squash with cranberry stuffing. It was delicious. Then, she received a knock at the door. I already knew who it was, and I'm certain she knew as well.

"Excuse me, this will only take a minute" she politely said, before getting up.

"Good Evening, Kateri, can we talk for a minute?" Youngblood asked.

"I'm having dinner right now," she informed him, while holding the door slightly shut, so he couldn't look inside, but he noticed how meticulously she was guarding the door.

"Oh, I see, I'm sorry for disturbing you" he replied, flustered, and saddened by the events.

Once again, I felt sorry for Youngblood, and wished I wasn't a participant in his misery. There's no telling what he and the boys have instore for me this time when I leave. I might not be so gracious though, if they try to kill me again.

After dinner, we talked some more on her porch under the stars. We managed to get around to the discussion of relationships again. This time I went into details explaining my relationship with Nina. She seemed happy for me. I only hope that this put an end to her flirtation, because she was wearing me down. I'd never let her know that, and the Great Spirit forbid Nina finding out. I'm flattered that such a gorgeous and intelligent woman, would be interested in me, but I was happy with Nina. We talked for about an hour longer, before it was time for me to leave.

"Would you like for me to walk you to your vehicle?" She asked, smiling, as if I needed an escort.

"No, I think I got it," I replied, smiling in return.

"Ok, then drive safely," she said, and placed her hand on the side of my face, before kissing me on the cheek, and walking away. I felt relieved

that I had departed her company without breaking my commitments. She was a distracting temptation that I didn't need.

As I drove down Route 7 from the Sokoki village to Swanton, I observed the headlights of two vehicles coming up quickly from the rear. I just knew in my mind that this was trouble. As they got closer I noticed that they were driving the high-end SUV's that Winchester's men were driving. This time they didn't wait for me to stop and exit the vehicle. I guess since the others disappeared they deemed me a high threat. They drove beside me, rolled down their windows, and fired upon my vehicle with a barrage of bullets! I ducked down on the seat, swerving and losing control of the car, until I ran off the road and into a ditch.

The henchmen immediately pulled over and quickly piled out of two vehicles. I immediately shadowed myself and exited the vehicle through the passenger door unseen by the men. Winchester had sent his best henchmen after me this time; it was the tall brute with the deep Germanic accent leading the charge. They continued showering the car with bullets for about a minute, which is actually a long time to fire upon anything with automatic weapons. I watched them from outside of the vehicle, as they turned the vehicle into a bullet ridden coffin. When they finally finished, they looked inside the vehicle only to find that it was empty.

It's not an easy thing standing by and watching someone trying to kill you. I was angry and wanted to return the favor. I wanted to kill them where they stood. I could feel the flames burning inside of me, literally, as I began to get hot, not speaking figuratively, but physically hot. I could see steam flowing from my hands, which has never happened before now. I would surely give away my position and had to calm myself down. Then I went through the men hitting and scaring them senseless, while shadowed. Some tried to escape, but I was too fast, as I intercepted them. I wasn't going to kill them, but I would give them a scare and beating that they would never forget.

After I finished beating and disabling the men, most of them were unconscious, except for the tall man, their leader. I reappeared, so he could see me. His eyes widened with fear, as I flashed an insidious grin at him. It was enough to tick him off, as he reached for the gun lying beside him, but when he turned to fire I was already gone. I was back at their vehicles. I had lifted the keys off one of the drivers during the fight and disabled the other vehicle, leaving them stranded. I doubt if I'll see these men again, after that, but I'll visit Winchester's dreams later tonight.

I returned to the hotel and dreamscaped with Winchester. I wanted to see if he knew anything about the missing agents or children. His dreams were dark. He vehemently hated the Abenaki with what he considered to be just causes. I thought his wife divorced him, but she died due to the mystery illness caused by the factory. The doctors stated that it was some sort of immune disease that they had never seen before. She was the one in charge of operations at the factory, and was just as intelligent as she was beautiful. I guess she would have to be an equal to be his spouse. Winchester blamed her death on the Abenaki's curse, like most of the town's people.

Winchester didn't know who or what was behind the killings in the forest, and judging by his dreams he was already in enough pain from the death of his wife. It was obvious that he loved her very much. He just didn't know how to deal with her death, so he lashed out at the Abenaki. Although he tried to kill me twice now, I didn't interrupt his dreams. He was grieving in his distorted, demented way, but he was really trying my patience. Perhaps after he hears or doesn't hear from the latest men he sent to kill me, he'll give it a rest. Although I doubt it, he's used to getting his way, as he stated to me.

This morning I didn't wake to my owl friend on the window sill, but to the pounding of someone on the door. It sounded as if they were going to break the door down, so I yelled out to them.

"Alright, already, I'm up," I said in an aggravated tone.

I sensed several human energy signatures outside of the door. I know those thugs aren't back for more of what I put on them. I looked out the peep hole of the door and discovered several FBI agents from the task force and two sheriff's deputies. As soon as I opened the door, they swung it opened and burst in.

"Special Agent Sands, you're under arrest for the suspected murders of Agents Bellamy and Gladden." the FBI Agent said as he turned me around and placed the handcuffs on me. *"You have got to be kidding me,"* I replied, as I allowed them to take me into custody.

Agents Bellamy and Gladden were the two agents that followed me into the woods. I had no idea they were missing. I felt sick at the possibility that they met with the same fate as the goons that I led into the forest. I thought they had made it out of there. I didn't hear any screams or anything, but then again, I didn't wait around to see if they had made it out, after finding that lair inside of that decrepit looking tree. I didn't kill them, but I might as well because I led them there. Now I know what deaths the owl was trying to warn me about that morning with the presence of the dead rabbit.

CHAPTER NINE
THE LINE-UP

My reputation was quickly becoming legendary. It had taken on a life of its own. The Agent that saved the reputation of the bureau and the man without a gun were amongst several of the lore's going around. Agent Whyte wasn't taking any chances when he sent agents to pick me up. There were several deputy sheriffs with them as well. It's not like they didn't have enough federal agents in the hotel. Whyte knew of my involvement with the ViCAP and knew of the reputation of the teams. He was probably one of the agents who assisted in propagating the term Freak Show and calling me Freddy Kruger.

Agent Whyte didn't know the exact nature of my abilities or talents, but he wasn't taking any chances nor were the agents and deputies that showed up to arrest me. They had their weapons drawn and went through the regular procedures for the apprehension of a suspect. The deputies placed handcuffs on me like I was a common criminal, and escorted from my room. You couldn't tell that I was once one of them or that I was a fabled legend of the FBI. *Stars burn out quickly.*

When I arrived at the sheriff's station I felt the strong presence of supernatural energy being emitted from within. It was already a busy day at the station, even at these early hours of the morning. The main floor was packed, as I attempted to locate the source of the supernatural energy, but couldn't. Swanton's misdemeanor rate had more than tripled with the influx of visitors since the children mysteriously disappeared. There was the press core visiting, which included television, radio, newspapers and magazines. They also had regular citizens visiting, which included sightseers, religious zealots, supernatural, paranormal geeks, and the alien abductee fanatics with their entourage of television, magazine and book writers.

Swanton's misdemeanor and felony rate was at an all-time high also, with the murders in the forest. Murder was a non-existent crime in Swanton until now. They had an occasional bear or wolf attack due to living so close to the wilderness, but the rate of attacks was consistent with any other wilderness town.

They took me upstairs to the second floor, where the investigations were conducted. The FBI had appropriated a large portion of the floor and made it the task force area. As I was walking up the stairs, the supernatural energy became stronger. When I entered the interrogating area, I saw Matunaagd Youngblood, and the Abenaki men scattered around the floor, at different desks with handcuffs on. There were a few other people being interrogated as well, but mostly the Abenaki. I was certain that they were emitting the supernatural energy.

I also wondered about this line of questioning; some would consider it profiling, judging by their line-up. They had rounded up several Abenaki men and now me, a half-breed Black man with Native American ancestry, go figure.

They took me inside the conference area that was separated from the rest of the floor and interrogated me in private. They at least granted me that common courtesy, as a law enforcement officer. I spent most of the day being interrogated by Agent Whyte on the missing FBI Agents who followed me into the forest. It was a task he didn't trust to anyone else. We went back and forth endlessly, as I tried explaining to him that I had no idea what happened to them. I didn't even know they were missing until the FBI informed me. I was saddened by the news and felt guilty about their disappearance. I was the one who had them follow me into the forest and loose them. I had no idea that this would occur. It was broad day light when I gave them the slip.

Agent Whyte was enjoying interrogating me and treated me just like a criminal. He even had me stand in a line-up for an unrelated case, just to *bleep* with me. He denied me my common right to a telephone call and an attorney. I didn't need an attorney and Whyte knew that with one phone call I would be released. After eight hours of grueling interrogation with no food or drink I was finally given a break. I don't think this was done out of the kindness of his heart; I think he needed a break.

I was given permission to use the restroom, and a bottle of water, while I waited in the main squad room for the next rounds of interrogation by Special Agent Whyte. That's when all hell broke loose. The Chief of Wildlife and Game entered the second floor with several of his officers and two FBI Agents. I could tell by the expression on their faces that something grave had occurred.

While I waited in the main room, I still felt a supernatural presence within the area. Youngblood and the other Abenaki were no longer in custody, as I looked around the room. There were only law enforcement officers present. I was in a precarious situation being handcuffed. I could have tried to break the cuffs with my supernatural strength, but I would have opened a brand-new bag of questions, so I remained quiet for now. Besides, I wanted to hear what they had to discuss, as the Wildlife chief addressed them.

"A swarm of ravens attacked several wildlife officers in the Black Forest earlier today while searching for the tourist reported missing. They reported that these particular ravens had red eyes instead of black. One raven flew directly inside the mouth of one officer, killing him instantly. The swarm killed two more officers, and left their bodies mangled and eaten, as if piranha attacked them. They took out the eyes of another Wildlife officer, and most likely blinding him for life; he was the lucky one. When we arrived on the scene minutes later, we observed the swarm heading north in the sky. In all my years on the job, I've never seen anything like this before. Now you tell me what the hell's going on around here, Agent?" the Chief of Wildlife Protection demanded.

"Ravens can't devour grown men like piranha, and leave nothing behind but skeletal corpses, what in the hell are we talking about here?

There has got to be a reasonable explanation for all of this, and we just have to keep our heads together and find out what it is." Whyte suggested.

"You tell that to the man that was there and saw it with his own eyes, when he had them, or perhaps you'd like to tell that to the families of the dead officers. In fact, you tell me what in hell did this in a manner of minutes until we responded, and about the swarm of ravens I personally observed leaving the scene!" The Wildlife Chief bellowed, and threw several photographs of the attacked officers on his desk.

Agent Whyte fumbled through the photographs, shrugged, and then looked at the FBI Agents who accompanied the Chief to the scene. They nodded their heads acknowledging the pictures. This infuriated me, because I'm just finding out about the deaths of the FBI Agents that followed me into the forest and now this. I told Whyte to quarantine the Forest when I first arrived here, but because it came from me, he had to dismiss it.

"Wasn't it you who got Wildlife involved with your bear stories? Why not blame the ravens now?" I blurted, condescendingly from the back of the room.

"If you don't have anything constructive to contribute to this, I suggest you shut your mouth, Mr. Sands, you're still under arrest and an official suspect in this case." Agent Whyte blustered, as the Chief of Wildlife raised one eye brow and looked at him like he was crazy.

"It feels good to take your incompetency out on others, doesn't it big man? I told you to quarantine the area at the first meeting I attended, but you weren't having it. Now tell me what the death count is since then?" I retorted, as he stormed in my direction while I was handcuffed.

Agent Jackson intercepted him by stepping in his path to restrain him from doing something stupid. Then chaos set in. The entire squad room was in an uproar with law enforcement personnel from different agencies bickering with each other. Then I observed one of the agents methodically rise from a desk he was occupying. He moved robotically, as if he was being controlled or possessed. I observed him looking in my direction, like he was looking at me, yet staring straight through me. His eyes were fixed in one direction, and didn't blink.

"Leave this place, Shaman, leave this place before you die!" He said, in a robotic manner, and then he drew his service weapon and aimed it at me.

"Gun!" I yelled out, to inform the rest of the station, as I dove behind the desk in front of me.

He shot one of his fellow agents standing behind me, and continued shooting, while everyone took cover. They drew their handguns and commanded him to lower his weapon, but the agent didn't adhere. I continued to observe him from behind the desk. He couldn't hear them, he was in some sort of trance or possessed. They shot him multiple times and killed him.

When the smoke had cleared, there were two FBI Agents killed, including the assailant, one Swanton Sheriff Deputy, one civilian being questioned like me, and one injured Franklin County Deputy. I remained on the floor, with my back against the desk, in disbelief at what just occurred. There was nothing I could do, but remain there with my hands cuffed. I haven't felt this helpless since I was a kid suffering from nightmares.

I was finally given the opportunity to make my one phone call. I did exactly as Whyte suspected and called Steve Weiss. Steve was the new Deputy Assistant Director in D.C. He sounded surprise to hear from me, like he didn't know I was on the case, but elated after hearing the tragic news the bureau received about the shooting. I gave him a quick sitrep (situation report) on what I knew, and my suggestions on moving further.

"I suggest you have the Forest quarantine from hence forth, Steve. I'm certain those missing tourists were probably part of the paparazzi. The town people around here are too afraid to even come out after dark, let alone step inside that Forest."

"Will do, is there anything else that you need?"

"Yeah, Whyte isn't the man for this type of situation. He's too closed minded and lacks imagination," I informed him.

"I know, I already have someone in mind. This case has fallen apart around him, and the task force has lost confidence in him. I think you'll like who I'm sending. Just call me if there is anything else you need. You always know how to reach me," Steve said, and hung up the phone.

I went to the bar in the hotel after being released from custody to see if I could order some food before going to bed. I was tired, hungry, and felt miserable about what happened at the Sheriff's Office and to the agents following me. I was expecting it to be empty as before, but it was packed with law enforcement. The FBI had sent in the reinforcements with other agencies accompanying. It looked like a law enforcement convention. At least they could handle the civil unrest about the town, because they have no idea what they're facing.

I made my way to the bar with glaring eyes watching me. It felt like I was walking the plank for desertion or mutiny. An even better analogy would be walking in front of a firing squad, as they uttered and blurted out rude obscenities, and hateful stares at me. Funny how quickly I went from being the Bureau's savior to their most *detestable*. I asked Jock if the kitchen was still open.

"Yeah, but the food is better at Kelly's if you ask me." He solemnly hinted.

I had been eating at the hotel bar since I arrive without such a suggestion. I knew Jock wasn't a racist, but he could clearly see the hate and tension directed towards at me. He was doing what a good bartender would to relieve a potential volatile situation. If it meant getting one person out of the line of fire, as opposed to the mob, the choice was simple, especially with a mob of trained armed men.

"Ok Jock, I'll do that," I said, in a low tone, and slipped a five-dollar tip on the table to show him I understood.

I thought about changing hotels, but staying there gave me an automatic alibi with whatever occurs. I had a platoon of law enforcement personnel that could testify to my whereabouts at certain times of the day and night. I departed the hotel's bar without incident and drove to Kelly's Bar & Grill. When I arrived at Kelly's, I looked inside the storefront window and observed a crowd of townspeople. It seemed like a good ole boy Irish Pub. This wasn't the establishment that I wanted to enter with the climate of the city as such. I'd rather beat up on agents, if need be, than to get into it with some emotionally distraught citizens.

I had passed a nude bar on my way to Kelly's. It said food, drinks and a good time on the outside. I was only interested in the food, preferably to go. Most strip club bars are liberal. They leave their baggage at the door, and concentrate on the women and having a good time, as the sign stated. I would have just gone to my room for the rest of the night, but I hadn't eaten all day due to Agent Whyte's interrogation.

CHAPTER TEN

PADOGIYIK

I could hear and feel the muffled sound of the thumping bass vibrating against the door, as I paused to ruminate my decision to enter. Then the growling of my stomach settled the indecisiveness without argument. When I opened the door, the thunderous music poured out into the street with the stale smell of tobacco smoke, as two large doormen impeded my progress for a quick pat down. I was relieved that no one in the audience paid any attention to me, as I walked to the bar for service.

The stage lights were flashing, and dizzyingly reflecting against an old disco ball that sent shards of light cutting through the pollutants of the murky smoke-filled room. I wasn't sure if it was the lights or the smoke, but my head was spinning faster than the dancers on the poles. I had been spending too much time in the dark, and my acute senses weren't prepared for the sudden infusion of simulants. I took a seat at the bar, closed my eyes for a second or two, and adjusted my sight to the new environment at Nightingales Exotic Dance Club.

They were playing 'Sweet Dreams' by the Eurhythmics, of all things, on the stereo. It was an old tune, but apropos for what the girls were doing. There were three stages with tables situated around them. The stage in the middle was the center stage. It was in front of the bar and bigger than the others. The other two stages were located east and west of the center stage. There were exquisite murals of nightingales painted on the walls and ceiling like Michelangelo visited. It seemed out of place, like it should be in a museum exhibit. I smiled thinking this could only be Tahki's masterpiece, but how they got the shy young woman to grace this place is a mystery to me. I quickly searched for a signature, but couldn't find it.

The dancers and waitresses were hauntingly beautiful and alluring. They were the only thing overshadowing the magnificent mural on the walls. The men in attendance were mesmerized by the half-naked beauties with their eyes locked in on their every movement. Nothing else seemed to matter, as their zombie-like stares blocked out the world.

The women had exquisite tattoos of different colored birds adorning their bodies, in various places, assorted sizes and colors; ranging from black, to midnight blue. There were even multicolored ones, yet they were all similar. I'm guessing they were supposed to be nightingales, but they reminded me of the pesky ravens that I've seen infesting the town. Nightingales are known for their gorgeous looks, and singing the most beautiful nocturnal songs in nature, and I must admit, the dancers and waitresses here were true to the symbolism.

There was also some ancient writing that I had never seen before inscribed near the tattoos of the birds. It wasn't hard to see why the men were mesmerized by theses harlots. They were from different nationalities, even Native Americans, Abenaki no doubt. I guess beauty, lust and sex have no prejudices or racial barriers, yet there wasn't a Native American male in the audience. It reminded me of the Cotton Club in Renaissance Harlem. Perhaps this type of servitude was considered acceptable, even during times of hate.

The unbelievable beauty of the dancers was beyond enticing, as I watched them through the mirrored wall behind the bar. I ordered a cheese burger with fries, and drunk a Corona while I waited for my carry out. I didn't bother turning around and looking at the ladies. I could see everything through the mirror and it didn't invite any unwarranted attention. I just wanted to get my food and leave without any hassles or temptations. Then I felt their presence, as they entered the door. Their energy was incredibly strong collectively, as my amulet lit up like a beacon in a lighthouse under my sleeves. It wasn't very noticeable, but it could be seen through my shirt and sport jacket.

The bartender looked at me, but dismissed it without inquiries. The customers paid no attention as they were enthralled in the ecstasy of the beautiful women. Then seven men stepped into the bar. All of them were supernaturals, and kind of favored each other, as if they were brothers. I could feel the high-energy levels emitted from them. You would think that the entire bar felt what I did the way they stopped and stared at the group.

They all had their reasons for watching them. The men in the crowd were looking because of the commanding physical presence the group displayed. They were all about 6 feet 4 inches, some above, and they were all muscular, like a football team. The women in the club looked for obvious reasons; they were handsome, physically fit, and hopefully bringing in seven wallets filled with money. The doorman stopped them at the door and spoke to them. It was all the time I needed to examine the group.

They were blonde with differing hair styles; long hanging hair like mine, some had it pinned in the back in a ponytail, and of all things dreadlocks. Some wore their hair short and even close cropped. Some had beards, ranging from close shaved to full beards and others were clean shaven. Two of the men had walking sticks. One was cylindrical and metallic in origin; it looked like an expensive platinum staff with some sort of runic writing and symbols etched on the side.

The other walking stick was larger, thicker and composed of solid oak. It could have easily been a club; it had a handle or grip that was shaped like some axes that I've seen. It also had runic words and designs carved into the woodwork, both sticks looked like they should have been in a museum somewhere. The surprising thing about all of it was that none of these men needed walking sticks or canes as fit as they were, and neither of the men carrying them walked with an impediment. In fact, the club shaped walking stick was carried by the largest man of the group.

The short haired man, leading the others, slipped the doorman some money, who looked at the bill and was clearly pleased by it, as he generously shook his hand and thanked him. They proceeded inside a few steps and the leader of the group stopped, as did the others. He was clearly the leader of the pack, you could tell by his countenance, and the look in his eyes, that he was the Alpha male.

They meticulously, yet quickly, examined their surroundings; absorbing the crowd, the atmosphere, the layout of the club, and the people within it. They were looking for me, the other supernatural within the club. It took them a minute, but they felt my presence, as I did theirs. I saw a small grin come over the leader's face, as our eyes met in the mirror. Then the others zeroed in on my energy.

It didn't take long before the male customers lost interest in the group, and once again became absorbed in the enchanted seduction of the beautiful dancers and the waitresses. The working women did no such thing and were quickly all over them. I felt a little slighted that I wasn't given that sort of treatment. Perhaps they were regulars, but I doubt it.

The waitresses immediately escorted them to the west stage where there were three empty tables placed together. Four dancing girls joined them soon. Lap dances came next and the waitresses followed with bottles of Grey Goose Vodka. None of the dancers approached me. I guess they could tell I didn't want to be bothered. I never turned around from the bar to acknowledge them or partake in the festivities. They only saw my back, but occasionally one or two would observe me in the mirror, as did the leader of the group. Just when I had finished my beer a waitress approached me.

"The gentlemen at the table would like to know if you would join them for a drink," she said smiling.

At that point, I turned from my mirror view and looked over at them. Their leader raised his glass with a smile further inviting me to join them. It appeared to be a friendly gesture and I was curious to know their intent, so I accepted the offer. They had taken their coats off and you could see the muscles bulging through their shirts, with every movement and flex of the arms. The leader of the men stood up when I arrived and offered me his chair while the others remained seated, drinking and enjoying the dancers.

"Hello Agent Sands please have a seat," he said with a Scandinavian Accent. I wasn't certain which country, Finnish, Norwegian, Swedish or Danish.

I was taken by surprise that he knew my name and I knew nothing about my strange supernatural host. The other men looked at me momentarily and continued with their merriment, as I sat down. The leader went over to the next set of tables where some townsmen were seated and took one of the empty chairs from their table without asking. He towered over them standing at 6feet 5 inches and a muscular build. The townsmen offered no resistance to the rudeness, and continued with their hypnotic gawking with the dancers.

"Thanks for joining us for a drink Agent Sands," he said.

"And who are you?" I asked.

"My name is Eirik, and these are my brothers, Gunnar, Brandr, Nidhogger, Asger, Egor, and Egil," he said proudly, pointing to each of the men, *"Perhaps you've heard of us, we're known as the Golden Seven or Padogiyik in the Abenaki language."*

"Yes, I've heard the legends of the Thunders, but I just thought it was that, a myth," I replied, as he laughed.

"Legends indeed," he laughed aloud, *"Did you hear that brothers,"* he blurted out and downed his drink.

Most of his brothers were too busy entertaining the women, and didn't really pay us any attention, except for Nidhogger, who wasn't entertaining with the ladies, and Gunnar, who was multitasking with the ladies while watching Eirik and me. Gunnar at least acknowledged me with a smile, and nodded his head, as I nodded in return. Gunnar was the largest of the brothers, and had the ornamented club-like walking stick by his side. The platinum walking stick was carried by Asger.

Nidhogger was quiet and basically kept to himself. He was observing me in the mirror, but didn't acknowledge me when introduced. He was dressed in all black and had a grim, eerie-like demeanor. You could tell the family resemblance within all the brothers, with their golden blonde hair and chisel features, but Nidhogger had a dark side about him, unlike the others.

Nidhogger's hair was long and stringy in a grunge like style, kind of oily. He had a tattoo of a small tear drop on his face, it was a hollow tear drop outlined in midnight blue ink. He wore a sleeveless shirt and had the tattoo of a hawk wrapped around his left arm, like some Asian gang's wear. It was an exquisite work of art, which looked extremely expensive. He seemed to have a fascination for birds just like the ecdysiasts of Nightingales. I could tell he wasn't the friendliest of the brothers and kind of anti-social.

The other brothers were festive and the best way to describe their differences was by their hair because they shared the same chiseled facial features that women adored. Eirik wore his hair cropped short and facial hair the same. Gunnar and Brandr wore their hair long, wavy and down to the shoulders, like Vikings and woodsmen. Gunnar had a full beard and Brandr had a goatee. Asger's hair was medium length, curly, and his face was clean shaven. He looked more like an Ivy League collegian or young Wall Street businessman. Egor's hair was pinned back in a ponytail, which appeared to be long and wavy as well, and clean shaven. Egil wore his hair in blonde dreadlocks, like the Rastafarians do, and had a closely cut beard, like a five o'clock shadow. He was the splitting image of Eirik. They truly were a diverse bunch for brothers.

Eirik poured us both a drink then raised his glass, as I did in return. We downed the double shot of vodka and he quickly poured another. I needed the distraction from thinking about all the previous events of the day, the missing agents, the murdered ones, and the suicide shooting. Getting drunk with strangers wasn't the answer, especially supernaturals, but it was a start. They were in here for a reason other than the festivities, and I'd say that reason was me, judging by their predisposed knowledge of me. I broke the ice before drinking the next shot.

"So, what business do you have in Swanton?" I didn't know if they were residents, but it seemed like a clever way to break the ice for further inquiries.

"We are here on a hunting expedition," Eirik replied.

"Oh really, and what game are you hunting?" I asked.

"We're here for the beast of the forest," he replied, directly and without beating around the bush.

"Do you know what kind of beast is doing this?" I asked.

"Not, yet, but it doesn't matter. They all go down the same way," he replied, smiling and pouring us another shot.

"You do realize that this is a federal investigation," I replied, as an agent, since he already knew my other identity.

"Oh, we won't get in the way. In fact, they won't even know that we were here, unless you tell them. Just let us do what we came here to do and all is well. Hell, we'll even let you in on it and take the credit for it," he said, and raised his glass again, inviting me to join him.

These men were dressed in expensive clothing and spending like they had money to burn. They were mercenaries for hire, but who hired them? Since we were being frank with each other I thought I'd pose the question. You never know until you ask, I always say.

"May I inquire who hired you?"

He was just about to drink from his glass when he paused and stared at me. He looked at me, as if he was trying to read my thoughts, and then he smiled and drank from the glass in his hand.

"That's confidential information Agent Sands. Our client wishes to remain anonymous. Are you going to have a problem with us?"

"Not at all, if that is all you came here to do," I replied.

What did I care about a bunch of mercenaries killing the beast and ridding this town of a killer? They seemed like they knew what they were doing the way he nonchalantly boasted about killing it. These were the first supernatural mercenaries that I've met. I guess you can find us in a multitude of trades like any other.

"Well, our client did want us to kill you as well," he said, dispassionately and filled my glass again without the slightest pause in emotions. Killing had become easy for him. It was a part of his life.

"And what was your response," I inquired, curiously?

"We're only here for the beast, Agent Sands. We only hunt supernaturals with malefic intent. Although I must warn you that we never break a contract and vow to see it through until the subject is terminated. Now please don't let me drink alone," he said and lifted his glass in a toast again.

As I drank another glass of vodka with him, two of his brothers, Egor and Egil, departed from the tables with two of the dancers. Eirik's expression was paired with disapproval and concern. He didn't set himself above his brothers, yet he was still separated from them like any good leader. Then a waitress brought my long-awaited carryout meal at that time.

"Well I appreciate the conversation and the warning. It's been a pleasure, but this is where I must bid adieu."

"I understand Agent Sands and thank you for having a drink with us." We both stood up and shook hands before I departed.

There was only one man in Swanton that could afford to hire mercenaries of Eirik's caliber and that was Winchester. I already knew he wanted me dead when he sent the last goons to follow me. I will pay him a visit in his dreams later, but for now he wasn't my immediate concern. Eirik and his brothers seemed to be very capable killers and hopefully they would slaughter the beast. The beast or whatever it is murdered several agents, but there are no signs pointing to the fact that it killed the missing children of Swanton. The beast killings seemed to be restricted to the forest. There is something else going on with the missing children.

When I departed the bar, I felt the supernatural signatures of the Padogiyik following me. It wasn't as strong as when it was in the bar, which meant it wasn't all of them. This night couldn't get any more interesting. I jumped into the car and pulled off casually, as they followed. I wasn't in a rush to lose them, but I was interested in why they were following me. I pulled off to the side of the road, when I saw the opportunity. I spotted an empty field off the highway with no homes or buildings within miles, Swanton was rural like that. I got out of the vehicle and walked into the wooded isolated area and stopped when I felt I was far enough within it. As I turned and faced my pursuers, I discovered that it was Gunnar and Brandr, standing about 30 yards from me.

"Can I help you, gentlemen?" I called out, as they walked towards me.

They just looked at each other and smiled. Then Brandr went inside the inner pocket of his long coat and pulled out a cylindrical metallic stick, which favored the walking cane of Asger, but much smaller. He gripped the object with two hands and pointed it towards the sky, as did Gunnar with his ornamented oak waking stick. Then I heard the roar of thunder in the sky, as if the heavens had parted and two steady lightning strikes came down from the sky and hit the walking stick and the metallic object. To my surprise the walking stick became a double headed axe made of pure electrical energy, and ornamented wooden handle was its shaft. The cylindrical object that Brandr held was the hilt of a Katana Sword and the electrical energy took on the shaped of its blade.

I must admit, I was impressed. My first thought was how cool these weapons are and how in the hell could I acquire one, until Brandr took me by surprise and fired a lightning bolt at me. I jumped out of the way, as the lightning bolt just barely missed me, and struck a tree. The bolt caused the tree to catch on fire. That bothered me more than him firing upon me.

Next Gunnar took his turn at firing at me. I ducked his bolt also as it hit the trees. I was using my full speed to elude the lightning strikes, and still I was just barely escaping them. I felt like a kid playing dodge ball in the playground, but this was a risky game. If they repeated their strikes or struck together I would definitely be hit, but I don't think that's their intention. They were testing me to examine my abilities.

"Ayv wiwadvhv nvgi ganolvvsgv, hnadvga gadousdi Ayv adanetsedi"

I summoned the only element that I felt comfortable in manipulating, the wind, and guided a strong gust towards them. It was strong enough to knock them backwards, and off their feet. They weren't expecting it because they didn't know what I was capable of doing. They recovered quickly and began firing synchronized bolts at me. Again. They were testing my skills, but it was a deadly test. As I avoided being struck, the fire in the forest grew. They were reckless and their nonchalant attitude towards the forest angered me. I had to end this little sparring session before they burned down the entire forest.

I retaliated with a stronger, more turbulent gust of wind. This time the brothers were prepared and didn't try to fight it, they allowed the wind to carry them, as they were swept off their feet. They went backwards with it like they were riding a wave, yet on their backs. It was similar to the way rockers dive into the crowd and surf on their backs. The brothers were just as athletic as I, and did a summersault in midair, and landed on their feet. It was impressive, but by the time they landed I had already shadowed myself, and quickly ran towards them under the cloak of darkness.

They were looking for me at the last position they had saw me, but I was standing behind them. Just before they became aware of my energy signature I delivered a right-hand jab to the temple of Gunnar, and a left cross to the jaw of Brandr with speed and strength, knocking them both unconscious. Their weapons fell from their hands, as they went down, and were no longer activated by lightning. I curiously picked up Gunnar's exquisite walking stick to examine it. It truly was a work of art.

I held it to the sky, as I had seen them do, and to my surprise the handle activated the double headed lightning axe. A surge of electrical energy flowed into the axe. It was now heavier and uncontrollable as the power kicked in. I grabbed the handle with two hands to control it and even then, it began to shake wildly, as I held on.

Then the energy from the sword wrapped around my hands like gloves, as if it had grabbed me, instead of the other way around. The energy crawled up my arms, as it made its way upward, enmeshing with the crystal, and causing it to glow. It wasn't an overload of energy, as it spread out through the rest of my body and creating a symbiotic relationship with my energy. It felt good, and gave me a tingling sensation throughout my body that made the hairs on my skin stand up.

Now the axe seemed lighter and my hands were no longer shaking. I could now hold it with one hand, as I had seen Gunnar do. The axe felt as if it was a part of me now, an extension of me like the rest of my appendages. I swung it, cutting through the air swiftly, and with ease. It felt like I wasn't holding it at all, how did they manage to fire the lightning charge from it?

"Well I'll be damn, look at that!" Gunnar said, waking up surprised to see that I had activated the axe, *"No one has ever been able to wield our weapons except for us and those who gave them to us."*

Then Brandr woke up amazed, as well, at the sight of me wielding Gunnar's axe. He immediately hopped to his feet and activated his sword in defense.

"It's ok, Brandr, the shaman doesn't mean us any harm. We attacked him remember," Gunnar said getting to his feet. He was clearly the older of the two.

"How is he able to do that?" Brandr asked loudly.

"Good question, who are you, shaman, and how are you yo able to activate the Thorenson Weapons?" asked Gunnar.

"This is all a mystery to me as it is to you. I didn't even know they had names, let alone know how I'm able to do this," I replied, perplexed.

"Our weapons were gifts from the Valkyries, and no one has ever been able to activate them except for us and Valkyries until now," Gunnar repeated.

"Perhaps he has the ancient blood line like we do," said Brandr, still astonished.

"Are you from Norsemen lineage, shaman," Gunnar asked.

"No, I mean, not that I'm aware of," I replied.

"Well which is it?" he hastily asked.

"No, I'm the descendant of Cherokee Freedmen of North Carolina," I said, bothered by the question.

"Norsemen have a long history with the Native Americans, since they cross the ice to get to here. Perhaps our bloodlines have common ancestry from then," he retorted with a smile.

"No, just Black, and Native American!" I snapped at him, and he returned with a puzzled look.

I know Gunnar didn't mean any harm when he asked about my heritage, but it was a sensitive subject with me. It always has been, and probably always will be. I've been profiled, ostracized, and discriminated against all my life, being biracial. The word race itself indicates some sort of competition where ethnicities compete to see who is dominant. I was fed up with the whole concept.

Gunnar held out his hand, after I snapped at him, in order to receive his axe, which I obliged. The tingling symbiotic sensation was broken immediately, as he looked me in the eye intensely trying to figure me out. I was a conundrum to him, as well as myself. They were looking at me like some sort of freak side show attraction, reminiscence of my days in Quantico with the ViCAP Unit. I turned away from their glares and focused my attention on the burnt trees.

"Sorry about that shaman. I guess we got a little carried away. We just wanted to see what you were made of," Gunnar said.

"So, the Valkyries are real?" I asked.

"Man, where have you been living, under a rock? They're as real as you or me," Brandr replied.

"You can say that. I didn't know any of this existed until over a year ago. So, are there warrior angels?" I inquired.

"Yes, they are that and so much more," Gunnar replied.

"And are there other angels?" I innocently asked.

"For sure, man," he quipped, and then Brandr chimed in

"You mean to tell me your name is Christian and you don't believe in angels? You've got to be kidding me. Your name means follower of Christ."

"I guess I just don't travel in those circles," I quipped.

We sat down and had a friendly conversation about angels, their heritage, and mine. These men truly were sportsmen in every way. They relished the challenge of a good fight and knew how to accept defeat. To them defeat was a temporary thing in which you learned from and become stronger from the battle. We talked for quite some time in the woods and became friends.

"Will you honor us with a contest?" Gunnar asked.

"What type of contest?" I replied.

"With the Thorenson Weapons, of course," he informed me, and Brandr threw me the hilt of his Katana sword.

I gripped it with two hands, as I've seen him do, and lifted it up to the sky. The thunder roared in the sky, and the lightning came down striking the swords hilt, and creating a blade of lightning. I went down to my knees with the initial bolt of lightning, but I surprisingly held on to it. I was used to managing the surges of energy from my crystal, and it assisted me in handling the lightning blade.

We sparred into the wee hours of the morning, switching off weapons. I'm uncertain where I learned of how I knew how to wield such weapons, but I picked it up quickly, like I had been doing it all my life. I was a natural at it, but I had the strangest feeling that the brothers already knew this little secret. Is this why Gunnar asked me to honor them with a contest? Perhaps I'm reading too much into it.

There were so many things I was learning about myself during my vision quest. The more I learned the less I seemed to know. Asku and others have said that I'm like no other shaman and it's started to look like they're correct. Asku said, he believed I could achieve the ability of the celestial energy manipulations like the angels. I dismissed that notion up until now, because I've never seen an angel, but how else could I explain these magnificent weapons of the Padogiyik, and my puzzling abilities. They claim to have personal contact with the Valkyries, their patron angels. It was a lot to think about, but at some other time. I still had a case to solve

When I returned to the hotel, the lobby bar was still filled with law enforcement personnel. I'm like Jock; I don't know where they get the time to socialize as such. I guess there are just too many of them up here now and they're running into each other. That only meant there would be more of them running into me. I can envision the chaos at their command center. It was something that I didn't miss. I guess what happened with Agent Robinson and the other two missing agents still had everyone a little on the edge. This was an inconvenient time to run into them while they were drunk and end up having an altercation.

I lowered my head and quickly made my way to the stairs. I saw the receptionist giving me the evil eye in my periphery.. By now the entire staff has heard about my arrest and implications in the disappearance of the FBI Agents. The hotel was filled with malcontent agents discussing it. Besides, Agent Whyte's intent was to embarrass and defame me in public. That's why he handcuffed me and made such a grand spectacle of the situation by sending a garrison of men to arrest me.

I couldn't wait to get out of my clothes and take a shower. I reeked of smoke from the forest fire. After showering I threw my cold burger and fries from Nightingales into the microwave and wolfed it down. Then I spent some time lying on the bed dreamscaping. I opened all channels for whatever and whoever wanted to communicate, but there was nothing, so I reached out to Steve in dreamscape.

I gave Steve a more detailed description of what I noticed at the sheriff's station, about the shooting. I informed him that I believed Agent Robinson was possessed when he pulled out his service revolver and attempted to kill me. I also told him that I felt several supernatural forces at play in Swanton since I arrived.

Steve informed me that Agent Whyte was being replaced by Agent Halifax. I knew Agent Halifax from Langley. We weren't friends or anything like that, but we were civil towards each other. He was a good agent and a fair man. Steve had personally picked him for the assignment. He was a part of the family, as Steve put it, and would cooperate with me in any way, and with whatever I needed while investigating the case.

I also discovered, while in Steve's psyche, that he had previously reached out to Nina and asked that she speak to me about investigating this case. They both had manipulated me into taking this case from the start. I didn't expect this from either of them. Steve was the closest thing I had to being a best friend. He was someone that I considered as a brother, but the real shock came at the discovery of Nina playing a part in this deception. I trusted them both with my life and would have easily given my life for theirs, but I loved her explicitly. I didn't think there was anything we couldn't tell each other at this point. I called her immediately after dreamscaping with Steve.

"I just didn't know how you'd feel about it. You know I've been talking to Gracie and Steve since the Coyote case," she said.

"So, that's what you meant by the bureaucratic timing?" I replied.

"Yes dear, Steve wants you back, but his hands are tied right now. Also, I knew you'd be less restricted on the case if you worked on it with Indian Affairs."

"I understand," I told her.

"You're not upset?" she asked.

"No, I'm fine," I replied.

Sometimes I wish I could invade Nina's dreams. We discovered that her gift was a defensive one that allows her to protect her dreams as well as others, sort of like a human dreamcatcher. She's a natural protector. I believe she has other talents, but she won't take the time to explore them. Her family is gifted like mine.

I was having a much needed and sound sleep until it was invaded by a gorgeous woman dressed in a white in color, sheer, see-through negligee and her face covered by an elaborate Victorian style mask, which was black in color and ornamented in diamonds and gold. I had never seen anything so exquisite, as she stood in the middle of hotel suite.

Her body resembled Nina's or at least that's what she wanted me to believe, as she approached the foot of the bed. She crawled on the bed towards me, and straddled me while I remained lying down. Then she moved forward lying on top of me with her warm -sheer naked body, and began kissing my neck. She was a seductress in every way, she even smelled like Nina. I held her face within my hands, as she willingly accepted. I slowly removed her mask, and to my surprise it was Nina or at least she had all the facial characteristics of Nina, except it was the supernatural energy signature of someone or something else.

I slowly and carefully placed my hands around her neck, as she continued kissing me and smiling. I raised her upward from me by the neck, as she smiled. She was under the impression that I was about to get kinky with her, but with lightning speed, I moved from the bed, and forcibly flung her to the wall of the hotel suite, in one quick supernatural motion. My hands were still wrapped around her neck, as I suspended her from the floor while pinning her up against the wall. Her smile faded quickly, as she squirmed under my powerful clutch.

"Who are you?" I asked, still holding her upwardly the neck.

I was angered by the deception, and invasion of this wicked thing. I was going to drain it dry! My hands were locked firmly around its neck. I was prepared to snap it, but this thing was powerful. I could feel its energy surging through me, as my arms began to shake, and my energy crystal radiated. Then with an explosive telekinetic force, it knocked me backwards; flinging me several feet, and crashing me into the opposite wall. Then it sent the dresser crashing into me. When I removed the dresser from off me, the doppelganger was no longer present.

I immediately reached for the cell phone on the nightstand. I knew it wasn't Nina, but I had to make sure she was alright. I didn't mention my previous encounter, but she was curious as to why I was calling since we had just spoken before going to bed. I didn't realize that it was three-something in the morning until Nina mentioned it to me. I told her that I had missed her and wanted to immediately let her know. She was tired and had to get up in a few hours, so she accepted the canard for now and went back to sleep. I'm certain that we will revisit this later.

The next morning, I decided to spend the day in the Black Forest. It was a risky move, but I owed it to the FBI Agents. I was the one that led them to their deaths, although unknowingly. I stopped past the tribal council to pick up some supplies before heading to the Black Forest. Sam Yellowbear was kind enough to lend me a wigwam and some other supplies for a day/ night out camping in the forest. He thought I was crazy after what happened to the BIA Agents and others found missing or murdered in the forest, but I assured him that I would be alright.

I pitched the wigwam near a tributary of the Missisiquoi River and spent an excellent day in the forest bonding with nature and meditating. I fished in the river for supper and ate berries and honey for desert. I was rustic in every way and it felt like I was back in the Smokey Mountains. Several animals approached me on their own terms and in their own time, but there was no supernatural intervention outside of the mysteriously looming supernatural energy field that persisted.

Then I heard someone approaching from a far, I was still in the lotus position meditating at the time. I was surprised when I discovered that it was Matunaagd Youngblood. He thought he was sneaking up behind me, just as he attempted to sneak up on Kateri and me at her cabin. I must admit he was good and would have succeeded if I didn't have supernatural abilities to warn me of his approach. I spoke to him before he got close without turning around or exiting the lotus position.

"Hello, Matunaagd, can I help you?"

He stopped in his tracks, surprised that I knew he was there. He paused for a few seconds, and then finally responded.

"I had to see it with my own eyes, when Sam told me you were camping out here," he said from behind me.

"And you're not afraid to be out here?" I asked, as he laughed hardily moving closing to me.

"Haven't you heard? They aren't killing Abenaki in these woods. This is the sacred burial grounds of my ancestors. I have nothing to fear here," he said, moving in front of me, as I opened my eyes.

His point was valid, there were no Abenaki killed or missing in the forest. This was one of the main reasons why the town's people were suspicious of the Abenaki. The more Youngblood talked, the more suspicious I became of him.

"Yes, that is correct, no Abenaki have been killed or missing since this has started," I repeated to him looking him straight in the eyes.

"You have balls, Agent Sands, I will say that about you," he said, turning and looking at the Wigwam and the fish slowly cooking over the fire.

"I would offer you a meal, but I only caught enough for me to eat," I said

"No, it's the right way, in harmony with the Earth, never waste what Mother Earth provides as a gift," he replied.

"So, do you come here often?" I asked. I was still curious about his motives for seeking me out.

"As much as I can," he replied with the slyest grin.

He knew where this conversation was heading, and seemed to enjoy the fact that only outsiders where being killed in the forest, but I continued anyway.

"So where were you during these killings and abductions?" I inquired.

"It depends on the particular day," he replied, "Why, am I a suspect now?"

"Everyone is a suspect until proven innocent," I told him.

"And here I thought you said you were a friend of the Abenaki," he said, as his sly grin curled up into a smirk. Then I addressed him in Algonquin.

"I am a friend of the Abenaki, but if the Sokoki are guilty of the crimes committed here, I will arrest them by the letter of the law."

"That's what I thought government man," he replied in Algonquin, and turned to walk away.

"I will provide you with the dates of the killings and abductions. I'll need you to account for your whereabouts," I said in English, as he walked away.

"I wouldn't expect anything less. You know where to find me," he replied, sarcastically without turning around.

Matunaagd Youngblood just reserved a seat on the top of my suspects list. It was clear that he moved freely back and forth through the forest without reproach. He also hated the town's people, vehemently. He was right about one thing, I did know where to find him, and therefore it wouldn't be hard to track him. I finished eating my fish dinner, packed up and departed shortly after my encounter with Youngblood.

During the drive back to town, I thought about Youngblood and how he disturbingly seemed to appear at inappropriate times and conveniently disappear at critical ones. Yes, I was keeping tabs on him. He disappeared right before the attack at the tribal council and reappeared at Kateri's cabin. He disappeared right before I was attacked at the Abenaki village before storming away angrily. He was mysteriously at the FBI building during the possession of Agent Robinson and now he conveniently shows up in the Black Forest when all citizens and tourist have been warned to stay out. He even bragged about visiting the forest frequently. I'd say I have a good suspect in hand.

I also thought about the dead FBI Agents and how guilty I felt. I was hoping to catch more than just fish while in the forest. I would have thought it strange to be in an ancient burial ground and not have any interactions with the departed, but this supernatural energy field was blocking all communications with the other side.

CHAPTER ELEVEN
MSKAGWEDEMOOS

I had picked up a tail once I made it back to town. Whoever it was, they were good, I didn't notice how long they were following me. Then again, I had a lot on my mind. I was totally absorbed in the case. I wouldn't have noticed them at all, if it wasn't for the yellow light that I ran, and forcing them to run the red light. It landed them in the middle of the intersection with oncoming vehicles blowing their horns at them. It was a government issued vehicle. Steve assured me that I would be left alone on the case. I guess someone didn't get the memo. Oh well, I was heading home anyway. One less agent to baby sit, one less dead agent caught in the crossfire.

As I got out of the vehicle, the other car parked and waited for me to enter the hotel. I was tired and really didn't care who was in the vehicle following me. I just wanted some uninterrupted sleep for a change.

When I entered the hotel's lobby, the unsociable desk clerk that was on duty when I checked in notified me that I had a message. Her attitude towards me hadn't changed, but I guess whoever gave her the message must have tipped her well. I positioned myself in front of the mirror near the front desk to observe if my escorts would enter the lobby, as I read the message. It was a message was from Eirik, requesting that I meet him at Nightingales before closing. It was already 1:30a.m. and it closed at 2:00a.m., so much for resting. Then with the worst of timing, I observed

Agent Jackson enter the lobby through the mirror. She was my tail for the night. She watched me looking at her and tried to play it off. I really didn't have time to play around with her, so I went directly towards her.

"Good morning, Agent Jackson. I'm glad you're alright. That vehicle almost hit you in the intersection." She just rolled her eyes at me and didn't respond.

"Look, I don't know if they told you, but I've been given the green light by your superiors in D.C. You don't have to follow me any longer." I assured her.

"But you're my only lead, I figure if anyone is going to find out what's going on here, I might as well follow the person with a reputation for strangeness." She replied with a scowl.

"Well, I'll try and take that as a complement. What is it they say, you're either very brave or very stupid, and you don't strike me as being the later, Agent Jackson. But you know the last two agents didn't fair very well following me." She looked at me with dagger eyes, and she was right to do so. That was totally out of line.

"No one told me to follow you, Agent Sands. I'm doing this on my own." She replied, despondently.

I didn't have time to apologize or continue this discussion with Agent Jackson. I would have loved to have just blended into the shadows and lose her, but the lobby was fully lit and her eyes were fixed on me. Besides, she was better off not following me, and if rudeness is what it takes, then so be it.

"Well, I'm going to the strip club right now. I'm not certain if you're into that sort of thing, but you're welcomed to ride with me. I would hate to see you get into an accident trying to keep up."

"Was that the message received at the desk?" she asked, looking at the note in my hands.

"I'm going to have a beer and enjoy some entertainment," I replied, balling up the note, and ignoring her last comment.

Agent Jackson was very attentive. I wasn't certain if she would take me up on my offer or if she believed that I was going to the strip club this early in the morning. She wasn't easily dissuaded. Either way, it's better to babysit her by my side then having her getting injured following me or worst. I'll have to figure out the rest as I go.

Agent Jackson was smarter than the others. She knew exactly where the action would be surrounding this case. The only problem is following her source or lead could get her killed. She never spoke out against me when Agent Whyte was bashing me. She didn't agree or disagree, although she did intervene before he rushed me at the sheriff's office. I'm certain she'll climb up the hierarchy of the Bureau in no time. She understood how to play the game. She had the intelligence, the looks and knew how to use them both to get ahead in a competitive male driven agency.

When I arrived at Dame's, Eirik was waiting patiently outside smoking a cigar. I didn't see his brothers or any other patrons, just him. The place appeared to be deserted. The lights were still on and there were cars parked in the small parking lot, but there was no pedestrian traffic coming and going, as I observed before. It was late and about to close or they were closed already. My brief encounter with Agent Jackson didn't save me any time for sure, and now she was with me. What the hell was I thinking about bringing her along? I must be tired or completely lost my mind. I really thought she was going to back down when I stated that I was going to a strip club.

"There, satisfied Agent Jackson, it's a strip club. Wait here in the car until I come back," I told her, but I might as well have been talking to a brick wall.

"Yea right; is that the person you've come here to meet? I'm coming along," she responded with a hint of skepticism, as she got out of the car. She didn't trust a word I was saying. Agent Jackson was the pessimistic *'Missouri'* type who had to be shown the facts.

"Well, I hope you enjoy the show," I said slyly, and glancing at her through the corner of my eye.

"Man, it took you long enough," Eirik said with a disapproving scowl.

"You're lucky I'm here at all, tired as I am. Now what's this about?" I asked.

"What's she doing here," he blustered, looking at Agent Jackson.

"This is Agent Jackson, she's...," but before I could complete the statement he interrupted me.

"I know who she is. I can smell a cop a mile away, but why is she here?" he further questioned, now staring at her with disgust.

It was clear that Eirik didn't like law enforcement very much. I still don't know why they took a liking to me, especially since Winchester sent them to kill me.

"Look, she only wants to solve this thing like the rest of us," I replied.

"This is a bad idea, shaman," he said, shaking his head in contempt.

"What did he call you?" she asked alarmingly, but I ignored her.

"She's alright," I replied.

"Are you kidding me? She's a sindigent," he said, as his face squinched up even further.

A sindigent is a derogatory term used by supernaturals to describe anyone who doesn't possess supernatural abilities. I've heard the term used before during my travels in the spiritual realm with my spirit guide, but never in the phenomenon realm. It isn't a term used to describe all humans because there are some people who aren't born with supernatural abilities, but gain them through other means. Although Eirik was correct in his assumption, this could be a grave mistake bringing her along, but I needed to babysit her until I found out what this was about.

"She's with me, I would have preferred to exclude her, but she's here now, so can we move on," I demanded, in a flustered tone

"Seriously," he replied with raised eyebrows, in a sarcastic display of pessimism.

"It's complicated," I uttered, twisting my lips, *"Now do you want to tell me what's so urgent that I had to come down here?"*

"The last time we were here together two of my brothers went missing that night. They went off with two of the dancers from here, and we haven't seen them since."

"Yes, I remember all of you getting cozy with them, but what does this have to do with me?"

"My brothers and I ran across the Mskagwedemoos (M-ska-gwe-demoos) while looking for the other two. They didn't tell us much before dying, but they had tattoos like the dancing girls from inside."

"Wait, did you say, Muskweed-demon?" Agent Jackson, blurted out sarcastically with a smile, as Eirik snobbishly frowned at her, but I wanted to know, also.

"I've never heard of the Mskagwedemoos either," I quickly interrupted.

"The Abenaki also refers to them as the P-skig-demo-os," Eirik sighed, as if we should know now, but he could tell by our expressions that we were clueless.

"I swear on the Valkyries, man, what am I working with here? You people have never heard of Mskagwedemoos!" He huffed.

Agent Jackson suspiciously lifted one eyebrow, as if listening to the rantings of someone insane. I knew that whatever he was talking about was factual; I just didn't know the vernacular.

"The Mskagwedemoos are an ancient cult of sirens. Some people refer to them as witches, as well," Eirik interjected.

"Impossible, we would have been able to pick up on their energy signatures the first time we visited Nightingales," I replied, as Agent Jackson turned to me with a dumbfounded reaction, but I continued to ignore her.

"Yes, that was the first thing I thought, but it's true. They've found a way to mask their energy signature," he informed me.

I was puzzled and intrigued, but I still wasn't following him. They had already questioned them, and killed them. How exactly do I fit in?

"Once again, how does this involve me?" I asked, as Agent Jackson gave me this incredulous stare, but continued to remain silent. She couldn't believe the discourse she was hearing.

"I think the Mskagwedemoos are the key to all that's happening around here. They possess the souls of men. Didn't you have an incident with possession at the police headquarters?" Eirik inquired.

"How do you know about that?" I retorted, curiously and with interest now, as I listened attentively.

"I have my means," he replied, grinning.

"Wait, so you're saying that Agent Robinson was possessed by sirens? You have got to be shittin' me," Agent Jackson blurted out in disbelief.

"Please send her away," Eirik quipped, in a frustrated tone, as if he was being pestered by some nagging kid. I couldn't help but laugh at this point at the antics between the two of them. It was like watching siblings fight.

"I'm just getting started blondie, who exactly did you confess to killing? She asked, adamantly.

"Can I continue," he said, annoyed at us both now, and ignoring her questioning.

"Mskagwedemoos control and possess men through suggestive whispers in the ear, through song and some say through dance. They are like black widow spiders; they kill their sexual partners after conjugating. They also can kill men, as well as kill or enable some supernaturals with their deafening screams." Eirik further briefed us.

Eirik and his brothers were on a revenge rave, and the suggestion was to sever the Mskagwedemoos' heads quickly! My question to him was how would we get any answers or leads in finding his brothers if we killed them all. He told me not to worry about it because he had a plan for that when the time comes. My main mission now was to stay alive and protect Agent Jackson, which really meant I had to fight for two. Eirik looked at me, as if he knew what I was think

"It's all about keeping your head. You'll be alright, just watch how we do it, and take it from there. I just wished you would've come alone. This is no place for a sindigent," he said with a smaller frown this time, which appeared only on the right side of his face.

Eirik's expression was more about concern than anything, as he was warming over to accepting the fact that Agent Jackson would be a part of this, even though he objected. Agent Jackson was still in disbelief and dismissing what she was hearing. She looked at Eirik, as if he was a crack pot or someone on drugs.

"You're not buying any of this bullshit, are you?" Agent Jackson asked me, as Eirik looked at me with a frustrated and impatient look.

"Can you trust her to at least keep her mouth shut?" Eirik asked in a perturbed voice.

"Who in the hell do you think you are?" she asked angrily, and then Eirik lost his temper. He glared back at her furiously, and turning his once blue eyes into all white, and glowing.

"What the fuck!" Agent Jackson alarmingly drew her weapon.

"Go ahead shoot!" Eirik quickly retorted with a sinister grin.

"Agent Jackson, I assure you it's alright," I said in a calming and reassuring voice.

She backed slowly away from us, still pointing her gun with shaky hands, and then with lightning fast, supernatural speed, I disarmed her. She was surprised and confused by my unnatural speed, and appeared like she was about to pass out. I held her in my arms and looked her in the eyes to calm her down. She was terrified and shaking. I needed to distract her attention away from Eirik, who wasn't helping in the matter. He continued smiling at her with what could only be described as the eyes of a demon or at least in her mind.

"Listen, I made a terrible mistake in bringing you here. I wish there was an easier way of telling you this," I said, turning from her and giving Eirik a disapproving glare.

"What you're about to witness is beyond your beliefs. You can walk away now or learn about the world beyond this veil of existence; the world within the shadows. Monsters do exist, Agent Jackson, but we're not the ones you should fear," I said, and gave her back her gun, as Eirik calmed down, and his eyes became blue again.

"So, what are you?" she uttered, trembling.

"That's not what's important right now. Are you any good with that weapon?"

"I will be if I know what I'm dealing with," she replied.

"Hopefully you won't have to use it, but if you do aim for the head, that will at least slow them down," I advised her, as her eyes grew larger in disbelief.

"I don't know what type of badge you're carrying, but we just don't go around killing people!" Agent Jackson bellowed.

"I'm telling you this is a bad idea bringing her," Eirik reiterated, shaking his head at her again in disapproval.

"Who can she tell? She'll either end up dead or in the loony bin like me," I replied, as Jackson looked at me in surprise by the statement, "I'm just saying, you signed up for this," I further added looking at her.

"So which hospital were you at, and do you think they'll have room for me when they check you back in?" Agent Jackson sharply asked.

"When we go in there just follow our lead and play it cool. Can you do that?" Eirik asked Agent Jackson who sharply rolled her eyes at him and smirked. She didn't care much for him as well.

"Now that we're one big happy family let's go inside, my brothers are waiting for us," Eirik said smiling.

Eirik and his brothers were mercenaries foremost, and killing didn't bother them in the least. In his head, everyone in the club was already dead. His only concern was keeping one alive to question her on the whereabouts of his brothers. We are from a different cloth. Each killing and victim meant something to me and just added to the nightmares. I remembered each one of them. I guess it's different when you can speak to the dead and they aren't a passing memory.

Once we got situated inside Eirik joked with Jackson about being resistant to the charms and whispers of the Mskagwedemoos allure. Women are immune to the effects of Mskagwedemoos, but I think he was referring to Jackson as being a Lesbian. He acted as if he knew for certain. He and his brothers reveled in the pleasures of the opposite sex more so than the prophecy of my polygamy. Jackson ignored him, and didn't deny his taunting or allegations. She absolutely didn't like him. I really don't think he cared one way or another about her. He probably thought she was going to die in a few minutes anyway.

When we entered the club, there were several large-sized men who posed as body guards, bouncers, protectors or whatever else you wanted to call them, inside the club preparing people to leave. Eirik made his way to the back of the club at this point and asked Agent Jackson and I to lock down the front door, while he let his brothers in through the rear door.

Agent Jackson was under the impression that flashing her badge afforded her with a level of respect and compliance, but that wasn't the case. Seeing the badge only freaked them out and placed them in a defensive demeanor, like criminals get when they're hiding something. One of the bouncers immediately went into action upon seeing the badge and swung at her. I intercepted his punch in mid-air, just before it reached her face. It was just natural reflexes to defend her, and it didn't occur to me until afterwards that I was using my supernatural speed. I held on to his fist while squeezing it in my hand and crushing his bones, as he went down to the floor.

Agent Jackson was astonished by my speed and strength, but it didn't prevent her from reacting under pressure, as she quickly pulled out her weapon and had it pointing at the other bouncer. She ordered him to lock the door and take a position away from me and his partner, who was on his knees wincing in pain. I let go of his fist, and then I knocked him unconscious with a blow to the temple. Agent Jackson attempted to handcuff the other, but then the other bouncers rushed us.

Jackson quickly hit the bouncer closest to her across the face with her weapon, and then landed a crossover punch to the side of his face with her left hand which was wrapped in her handcuffs like brass knuckles. I've never seen anyone use them like that before, but it was effective, as it knocked him out also. The other four men hurrying over to assist were quickly knocked unconscious, as I moved through them with supernatural speed.

Jackson was shocked even more so know after witnessing that, but it wore off quickly with what she observed in the back of the club. Eirik and his brothers had declared all-out war! They were brandishing the Thorenson Weapons that the Valkyries had gifted to them. Each brother had a different lightning wielding weapon, like I experienced while sparring Gunnar and Brandr.

They wielded the power of lightning like the Norsemen Thunder God. They were equipped with swords, a double headed spear, and axes. Eirik had an ornamented double edged Great sword, Gunnar had a large double headed Viking Axe, Brandr had the Katana, Asger had a double headed spear and Nidhogger had two arm length axes that were between the size of a tomahawk and full-length axe. I don't see how anything stood a chance against them as a team, and this is probably why Winchester hired them. I'm not sure if he knew exactly what they were capable of, but if he's as rich as I was told he could afford to purchase information about these incredible mercenaries.

They each had some sort of signature move that was congruent with the type of weapon that they used. Gunnar swung his double headed axe like a baseball slugger who was ambidextrous, severing heads to the left and to the right of him with power and precision. Brandr used the samurai style of Jigen-Ryu during his attack. He used upward and downward movements with the sword creating the perfect eight as he sliced his way through the Mskagwedemoos. Asger moved like a ninja whirling his double headed spear, like a Wushu Master, around his back and above his head, spinning and bending, as the spear never stopped moving or taking their heads with both sides.

The most prolific of the brothers was Nidhogger. He used his two axes to sever the heads of Mskagwedemoos while spinning in a circular motion using both hands like the blades of a helicopter or blender. Eirik combined the styles of all the brothers. He was a master swordsman with the Great Sword. He swung the sword creating the figure eight while carving through the Mskagwedemoos using both edges of the blade. He spun and twisted, swinging the blade behind his back and changing hands in the process. Each movement was precise and each movement was deadly efficient, as he killed Mskagwedemoos within his circumference. All the brothers hit their mark with accuracy, as headless bodies hit the floor. It was extraordinary to say the least.

These Mskagwedemoos were the daughters of nymphs, witches of the ancient ranks that used men as toys of pleasure and to do their bidding. They were warriors and wouldn't go down without a fight. They were armed with katana swords, and fought back with skill and a level of mastery of their own, but we had caught them by surprise this night and they were clearly outmatched.

I was astonished, as Jackson, watching the brothers work as a team. Jackson was mostly shocked rather than admiring what she was witnessing. She had never seen supernaturals battle. The speed alone had her in a daze, as she tried to keep up. Each of them working in unison and protecting the other's back. It was like watching an orchestra in concert, individuals moving in synch. Each one of them aware of the position of the other, like they had some innate sense of where the others would be, and what they'd be doing.

They were like any well-coordinated team at the top of their game, like the Lakers with Magic or the Bulls with Jordan, except these were mercenaries and their confetti was blood, guts and severed heads. Jackson vomited looking at the beheading or perhaps it was the smell left behind by these witches lying on the floor.

A few of the Mskagwedemoos attempted to escape to avoid facing the slaughter the brothers were dishing out, so they ran towards Jackson and I guarding the door. As one approached Jackson, she shouted a warning to her.

"Halt, put down your weapon!"

She was still abiding by law enforcement procedures after all she had witnessed. She shot at her several times. I don't know how, but she managed to hit her, even with her supernatural speed, but the bullets didn't stop her. They continued to charge with their swords drawn, as I intervened.

I had to do it the old fashion way. I didn't have a sword, but I was faster, and stronger than the Mskagwedemoos. I rushed the advancing siren and twisted her neck with my strength and speed as I went by her. I thought this would be enough, but the siren got up from the floor with a broken neck and her head twisted the wrong way. It was by far the freakiest thing I'd ever seen, and once again, Jackson bent over and began heaving, but there was nothing left to vomit up. Her body was still going through the motions; it's what we refer to as dry earling, which is more painful.

"You have to take its head," Eirik yelled over to me.

Even while fighting he kept his eyes on us, as well as his brothers. It was obvious that they had been doing this for quite a long time, as I was learning, and witnessing a lot this night. I ran over to the siren and ripped off its head, as blood rushed out her jugular like a hydrant before her body hit the floor. I immediately dropped the head. I didn't have time to react to what I had just done, because another siren had zeroed in on Jackson who was completely out of the fight now. She was a target, sick and defenseless, and they knew it.

I hurried over to her, and caught the siren, as she swung downward upon Jackson, and I jammed the blade into her own belly before ripping off her head! She would've killed her if she didn't pause to savor the kill before doing it. They enjoyed killing, just as much as Eirik and his brothers. It was just a means to an end for me. I derived no pleasure from it.

"Use the sword, shaman! Trust me; you're a natural at this. It's in the blood!" Eirik yelled out, laughing while engaged in battle.

I'm uncertain what he meant by that, but I'd rather not get into the habit of severing heads with swords. This seemed to be the thing with supernaturals. It's all about keeping your head, as Eirik put it. They reveled in it like kids in front of a television with their favorite video fighting game. They were making sport of this carnage, like a Sunday walk in the park. I've only used a weapon in the spiritual realm, and that was only due to convenience.

"But they're not human!" He bellowed, as if reading my mind.

I heard what he was saying, but didn't take the sword from the headless corpse. It was hers and I didn't want any trophies or spoils of this battle. I wasn't a Norseman nor did I ascribe to the Viking ways or codes of battle. In fact, I was sorry that I came and wondered why I was invited. Why Eirik wanted me to witness this is a mystery to me. It's clear that they had this well under control, and didn't need my help. His reasoning was a bit shaky, to say the least. Then more Mskagwedemoos poured out from the basement.

I detached the heads of more Mskagwedemoos attempting to attack Jackson and me. I was no longer concerned about them fleeing; only protecting Agent Jackson. I would have thought ripping off someone's head would be an arduous task, by it was easy for me. It took a little muster, like popping the cork of a tightly sealed bottle of champagne, and watching its contents flow out. The demons were softer than regular humans, and thus easier to behead. My only problem was trying not to vomit in the process, which I did several times.

I was covered from head to toe in blood and puke. The blood trickled down my face like the sweat from running a marathon. When it was over the brothers weren't the worse for wear. They had the splatter of blood on them, here and there, but they weren't drenched in it like me. Once again, you could tell the rookie in the room.

"You should have listened to Eirik, Shaman, and allocated one of their swords," Gunnar said, examining the club to ensure that it was safe.

"You're all under arrest!" Agent Jackson yelled out, as she rose from her chair, trembling.

"I'm glad to see that you're still alive, Agent Jackson. I just knew that you wouldn't survive the night, but then again, you had someone protecting you, didn't ya," Eirik laughed.

"I need all of you to come down to the sheriff's station with me," she said, pointing her gun unsteadily with both hands, delusional, and still in shock.

"Or else what? Isn't that what you're trained to say next? You're gonna shoot us, Agent Jackson? Well go ahead, you've seen how well your bullets worked here," Eirik said while steadily walking towards her, and stopping within inches of the gun barrel.

These supernaturals were mercenaries and didn't think twice about killing, but I knew they wouldn't kill her, as I watched it play out this time. They were mercenaries, but they lived by a code and were honorable. It's a funny thing to say about killers, I know, but they had fought side by side with her now, in the trenches. No matter how she survived, she survived and that gave her a level of respect, and acceptance. After a minute, Jackson lowered her weapon, as Eirik smiled and walked away.

They claimed their agenda was similar to mine, and they were after the thing that was killing the people of Swanton, but all I saw was the useless killings of several bouncers and Mskagwedemoos, who may or may not have information on the missing men or the killings. We'll never know because they didn't leave any alive to question, and even if they did, how would we question them?

"So, this is the big plan you spoke of? Kill everyone in sight, then what?" I asked Eirik furiously.

"Yes, it is, Brandr and Asger are tailing one of the Mskagwedemoos, as we speak. We let her get away through the back to find out where they're keeping Egor and Egil, and then perhaps we can get the answers we're both seeking," he replied.

"And what about all this carnage you left here, who's going to explain all these headless corpses?" Agent Jackson inquired about the possessed humans that weren't demons or sirens.

"Tell them, I received a lead from an anonymous caller, and I asked you to accompany me here. We weren't certain of the credibility of the caller, so we decided to check it out on our own. When we arrived, this is what we found," I informed her.

"And what about my weapon that was fired several times and the fact that you are leaving the crime scene?" she asked.

"Ok, tell them that several of the perps were still here when we arrived and got into a shootout with you before they escaped through the back door. I left in pursuit and will collaborate the story," I replied.

"Sounds a little shaky, if you ask me," she muttered with a frown.

Agent Jackson was really testing my law enforcement procedures, as she continued questioning the story, as if I was on trial, but she was correct, it was a little weak. Someone would be asking her the same questions. This was our code and our way of conducting business, unlike the ways of mercenaries who could just abandon the scene of a crime, especially one of this magnitude.

"No other guns were fired, just heads cut off with swords," she said rolling her eyes at Eirik.

"I can remedy that," Gunnar said, and pulled out a pistol, *"It was on one of the bouncers before he died."* Jackson gave him a stern look, as the big man handed her the weapon.

"What? He tried to kill me with it," he quipped.

"I thought bullets couldn't harm you," she replied. Gunnar just shrugged his shoulders, and walked away without responding.

"Savages," she uttered angrily.

"Look, we can just burn the entire place down, and there will be nothing left, no prints, no evidence just charred corpses," Eirik said while charging his weapon.

"No, you've done enough destruction for one night," Agent Jackson stringently replied.

"Ok then, I'm sure you can figure out the rest, Agent Jackson, or do we have to fire that weapon for you, as well?" Eirik asked, sarcastically.

Agent Jackson became enraged and began firing the weapon with little regard about hitting the brothers. She was an excellent shot and came within inches of hitting them as she fired around the club. Each of them looked at her curiously and clueless to the reasons why she was so angry, but never felt endangered or threatened in the least by her tantrum. She would have done great if this was an actual gunfight. Then she turned and looked at me disappointingly.

"Are there any laws that you follow, because right now I'm looking at a bunch of vigilantes!"

She was rightfully just in her convictions. I hadn't been associated with the actual killing of citizens, even possessed ones without at least attempting to drive out the demon, and using guns were so far behind me, I can't recall the last time I've touched one. I never carried when I was with the FBI ViCAP Unit, and now they wanted me to brandish a sword, the weapon of a woman that I killed.

I paused to observe the carnage surrounding me. There was blood everywhere; splashed and smeared across the walls, and crimson pools streaming from headless corpses on the floor. I walked amongst the corpses and stopped in front of one of them with her head lying next to her. She was a Native American, an Abenaki woman who left the village, no doubt. Then Eirik approached me.

"You feel something for these creatures?" He inquired.

"Of course, he's a shaman, remember, these creatures are disciples of the earth and follow the same principles as shamans, like the *pentagram. They just use their natural magic for darkness,"* Nidhogger blurted out while eavesdropping.

"No, he's more than that. He can wield our weapons," Gunnar interjected, as Nidhogger quickly turned and stared at me in disbelief, but Eirik didn't seem surprised by the news.

"Yes, Brandr and I discovered that when we first met him. We wanted to give him a proper Thorenson introduction."

"I don't know how to respond to my ability of using your weapons, it's just as much a mystery to me, as it is to you. I can tell you that shamans do believe in the principles of mother earth and its elements are represented by the pentagram, Earth, Air, Water, Fire and Spirit. Like any other philosophy, the interpretation varies from group to group, cult to cult, religious sect to sect, and their values can be twisted, and debased like anything else. The Holy Wars were based upon bringing Christianity to the heathen savages of Africa, yet these people weren't savages and they believed in Islam, which believed in the same God of Abraham, as Christians. In short, yes, I do feel remorse for killing them. These were ordinary humans before they became corrupt and turned to the black arts."

"He's of the Fourth," Eirik interjected.

The brothers remained quiet after that, as if he just shared some startling, world shattering news to them, which made no sense to me whatsoever, as Agent Jackson just listened to it all in disbelief.

"And what exactly is the Fourth?" I inquired.

"All prophecies will be revealed in time. Just pay attention to the signs," Eirik stated, sounding a bit like Asku now.

I wasn't in the mood to play 30 questions with him after that massacre, so I accepted his riddle and knelt beside the headless corpse, and examined her tattoo. Besides the elaborate Ravens that adorned all of them there was some sort of writing among the designs that I had never seen before.

"What does it mean?" Eirik asked, watching me scrutinize the inscription.

"I don't know, but I believe it has something to do with their masking abilities, like a rune or something." I replied.

"But I thought you, shamans, had the gift of speaking in tongues," he retorted.

"Yes, we do speak in tongues, but that doesn't mean we can read the languages that we speak," I informed him.

He frowned at my answer and shook his head in disappointment. I still don't know why he wanted me present for this. I got up from the floor and took a panoramic view of the club and the handiwork left behind by the brothers, it was a graveyard.

"You must think of us as money hungry mercenaries, Shaman, but this is what we do. Somebody has to fund our quest to exterminate scum like this," he said, as one side of his mouth curled and accentuated the scowl on his face from the distain he felt for the Mskagwedemoos.

It was as if he knew what I was thinking again, but why was he justifying any of this to me? He was right about one thing; I had no right to judge them. They handled their business differently, but we both hunted evil and dealt with issues outside of the normal scope of the law. I could tell that he really cared about his brothers, and generally had a sense of care for the welfare of Jackson and me, as he demonstrated during the battle. I guess it was their cavalier attitude and nonchalant way about killing that just didn't set right with me. It wasn't my way, it wasn't in accordance with my beliefs, shamanism. Killing was a last result for us.

I had gotten more than I bargained for partnering with the Padogiyik, minus two. The body count was extremely high, and I have a feeling it would get even higher until they found their missing brothers, and the beast. I was in too deep now to turn around, I'll continue to follow them, and perhaps I can prevent some collateral damage. Besides, this was the first lead into supernatural causes for the murders, which is congruent with my ideas on the case. The Mskagwedemoos have the ability to possess

Agent Robinson and their M.O appears to be the abduction of men; case in point, the abducting of Eirik's brothers. This would account for at least part of this investigation which was spiraling out of control with the elevated body count and missing Padogiyik.

We left Agent Jackson to clean up the mess at the club and answer any questions. I would back her up, and soon come under the bright lights of an interrogation as well, but I always had Steve and Nina to fall back on for assistance.

CHAPTER TWELVE

BLACK ROSES

Brandr and Asger were on the trail of the fleeing siren, who was too excited and afraid to pick up on their energy signatures in pursuit. The brothers couldn't rely on tracking the siren's energy signature because it was cloaked some kind of way, but they didn't need it. The brothers have been hunting supernaturals for years and had other ways of pursuing her. We were a few minutes behind Brandr and Asger in pursuit of the siren and pulling up the rear.

We met them in a remote location in the Northwest section of the Black Forest. The Mskagwedemoos were nestled in a huge three-story cabin, miles away from the vacationing cabins and time shares area. It was starting to make sense to me now. I was looking for something other than a bear that caused the horrific murders and disappearances in the forest. I doubt if they left behind the mangled remains of the others, but there was always room for the anomaly when dealing with supernaturals.

At the least the Mskagwedemoos might have some information about what is going on in the forest, especially with this massive energy field. It could be some sort of defense mechanism set up by them, they've already displayed the ability to mask their energy signatures, and what was this energy field if not a huge cloaking device. But why was it at the Abenaki Village? Some of the Mskagwedemoos were Native American, but not all of them.

In this section of the forest the trees and foliage seemed to be thicker than the rest. There was no moon in the sky to illuminate the darkness, and even if there were, the thick towering trees with a veil of black leaves would have completely blocked it out. Something else illuminated the darkness this night, as the trees appeared to be on fire with little sparks of flame. There were hundreds of ravens, perched upon their limbs, peering silently in the dark with scarlet red eyes. Like fireflies glowing, and lighting up the night, they provided crimson stage lights for the task at hand. They're the spectators of the macabre; connoisseurs of death, and messengers from beyond. They could sense death lurking in the air, and waited patiently to feast upon its spoils, like a symbiont.

We remained a good distance from the cabin and out of sight. Our plan was simple, surround the cabin, close in slowly, and then attack from all sides. It was the ways of the Vikings and guerilla warfare. The forest became still as we made our move. Nature speaks to all of us, if we know how to listen. The Mskagwedemoos didn't need to sense us, all they had to do is recognize how still and quiet the surrounding forest became as we approached the cabin.

Shamans are more in touch with nature than other supernaturals, perhaps it's our animal spirit guide imprinting. I was still new at being a Shaman, but I had achieved one with nature early in my vision quest, and right now she was telling me that something was off! She was telling me that something was uncannily wrong in this stillness. It was a little too vast. The brothers had already divided and surrounded the house. I was with Eirik when I informed him of my concerns.

"Something's not right here, Eirik."

"What's wrong?" he asked.

"I don't know, but trust me something isn't right," I replied.

"You're just feeling the nerves before a fight, we all experience it. It'll be alright once we begin," he said.

I stayed behind as he continued his approach. I could see and hear better than they could in the dark, so I relied upon my panther imprinting.

It didn't take long before I heard it, the movements of something behind us in the dark forest. I immediately shadowed myself and took a closer look. Then I heard their song, like a soft whisper, flowing through the forest, like a heavenly lullaby to a child, yet this was a deadly hypnotic melody that entraps the souls of men.

Then before I knew it, they rose from the settled black leaves on the ground, moving to a primeval rhythm that was intoxicating to watch. Their hips rolled slowly left to right, while their arms flowed gracefully, imitating the wind, and inviting you in. It appeared as if various parts of their body were moving separately, yet elegantly in a well-coordinated harmony, like the gliding movements of a snake. This was a stupor no ordinary man could resist, and even I was captivated by their muse.

There were four of them, beautiful, dark and erotic. They reminded me of a rare Halfeti Black Rose that I've seen before; as beautiful as the midnight sky, rare and exquisite, yet their thorns are the sharpest of any rose. These Mskagwedemoos were no exception with razor sharp claws on each finger. Some were completely naked, while others scantly covered their breasts or genitalia with a mesh composed of leaves and vines. Their hair was long and jet black, like the raven's wings, but thick as moss, and resembling dreadlocks, swinging to each subtle and meticulous movement, as a conductor leads an orchestra.

Now I understood the symbolism of the nightingales, and their beautiful nocturnal songs, in reference to these sirens, beautiful hypnotic songs. I would have fell victim to this trance, but the distracting light from my amulet kept me grounded, as its warning shined brightly from beneath my sleeve. It seems a shame to kill something, so beautiful, but this beauty was laced with pure evil. I know this was necessary, but I still didn't like it. I didn't enjoy killing anything, unlike the brothers who seem to relish it. This is just one big hunting expedition to them, no matter the risk.

I moved in quickly using my supernatural speed, but these weren't like the Mskagwedemoos at Nightingales. They moved almost as quickly as me, and could see or sense me, as they ducked and dodged my advances. They swung their razor-sharp claws in defense, swiftly cutting through the air, left and right, in an attempt to strike me. We sparred like this for several minutes, swinging and ducking each other's advances. Then they used the leaves to do their bidding; moving and twirling them, while attacking me from all sides. I was cut several times, until I summoned the wind. I hit them with several strong gusts, throwing them off balance, and knocking them down while I swooped in to severe their heads, one by one.

They disintegrated into the black ash that I've witnessed the demons turn into, and depriving the ravens of a meal. I knew they were different than the others. They never were human, they were demons. We were getting closer to their master or mistress, as we climbed up the chain.

I was ready to depart when something grabbed my foot from below the soft black soil. It was most likely a siren no doubt, hiding below; where the others rose. I couldn't see it or my foot, submerged in the dirt, as it pulled me deeper and deeper below. Its claws sunk deep into my flesh. Its grip was strong and tight, as I struggled to free myself. There was no using the elements, as I sunk into the cold black earth below. So, I dug downward in a last-ditch effort, to find its hold on me and relieve it of its energy life source. I was finally able to grab a hold of its arm, and all I heard was its agonizing screams from below. I could see the light from my energy crystal surge through the cracks of earth, as its arm faded into the grainy black ash within my grip.

I limped back towards the brothers, fearing that it might be too late, and find them enslaved by the siren's charms, but it didn't affect them. Which posed the question; why and how were the other two brothers taken so easily? There was no time to ponder these questions, as their slaves rushed out of the cabin, the men they possessed. They were armed with swords, as they hurried to their deaths. I was upset these innocent men had to die and wished there was another way. My first choice would have been to knock them unconscious, but they would only get back up and attack again, as demonstrated at the club. The brothers weren't taking any chances or wasting anytime with the armed men, as the cut them down like weeds in a field. Egor and Egil weren't among the possessed.

Then a second wave of Mskagwedemoos came from the forest. It didn't make much sense to remain shadowed since they could see or sense my presence anyway. I used the wind once again, moving through the

Mskagwedemoos attacking from the forest. I couldn't believe their numbers, and how quiet they were in the forest. They were well disciplined and trained, deadly, yet beautiful. It was like destroying a Picasso, but they wouldn't hesitate for a second to sever my head.

They were dressed in all black, from head to toe, to blend in with the darkness. They had war paint going across their eyes which created a dark linear mask from ear to ear. The colors of war paint varied from red to black and blue, all dark colors. I didn't know the significance of this display, but most tribal war parties do this, except these Mskagwedemoos were from different nationalities. They had blended in well with the dark forest.

I moved in with ease killing the first few, except they didn't turn to ash. These were human disciples that were turned into slaves. They weren't as quick as the demons, therefore I shadowed myself, to see if they could sense me, and they didn't. I continued moving with ease through the gang of Mskagwedemoos, until I was hit several times by their sharp claws. The demons Mskagwedemoos were deceptively hidden amongst their human disciples; therefore, I went back to my previous strategy and manipulated the wind to assist me.

"Ayv wiwadvhv nvgi ganolvvsgv, hnadvga gadousdi Ayv adanetsedi"

The human disciples of the Mskagwedemoos wielded the katana swords, as before, against the Thorenson Weapons of the Padogiyik. The brothers managed to make their way back towards one another and fight as a unit, as they used the full strength of their weaponry. The dark forest was illuminated like some sort of light show where the brothers were fighting. There was a giant size electrical sphere surrounding them, and anything within it fell victim to the electricity or to their blades. I've never seen anything like it, as they electrocuted some Mskagwedemoos to disable their advances, while severing the heads of others, and then coming back to the ones that were disabled and severing their heads. It was an incredible show!

Then I saw something that I had never seen before. Eirik was not only using his weapon to wield the lightning and severing heads, but with his free hand, he was manipulating the lightning, as I would manipulate wind, fire or any other elements. I didn't see the other brothers doing this. I didn't know if it was something that only he could do. It was extremely effective, but very destructive to the surroundings. Once again, the trees became collateral damage under the lightning strikes and electrical sphere of their weapon.

We continued battling amongst the burning trees. Some falling from the blazes and others sending their burning timbers scattered in the winds. No one seemed interested in the destruction caused by the growing flames. Several Mskagwedemoos were caught in the blaze, those that were human died screaming, while the demons managed to shake off the flames or fight while on fire, until we took their heads.

I was drenched in blood, from head to toe, like a battlefield surgeon, yet with an opposite purpose. Not to save nor spare, grant clemency nor judge; we were here to take, and give nothing in return. The cost of our bounty was non-negotiable; we sought death, and nothing more.

We fought into the dawn, as headless corpses lay amongst the smoldering ashes of the forest. The fire consumed most of them, and their blackened remains blended in with the burnt foliage. I'm certain they weren't the only ones that died in this destruction. Besides the murdered trees, everything that lived in them or around them may have died as well, except for one thing. The silence of the ravens ended with the dawn. Their squawking could be heard for miles. Perhaps they were annoyed that the flames consumed their feast or that their homes were destroyed. Then again, they could be lamenting the fallen Mskagwedemoos in their symbiotic relationship.

No emergency personnel arrived to extinguish the flames. We were too deep inside the forest, and Steve pulled a few strings to get the forest quarantined by the CDC. It was a step to prevent tourist and the media from entering this death zone. I did the best that I could while fighting to contain the flames, but it wasn't good enough. Victory favored us with the dawn, but the immediate surrounding forest was laid to waste.

It was light outside and there were a few wounded Mskagwedemoos still alive. Perhaps these will be the ones we question, but I doubt that was our purpose. It's as if they already knew their brothers weren't alive; the way they fought, and granted no quarters. Then from out of nowhere, Asger yelled in agony. He was hit hard from the front, and then from the back. We watched his movements, as he twisted around, but we couldn't see his attacker. Something had slashed deep inside his chest and back. Then he was raised off his feet into the air, and then his head was ripped from his body, mimicking what I was doing to the Mskagwedemoos. His head was tossed in my direction, and then his motionless, suspended body fell to the ground.

We had found the beast!

Gunnar hollered, as he rushed towards Asger, like a berserker with his sword held high, only to be slashed across the chest, and knocked several feet backwards. Then Brandr was attacked in the same fashion. Eirik told the brothers to regroup, as they came together and created the electrical sphere surrounding all of us, but it did no good against the invisible predator that came in quick and hard slashing at will.

I couldn't see the beast, but I realized that this thing was strong, with deadly sharp claws and tall by the way it lifted Asger. I warned the others to stay low, but they were caught in the heat of battle and in revenge. They broke rank after the beast penetrated their electrical sphere and went with Plan B, which was to separate and spread out, making it harder for the beast to concentrate on them as a group, but even this plan failed. The beast was moving faster than any supernatural I've ever seen; I was fast, but the beast was faster!

The remaining Mskagwedemoos retreated to the cabin, as we defended ourselves from the unseen beast. I shadowed myself, but even I felt the sting of its claws, as it grazed my back. It could see my shadow and caught me, as I was ducking. In the light of day, a trained eye could see my shadow, and this beast was no exception, judging by the way it slashed me. Now I had to rely on my panther imprinting again, to withstand the beast advances. I could smell it unlike the others. It was a very profound and foul stench that I'll never forget.

When the smell came close to me; I ducked here and there, avoiding its swings. As the wind brushed across my skin, I rolled on the ground to another location, but as soon as I was in the clear, it was on me again. It was attacking me and the brothers with speeds that we couldn't fathom. It was like the beast was everywhere, one second attacking me, and the next second on one of the brothers, and moving repeatedly through us. The stench was everywhere and I couldn't get a fix on it to warn the brothers, only when it came close to me was I able to avoid it, and just meagerly at that.

We were literally sitting ducks, as the creature had its way with us. The tables had completely turned and now we were the hunted and the Mskagwedemoos had the advantage of a stealth weapon. I think this was the message the beast was trying to display to me when he tossed Asger's head at me. We were getting mangled in the early morning of the new day. I knew when to retreat from an unwinnable fight, and I would definitely categorize this one as such. Now I had to convince Eirik and his brothers to retreat. This was a foreign concept to them.

They followed the Viking's code; to die gloriously in battle with weapon in hand. We were clearly outmatched and getting the life beaten out of us. The Golden Seven was now down to four. They would have fought until the end, and died just as Asger, but this wasn't my code. I say live to fight another day, perhaps when the odds are in our favor or at least equal. It was time we cut our losses.

"It's time to retreat, Eirik. We can't fight what we can't see. We need to pull back and regroup," I advised him.

"Do as you please, Shaman, but this is one fight that I won't be retreating from," he replied, anxiously looking around, and preparing himself for another attack.

"Look around you man, Gunnar and Brandr are badly wounded. What good will all of you dying accomplish this day? We must live to fight another day for vengeance," I said.

He paused briefly and assessed the situation of his remaining brothers as we waited for another round of attacks from the unseen beast.

Nidhogger wasn't injured, and seemed to be enjoying himself, as he waited for a glorious death. He was the quiet one, but he was the fiercest when it came to battle. It was like some type of trigger went off inside of him and he became a different person while fighting. He went from a quiet introvert to this killing machine! You would never suspect this from him by looking at him. His fighting style was low to the ground which protected him from the advances of the monster, but he still couldn't see what to hit.

"We're like sitting ducks, sheep waiting to be slaughtered. Let's get Asger, and get the hell out of here. I promise you I'll help you seek revenge," I implored him.

He finally gave in and told his brothers to retreat. Gunnar slung Asger over his shoulder and we rushed from the forest using all the strength and supernatural speed we could muster; our lives depended on it. This was the first time I'd been beaten like this, and judging by Eirik and his brother's reactions, it was their first beating as well. We could barely defend ourselves, and relied on instincts and impulse after the first strike, but those first strikes were beginning to take a toll and the damages were surmounting.

We retreated to the house that Winchester provided for the brothers on the outskirts of town. It was a single-family home with no other homes within miles. I guest he didn't want them to run into me in the hotel like the boosters. Gunnar and Brandr were badly wounded, but would survive. All of us were healing exponentially, but the quickness of the beast didn't allow us to heal while on the battle field. We all would have eventually ended up like Asger, dead.

"So, Shaman, what's your big plan for revenge," Eirik asked, sarcastically?

"I don't know yet Eirik, but there has to be a way of meeting this thing on equal ground," I replied.

"Well you let me know what you come up with, my brother, and I need to say goodbye to our brothers," Eirik said.

"I understand, I'll get back with you later," I replied.

"No, I would be honored if you stayed. The more brave souls to send them off, the better," he said.

I remained and assisted with the burial ceremony of Asger. Now there were only four brothers remaining from the proud and honorable Golden Seven. I was honored that they wanted me to stay. It felt good to be accepted as one of them. They were great warriors. It was obvious by the way they fought. The Valkyries chose well.

CHAPTER THIRTEEN

THE VALKYRIES

The brothers didn't waste time preparing the burial for Asger and the other two missing brothers, Egor and Egil, which they accepted as being amongst the fallen. It was considered offensive in Vikings tradition to wait to bury their dead, and appropriate to send them off on a swift journey. I assisted them with the burial arrangements. Preparing the headless corpse of Asger had to be one of the most difficult and bravest things that they've had to do since becoming mercenaries.

It took most of the day to prepare for the burial ceremony which took place in the rear of the house. It was a burial by fire in the Viking Traditions of the past. The brothers used their weaponry to cut down several large trees, nine to be exact, and then stripped them down to only their trunks. They took precautions to preserve the trunks of the trees from burning. The trees were placed into three overlapping triangles, creating the symbol of the Val Knut, as explained to me. This is the Viking symbol for slain warriors

We dug a circular containment ditch around the large Val Knut, and within the three empty spaces of it, igniting materials were placed to keep the fire burning with a good blaze. In the center of the three triangles was a wooden bed where they placed Asger and items belonging to the other fallen brothers. He was dressed in a purple robe resembling those of the Norsemen, and on the chest of his robe was a crest adorned with a beautiful

Verreaux's Eagle Owl. I found this particularly interesting, considering my newly found owl friend, compounded with the fascination with birds in the town, and the omnipresence of blackbirds.

Gunnar informed me that they all had different raptor signs, but nothing like a spirit guide, just the symbolic representations of birds of prey. Eric's symbol was the Eagle, Gunnar's was the Vulture, Nidhogger's symbol was the Hawk, like his tattoo, Brandr's symbol was the Condor, Egor's was the Osprey and Egil's symbol was the Falcon. They traveled with their burial robes, expecting death and accepting it. I guess that's why they lived life to the fullest, knowing that death was always around the corner.

Although it was an accepted way of life for them, the deaths of his brothers hit Eirik hard. He was the oldest of the brothers and the leader. He looked at it as a failure on his part, but neither he nor they let their sorrow prevent them from sending their brothers off on their journey. As they lit the fire where Asger laid, the flames quickly devoured his body. It was a huge flame that reached high towards heaven, in the clear night sky. Then the brothers recited an ancient Norsemen burial chant. I understood the words and repeated it after them to honor the slain.

May the sword swing just,
When the flames carry my dust,
And Valkyrie Wings provide the wind
As I sail to the ocean's end

My pledge is simple,
Yet no harder to keep,
Like the stones of a great temple,
Its mortar runs deep,

We keep our wit, as death takes tally,
As Men, not boys and never with fear,
Never too quick, and never to dally,
We go with joy and never with tear

As the hordes rush in,
Never to yield,
No swords or shields,
Shall rest till then

May the sword swing just,
When the flames carry my dust,
And Valkyrie Wings provide the wind
As I sail to the ocean's end

I hear the wings of Victory,
As my time grows near,
Let there never be doubt,
That I withstood the test

And throughout history,
To whoever should hear,
Let there be no doubt,
That I've given my best

From the earth I lay,
From the fire I rise,
To the one God I pray,
That my soul never dies.

May the sword swing just,
When the flames carry my dust,
And Valkyrie Wings provide the wind
As I sail to the ocean's end

Then they pulled out their weapons, placed their lightning blades together, and they fused into one great lightning rod that shot upwards, piercing the sky. I heard a thunderous boom, as several stars in the night sky began to fall from above. It was a wonderful magnificent sight to witness as they tumbled downward from the sky like fireworks in July. They became larger and brighter as they fell towards us. The brothers heeled their weapons as they approached.

The brightness blinded me, but the brothers were unaffected by the light. They had seen it before, several times, and their eyes were accustomed to the glare now. I had to close my eyes because the intensity of the light was too great for me. My crystal was shining just as bright as the stars that fell upon us. I went down to my knees and attempted to shield my eyes with my hands, but to no avail, and then it disappeared.

When I opened my eyes, my crystal was no longer shining brightly, but it glowed like a beating heart and we were surrounded by these wondrous and beautiful winged women. They were dressed in exquisite chainmail armor with pristine white, short dress togas beneath it. Some had shields swung around their backs, but all with swords. These were the Valkyries that Gunnar told me about. I would not have believed it if I hadn't seen it with my own eyes. Each one was as beautiful as the next. Then one of them with golden blonde hair spoke to Eirik and his brothers in the ancient Nordic language of the Vikings. Speaking in tongues has its advantages, as I understood what was being said.

Her name was Freyja, and she was the leader of the Valkyries. They came to give their condolence s and stated that Asger fought with a brave heart and soul. She told them to be strong and forever fight the good battle. I felt all their eyes on me, as I tried not to stare back. I was like the kid let loose at the toy store and not knowing where to turn or to go because of all the wonderful goodies surrounding him. I've never been surrounded by such ethereal beauty, and didn't know how to react. I was quiet and still as a church mouse, as I felt the warmth of their energies surrounding me and embracing me. They smiled at me, as if they could read my thoughts. Then the angel next to Freyja with curly, fiery red hair spoke to me, as my panther would through telepathy.

"There's no need to fear us Christian, each of us can hear your thoughts. It's alright to gaze upon us. We're appearing outside of the light, so we can show ourselves to you, and that you should know that we and

heaven exist. There are remarkable things in your future, just let your spirit guide you, Cheveyo, and you won't go astray. But remember that a part of you is still human; therefore, you have faults like humans. You mustn't let it distract you or be too hard on yourself. The good will prevails in the end."

Then I saw Asger rise from the flames. He was dressed in armor like the Valkyries. He said his last goodbyes to his brothers and informed them that Egil and Egor were calling to him from the halls of Valhalla. It was a tearful sight to see, as they embraced. Gunnar, Nidhogger and Brandr had tears in their eyes, as Eirik stood strong and embraced his little brother for the last time. Then Asger and the Valkyries appeared as bright lights again. I shielded my eyes, as they ascended into the heavens as the stars that fell from the sky.

I had no idea what the Valkyries were attempting to tell me, I was so overwhelmed just by the sight of them. The brothers were filled with tearful joy now that they had a chance to see their brothers off. Now I understood why they didn't fear death. If you live as a righteous man, no matter how others view you, there is something better waiting for you on the other side. These brothers were above just being mercenaries; I now knew and understood that.

Eirik and his brothers took some time to drink and reminisce about their fallen brothers and accepted me into their circle. They nor did I understand why the Valkyries chose to reveal themselves to me, nor did we understand why I could activate their weaponry, but their message was clear that I had bigger things in the horizon. Whatever my path may be, I was elated to have met the Padogiyik.

I inquired later, as we were drinking, about the weapons of Egor and Egil. They informed me that Egor wielded a bow with lightning arrows that appeared whenever he pulled back on the bow and Egil, the youngest brother with the dreadlocks, was being trained in all the weaponry like Eirik, but used two Wakizashi swords. He was the favorite of all the brothers. Little brothers tend to be that in large families.

They also informed me that their weapons are passed on to the next Golden Seven when they die. Sometimes the weapons may vary or change, but they are all lightning weapons from the Valkyries. They also informed me that in every other generation exactly seven brothers will appear in the ancient blood line, no more, no less, just seven, and the Valkyries will appear to them and begin their training. Then I went on to inquire about something that was nagging my conscience since we fought the Mskagwedemoos.

"So, tell me, Eirik, why didn't you and your brothers fall under the Mskagwedemoos charms when we were fighting them?"

"As long as we're in possession of our Thorenson weapons, we're immune to such trifles. We must die on the battlefield, and in combat," Eirik advised.

"Didn't Egil and Egor have their weapons with them?" I further inquired.

"Yes, but it must be activated or charged before it can assist in that manner," he informed me.

"I have one further question that's been burning on my lips since the Valkyries appeared. Can you tell me the name of the curly red-haired Valkyrie?" I asked.

"Sure, my friend, her name is Kara, the Stormy One. She's the most aggressive and hot tempered of the Valkyries. Some refer to her as the Tempest or Thunderstorm. It is rumored that she is a demi-goddess; half-human, half goddess," he replied, to my surprise.

"Are there really such a thing as demi-goddess?" I inquired

"Well, there's half-human, half-angels, right? So, why not?" He retorted.

"Why do you ask, as if struck by lightning?" He inquired, a little inebriated, yet still able to see the astonished look on my face when discovering the Valkyrie's name.

"More like an epiphany, Eirik. My mother and grandmother use to tell me that my guardian angel's name was Kara, each night as I prayed.

I thought it a little strange at the time because I've never heard of any angels named Kara. She also told me that Uriel, and Esther were my guardian angels as well."

"Yes, an *efifany* it is," he hiccupped, pronouncing it incorrectly from the alcohol consumption.

Suddenly I reflected upon what Asku had told me about my journey before I left Cherokee. He said my journey would be stormy with a lot of thunder, but I wouldn't be alone. Once again, his visions were sound. Kara is the storm and Eirik and his brothers are the thunder. Perhaps everything my mother and granny told me was correct also. I had a strange feeling that this isn't the last time I would see or hear from Kara and the Valkyries.

I decided to call it a night before it became too late. I still had some work to do. This ceremony had been filled with tears and joy. All of us could only hope for an ending like Asger was given. I had no idea how to defeat the beast of the forest. I was tired, beaten and looking forward to lying down after all we've been through. Perhaps after some rest I'll be able to think clearer. We had just got our asses handed to us, gift wrapped, and served on a platter by something we literally never saw coming. It would have killed all of us.

One thing is for sure; only strategy and planning would assist us in defeating the beast. This sounds like something I need to consult with my spiritual guide before moving forward. I thought things would become easier with my new abilities, but it only took me to another level of complications; the gift and the curse.

CHAPTER FOURTEEN

POSSESSION

When I arrived back at the hotel, there wasn't anyone in the lobby for a change, except for the desk clerk with the bad attitude. This was a welcome relief, because I wasn't in the mood for anymore confrontations with the FBI, Sheriff's Department or anyone else who wanted to take a shot at me tonight. I didn't mind the contemptible stares of the desk clerk. She never said anything to me and it suited me just fine. I was so used to her rude disposition that I no longer gave her the pleasure of looking her way, but no soon as I passed her, I heard the strangest thing.

"This is no place for you, Shaman," I heard someone say from her direction, in a deep and raspy voice. The person was speaking Algonquian.

"Excuse me," I replied.

I was totally taken by surprise and looked in her direction, but expected to see someone else. It wasn't the light toned voice of the rude young desk clerk, and then she gazed at me with an ominous stare.

"You're not wanted here Shaman. You will find nothing, but death here. Leave here before you die." This time she wavered in tongues (languages), vacillating between Algonquian, Tsalagi and the ancient Proto-Algic language.

It was clear to me that the desk clerk was possessed. She looked horrible and was speaking in tongues. Her speaking to me in any language was a sure indication of that. She's only smirked and frowned at me since I checked in, except for when she gave me the message from Eirik. She was probably tipped generously for delivering the message. She's always looked at me as if she just ate something disagreeable, as if I upset her stomach.

"Who are you?" I asked.

"Leave here now or I will cut out your heart," she replied.

She picked up a letter opener from off the desk, leaped onto the check-in counter, and crouched down on it, swaying back and forth, like a monkey; shifting her head, left to right, while swinging her arms with the letter opener in her right hand. Her eyes were bulging, as if they were ready to pop out of their sockets, and then she leaped towards me. I moved with supernatural speed avoiding her leap. I was behind her without her knowledge. She looked in my previous direction, paused, and then titled her head upward towards the ceiling like a predatory animal sniffing the air for its prey.

"Oh, there you are, you're fast Shaman," she said, and turned towards my direction, *"But I can smell that heavenly stench on you a mile away."*

"I took a shower this morning, but I guess the smell of the forest had its way with me," I replied sarcastically.

She charged at me again, and I quickly moved across the floor. I could have easily killed her with one blow, but she was an innocent young woman; rude, but innocent. On her next charge, I knocked her out with one swift blow, and caught her in my arms before she hit the floor. I carried her down to the basement of the hotel, kicked open the laundry room door, and took her inside.

I learned to exorcise demons during my training in Cherokee, North Carolina with Asku, if you want to call it training. He threw me into deep end of the pool, so to speak. He left me in a room with someone who was possessed, and told me I had all the tools that I needed through my travels in the spirit realm to exorcise the demon. Now this I understood perfectly clear. Asku exorcises demons externally; by pulling them out of the possessed. I go inside the person's psyche (internally), and exorcise the demons from the spiritual realm. Knocking Gale unconscious not only provided me with control, but a way to communicate with whatever was inside of her through dreamscape. I would exercise this demon from within the spirit realm.

When I laid her down on one of the folding tables she jumped up immediately, and tried to attack me again. This time I placed her in a sleep hold until she went unconscious. I didn't want to hurt her by striking her again. I placed some distance between us and entered dreamscape. I had no idea how to exorcise someone, but in the spiritual world where dreams reside; I felt right at home. I'd been tormented for years in one way or another in dreams, now it was my kingdom. In dreamscape, I ruled like a prince and fought like a warrior.

It was dark inside Gale's dreams. I didn't even know her name until now. Whatever was possessing her had made itself at home, as if it was going to stay awhile. I was standing outside of an ancient Aztec Temple of Central America, in a barren wasteland with nothing else in sight. The ground was completely covered in black, grainy, smut-like sand. It reminded me of the demon- ash. The wind was howling, and carrying the black smut, as it twirled and whisked through the air.

There was no sun in the sky, just blackish-grey clouds which seemed to envelope the entire area, like the grey and black mold one finds on putrid bread. The thunder roared from the clouds, as lightning jumped from one cloud to the next, but there was no rain or even the slightest trace of moisture in the air. The only brightness in this gloom came from the crystal around my arm.

My Black Panther Spirit Guide Ebony was by my side, and ready for battle. I didn't even have to look, I felt her every move. She and I were linked spiritually. I should not have been surprised by what I saw next, yet it sparked my curiosity all the same, in the dark ominous sky was a flock of black birds heading my way. They were literally everywhere. This was past the point of being coincidental. They were linked to whatever was going on around here. Ebony began to growl, sensing danger, as did I. The birds dove towards me, but not close enough to be a threat, and then back towards the temple where they continued to circle above. I had seen enough of these creatures to last a lifetime, and wouldn't miss seeing another one.

As I walked towards the steps of the temple, the birds descended upon the steps and came together forming the figure of a man at the top of the high rising steps. It was dressed in a long, loosely fitted, black hooded robe, and carrying a long staff, as wizards and mystics do. I couldn't see its face under the hood. There was a raven flying above the figure in the sky and landed on its left shoulder, as it stood at the top of the steps. I almost wanted to laugh because it reminded me of those old pirate movies with parrots resting on the shoulders of the nefarious captain, but this was no laughing matter.

"You're brave, Shaman, and that's good, because you will be tested," the figure said, in a deep and raspy voice, like Gale was previously speaking.

Then the raven flew into the air and grew, as it flew upward until it was the size of a bear, but with wings. Ebony growled loudly and took on the challenge. She charged in the direction of the large bird and grew larger, as she ran. She leaped into the air and swung at the raven, nicking its wing, but not enough to ground the large bird. The raven flew further into the sky avoiding any additional attacks, and circled the panther in the dark skies, as birds of prey often do before swooping down for their attack. They went back and forth at it for some time, as I engaged the hooded figure.

"What is it that you want?" I asked.

"I'm here to kill you," it replied.

Suddenly the ground turned into quicksand around me, as I sunk into the bottomless pit. This was child's play for me. Things I experienced countless times before, as a kid and so much worst. I rose from the quicksand covered in the thick heavy mud and levitated into the air. I clapped my hands together with force, while extending my arms forward, and driving all the heavy mud from me and flying towards the hooded figure.

The mud completely covered the figure, as it dried quickly and encapsulating it in a solid rock tomb where it stood. I was getting ready to shatter the mold and hopefully obliterating the figure within, but then it began cracking on its own. I observed a red glow, like the scarlet eyes of the ravens, being emitted through the cracks from within the erupting mold. Then it shattered, bursting into pieces, as the figure reappeared. It was covered in a red type of energy that soon dissipated.

These were only mind games in the spiritual realm, tricks for kids; compared to what I could do here. As I approached the hooded figure, it tried one last time to deceive me with illusions, but I had been trained well by Asku and my spirit guide to expect this from a cornered creature, as they attempt to make one last desperate attempt. This time it mimicked the image of Gale, and surrounded me with several clones of her. The energy crystal around my arm was glowing fervently, as I grew tired of playing these feeble games, and with one swing of my hand, I snatched all the energy from these chameleon demons, and turning them into black ash. I was ready to do the same to the hooded one, but it retreated quickly into the temple.

When I entered the temple, I immediately stepped inside of a ghost town, instead of a temple. Apparently, the entrance was some sort of portal. This wasn't the same ghost town I experienced when I was pulled inside of the mirror by the apparition. Although I didn't spend an extended period of time in the mirror, this one was quite different. Instead of dust and dirt being blown in the wind, it was cold outside; snow was being carried by the wind. There were several inches of snow covering the ground, and the huts that were used as homes. These structures were used by the Inuit Native Americans of North America or Eskimos, as some call them.

There were no visible tracks outside, but that was to be expected with the snow, but when I walked inside several of the huts, but here was no one insight. All their belongings were still in place, clothing, food, etc. preserved by the wintry weather. The tempestuous winds were beginning to pick up outside, and creating a faint white out with the blowing snow.

My panther vision was useless in the snow, but my energy crystal was glowing brighter than a star. I partially rolled up my sleeve, and expose its full radiance, and in a nick of time, as they approached from all sides. This ghost town was now inhabited by demons.

Although the steam from their breathing covered their faces, I know what lies beneath their murky hot breaths. These hairless, eyeless creatures stand at about seven feet tall, with sharp fangs, and long tongues. Their skin was white as snow, unlike others that I've vanquished with colors ranging from neutral to black.

They seemed immune to the cold, as they approached slowly and methodically, melting the snow with each step, and hiding their tracks. Thus, there was no trace of the demons after its pillaging. Then they ran on all fours like animals towards me. I wanted to vomit smelling their wretched stench in the distance as they charged.

Now these I know how to handle. I've been fighting these things in the spirit world for several months during my training in Cherokee with the use of my energy crystal. Wielding energy was relatively easy due to my training in manipulating and wielding the wind. I could only wield the energy from my crystal while I was in the spiritual realm. This was handy since there are no elements to wield in the spiritual world; they don't exist, except for the brimstone fires of Hell. I wielded the energy from my crystal as I did the wind. I could extract or absorb the energy from supernatural beings in the spiritual realm just as I could in the noumena world.

I was surrounded by a horde of demons, as my energy crystal glowed like a star, ready and willing to do my bidding. I rolled up my sleeve, and prepared myself for the attack. They attacked from all sides; most of them were running like dogs on four legs. I ripped the energy out of the first wave of demons attacking from the front, as they crumbled into black ash. Maneuvering their energy with my hands, I spun around in a 270 degree turn to harness its speed, and to gain more momentum. I spun downward to the ground and threw the energy blast to my left, killing another wave of demons attacking. I turned to my left while still kneeling on the ground, and ripped out the energy from the next wave, as they fell to ash. I pulled their energy towards me as before, except spinning upward in a 270 degree turn to vanquish the attacking demons from the right.

I continued killing the horde in this circular fashion, as I had practiced on numerous occasions in the mountains of North Carolina. It was a graceful dance, like a ballet in the snow, except I was using the circular tactics of Aikido, which is called Irimi. I respect the principles of Aikido because it follows the concepts of Ki; the way of harmony or the moving Zen. It utilizes the energy and power of its attacking opponents against them. It's a defensive art.

I continued fighting these demons for what appeared to be hours, as the snow flew in all directions around me, like a child kicking up the rain from a splendid summer down-pour. I didn't tire because I was only transferring or redirecting energy from my attackers and using it to destroy them; Irimi.

The snow surrounding me had melted from the hot ash left behind by the demons, and leaving only a black circumference around me. I continued walking around the uninhabited village to see if the thing I followed in here was anywhere around, but it wasn't here. I did find a sign in the snow that said Lake Anjikuni Inuit Village. I didn't feel the presence of any other supernatural beings present, so I left the way I came in, and discovered Ebony, my spirit guide, still toying with the bird.

She was taunting it as a domestic cat would with a mouse or other prey. She was killing it slowly, and having fun doing it, until I told her to finish it. With one lightning fast move, she leapt into the air, grabbed the bird by the neck, and strangled it. She then proceeded to eat the bird. It was a horrific sight. Neither the hooded being nor the raven was up for the challenge. Now the demons were completely exorcised.

I woke up a little before Gale in the laundry room. I never turned on the lights in the room; I didn't need it to see. She woke up terrified and trembling. She had no idea where she was, how she got there or what had occurred. I shadowed myself and blended into the darkness. There was a slant of light coming inside the room from the door, and of course she gravitated towards it. She quickly opened the door leading to the hallway and realized her location. She quickly dashed upstairs like she had seen a ghost.

I stayed behind for a few minutes and wiped my prints from everything I touched in the room before walking upstairs. What seemed like hours in dreamscape is only a matter of minutes in the noumena world. No one had noticed her missing in the deserted lobby. She was still trembling with tears in her eyes and a black eye when I entered the lobby.

She knew she had been violated, but had no idea by whom or what occurred. She couldn't even notify the authorities. What would she tell them except she woke up with a black eye in the laundry room? She was in a hotel filled with law enforcement officers and no one saw a thing. This takes the adage of *there's never a police officer around when you need* one to a whole new level. Then again, the best place to get away with anything is right under someone's nose, and in plain sight.

"Excuse me miss, but are you alright?" I asked, while approaching her.

"Stay the fuck away from me," she yelled, in an angry, crying voice. I stopped my advances towards her immediately, and placed my hands in the air.

"I just want to know..."

"Leave me the fuck alone," she yelled again at me, crying before I could complete the sentence.

I turned around, and retreated towards the stairs. I guess she was all right because she was back to treating me like garbage again. I know it's wrong for me to feel this way, but I took satisfaction in the fact that she was scared shitless, and had a black eye from the hard jab I delivered. The first thing on the list of training, if I survive this case, is to delve more into the expulsion of demons and possessions. There's just so much to learn, now I see why it takes shaman apprentices decades to master the shamanic arts.

It had been one hell of a day, and once again I thought about just leaving this damned place. The town's people didn't want me here, the Abenaki didn't want me here, the FBI sure as hell didn't want me here, and the supernatural didn't want me here. The only thing that was keeping me here was my promise to Nina and I knew Steve was really depending on me to solve this thing, even with the reluctance of the bureau.

I had packed a dreamcatcher in my luggage for such an occasion, but it was lost in the wreckage. I haven't used one in over a year. I didn't need to use it in the solitude of Cherokee County, but I needed to get some uninterrupted sleep tonight, without the invasion of spirits or others reaching out to me in my dreams. It had been a long-fought day; therefore I created a dreamcatcher by drawing it on the wall over the headset of the bed, and then enchanting it. This was a little trick Askuwheteau showed me during my shamanic tutelage.

I was awakened by the loud blast of the television around three-something in the morning. I never watched television so it was strange for it to be on at all. When I looked over at it, there was nothing but a blank, snow filled screen with the volume blaring, and nothing else. I turned the television off and went back to bed. About twenty minutes later, the television turned itself on again. Now I knew it wasn't a coincidence.

I grabbed the plug to pull it from the socket and a surge of electrical energy rushed out and caused me to shake momentarily, like when you get a chill, as I held on to the connection. This would have electrocuted an ordinary person, but the conductivity only jolted me as it surged through my body and into my energy crystal. I was only a conduit for it like supernatural energy. The television remained on even while it was unplugged, and then I heard a voice speak in the ancient and lost Algonquin language.

"Leave this place; leave this place before you die."

The television went dark afterwards, and the energy surge disconnected. It was the same message that I've heard repeatedly since I arrived here. The citizens on the streets of Swanton before going into the sheriff's station, Agent Robinson before he pulled out his service revolver and began shooting at me, and Gale. They were possessed by this same supernatural being. The supernatural energy that was fused in the electrical current was the same signature that I had experienced in my dreams with the masked woman. Electricity was energy and could be controlled like any other element, but there was no hiding your energy signal from me. It was unique like a human finger print.

I always kept an open channel to communicate with other supernaturals. I had no runes, spells, or totems to prevent them from communicating with me. I hadn't even used the dreamcatcher for years until tonight. I had learned to accept my abilities as a gift, instead of a curse. This supernatural entity didn't want to communicate; it only wanted to scare me away from Swanton. It looked at me as a threat, and it was right to do so, if it was behind what was going on here. As much as I wanted to keep my channels open to communicate, this was a hindrance and I had to put an end to it.

Since it couldn't enter my dreams with the dreamcatcher present, it used other physical means to show itself, therefore I drew runes on the four walls of the hotel suite, representing the North, South, East and West. I hid the runes from the view of anyone entering the suite. Then I sat in the middle of the floor and charged the runes with a protection spell to prevent any supernatural beings from entering. I had enough things to worry about besides a nuisance supernatural disturbing my sleep. Its biggest mistake was giving me its energy signature, now I knew it, regardless of what form it presented itself in.

I didn't go back to sleep, and decided to invade the dreams of the desk clerk, Gale. She was still shaken by the experience she had last night. She quit her job last night and had the manager come in and relieve her of duty. I'm surprised she waited for him to come in before departing. She thought she was abducted by aliens, but wondered if I had something to do with it.

The mind is an amazing thing. Her subconscious probably had some residual memory of me being inside her head. Perhaps it was just the way I showed up so quickly that creeped her out. It's easy to resent and pin something on someone you already dislike. That's exactly what was happening to the Abenaki.

I still had enough time before the sunrise, and decided to go witch hunting. I was fed up with all the killings of innocent possessed people. Eirik and his brothers only saw red at this point, and anyone who got in their way would surely feel the lightening death of their blades. I visited the cabin in the woods first. It was vacant, as I thought it would be, but it was worth the chance.

Then I went to the one place that stood out in the back of my mind. It was where the Mskagwedemoos in the forest came from. They were never in the cabin; I remember only seeing their male slaves running out to be slaughtered by the Padogiyik. They came from that ominous looking tree that I discovered and forgot about until now!

I shadowed myself for the duration of my travels through the forest. The tree was only a couple of meters from the cabin. I spotted several Mskagwedemoos outside the perimeter of the tree nestled in the forest surrounding the isolated atrocity.

I quickly sped through the darkened forest, using my supernatural speed, and killing them one by one without prejudice. My rage had taken over at that point and the fires from within unknowingly took over. My clothing was the first thing to burn off, as my energy crystal fell to the ground. Then my skin singed quickly, turning black and peeling right off, as my flesh followed. You could see the fire moving across my body like a tsunami consuming muscles, veins and organs until nothing was left of me except the silhouette of my naked body created by the flame. I felt invigorating as if it gave me new life, energy, and power like I've never experienced. I picked up my energy crystal and continued.

There was no hiding this sight, as I moved towards the entrance of the tree. Before the crows could sound the alarm, I burned every one of them alive. The top portion of the tree was on fire at this point, if it wasn't dead, it gave off the smell of death now, as I moved down the narrow passage towards the cave. A horde of Mskagwedemoos screaming at the top of their voices with their collective deafening cries tried to attack me, but to no avail. With the wave of my hand, I incinerated them all. Wave after wave, you heard their agonizing screams, as I burned them alive. And when I got to the core of the cave, I let loose, and created a giant inferno in the enclosed cave that resembled a pressure cooker.

There was nothing left alive when I was finished. I departed the burning cavity still on fire, and the tree was still ablaze. I tried my best to calm down but I couldn't. I was still enraged and couldn't control the flames, so I sat at the base of the isolated burning tree, where there was no surrounding grass or trees, just cool and moist black soil. I could still hear their screams in my head, as I tried to calm down, but just became enraged again. In the dark and distance tree line, I thought I saw a figure staring at me, but when I got up to look again, it was gone. I probably didn't get them all, but I killed more than enough to cause a major ripple in their demonic numbers.

The dawn was peaking over the horizon when I finally cooled down. I was naked as a jaybird with only my energy crystal glowing in my hand. It had received a reboot last night and was bright as the sun. I collected some mud from the ground, placed it around the crystal and made my way back to my vehicle. I had a change of clothing in the trunk of the car. *Preparedness is the key to success.*

I drove back to the hotel, showered and remained up. I was supercharged from the energy that I acquired last night or early this morning, so I continued working. My first order of business of the day was to research the symbols that I discovered on the siren. I did this on my laptop while at the hotel, but I didn't come up with anything after hours of searching, so I called upon my tech savvy friend at Quantico, Carlyle. He previously assisted me with tracking the movements of the Coyote, eventually leading to his apprehension and death.

"Hello, Carlyle, how are you?"

"I'm doing great Chris. How are you, my friend?"

"I'm doing well. I can't thank you enough for what you did for me on the Coyote case," I said.

"Are you kidding me? I received a pay grade raise, and a call from POTUS (President of the United States) thanking me for my assistance. I

can't thank you enough, man. Did you enjoy that bottle of Dom and Cuban cigars I sent you?" he asked, zealously.

"Yes, thank you, Carlyle, I appreciate it, but I need to ask for another favor. I'm working this case for the Bureau of Indian Affairs, and need some symbols transcribed for me. I couldn't get anywhere with them and wondered if you could do some investigating, and see what you can come up with?"

"It would be a pleasure, Chris. If Kindle can't solve it, no one can," he replied.

"Who's Kindle?" I asked, curiously.

"Kindle is only the sweetest and fastest, mega-data computer in the bureau. Send me what you got and I'll get back with you," he replied

"Ok, thanks, Carlyle, I owe you one."

"No, you don't my friend. I'll talk to you later."

Carlyle is one of the most brilliant and eccentric tech minds at the bureau. I will surely mention his service again to Steve after this thing is over. Even if he doesn't get anything for me, but if anyone can, it will be him.

My next order of business for the day was to look into some theories I had on the beast from the forest, which meant I had to get access to the FBI files relating to the citizens missing in the forest. This was something that I didn't look forward to doing. I was the most hated man in law enforcement right now, but I had to bear it for the common good.

I endured the glares, smirks and scowls of over a dozen law enforcement officers and agents on the Task Force. Some spoke harshly under their breaths of me while others vocally cursed and beseeched me out loud. I felt like Judas walking before the other apostles. I asked the desk sergeant if I could speak to the new FBI SAC Agent Halifax. Steve informed me that I could count on his cooperation.

Agent Halifax bared no ill will towards me as Steve had stated. He was one of Steve's appointee's and considered to be in the family. He brought me into his office and offered me his full assistance. I looked over the files in his office. It didn't take long for me to find what I was looking for. He extended the full service of all the agents under his supervision and made sure that they heard what he was saying, as I was leaving his office. He didn't care what the other agents thought or said about me; he even reprimanded a few of them for staring at me as I departed.

I discovered during my research that all the killings and abductions in the forest occurred during daylight hours, like the attack on us. We were defeating the Mskagwedemoos until the beast showed up after sunrise. My theory is that it needed the sunlight in some way. Perhaps it gained its strength or masking powers from the sun. We had to attack the beast at night, when it is weakest or at least that was my theory.

Carlyle returned my telephone while I was driving to meet up with Eirik. Kindle had worked her magic and found out about the symbols tattooed on the Mskagwedemoos. The symbols were a branch of ancient Mesopotamian Cuneiform writing. The symbols represented the letters CRO or Crow in English. The raven was considered a bird of deity in the Mesopotamian culture. It seems like there is a lot more behind these blackbirds here than just being pests. I have the uncanny feeling that my encounter with them wasn't quite over.

I shared my hypothesis with Eirik and his remaining brothers, Gunnar and Nidhogger, and Brandr, who couldn't wait for revenge. I also shared the information I discovered about the Mskagwedemoos tattoo, but they weren't the least bit concerned with the Mskagwedemoos at this point, it went in one ear and out the other. They didn't consider them to be a threat. Their singular focus was the beast.

We ventured out that night, first paying the Mskagwedemoos a visit at the cabin, but they had vacated the place long ago. All the furniture and everything else were still there, but they were nowhere to be found. I still couldn't sense their presence, as before. I believed that their tattoos were linked to some sort masking spell for their energy, but it was only a theory. I guess we'll never know for sure. It would be impossible to track them down with this ability, so we moved on to tracking the beast

CHAPTER FIFTEEN
GICI AWAS (THE BEAST)

The beast didn't leave any footprints in the forest to follow. Its invisibility wasn't like anything we'd ever seen; therefore, we relied on my panther imprinting to track the beast. My panther imprinting coupled with my ability to sense the energy of the beast made me the perfect candidate for the job. I had its stench committed to memory.

I picked up the trail of the beast quickly. It visited the forest daily and followed the same trail. I didn't expect to still smell the creature in the forest, but it was still pungent. If you can imagine the smell of a herd of buffalo in the heat of summer, but in an enclosed environment, this would be the smell emitted by this thing. I had tracked the beast through the forest to Lake Champlain where the trail ended.

"Within the chaos, there's always rhythm," I said, lowly, under my breath, and looking out into the murky vast waters.

"What was that?" Eirik quickly and petulantly inquired.

"The trail ends here, at the lake," I replied.

"Damn it!" He bellowed.

"So, why don't you use some of that shaman hocus pocus and go to the other side, and find the damn thing?" Gunnar blurted out heatedly.

The brothers were so set on revenge that they became angry at me when the trail ended. I wasn't a very patient person to begin with, therefore it took every fiber of patience that I had not to fire back at them. I had to remain calm and be the sensible one, so I kept my cool and attempted to calm them down. I understood what they must be going through, but I learned a long time ago, while working with the FBI ViCAP Unit, that getting emotional at times like this was the worst thing you could do.

"Look, the trail isn't gone," I said, enthused and looking out at the lake.

Eirik and his brother's vision was nothing compared to my night vision, so I had to take my time and show them what I was observing. In the middle of the lake I saw colliding waves crashing into each other like it was crashing against a wall. This effect is known as destructive interference, but I've never seen it so pronounced. This wasn't normal for a lake, even one this large. There was something beneath the surface of the lake causing this anomaly and gave cause to investigate. I also didn't think it was a coincidence that the trail stopped near the lake.

I remembered that there was a dock with some boats nearby from spending time in the forest. We ventured up the coast, and commandeered a vacant vessel on the pier. I learned that Nidhogger was more than just a quiet assassin, he was also skilled in jacking engine related carriages, cars, boats, planes; you name it. We went out to the middle of the lake to the wave disturbance. It was larger than we had envisioned, once we came upon it, so we anchored the boat away from it. Before we took the plunge into the unknown, I asked my newly found brothers to allow me to say a Cherokee prayer before we disembark. Who knows what awaits us down there or if we'll return.

"As the Moon follows the Sun
Until my last breath is done
I will follow the path of the Warrior

I will stand in the dark
When all hope seems lost

Like the Great Oak's impenetrable bark
I won't waver or bend nor abandon my cause

On this pledge I rest my soul
Like the bonds of the wolf pack,
My resilience will never unfold,
And my courage remains intact

In the thick of battle
You'll never see me cower
When others seem, shaken and rattled
It is I, who shall find strength in that hour

As the Moon follows the Sun
Until my last breath is done
I will follow the path of the Warrior"

We didn't waste any time afterwards, thinking about what lies beneath the surface and just dove in, head first and fully clothed; five brave souls with reckless abandonment. We swam near the wave disturbance and noticed that the crashing currents seemed to cancel each other and resulted in a somewhat straight line or tunnel in the middle. It wasn't a whirlpool sucking things within it, but it looked like a tube and the medium was calm inside. We swam to its edge and took in a deep breath before going inside. There was no turbulence within the wave tunnel which allowed us to swim downward quicker than normally possible. It was like a superhighway in the water, a wormhole. It was exhilarating and exciting. I felt like a kid at the water park on the giant water slide.

At the end of the wormhole, we rose slowly and quietly into a halcyon cavernous pond. We remained in the water like crocodiles with only the top portions of our heads seen out of the water. We bobbed silently in the water to expose our noses, and catch our breaths from the invigorating ride, as we scrutinized our surroundings. It seems like these things didn't know of any other way to live than in caves. I felt like Alice in Wonderland, following the rabbit.

The first thing that caught most of us was the smell. It smelled like the rotting stench of death inside the cavern. The aroma was so pungent that it caused all our gag reflexes to involuntarily react. Some of us vomited in the water while others jerked in seizure-like motions to hold it in.

There was a matrix of tunnels leading from the cavern. Surprisingly, it was dimly lit by torches that were meticulously placed in crevices along the wall. This wasn't the work of an unintelligent beast, but one with the same cerebral capacity as man. We also surmised that it couldn't see in the dark if it needed the torch light. Perhaps we can use this to our advantage later. This thing could have even been humanoid if it wasn't for what we found next.

The moist blackened soil outside of the pond was filled with the remains of human skeletons. This carnage was indiscriminate with bones of assorted sizes and ages, including a few children. These things had brought them here from topside and immediately feasted upon them. There were no signs of a fire prepared for the cooking of flesh, as cultured societies do, even human cannibals. These things ate their prey like any other common senseless predator, relying only on instinct. It might as well have been a bear like Special Agent Whyte wrongfully surmised.

All I could think of were the bones of the children it consumed, and wondered if this is what happened to the missing children? This thing was fast enough to get around the town, and it could cloak itself, at least during the day. The children could have been taken during the wee hours of dawn, which could support my theory of them utilizing the daylight for cloaking and attacks. I seriously don't think these are night creatures judging by their use of torches, but now we must contend with the fact that we were dealing with a highly intelligent being with an appetite for human flesh.

Matunaagd stated that the beast only recently began feasting on human flesh, but there was a graveyard of bones lying around. Most of the bones were old, and perhaps it did lose its appetite for human flesh, until something aroused it. Perhaps the polluting of the waters by Winchester, as the Abenaki suggested. There was no doubt at this point that we had hit our mark in finding the beast's lair, except once again there were no tracks found leaving the pond, and the smell of the beast, and its energy signature was all around the cave, making it hard to determine which of the tunnels to choose. Therefore, we decided to pick a tunnel and just follow the torches to see where it leads us.

There was a strong wind flowing through the tunnels of the cave which indicated that there was another entrance by land somewhere around the lake and that the tunnel system was extensive. I couldn't hear a sound due to the wind whistling in my ears. At least we were down wind in our search through the labyrinth of tunnels. This way I could smell them before they smelled us. The tunnels were wide and the ceilings were high, which confirmed our theories about the beast's height

The ceiling of the tunnel was perforated with huge holes of diverse sizes and shapes. It looked like a matrix of honeycombs. This also worked to our advantage since it absorbed our sounds in the cave and swallowing any sort of echo that would normally be in such vast caves. I must say this beast's intelligence was very questionable when it came to the security of its lair, because it didn't afford him any warnings of intruders, no sounds, no smells, and apparently, no sight; judging by the dimly lit cave. The most basic animals and insects in the wilderness provide their lairs with some sort of basic defense against predators. I guess it considered itself an apex predator with no enemies, but we were about to put that to the test.

We had ventured to an open area that was about fifty square yards, half the size of a football field. The honeycomb ceiling had dropped tremendously and the lighting was even more dimly lit than before, making the area almost completely dark. We could see a handful of torches around the perimeter of the area, but they were like candles burning in the distance. Then a smell hit us. It was something different than the smell of the beast. All of us knew this smell. Then I saw the body parts of several humans piled up in the corner of this dark chasm. This was the rotting flesh of recent victims. The brothers couldn't see, as I could in the dark, so I informed them of the macabre.

We stopped to discuss whether to continue due to the disparity. Eirik asked for my assessment, but nothing had changed since we entered the cave, I sensed its presence and smelt it, but it didn't fluctuate. The changes gave us reason for concern, but in our assessment of the height of the beast, he couldn't access the lower ceiling of this area for an ambush. I did observe that the tunnels continued as normal on the other side of this area. Perhaps the beast went around this area in one of the other tunnels and just used this area for refuse. We decided to continue, but with caution. The brothers were eager to see if Egor and Egil were among the remains, and I was curious as well.

There was no discussion on which way we were going at this point, we made a straight line towards the mangled remains. Eirik illuminated the dark area with his lightening sword. We were trying not to draw the attention of the beast, and catch him by surprise, so they didn't use their weapons for light, and relied on my vision. It worked up to this point, but Eirik just had to view the carnage for himself.

In the corner where the scattered corpses lay, the brothers noticed the mangled headless corpses of Egil, Egor. There wasn't much left to go on, except for their ripped and shredded clothes. It was confirmed now. The Mskagwedemoos had lured them into the clutches of the beast. We paused for a moment, and as they stared at the ghastly sight. I looked up and noticed; encased in the wall of the cave was Egor's head, and about a foot away there was another hole in the wall with Egil's head. The brothers immediately diverted their attention to see what had me so enthralled.

Eirik shined his light towards the walls, and they spotted the horrifying sight. There were dozens of heads surrounding the entire 50 square yards of this chasm, like a trophy display. Now at least we knew the purpose of this area. It didn't take long before I discovered the decomposing heads of the missing agents and the goons that Winchester sent after me. The beast left this carrion here so we could see his latest trophies. I think we might have underestimated the intelligence of this thing. Then I told the brothers to stop! I now sensed and smelled the stench of the beast become stronger, but I still couldn't pinpoint its direction.

We moved towards the exit, as the brothers prepared for battle. Could we have been wrong about its height? They gathered in a circle to protect each other's back, as we neared the center of the area. I shadowed myself and split from the group, as a recon soldier. I was hoping that my shadowing worked for me now that we were in the dark. Then we heard the beast make a loud screeching sound that resonated throughout the cave and tunnels, even in the sound attenuated area.

This was only a scare tactic, used since prehistoric man and other animals to throw off your enemy or opponent. It didn't work in scaring us, but it did make it harder to pinpoint its location. The scare tactics confirmed my theory about its use of the light to become invisible. Why use scare tactics when you can just go attack us while stealth? Now I felt a sense of confidence, like maybe we can defeat this beast, if we can see it.

As we looked in all directions waiting for the beast to attack, Brandr was quickly grabbed and lifted into one of the shafts in the low ceiling. We could hear him fighting with the beast and saw the illumination from his weapon while the annoying screeching sounds of the beast continued resonating throughout the cave. Then we no longer heard any movement emitted from the ceiling nor see the illumination of his weapon. Several seconds later blood and other body fluids began dripping from above, and then his weapon fell and hit the floor.

The brothers quickly fired lightning bolts into the honeycomb matrix, but it did no good, Brandr was already gone. We knew for a fact now that it couldn't stealth itself in invisibility without the sun. It was using the honeycomb matrix in the ceiling as a defense mechanism, and to attack us.

The brothers got in a low defensive position to protect from another aerial attack, and so did I. Then it came down, and for the first time we saw the beast. It was hairy all over like a Sasquatch, with long black hair that covered it like fur, long sharp claws, and its teeth were composed of several long fangs of the same width, like piranha, and scarlet red eyes, like the possessed ravens. It was at least 7ft tall standing, but it was hunched down on all fours, like a bear. The brothers activated their lightning weapons and prepared for battle, and then one by one, they rained down from the low hung cavernous ceiling. We were under the impression that there was only one of them, but there were hordes of them. This would explain how they quickly defeated us in the forest. It wasn't that they were so much faster than us, but there were more than one of them cloaked and attacking.

It didn't consider us as a threat, and began their attack. I was a likely target without a weapon, but I managed to dodge the grasp of the first beast, and rolled, as I did on previous encounters. It wasn't as fast as before, but it could still see me, like wolves, it could see through my cloaking with other means. Then all hell broke out. The few lights that surrounded the perimeter walls of the area went out one by one.

We thought the beasts were blind in the dark, but we were wrong about that, like other things about it. The beasts were smarter than we anticipated. It knew our every move and baited us to this trap from the start. We were under the false notion that we had the upper hand and its security set up was feeble, but nothing could be further from the truth. It chose to come in and out the way we came to lead us or anyone else tracking them to this place. It had another way in by land, this created the downward wind, which obstructed our hearing, and sense of smell.

The elaborate honeycomb matrix was like hundreds of speakers that absorbed every sound and the wind in the tunnels pushed the scent of anything approaching upward into the matrix. It carried every sound, smell and sight directly to the beast. They could hear us, smell us and see us from the start. Now we discovered that they could see in the dark which meant the torches were placed in the walls just to lead us to these killing grounds, like crumbs left out for prey. I should have known better, being in touch with nature. All cave dwellers and burrowing animals have the ability to see in the dark, in some way, even moles. This thing was an Apex predator, and used to killing men. It's been killing men for a very long time.

The brothers lit up the area with their lightning weapons, but the beasts were distracted. They came from above, some landing on us and bringing us down, while others swarmed and knocked us down, and with each hit, a deadly slash or a bite from their sharp claws and fangs. They attacked us on all fours like bears, but faster. They didn't fight in the manner the Mskagwedemoos did. They used guerilla tactics like the Apaches. They ran in slashing and kept running, never presenting a still target to fight in the dark, they kept moving.

The brothers fought hard until the end. They were able to kill some of the beasts, but there were just too many in the dark. First Gunnar went down, and his head was severed. It took some time before Nidhogger went down. He managed to kill the majority of the beasts before losing his head. I used the wind as my weapon, as I managed to whirl some of the herd away, but they were smart and didn't fight together as a group. They were sporadic and random in their attack.

Eirik was wielding his sword with one hand, and lightning with the other, but there were just too many in the dark for either of us to handle, even as elementals. I watched them swarm him like sharks in a feeding frenzy, as they took his head. I was alone now, in the dark, a place that I was more than familiar with from my nightmares. The only thing that was keeping me alive to this point was my speed and ability to see in the dark. I didn't provide them with a target like the brothers. I was a quick learner and moved as they did, but even then, they were taking me apart with their numbers.

I began to slow down, exhausted and injured, until there was no more rolling or out maneuvering to be done. I was literally on my last leg. The beasts had maimed my other legs to slow me down, and my healing abilities were slowed due to the frequent slashes and bites. They had backed me into a corner in the dark. I looked over at Eirik's headless corpse. I only saw pieces of Gunnar and Nidhogger lying around like the body parts discovered in the forest. They ravished their bodies quickly and began on Eirik.

While I was distracted, I didn't see one swinging down from the shafts, as it slashed me, and another knocked me off my feet, and flung me several feet in the opposite direction. I slammed against the wall hard from the force of the hit. I was hurt badly; lying against the cold dark wall of the cave with blood running from my mouth and who knows where else

Now these mammoth sized Sasquatch cannibals with their amber colored eyes fixed on me, approached for their final conquest. This time they immolated wolves instead of bears, as they hunched their backs and growled at me. I could see their fangs, as their upper lips trembled in anger, and smell the odious stench of their breaths, as they moved in closer. They took meticulous steps, slowly towards me, as if walking on pins and needles. I could see their shoulders move up and down like fulcrums with each carefully placed step. I wasn't certain if they were humanoid or not, the way they were acting on all fours, and mimicking quadrupeds.

I was alone again in the dark; a place that I was all too familiar with in my dreams. I had grown accustomed to it. My nocturnal instincts from my panther imprinting made it even more second nature to me. They had my back against the wall, injured and beaten badly, but I refused to go out being eaten by these wretched smelling beasts. I'd rather die by my own hands, and hopefully kill them in the process. I rolled up the sleeve of my tattered shirt and quickly yanked the glowing energy crystal from off my arm and dropped it on the ground. The crystal that was given to me for protection would now serve to protect and kill me in the process. It was the story of my life, the gift and the curse.

The energy surging throughout my body jerked me, like being in a horrific car accident or having an epileptic seizure. All my muscles contracted at once, and every axon, synaptic vessel and receptor of my nerve fibers felt as if they were on fire. My veins expanded and you can see them protruding from my skin. Shockingly the energy surge also revitalized me, as it entered my broken body. I could have just absorbed their energies until all of us died, but I wanted them to suffer for what they did to my friends. I had the consciousness to summon the elements of air and created a whirlwind, while being bombarded by the surging energy, and then I summoned the element of fire in a last-ditch effort before dying. I was channeling their energies into the fiery whirlwind like I've never channeled before.

"Ayv wiwadvhv nvgi Ganolvvsgv, ale atsilv, hnadvga gadousdi ayv adanetsedi"

The entire area was filled with the burning twirling flames, as it grew larger, and the heat grew stronger; sucking in and killing everything within its grasp. Eirik was wrong; I could kill them without severing their heads, I could incinerate them in this inferno. It felt liberating, as I released the fire, again. I felt elated and exhilarating with the taste of the blood and revenge, as my main objective. I wanted them dead like none other. They were going to pay for what they did to my friends. I could feel the hate burning inside me, but it felt good. These were the feelings that I tried to avoid when using fire; the hate, the power, and the evil that came with it.

Some of the beast attempted to escape through the honeycomb ceiling, but the flames just expanded with the assistance of the whirlwind into the shafts killing them there as well. The flames went wherever there was air, like a moth to a flame, engulfing the oxygen and everything else that crossed its path. All you heard were their agonizing howls in the inferno. It was like music to my ears. I was overjoyed with a heinous smile on my face at this point. I could have done cartwheels in celebration of their deaths.

It felt as if my eyes were on fire and burning like everything else inside the cave. Then I fell to the ground from the overload of energy. I knew this was it, now it was time to die, but I enjoyed every minute of seeing them burning and screaming in the flames. I could feel my heart about to explode, like I was having a heart attack. I struggled to reach for the crystal lying on the ground. Every movement I made was unbearably painful, and then I saw the strangest thing. I saw the figure of a man within the whirlwind of flames, standing inside of it, unharmed and staring at me, like the figure I saw staring at me in the forest when I burned down the witch's lair.

I don't know if I was unconsciously seeing a mirage while I was passing out or if it was a product of this world, but it was peculiar, even for me. I managed to just barely touch the crystal with my finger tips and then I passed out from all the energy surging through my body. I knew this was the death of me, but I woke up later to my surprise, naked, with a nose bleed and splitting headache. It felt like someone had hit me with a baseball bat, yet I also felt energized by the absorption of energy. The walls of the cave were black as coal with steam was rising from them and filling the hot and humid cave. It was the water that surrounded the underwater chamber attempting to escape the heat that just turned it to steam.

I couldn't feel anything supernatural within the cave. I was the last man standing. There were no signs of the brothers or the beast inside the cave. The whirlwind of fire was so intense it cremated them and everything else in the cave, living and non-living. The only thing that remained was their ashes, the steam blackened walls and the crystal, which was no longer glowing. The crystal was created from rock and heat, so it was in its element, like me apparently. There was no sign of the deer hide binding that I used to tie the crystal around my neck. It had been rendered ash like all my clothes.

I had the power within me to kill the beast from the start, but I would have killed my friends in the process. I had no control over it. It was a catch twenty-two scenario. I was elated to be alive, but any joys were smothered by the blackened charcoal surroundings and ash which now entombed my friends.

It was odd, but I felt good inside, in fact I felt better than good. The raging fire from within me was wonderfully euphoric! I was refreshed and energized. I felt more alive than I had ever before. It was as if I just completed a full course treatment at a luxurious spa resort and received the King's treatment. The power that I released was intrinsically healing. I felt as if I was reborn.

There was no way for me to provide a proper burial for my friends, so I picked up some ash from the floor of the cave with one hand and grabbed the crystal with the other. I made my way through the humid steam filled cave to the water portal that brought us here. I noticed the burnt, steamy walls of the cave for quite some distance, as I journeyed back. If there was air, the fire traveled towards it in the tunnel like a vacuum, expanding and engulfing the air. As I approached the water the black walls began to fade, but steam remained in the air.

When I reached the banks of the pond, I drew the symbol of the Val Knut in the dirt, and recited the Viking Prayer they taught me. Afterwards, I tossed their ashes into the water. I really can't put my finger on it, but it is as if Eirik knew all of this was going to take place, and asked me to stay for Asger's burial, so I can see what to do. Now at least they had someone to recite the words of the fallen for them. It wasn't much, but it was something. Then I recited a Cherokee prayer for the fallen.

I give you this one thought to keep,
I am with you still, I do not sleep,

I am a thousand winds that blow,
I am the diamond glints on the snow,

I am the sunlight on ripened grain,
I am the gentle autumn rain,

When you awake in the morning hush,
I am the swift uplifting rush,
Of quiet birds in circle flight,
I am the soft stars that shine at night,

Do not think of me as gone,
I am in each and every dawn,
Do not stand at my grave and weep,
For I am not there, I do not sleep,
Do not stand there at my grave and cry,
I am not there, I did not die.

I give you this one thought to keep,
I am with you still, I do not sleep,

It was uncanny the way Eirik and his brothers seemed to have some sort of innate knowledge about me, my abilities, and my journey with them. It was like I was predestined to meet with them, especially when the Valkyries appeared and expressed that they knew me. I had my doubts about angels up to that point. It was like a planned meeting to reassure my beliefs, and introduce me to Freyja, the leader of the Valkyries, and Kara, my supposed guardian.

It turned out that the Padogiyik or Golden Seven had more faith than I, but it's easier to believe in something when you're in close contact with it. I was so quick to pass judgment on them. Asku told me during our dreamscape, before I left Cherokee, to be careful not to prejudge, and that it would be hard for me to distinguish friends from enemies. Man, he was on point with that advice and prediction.

I didn't expect the Valkyries to show up in the cave during my prayer, besides I didn't have the Thorenson Weapons to summon them, nor the heavens above. This was now a tomb that harbored the memory of my friends and the evil that was destroyed. I had learned a lot from these brave brothers, and loss a lot this night. They were fighting in something bigger than the case that I was investigating; they were waging war against evil. I will mourn them and remember the way they lived.

This night displayed the paradox of my abilities, as a gift and a curse, more so than any other night. The very thing (energy crystal) that was supposed to save my life, placed me in jeopardy, and the absorption of energy that was supposed to end my life, saved it. There is no way Asku or anyone could have predicted this night. I'm surprised that I'm alive.

Once again, I was going at it alone. All my life all I wanted was to fit in and be a part of something, but it seems like fate has something different planned for me. Even as a shaman, I've discovered that I was different from other shamans. I had to accept the fact that I was never going to just fit in or be anything average. I was deeply saddened by the turn of events, as I looked over the cave for the last time, and it brought me back to my old saying, *"Within the chaos, there is always rhythm."*

The Abenaki tales or rumors weren't too far off from the truth. They said the spirit of the lake sent the Wendigo to take their children. I'm not certain if these creatures were wendigo, but they did come from the lake. Who or what sent them is still to be determined, but when I discover that answer, I'm certain it will point me to the real culprit behind it all. I dove back into the water, leaving that damned place behind me.

My ascension towards the surface was just as smooth as my descent through the wormhole. The boat was no longer anchored where we left it; I assumed the owner came for it. It was going to be a long swim back to shore in the dark lake, but it didn't pose a problem for me with all the stored-up energy I had absorbed.

When I reached the shore of the lake there were a few people on the pier. It was dark outside and judging by the night's sky I didn't have much longer before it became daylight. I shadowed my naked body, as I made my way to the vehicle. There was no way I was going back to the hotel naked. I couldn't properly shadow myself under the lights of the lobby, so I went to the only friend I had left in Swanton. I was naked and needed to get some clothes before the sun rose and the closest place to here was the village. I hated burdening Kateri in my predicament, but I didn't have a choice.

I drove to the Abenaki Village, and as usual, I parked the car, which seemed like a hundred yards away from the actual village, and walked. The mist-like fog was thick as ever in the village during the dark hours of the morning. I still didn't know what to call it, mist or fog, because it didn't seem to have any time constrictions upon when it appeared. It had a mind of its own and seemed to defy the natural laws of weather. I guess I'll just refer to it as the Abenaki, and call it Chibaiskweda.

You couldn't see more than 5 feet in front of you, as it blanketed the area. My energy crystal was the only light out this morning, glowing from the mysterious energy field that also shrouded the village. It assisted me during the dense Chibaiskweda, but it could do only so much in this soup. There was no one out in the village, and with the Chibaiskweda so thick, I didn't worry about shadowing myself while I walked naked through the village. It took quite some time to find her cabin. My panther vision couldn't assist me and the supernatural energy field prevented me from sensing her energy, but I found her residence.

I knocked gently on her door, so I wouldn't wake her neighbors. I was naked as a jaybird, with only the glowing crystal in my hand. I didn't worry about explaining it to her, I had more important things to figure out and my current condition would trump any questions regarding a crystal that glowed. I could easily say that it's a new camping device that uses the same glow-like substance in glow sticks that cave and scuba divers use.

Kateri stood in the middle of her doorway staring at me for several seconds. She gave me a very good look over before inviting me. There was no mention of the glowing crystal in my hand, as I thought. Her eyes were fixated on the naked man at her door in the wee-hours of the morning. She invited me in and provided me with a towel, and stated that she had some clothes that might fit me, as I waited in the living room with the towel temporarily wrapped around my bottom. She had a myriad of questions about how I ended up in this situation, but settled for the only answer I provided; that I was working on the investigation and ran into some trouble.

"I've laid some clothes out for you in the guest room, but you need to take a shower first, you smell like the lake. I left some items in the bathroom for you, as well," she said, and showed me to the rooms.

After showering I dressed in the clothing laid out for me. It was a lumber jack shirt or at least what I called the flannel type shirts with checked crisscrossing strips, a pair of blue jeans, and an all-weather, black duster with a hood, that had a black bandana in the pocket, and a pair of black boots. The clothes miraculously fit perfectly. It was obvious that she used to have a significant other that used to live with her or visited. I'm betting that it was Matunaagd Youngblood, who was identical to me in physique. I joined her back in the living where she had a cup of coffee waiting for me.

"The clothes fit perfectly, thank you very much," I said.

"I'm sorry, but I didn't have any undergarments for you to wear," she replied, smiling and handed me the mug filled with coffee.

"This is more than enough. I'm sorry to inconvenience you like this, but I didn't have anyone else to turn to. I'll return the items once I get back into town."

"Please don't. They're yours to keep. The person they used to belong to is no longer around, besides you'll need them if you are going to be wondering around these parts," she replied with a melancholy look.

It felt as if she was talking about someone that died or they were no longer seeing each other. Either way it seemed to make her sad discussing it, so I didn't inquire about it.

"*Thanks again. I really appreciate it,*" I replied.

"*It's not a problem; I told you to call me if you needed my assistance. I noticed that you were carrying something when you came inside,*" she inquired.

"*Oh, it's just a memento from a friend. I lost the neck rope wandering around tonight,*" I vaguely informed her.

"*I see,*" she retorted, and got up from the sofa, "*Well, you're welcome to stay here, if you like, before heading back down the highway, but I have to be getting up in a little while for work.*"

"*I think I'll take you up on that offer,*" I replied. I was tired after having a long day myself, and it was far from over.

"*You know where everything is located,*" she said, and placed her hand on the side of my face, staring into my eyes, and smiling, as she has done on previous occasion, and then departed for her bedroom.

"*Thanks, Kateri,*" I replied, as I watched her walk away. She looked back with a welcoming smile, and left her bedroom door open. I knew exactly what she meant. She was inviting me to join her, but left the decision to me.

I was tired after a horrendous night where I almost lost my life and lost several good friends. After Kateri went to her bedroom, I placed the coffee mug on the table and went to the spare bedroom and flopped down on the bed like a log.

While I slept, I was awakened by the silhouette of a bright light surrounding the contour of my door, as it appeared beyond the door, and when the door opened I could see the outer figure of a perfectly sculptured woman. As she came closer, and the light from behind her was drowned out, Kateri was standing in front of me, with her hair hanging down to her shoulders, naked and looking like a brown goddess.

I wasn't certain if it was one of my dreamscape affairs or real, but it felt real. She smiled and didn't say a word, as she lay on top of me in the bed and began kissing me. I was completely submissive to her charms, as my clothes came off one by one. It was like I was under a spell or something, but I wasn't trying to resist, it was pure bliss.

We had turned off the world this night and let the worries and problems of this realm escape us for a few moments of ecstasy. If I was dreamscaping it made it all the better, because I was all in. I not only wanted this, but I felt as if I needed it, like a hunger or addiction that I couldn't do without. I yearned for her with a deep burning inside, and made love to her over and over throughout the night. My animal side was awakened and the panther took complete control, as she accepted all I had to give with the same intensity and drive. We were locked like magnets with a force that I can't describe, a magnetic energy that surpassed any that I've ever experienced. It seemed beyond this realm of reasoning.

After exhausting each other, and sipping the last drop of energy from deep within, we fell asleep. I hadn't slept like this in years it seemed. I never knew this type of sleep as a boy or adolescent, the type of rest that could last all day.

I jumped out of a dream in the morning, and fell out of bed. I was naked on the floor of Kateri's spare bedroom. I thought I had fell asleep with my clothes on, but observed them scattered on the floor. They were the clothes she provided me when I arrived at her door step, nude, and after killing the beast of Lake Champlain. I dreamt of making love to her, but it was only a pleasant dream, at least I hope it was just a dream. I was distraught, exhausted, and mourning the deaths of my friends. Brothers who had taken me in as family. That was only part of my discombobulation this morning. I also dreamt of another barren deserted ghost town. This time the sign I discovered said Kanawha River Village.

It was well past noon when I checked the clock. I got out of bed and searched the cabin for Kateri, but she had departed. Then I saw the note on the coffee table that she had left.

"Good morning, Chris, and thank you for a lovely night. I enjoyed it immensely. I departed for work, and left some breakfast in the microwave for you; hopefully you don't wake too late for it. Have a wonderful day and I'll talk to you later, Kateri".

Damn! Her note confirmed everything that I was hoping didn't happen. I wasn't dreamscaping last night and my night spent with her really occurred. I sat down on the sofa after reading the note, and just ruminated about the cluster fuck that I was in, but I couldn't linger, because I was still in Swanton in an official capacity.

I pretty much wrapped up the investigation into the killings in the forest which included Agents Stone, and Wankaego, but how could I muster up a report about cannibalistic underwater cave dwelling monsters that look like Bigfoot with the ability to blend into the forest, like a chameleon. I was certain that I could tell Nina the truth about the case, but I was flustered about how to begin to tell her what occurred later this morning. I'm certain I could muster up a plausible excuse for the public about the Agents, but there was no excuse for what occurred between me and Kateri.

The only thing left now was the open case concerning the missing children of Swanton. Although there were bones of children in the underwater cavern of the beasts, my gut tells me that they aren't the culprits. They limited their attacks to the forest and there aren't any indications that they wandered outside of the forest. There aren't any mutilations outside of the perimeter of the Black Forest. In fact, the only crimes to take place outside of the forest were the abduction of the children and aggressive acts taking place as an aftermath, namely the citizens of Swanton versus the Abenaki. I believe that the supernatural energy that's been covering the forest and the village may have something to do with the missing children. My gut instincts just tell me that they're related.

CHAPTER SIXTEEN

NIXKAMICH

When I returned to the hotel I was looking forward to taking a long hot shower in my room and attempting to figure out the rest of this cluster fuck supernatural primordial shit that's been eating away at this town. I was still guilt ridden from what occurred at Kateri's. There was nothing more I'd rather be doing at that moment than in her arms, but now I wished to heaven that it never happened. I wished I could wash it all away, so I looked towards the water once again for redemption and peace of mind. It always seemed to relax me, and wash away the dirt of this world.

I immediately slipped out of my clothes and took a nice hot shower. I intended to be in there for as long as it takes. I was in no hurry to leave because I was in no hurry to face what I had to do next. I had to inform Nina of my infidelity. She needed to know about the rat that I am. Perhaps this was the sign or symbol that the owl was portraying to me when it perched on my window seal with that rat.

I couldn't hide this from her, especially when I connect with her during dreamscape, she would surely find out. What kind of a man would I be to even attempt to hide such a thing? I didn't want her to discover it that way, but I didn't want to callously tell her over the phone either. I was beyond confused about what to do, but one thing is for sure, she had to know.

Now all I could hear in the back of my mind were the words of Asku. He told me that I couldn't be with just one-woman due to the animal inside of me; panthers aren't monogamous. I worked so hard to prove him wrong, as many times as I turned down the advances of Kateri. I could blame it all on the fact that I was caught at a time when I was vulnerable from a near death experience and the loss of my friends, but most of the experiences I encounter with the supernatural could be consider as such. Although this time was a little different than the rest, I thought I was going to die.

The steam in the bathroom was thick as pea soup. I had been in there for at least an hour, soaking and sulking until my skin was wrinkled. I thought I had hit the bottom of depression before, but I must have found the sub-basement this time. I had infidelity on top of grief anchoring me swiftly to the bottom.

I didn't hear anyone enter the hotel room with so much on my mind, and lost in thought, but I heard the bathroom door open quietly. I thought perhaps they spoke, but I didn't hear them, due to my mind drifting off. Perhaps it's Agent Jackson concerned about me and let herself into the room because I didn't answer the door or maybe Kateri?

"Excuse me, but I'm in the shower," I informed the unexpected guest, but there was no reply.

The next thing I heard was the clicking of a round being chambered into the barrel of an automatic weapon, and then they fired into the shower several times. There was no place to run this time, and my speed couldn't assist me in this small space, as I felt each bullet piercing my skin and tearing their way through my flesh. Some burrowed straight through while others hit bone and fragmented, further ripping into my flesh.

I went down to my knees immediately from the initial shock. It felt like someone had jammed several small pieces of burning hot coals into my flesh. It stung tremendously, but it didn't hurt like I thought it would. In fact, I could feel the shrapnel moving and shifting inside my body, as if it was being pushed or pulled out. Blood was mixed in with water, as I watched them both swirl down the shower's drain like mixed syrup on an

Ice Cream Sunday. Then Agent Jackson burst inside the shower, stunned by what she observed, and stooped down inside the hot running shower. She didn't bother turning off the water as she got wet kneeling beside me.

"Don't worry Christian, stay with me; I'm going to get help."

She speed-dialed 911 on her cell phone for an ambulance. "Federal Officer down, I'm at the Swanton Inn, multiple gunshot wounds" she said, as we both looked at the bullet wounds spewing blood, and that's when to our surprise, we saw the most unusual thing occur. We witnessed the shrapnel being pushed out of the same wounds that they created. Astonished by what was taking place, she rubbed her hand over the holes in my chest and shoulder and within minutes they were healed without leaving a scar. It was as though it never happened. We heard the 911 operator on the telephone telling us that a unit was in route and requesting further information, but Agent Jackson just held the phone in her hand staring and examining the wounds, while rubbing her hands over my skin, several times.

"How in the hell is any of this possible?" she murmured, eyes wide open in astonishment.

"I don't know, this is as much a surprise to me as it is to you. This is the first time I've been shot. I guess it's the same, as the other supernatural things that I can do."

I attempted to get up, but she had me cornered, and wasn't trying to release me, as she continued staring into my eyes through the wet hair hanging partially over her eyes. Her t shirt was wet and exposing her hardened nipples. She had a late start and was just getting ready for her day when she responded from her room. Her pants were wet and tighter than they usually are and exposing the contour of her perfectly curved figure. Then we heard the 911 operator inquiring again for a sitrep of our situation.

"You'd better answer that before they get here." I informed her, still enamored and in a state of still life.

"But...what...should I say?" She stammered.

"I don't know, but I'd like to get out of this position before they or anyone else arrives." She didn't move, and continued to pin me down. "Carolyn, we have to move now," I told her and looked down at the telephone.

She immediately kissed me before I could say or do anything about it. I looked at her and cautioned her.

"I'm sorry Carolyn, but this isn't the place or time. Perhaps…"

"No, you're right, please forgive me, I don't know what I was thinking about," she replied, blushing from embarrassment.

"No, Carolyn, it's just…"

"I know," she quickly retorted and got on the cee phone with the operator while rising from the shower, "It was a false alarm. The Federal Officer isn't down."

"So, there's no need for an ambulance?" The operator inquired.

"No, there's no need for an ambulance." Carolyn replied.

"Ok, but I'll have to report this incident to the sheriff's office." The operator informed her.

"Ok, that's fine." Agent Jackson retorted, and hung up the phone. She closed her eyes and inhaled deeply after getting off the telephone, and exhaled slowly.

I had placed a towel on by the time she had finished and offered her a towel, as we both walked out of the steam filled shower. She asked me what had occurred and I informed her of the details. I could still see her visually examining me, but I wasn't certain if it was because of the intimate exchange we had or because of the anomaly with the gunshot wounds. My panther libido was still on overload after the kiss and I tried to hide it the best I could, but it was clear to me that she wasn't in a hurry to leave, so I politely asked her if we could resume the questioning after we both got properly dressed.

"Oh, yes, of course, excuse me, I'll let you get dressed and we'll resume this afterwards," she responded. Her face was blushing red, as she nervously fidgeted with her telephone which she was clutching since the shower.

I had a late breakfast with Agent Jackson and explained everything to her including what occurred the night before with Erik and his brothers. It was good having her available to talk to even though things became a little awkward earlier. I'm glad we didn't proceed with whatever we were about to do. I was already guilty and wondering if I could see Kateri again, I didn't want to drive away the only friend I had on the task force. We came to an agreement that I would keep her informed of my investigations while in Swanton, if she stops following me. It was for her safety, and she agreed. She realized after her encounter with the Mskagwedemoos and the Padogiyik that she was way out of her league in this investigation.

"So, do you have any idea who tried to kill you?" she asked.

"Yes, I do, but I thought he'd stop by now," I replied.

"Who are you referring to?"

"Mr. Winchester," I answered.

"Why does he want you dead?"

"He sees me as a threat to his kingdom. I may have roughed up a couple of his employees. He keeps sending them to kill me, and I keep sending them packing." I responded, laughing.

"You really are taking this lightly," she said with concern.

"Yeah, because I hate to think of the alternative and that it was a rogue FBI Agent, I mean there is a hotel filled with them, and not one responded to the gun shots fired, except for you."

"There were a few agents outside the door when I departed. I told them everything was alright, and it was just a misfire while cleaning your weapon," she replied, smiling.

"And they believed you? Everyone knows I don't carry a weapon."

"They didn't seem to care after finding out it was your room," she retorted with a giggle.

All I could do was shake my head, and we both began laughing at the same time. If it wasn't a rogue agent, then it had to be one of Winchester's henchmen payback. It didn't matter at the time because whoever it was would be in such a panic that I'm still alive I doubt they'll try it again. Besides, sooner or later it always comes out in the wash. After brunch, I telephoned Nina and briefed her on what really occurred with Agents Stone, Wankaego, and the others. She agreed to assist me with a plausible write up for the case, but I instructed her to hold off; I still wasn't convinced that all this wasn't tied together somehow. I informed her that I was going to remain in Swanton and dig deeper. She informed me that she would keep Steve abreast of my progress as well. I reserved telling her about my infidelity until this case was over and could tell her in person. I knew it would be just too much for either of us to deal with currently.

I decided that it was probably a good idea to revisit the resident medicine man of the Abenaki Village. I didn't have a clue where to start investigating the disappearance of the children, but perhaps I could pry something from Chogan's psyche. I waited until night fall to pay him a visit, and used my shadowing abilities to blend into the night, as I stealthily made my way towards his cabin.

When I arrived, I looked in the windows to see who was inside. His niece was in the kitchen preparing a meal, and he was in the living room, sitting in front of a television. I doubt if he had the capacity to watch it, but it was a nice gesture on her behalf. She was a good niece, and dedicated to her uncle. She was pretty, young and intelligent. She could have easily been somewhere else, instead of taking care of him, but she had a keen sense of family.

Chogan might be senile in this realm, but he might have a lot of knowledge to convey in the spirit world, at least that is what I was counting on. I remained shadowed as I entered the house unnoticed. I passed by Chogan and went to the kitchen where Tahki was located. I placed her in a sleeper hold that rendered her unconscious. Then I picked her up and placed her on the sofa in the living room. I didn't have much time, but time moves quickly in the spirit world. I wish there was another way to dreamscape with Chogan, but that energy field was blocking my communications in dreamscape, therefore I had to do a physical low jack, as I put it.

I placed a chair in front of Chogan's wheelchair and sat down. Nothing had changed in his demeanor since the last time I visited him. He still appeared to be in a vegetated state and repeating his name over and over, while rocking in his chair. I placed his hand in mine and began the procedure to dreamscape with him.

The walls of the cabins collapsed around us, and I found myself on a beautiful snow caped mountainside with a brisk wind whistling past my ears. There were snow flurries trickling down from the sky with a slight overcast. It was beautiful here. I smiled, because it reminded me so much of the Smokey Mountain Range of Cherokee, North Carolina, and the place that I was currently calling home. Although, I didn't summon my spirit guide, she was present. Ebony only appears when she senses danger, but it was placid and quiet here. I was looking forward to having an amicable pow wow with Chogan.

Then I saw him, but to my surprise, he was no longer in a wheelchair. He's probably been spending most of his time here, while in a vegetative state in the earth realm.

"You should not have come here, Cheveyo. There have been a lot of whispers from the other side about a Great Spirit Warrior with great things to do. They told of your arrival Half-Breed, but you are not needed here. Leave these affairs to the Sokoki," he said, standing upright without a wheel chair in sight. After all we were in dreamscape.

The old man wasn't senile at all in the spiritual realm. He was broken in the reality world, but here he was fit with all his faculties. He knew my Tsalagi name as well.

"I come here in peace, Chogan. I'm here to help the Abenaki in these times of great sorrow. I need to ask you about the mysterious energy cloud that has enveloped the village and the forest. I believe it is linked to the murders, and violence that has occurred here. I believe it holds the answers to the missing children," I informed him.

"You've been warned on several occasions to turn around, Half-Breed, this is not your concern; please leave these things to the Sokoki, or suffer the consequences," he warned me.

"But these things are my concern. I've been sent here to investigate this case by the Bureau of Indian Affairs. I've been sent here to bring an end to the violence, and make peace amongst the Abenaki and the people of Swanton," I advised him.

"You have been warned, Spirit Warrior." He said aloud, and raised his hands to the sky.

The thunder roared in the sky, and black clouds quickly rushed in to cover the sky. Then the mysterious mist, Chibaiskweda, came from out of nowhere, encapsulating us, and covering the entire mountain top. I was temporarily blinded by the mist, as Ebony growled, and then they appeared from out of the mist; several translucent beings. There were hundreds of them. I couldn't differentiate between them and the mist, where one began and the other ended. It appeared, as if they were one with it, as it moved mysteriously around them. This was one epic apparition, and within the midst of it, I saw several small, star-like, beams of light, shinning like pin holes in the thick Chibaiskweda.

The lights were different from the rest of the apparition; it was distinct and didn't waver in the mist as the translucent figures. I was amazed at what I was witnessing, it was magnificent! I could feel the power of the energy that it exuberated. It was the same supernatural energy as the mass that covered the village and the forest; they were one.

"Who are they?" I asked, in an astonished tone.

"Who they are doesn't matter. I've given you ample opportunities to depart. You were destined for something else. I'm sorry it has to end this way," Chogan replied.

He sounded sincere until he commanded the apparitions in Algonquian to kill me. My spirit guide and I took defensive positions, but the apparitions didn't move from their position. I could still feel their supernatural energy, but they weren't obeying his command. He yelled again, for them to attack, but nothing occurred.

"Why do you want to kill me, Chogan? I'm here to help the Sokoki," I said, and hearing me say it seemed like an old theme song of mine.

"You should not be here Spirit Warrior. What is happening here is for a good purpose," he snapped, angrily.

"So, you condone what is taking place here?" I inquired, curiously.

"This has to be done," he uttered, looking at the ground, and shaking his head slowly in a melancholy gesture.

Then, he ordered them again, in a firm and agitated voice to kill me, but the apparitions didn't move. It was apparent that he summoned them and at one time or another controlled them, but no longer. Since I first felt the presence of their energy it wasn't malefic in nature, yet, Chogan was asking them to harm me, which leads me to believe that they have done it before.

"What have you done, Chogan? What type of evil deeds have you had them performing for you?" I demanded.

"I only had them protect the village against those who would harm it," he retorted.

"Well, I guess they aren't listening to you today. It's clear to them that I pose no threat to the Abenaki or you, why can't you see that?" I asked him.

"Whatever good you think you're here to do will only be temporary, and then the village will be left unprotected again. Now prepare to leave, before it's too late," he barked.

"I don't want to fight you, Chogan." I warned him.

Then a mist of a different nature, black in color, surrounded him, like a funnel cloud. I could no longer see him, but I heard his agonizing cries. Whatever was happening to him wasn't pleasant, and when he stopped shrieking, the black fog dissipated. Then to my surprise, the old man was no longer old, but young, and virulent with the scarlet eyes of the Mskagwedemoos. It was quite clear that the Nixkamich was under their charm. His hair no longer scraggly and gray, but jet-black and long, as it sailed in the wind, as mine. The only distinction in our hair styles is that his was slightly longer, and adorned with feathers and beads.

He was wearing tanned buckskin pants, and the hide of a black bear with its head folded down his back like a hood. His chest was exposed under the bear hide with tattoos of symbols that I've never seen before. It was unclear what language or culture they belonged, but I would guess they were Mesopotamian or predated before that. Why he would be tatted like this is a conundrum. He also had bear pelt moccasins on his feet.

He was carrying a long wooden spear with several feathers. The spearhead was composed of the whitest, sharpest ivory I've ever seen. It seemed to have a translucent quality unlike any. There was a double headed tomahawk affixed to his waist, and something that I've never seen worn by the First Nation or any other. He had thick rope-like vines, creating a loop or ring on his back, and circled around his right shoulder, as it shifted and moved slowly like it was a snake. The vines reminded me of the ones I'd witnessed on the decrepit tree that led to the Mskagwedemoos cave.

This was no doubt his warrior attire while in the spiritual realm. I really wasn't up on the whole traditional costume thing; only the clothes that I wore before I came into the realm. I must admit the young Chogan looked fierce even without his weapons, but was he as skillful as me, in the spirit realm? I have the strangest feeling that I was about to find out.

He turned around with his head downward, and firmly planted his spear into the earth. Then he spoke in a low grimacing voice.

"I've given you more than enough warning, Spirit Warrior, now it's time you met your match."

I felt my spirit guide at my side without even looking. She was in the low ready position with her back hunched and ready to pounce. She only appears when I'm in dire need or summon her. Then she growled lowly, as I kneeled beside her. I placed my arm around her neck and began patting her the way she enjoyed.

"It's alright girl, calm down. I got this one," I told her, as her growls turned into purrs, and she sat down.

"I told you, I'm not your enemy, Chogan, but I don't think he heard me. He was now under their spell.

He quickly snatched his spear from the ground and attacked! The young warrior was fast, as he swung his spear with accuracy, cutting through the wind, as I quickly moved, dodging and blocking his attacks. We battled at lightning speeds. I could tell he was very skilled with the spear, but he was out of practice, and slower than I. He managed to cut me a couple of times before I dislodged the spear from his hands, and knocked him to the ground.

"I told you, I'm not here for this," I informed him, while on the ground.

He quickly flipped upon his feet, and from the squatting position, stretched out his right arm, pointed in my direction, and the animated rope-like vines quickly whirled my way with the force of a whip. Its speed was incredible, as it wrapped around me, before I could react. My arms and hands were tied down next to me to, like being tied to post. Then it became tighter, and tighter, squeezing me until I could barely breathe, as he held onto the other end.

My spirit guide was ready to attack at that point, when I instructed her to stand down. I just needed to concentrate. The vines were touching my hands and that's all I needed to drain its energy. The vines turned browned, and crumbled into dust; releasing me after I transferred its energy to my crystal. The animated vines remained wrapped around his right arm, ready to unwind. I didn't want to take Chogan's life energy; this is all he has left, being bound to that wheelchair.

"Please stop this, I don't want to hurt you," I pleaded with him.

He ignored my warning and picked up the spear. Its head began to glow, and then he shot an energy beam my way. The energy beam was a bluish color unlike the invisible energy from souls. I've heard of this energy in my spiritual travels, but this is the first time experiencing it. It's a form of plasma energy manipulated by ionized electrons.

I dove out of the way of the energy blast, just barely escaping its hit, but he didn't wait, and shot another while I was on the ground. I absorbed the blast, like any other surge that I've experienced. I wasn't certain what it would do; I've never been on the other end of being shot by an energy blast. It made me pause for a second or two, but I was fine, as my energy crystal began to glow from the transfer. The plasma energy wasn't as strong as the energy of souls.

He tried it again, except this time there was no pause in between from me. It took all the patience I had not to just fire back. Ebony's patience was coming to an end, as she began pacing, back and forth, ready to attack, but I had this under control. I had questions that needed answering, and I knew Chogan wasn't in his right state of mind. If the young warrior shaman had been practicing his skills, like I had been, over the course of years now, he might have been a formidable opponent.

I quickly rushed him, as he flung his vines, but my spirit guide intervened. She leaped into the air and snatched the vines within her teeth. She began pulling it like a game of tug-of-war that you would play with your large dog. She was having fun, as it threw Chogan off balance and gave me just enough time to tackle Chogan.

We wrestled for a little while, exchanging punches, but once again he was lacking in speed and skill. It was the comparison of an active warrior against one that was retired or a rookie. I put a good beating on him until he grew tired, but instead of quitting; he rolled towards the spear and threw it at me in a desperate attempt. I caught the energy spear, drained its power, and broke it in half. I'm not certain where he retained the ivory colored gemstone that stored the energy, but it was lacking also.

Even now, there was still no retreating for Chogan; he was possessed, as he charged with his tomahawk next. These witches had no remorse. I believe the Mskagwedemoos wanted me to kill Chogan because he was clearly defeated. He was exhausted and slow. I could have drained the life right out of him out of him, and ended this, but I needed some questions answered that only he could provide.

I swiftly side-stepped his attacked, and with the use of Irimi, I knocked him off his feet, once again, and took the tomahawk. This time, I jumped on him, and placed him in a bear hug. I was trying to put him to sleep, but was draining his energy in the process, so I pushed him away quickly before ending him. His eyes were no longer scarlet red, and had turned back to brown. Apparently, he was no longer possessed, as he lay on the ground before me.

"Have you had enough yet?" I asked, in a perturbed voice.

"Yes, I've had enough," he replied, holding his hand up in surrender.

"I don't want to harm you, Nixkamich, I came here in peace. I only want to ask you a few questions," I reiterated.

I thought perhaps if I called him by his honorable name and give him a level of respect; it would appeal to his sensibility. I didn't enjoy fighting him one bit. He stayed down this time, so I sat down in the lotus position near him, but keeping my distance. The apparition was still present, but wasn't communicating with me or Nixkamich. He sat in the same position, as I began to talk with a look of empathy on his face.

"You're the one that cursed the factory, aren't you? But that wasn't enough, was it? You brought this evil here, didn't you?" I inquired.

"I summoned them here to protect the village. I didn't know things would get so out of hand," he said, looking over at the apparitions, *"All was going as plan and..."*

Then my connection was abruptly cut off from Chogan in the spirit realm, and when I returned to consciousness in his cabin, I found him murdered in his wheelchair with blood flowing from his ears. I looked around him and his niece was no longer on the sofa. She had been abducted, no doubt, by whoever murdered Chogan. I checked his pulse to make sure and there was nothing. I looked around the house for clues, and then went outside. I didn't pick up on anything supernatural due to the energy field and didn't see or hear anything within miles with my panther senses, except the normal sounds of the wilderness. The blood flowing from the ears had all the indications that it was caused by a siren.

I telephoned the sheriff's department and called Kateri. She was the first one to arrive at the cabin. I told her that I came to speak to Chogan and discovered him in his wheel chair dead and his niece nowhere around, but her jeep still parked outside. The sheriffs appeared around the same time Youngblood did. I'm not certain who notified him, unless it was Kateri.

I tried answering all the initial investigative questions for the sheriffs, but Youngblood went into a tirade.

"Will this be another one of your cases that you just throw in the unsolved piles without even investigating the matter or can we get some justice? The First Nations People have been here thousands of years before your ancestors decided it was their right to occupy land that didn't belong to them, now we are the ones treated like we don't belong. We are minorities in our own land. If the crooked Winchesters of the world can buy justice, why can't we? I will promise you this. If you haven't found Tahki, and those who killed Chogan by the next full moon there will be retribution," he threatened.

"Are you threatening us," Sheriff Meehan, inquired.

"You take I any way you like, but by the full moon, there will be a reckoning," Youngblood blustered.

"That's it, arrest that man," Sheriff Meehan, commanded deputies.

"On what charge? "Kateri cried with tears in her eyes for the old man. She was also fed up with the treatment and disregard of the Abenaki.

"Threatening an officer of the law, obstruction of justice, and a public nuisance. Please don't make me arrest you also," Sheriff Meehan instructed Kateri.

"Is that how we get justice for someone murdering an Abenaki senior? Instead of finding the perpetrators, you arrest us instead? What's

wrong with this picture, Sheriff Meehan? What did we do to deserve such disrespect?" Kateri inquired wiping the tears from her eyes.

"Ok, you can join him in lock up. Now please remove them. This is an active crime scene," Meehan demanded, then looked at me, as if I was going to say something.

Then Kateri looked at me, and waited for me to say something to assist them, but there was nothing I could do. I didn't agree with the sheriff, but he had full jurisdiction over the crime scene, and they were civilians. They could be cited for everything he stated. I wasn't on good terms with the locals or the FBI, so I cooperated. Someone had to keep cool and bail them out. Besides, the sheriff and I will settle-up when this is all over.

CHAPTER SEVENTEEN
THE MALSUM

The next day I decided it was time for me to do some tailing of my own, and I started with my chief suspect. I tailed Youngblood for a full day checking out his routine and habits. Most of his day was spent at the tribal council conducting his duties as a council member. He didn't have two jobs like Kateri, who sat on the tribal council board, and was also the chief medical officer for the tribes. It was easy following him unnoticed in Swanton even with the mysterious supernatural shroud hovering above. I could sense him with no problems and shadow him when I needed. He made a couple of runs outside of the tribal council building, but it was business related to the council.

It wasn't until later that night that I followed him inconspicuously into the Black Forest, just short of the Abenaki Village. I was in the process of shadowing myself to follow Youngblood, and no soon as I did, I heard her voice scream from behind me, "Christian!" I turned around and saw Kateri, riddled with terror upon her face. I can imagine how this most look to her, half of me was shadowed and the other half was not. Unfortunately, I couldn't afford to stop to explain it to her, and risk losing the elusive Youngblood, especially when all my leads were running cold. I shook the visible portion of my head, left and right, with a sorrowful look upon my face before completely shadowing myself, and then continued to track down Youngblood.

I caught up with Youngblood using my shadow form and the cover of night to mask my image through the desolate forest. He had stopped a couple of times, as if he knew someone was following him, but he saw nothing. He looked right through me, as if he knew I was there. His instincts were keen, a little too keen. Perhaps I can get to the bottom of this mystery once and for all.

I followed him deep inside the forest, as he headed towards a glimmering light in the distance. I adjusted my panther's vision and observed a bonfire with several Abenaki men. They were covered from head to torso in red and black war paint, and wearing loosely fitted buckskin breechclouts, as they danced around the fire, chanting in Algonquian.

'With we who visit Ghosts
From the Sun Star of our birth
And in our Infancy which is from the Land of The Rising Star
As long as the Deer and Moose shall run free
And the Grass Shall Grow and the Rivers Run Swiftly
The Abenaki Shall Survive the Whiteman's Wickedness

And our Grandfathers Spirits
Have given us Guidance and Wisdom
To rise and come together to Dance
We have been taught to Love Mother Earth and to Respect Her
We are the Children of the Dawn
People of the East

May the Great Spirit and the Great Creator
Bless Us and Smile upon Us
May they be our guide, and our protector
May we forever walk this land with them by our side
To fight against those who seek to do us harm.'

In Algonquian, the chant sounded rhythmic and harmonious, like a beautiful song. Youngblood took off his clothes, placed on a breechclout, and covered himself in war paint before joining them in the ritual. They circled around the huge bonfire, chanting and dancing, as the timber cinders rose like stars to join the nebulous sky. Their eyes were the first to change into a deep amber color, like the eyes of the Gici Awas; the beasts of Lake Champlain.

Then the circle of men hunched their backs, and went down to their knees. They began crawling methodically around the bonfire, like animals, and then they began to shed their human skin, as their bones grew. It looked similar to the ecdysis process of a snake or molting of insects, but this this appeared to be more painful, as their chilling howls echoed throughout the forest. Just listening to them made the hairs on your skin stand up. Then their breechclouts dropped, as they shifted into enormously large wolves. These things were the size of bears! I've seen this done before with the Coyote, but never so gracefully in song and dance.

This explained a lot about Youngblood and the men of the Abenaki Village. The reason why they could see me when I shadowed myself is because they had other ways of knowing my location, like the wolves at Winchester's mansion. I thought it was time for me to get out of there, before they catch wind of me, but before I could turn around and depart, they were already heading my way. I didn't want to tangle with these wolves unless I had to, so I ran using all my supernatural speed, as they gave chase. I guess it's a canine thing, but they seemed to enjoy chasing me, as they howled behind me.

I ran through the forest towards my vehicle, but what good would that do, so I continued running. I wanted to run with the Malsum, as they say, to check out their strengths and weaknesses. I could hear their angry, man eating growls become louder on my tail. I should have outrun them by now with my supernatural speed, but they were right on my heels. Then one leaped from out of the dark abyss of the tree-line. Damn, for something so large they were fast! I've never seen a wolf that enormous in my wildest nightmares, as the Malsum emerged from their invisibility in the dark forest, racing towards me like a pack of stampeding buffalo.

These were no ordinary wolves, to say the least. I leaped into the nearest tree I could find. The Alpha tried doing the same, but only to fall from the first limb, as I made my way up to the top. The bottom limbs are the weakest; I've had lots of practice doing this back at home. They were big and fast, but not very agile, as I anticipated. I'll use this to my advantage.

They continued to follow me from the ground, as I leapt from branch to branch, tree to tree, in my attempt to escape, but they were steadfast in their pursuit. I must admit, this was exhilarating for me also, as my animal instincts kicked in. They split up, in an attempt to surround me, using stealth techniques. They were clever, but not clever enough.

They chased me through the forest until we came to some marsh lands on the eastern shore of Lake Champlain or the bogs as they call it here. It's filled with jagged and uprooted trees, stumps, and water that appeared shallow would drop 10 feet or more in one step. It contained mud-like quicksand and vines that would trap and entangle you sinking to the unfathomable depths. And that's just wat you can see, who knows what else lies beneath the water. These were the wetlands of the Missisquoi National Wildlife Preserve.

I just knew they would give up now. The reserve contained mud, snakes and hazardous terrain like a swamp with sharp sticks and trees coming from the bogs and no clear footage. They wouldn't be able to match my aerial game through this terrain.

The Malsum was relentless, and followed me through the preserve. They had adapted to the marsh-like terrain of the wetlands. You could tell they've hunted here on many occasions. They knew how to adjust their footing through the bogs. It was remarkable seeing them maneuver so swiftly through it with cat-like agility, but these were no ordinary wolves. Their size alone would mammoth any normal wolves. They could have easily been in the trees with me if it wasn't for their weight.

This is a strong Malsum, risk takers that were willing to follow their leader to the death, but their biggest strength lies within the pack and working together. I was having fun and stopped just short of the international boundary with Canada when I decided to call it quits. It was getting late and I had to get back. It was a wonderful reprieve, but I had my share of fun with the wolves for one night, even though they would have ripped me to shreds if they caught me. The wolves had a good scent of me now, but I had also learned a lot. They knew what I was capable of doing, but I wasn't worried about that. They've only seen me in retreat.

I would have easily suspected the Malsum of mangling the people in the forest, but I had already killed the beasts that caused that atrocity. Although I did have some questions for Youngblood, they could wait until later. I called upon the wind, and created a huge gust that caused the bottom branches and leaves to fall, and thus blocking their visual sight of me. This also temporarily prevented them from catching my scent from so far up, as I quickly departed. I felt no closer to finding this supernatural being than when I came to Swanton. I just knew for certain that it was Youngblood, but it wasn't shifters that I was after.

The next morning, I visited Kateri to explain what had happened to me. She didn't go on her rounds today and was still in her cabin, distraught and confused about what she saw. She didn't know what had happened to me, and feared the worst. As she opened the door and stared at me with quizzical eyes filled with tears.

"Hello, Kateri, I know you have a lot of questions." I said, but she didn't say a word and hugged me immediately.

"What happened to you? I saw you there one minute, and then you were gone, just vanished. I tried calling you, and looking for you, but I didn't want to go too far into the forest. The sheriffs are arresting people for entering in the forest. What was that? What are you?" She interrupted, hysterically with tears drowning her dreary and terrified eyes, as she held on to me for dear life.

"I am a shaman like we previously discussed. We call it shadowing," I told her, calmly, attempting to ease her fears.

"I've never seen any shamans do that before, I mean it is believed that they practice shape shifting and animalism, but only demons display shadowing skills, as you've displayed. We were under the belief that dream

walkers transverse the spiritual realm and the realm of the living freely, but never physically turning into shadows." Her voice trembled.

"Yes, I keep hearing that I'm unique, but this is all still relatively new to me." I smiled.

Then she let go of me and surprisingly began hitting me on the chest. They were only light punches, but hard enough to let me know that she was overly angry at me, but it was just the stress from fear that she was displaying. I let her continue until she finally stopped and broke down crying in my arms. I held her gently in my arms and attempted to calm her. After several minutes of crying, I assisted her in wiping the tears from her eyes. Then she placed her hand up to my face, as I have been accustomed to her doing now and stared into my eyes once again with those gorgeous big brown eyes. I thought I was going to melt at that point, and then she hugged and squeezed me as tight as she could.

We talked for over three hours, as I went into details, explaining my origins, dreams and experiences since a child. She prepared a small brunch for us, and afterwards she hugged me once again, before I departed. I didn't go into any details about Chogan's murder, because it was an ongoing case, but I assured her that I would be investigating it personally. I also didn't share the details about Youngblood and the Malsum's shape-shifting. She had been through enough shock and awe from the supernatural, compounded with Chogan's death, and getting arrested.

I think what I experienced at Chogan's was the break in the case that I was looking for, so I decided to go back to his cabin to see if I could make a connection with the Abenaki ancestor's, as Chogan called them. The spirit world was something that I was well versed in. The visions of light that I saw amongst the Abenaki Apparitions were the souls of the living, surrounded by the Abenaki. These could be the souls of the missing children. The one thing that I did realize is that they were one with the ominous supernatural energy field, which would account for its potency. There were literally hundreds of them, if not thousands.

The supernatural energy field was still covering the forest and the Abenaki village, as I drove through in route to Chogan's cabin. When I arrived at the cabin the police tape was still up and blocking the door. No one had been inside since his murder. The police were still looking for his missing niece, and had no suspects or clues. They didn't know if she was a victim or their lead suspect. The supernatural energy field was still present here as well.

The place looked the same as when I was last here, including the blood on the floor. I smelled the rot coming from the refrigerator even with the door closed. All utilities were still on in the cabin, but certain items perish even in the refrigerator after a while. I don't think this was something that a normal person could have smelt with the fridge closed. It was my heightened panther imprinting assisting me again.

I looked around the cabin for a little while. I didn't need to touch anything because I already had a connection with Chogan from our last dreamscape, but I wasn't certain if it would work without him being present and the supernatural energy field present. I was surprised that I could jump start my connection with him the last time in its presence. It was as if either he or the entity wanted me to discover what I now knew.

I meditated for hours, as I transverse the veil of the spirit world, but I didn't make a connection with Chogan or the Abenaki ancestors that I saw during my dreamscape with him. I didn't have a clue on how to bridge the gap and communicate with them. Then something caught my eye. It was like the mother of all epiphanies. The paintings on the wall of the cabin were more than just impressionistic art, as I slowly walked around the cabin, astonished and methodically examining them. Each one of them had a message to display.

The painting about the Black Forest and the mist is about the Abenaki ancestors that I'm currently trying to reach. The painting of the phoenix or birds on fire is actually the ravens that attack me, and I had to burn them. The women dancing and singing in the forest amongst the black leaves are the Mskagwedemoos that emerged from the leaves. The Angels over the graveyard are the Valkyries at the Viking Funeral, and how could I miss those damned amber colored eyes of the beast, Gici Awas in the cave! I thought they were stars in the cave.

Then there's the picture that I purchased with the Warrior, the leopard, the bear and the wolf. I see this painting every day in my room, and didn't catch it until now; this was my dreamscape conflict with Chogan. It was all here, before it even happened. Tahki was gifted indeed, not only as a magnificent painter, but as a seer. I should have probed and questioned her further. All the energy that was being emitted from the cabin; I thought it belonged to Chogan, I didn't sense any other energy signatures. That damn energy shroud is really making this case difficult for me.

Damn, I wished I would have known this before she was abducted; I would have loved to talk to her. I'd probably have this thing wrapped up by now. I just hope she's still alive. Whoever has her needs to pray that I get to them before the full moon. Then I turned to the unfinished painting on the easel of the wolves running under the full moon.

"Unfinished indeed," I said, verbally to myself. Then I heard someone approaching outside in the distance. I couldn't sense them due to the supernatural energy field, but that didn't prevent my panther imprinting from hearing them.

I hurried to peep out the window. He had my scent now; in fact, he had it since the first day we met at the tribal council. That's how he always knew where to find me. This day was no different than the rest, as Youngblood approached the cabin. I understood how I couldn't detect his supernatural energy at the village and at the forest, they were all places that the mysterious energy field had surrounded, but how was he able to mask his supernatural energy at the tribal council? I would have noticed his energy signature there on the many occasions.

Oh, I got it; he always left the council before I did. They have set up runes around the building, most likely protection and masking spells. I wanted to shadow myself and see exactly what his interest was in the cabin, but what good would that do? He already knew I was here and he would smell me regardless. It was time for us to sit down and have a heart to heart conversation.

He quietly approached the cabin in his routine manner. I've lost count on how many times he's tried to sneak up on me. He didn't understand the full potential of my abilities. He peeped inside the window first, to see what I was doing. I was sitting in one of the chairs in the cabin staring at the door when I invited him to come in.

"I was just thinking of you. Please come in Matunaagd," I instructed him without looking at the window. This time he didn't hesitate and walked towards the door and came inside. Never once did he question how I knew he was present. *"What are you doing here?"*

"It is customary for the council to look after the property of the Abenaki who have no surviving relatives. The property passes on to the council, in order to keep what little land, and property that we have in the hands of the Abenaki. I'm just here to check on it," he answered, staring curiously at me. I'm certain, he wanted to ask me about last night, but he waited for me to topic the discussion, but I wanted to play with him for a minute, as I did in the forest.

"So, you're already counting Tahki as being deceased," I inquired, to catch him off guard.

"No, I'm not, but just in case the sheriff's department decide to do their usual which is nothing, I want to be prepared," he answered, and walked towards the window.

"You mean like when the next full moon rises. Isn't that what you told Sheriff Meehan?" He just stared out the window without saying anything, so I continued.

"It has become more than just a coincidence of you running into me outside of town, Youngblood, why don't you tell me why you followed me here?" One side of his mouth curled upward, in the slyest grin, and his eyes closed slightly, as if squinting.

"I'm not the only one guilty of this. You followed me into the forest the other night when I met with the Sokoki." He replied, with a pompous sort of pride, as he sat in a chair opposite of me.

"It is part of my job to follow and investigate potential suspects," I told him.

"Well, I'm here to make sure you don't try to implicate any Abenaki for this or any of the murders that have occurred near the Abenaki Village," he responded.

"So, you call yourself policing the police or are you just making sure I don't come across any incriminating evidence that might link you to these crimes?" I inquired with raised eye brows.

"Neither you nor the sheriffs have anything on me or any of the Abenaki they gathered up. That's why you had to release us," he grumbled.

"You keep associating me with them. Don't you recall they escorted me into the station with handcuffs on?" I asked, as he chuckled.

"Yeah, I guess it doesn't matter what side of the law you're on if you're Native."

I could see the tension on his face begin to ease from the squinched up wrinkles that gathered on his forehead and seem to pull in his eyes, eyebrows and nose into one tense scowl that faded.

"You know that's the first time you've referred to me as a Native, instead of something less charming," I replied with a smile, and repositioned myself in the chair for the next question I was going to ask. "I've been meaning to ask you why you sent those men to kill me at the village."

"I didn't send them. When we showed up they were still half-crazed and with dilated pupils, like they were possessed. That's when we shifted and picked up your scent. The Malsum wanted to attack, but I told them to stand down," he answered.

"Why did you do that?" I inquired.

"I wanted to get more information about you." He grinned, leaned back in the chair, and folded his hands behind his head.

"And you've been following me since or only when I show up at the village or forest perimeter? If you showed up outside of that, I would have sensed you," I said.

"You were the only one seen when the Abenaki were possessed. I didn't know what you were capable of." He replied, and shrugged his shoulders.

"And the beast of the lake, did you know about that?" I inquired.

"Everyone knew about the killings, but if you're asking me if I know what is doing the killings, then yes, it is Gici Awas," he said.

"And you did nothing to stop it." I snapped, as I shook my head in displeasure of his inaction.

"As I said during our last conversation, it wasn't killing Abenaki. My people have lived on the lake with the Gici Awas for generations, unharmed. We hunt in the forest, and fish in the river and lake. It was the factory that angered Gici Awas and brought it out of the lake."

"Look, I think we got off to a bad start. I think we both want the same thing here, to catch whoever is behind these murders, and to ease the tension between the Abenaki and the town's people, correct?" I said to him.

"No, I'm only interested in the security of the Abenaki," he selfishly replied.

"But the security and of the Abenaki is predicated on clearing them on any suspicions of murder and catching this killer," I informed him.

"What are you proposing?" he asked.

"I'm not saying we work together, but there is a way you could help me," I told him.

"And how is that?" he asked, curiously.

"What is the most sacred place of the Abenaki ancestors?" I inquired.

"The Sacred Forest is the burial grounds of the Dawn's People," he replied.

"And where is the Sacred Forest?"

"You refer to it as the Black Forest. This is what the white man called it, since their children were taken and their men murdered in the forest," he replied.

"Is there one particular place within the forest that is the most sacred?" I asked.

"Yes, the sacred springs. That is where the burial ceremonies took place," he informed me.

"You mentioned the Dawn's People? Who are they?" I retorted.

"This is the true name of the Abenaki. We are considered the People of the Dawn because it is said that our ancestors would appear in the mist of the dawn and disappear within this same mist. You will find this mist at the ceremonial site just, as it was in the beginning, but your time is running out," he warned me.

"What do you mean?"

"Kateri informed me that Winchester and the townspeople plan on marching to the Abenaki village with guns two days from now."

"When did she tell you this, and why didn't she just come to me with it?" I asked

"Perhaps she was afraid you'd side with them, like you did when they arrested us," he complained.

"That's not what I was doing. We needed calm and rational heads, at the time. The both of you were too emotional, and that would have led to something neither of us could come back from," I replied, "How did she find out about this any way?"

"I don't know, probably from the clinic in town," he said.

"Look, I'll give the directions to the Sacred Springs, but I'm telling you this as a warning. If an armed mob comes to harm the Abenaki, the pack will kill them all, and then go into the town and do what they set out to do," Matunaagd threatened.

"I'm certain it won't come to that," I replied.

"Coming from the man who was rounded up and arrested like the rest of us. Excuse me if I don't hold my breath, and wait for optimism to prevail. The time for talk is over!" He bellowed.

"You don't believe that or you wouldn't be here, right now, telling me this," I informed him.

"If they show up at the factory to march on the village, they're dead, along with the town!" He reiterated.

I wonder why Kateri didn't come to me first with this. Was she upset with me? This is the longest conversation that I've ever had with Matunaagd. It was well over due and enlightening. I had gained his respect and trust. Even if I could divert Winchester's mob from attacking the village, if Tahki isn't found and Chogan's killer isn't brought to justice, my gut feeling tells me that the Malsum is warming up for something big, supernaturally big!

He gave me the directions to the Sacred Springs, and wanted to come with me. I informed him of the ramifications if something occurred and he was present, as a potential suspect. The FBI would only blame him. I remembered driving on Spring Road when the FBI Agents were following me. I pulled off the road to follow the directions of the murders in the forest, but didn't continue. For the first time, I was feeling positive about this case. I had directions and solid Intel. I couldn't wait to get started and drove immediately out to the springs.

CHAPTER EIGHTEEN
THE HANGING TREE

Spring Road was just like the other rural paved roads outside of Swanton, it stopped several miles before I got to my destination, and gave way to a forest trail that you could hike on foot or continue with an ATV. Once again, I was left to hike the road. I wished I had known about the roads here when I landed in Burlington. It is a thriving urban city, miles away from Swanton, and its rustic community.

The paranormal energy field wasn't any different in this part of the forest as the rest. It was just as thick, as I walked in the directions that Youngblood had given me. After about 15 minutes of walking, I heard children coming from the east end of the forest. There shouldn't be anyone camping or picnicking in the forest, so I paused and listened for a little while longer. Then, I saw children running in the nearby tree line. I hurried over, and followed them into the forest. I had to warn their parents of the potential dangers of being in the forest. The beasts were dead, but whatever had summoned them and whatever was possessing people was still out there, not to mention this mysterious energy apparition that I now believed belonged to the Dawn's People.

I continued following the sounds of the children into the forest. I could hear them and see them sporadically running and playing like children do. They had me chasing them in circles until I realized that I had followed them for at least a half a mile in the opposite direction of the springs, and I wasn't getting any closer to them. This was only a ruse, a supernatural vision or apparition, to lead me away from the springs. I could only smile at the attempt because they really had me going. I would have sensed this under normal circumstances, but this paranormal energy veil that the Dawn's People casted over the forest suffocated my supernatural senses.

I turned around and ignored the apparitions, as they continued trying to tempt me into going in the opposite direction. I heard the laughter of the children and saw visions of them. I regained the ground that I had lost, but not the time. As I continued walking, and I saw something in the trees ahead of me. It was on the way, so perhaps it wasn't another ploy to distract me. As I got closer, I realized what was in the trees, and I rushed over to them. There were several children with ropes around their necks, hanging from the trees. When I arrived to rescue the children, they turned into corpses, as rotting flesh began falling from their bodies.

Once again, I bent over to my knees, to catch myself from vomiting. This was not a day for holding down my supper. This tree was truly possessed. Then the rotting corpses of the children hanging from the trees began to speak to me.

"Turn around, turn around and leave now, before it's too late."

I've lost count at the number of times I've heard this warning since I arrived in Swanton. Then, as I turned to leave this wretched tree, I saw visions of Native Americans hanging from the tree, and then the visions switched to runaway slaves from the past hanging in the tree. I felt their pain and despair, as they hung there, and then suddenly, I found myself hanging from the tree. I couldn't breathe or speak, as I began to choke; dangling, kicking, struggling and squirming for air, as the noose tightened around my neck, using my body weight to strangle me.

I passed out, and thought I had died, but woke up standing next to the tree inside of another ghost town. I didn't have to look hard to figure out my setting this time; I was standing in the Lost Village of Roanoke, according to the sign hanging across the entrance. I knew the story of the lost colonist just like everyone else in North America.

The village was barricaded with a 10-foot-high, wooden post fence, like a fortress. It was erected to prevent the colonist from being attacked by hostile Native Americans. The first point in question is the name, Native Americans, which meant this is their home, their lands, and you are either an invited guest or you were trespassing on their lands.

The British colonist invaded the Native American people's land and created colonies without the permission of its tenants. They just boldly came in, staked lands and erected fortified colonies, as if it was their inherited right to take other people's land, and wondered why the Native Americans were hostile against them.

This was the fourth or fifth ghost town that I've visited since investigating this case in Swanton, and following the mysterious events leading to its resolution. I departed from the tree, and walked through the village, knowing fully well what to expect, the question is why these places? What is the significance of these places, besides being ghost towns?

The village was deserted like the others, except this time I was confronted with visions of black families hanging from trees; men, women and children, just as I was hanging. These were the Black Freedman that occupied Roanoke after the civil war. This is the Roanoke story that you never hear about, the one that remains hidden from the history books.

The island was given to Black Freedmen by decree of the Department of North Carolina and General John G. Foster in 1863 after the emancipation, but President Andrew Johnson abolished that decree two years later with the Amnesty Proclamation and ordered the return of the lands to the Southern Plantation owners.

Some of the Black Freedmen refused to leave their homes and community which they had built for several years. That's when the Southern Plantation Owners raided their homes and hung entire families to reclaim the land. My heart was filled with sadness viewing these atrocities. Although, these images were true; I know it was just something trying to get inside my head, a ploy by these demons to catch me off guard.

When I returned to the tree, I hadn't noticed the infamous engraving carved into it when I arrived, but it was there now. You couldn't miss it, on the tree, sitting in the middle of the town, or was it just placed there by my current hosts. The etchings were CRO, and many historians believe it to mean CROATOANS, but this would mark the end of my history tour, as the demons ambushed me.

This seemed to be a reoccurring theme since I've been in Swanton. I had adapted to fighting these demons, and it was becoming easier each time. My energy crystal was shining, and ready for battle, as I rolled up my sleeve, and prepared myself for another battle with demon horde. I continued using the principles of Aikido; Ki and Irimi, to vanquish the horde, but there were even more of them this time than before. They'd learnt from their previous battle, and brought in an army, as I attempted to fight them off.

There were just too many of them this time, their numbers never diminishing as they attacked with full vengeance. They had overwhelmed me like a tsunami claiming it spoils. The horde piled on me until you could no longer see any signs of me beneath the insidious mass. Yet, at the bottom of this pile-up, I was absorbing their energy, and turning them into ash, at a phenomenal rate. Then the mountain began to shift, jerking downward in paused sequences, until I could no longer safely absorb any more energy. Then I unleashed it all in one blast of light!

It resembled an atomic blast being ignited, as I obliterated the horde in one swift strike. Their black ashes fell from the sky like a volcanic eruption, as I emerged from the blast covered in black ash, from head to toe. The ash covering me was thick as mud, and you couldn't make out my face beneath its mask. My crystal was drained of energy, and so was I. There were no signs of any demons or any other supernatural presence, as I looked around, took in a deep breath, and exhaled slowly.

No soon as I relaxed, and thought it was over, I found myself gagging, and kicking while hanging from that twisted macabre tree off the road leading to the Sacred Springs. I literally didn't have anything left in the tank. Perhaps this was the intent or battle strategy of the demon horde from the start; to wear me down with numbers until I tire and use all my energy.

I was ready to clock out, and then I saw the Dawn's People in the distance. The noose broke, and I fell from the tree to the ground. I wasn't certain if they initiated the noose breaking or if they were just bystanders. Then I realized that I was standing near them, and viewing them from outside of my body. I thought I was dead for sure. My spirit had innately separated from my body. It is what people say they experience when they die and come back to life. I was like an apparition, myself. Unlike my travels to the spiritual realm or noumena world, I was here, in the realm of the living, the phenomenal world

I looked over and observed myself on the ground with the demon spawn surrounding my body and strangling me. I felt helpless watching them do as they pleased with me, yet I felt energized like I've never felt before. It was different from the energy from the crystal which was still depleted. Then I realized that I was thinking like a helpless human without any control of the spiritual realm. I was ready to rush over and reunite my body and spirit, but paused to ruminate. Why was I in a rush to reunite my body, and spirit, when I was already charged up and ready to go? These demons aren't the only ones who can possess. I'll just enter inside of them while in this ghost form and destroy them. Now this is going to be fun!

I entered these demons with ease. This is something they never expected, and never saw me coming. I ripped through them like a hurricane ripping through a shanty town, feasting on their energy, and destroying them from the inside. They only wet my appetite, as I hungered for more. This was a thirst that I've never known before. It was different than the emotional rage I feel when I summon fire. It's a craving similar to a heroin addict in need of another fix, an insatiable vampiric appetite. Then I observed more children falling from their nooses, and turning into demons. There were scores of them falling like leaves in the autumn, or grapes from a tree to satisfy my hunger.

The Dawn's People had disappeared, and my energy crystal remained depleted from my previous battle, but I didn't need them any longer. All I could feel was the thirst to devour more demons. The macabre tree was now an oasis to me, as I rushed towards it, like a man in a barren desert. I took the liberty to gluttonize myself on the horde, but still couldn't satisfy this unquenchable thirst, as I waited under the tree for more. I was now the savage, feasting on evil, and when nothing else fell from its limbs, I jumped into the tree and shook it in a mad rage.

After several minutes of shaking and scavenging the tree, I fell from its limbs onto the ground. I was sick now, like an addict experiencing withdrawals. It felt as if my blood was boiling, and thousands of needles were prickling my insides, as uncontrollable, painful cramping clawed into my muscles, twisting and tightening them as if strangling my blood flow. I was bawled into a fetus position, helpless and in pain. My body was still separated from my spirit, and I felt I could never go back, as the cold set in. My body had been without spirit too long.

Then the thick mist moved in again, and covered both me and my lifeless body. I didn't see the Dawn's People this time, but I could feel their presence; it was warm and soothing. The chill had left my body, and I discovered myself reunited with my spirit. I felt refreshed again, and my energy crystal restored. Now I know how the other side feels; the pain, and the hunger. Is this what they wanted me to feel? I never really thought about it until now, but all those years when I was dreamscaping, and imposing my will upon others; it was like a mild form of possession. Now I was the one possessed. Where do I begin to atone for that depravity?

My head was spinning from all the knowledge and experience that I was learning from the Dawn's People in such a brief time; brief in reference to the world of the living. Although, I still didn't receive the answers that I was looking for.

I stopped and refocused myself, while meditating under the tree. I had traversed the realms of this world and the spiritual world, but not completely committing to either. I had brought both worlds to me as these demonic apparitions were doing. This is what the Dawn's People bestowed upon me when they separated me from my body. It was something that I didn't even know I could do until now. It was a lesson in humility; wrath, greed, sloth, pride, lust, envy, and gluttony; the seven sins. I had to keep myself in check, and remain humble, even when fighting evil or it can seep in without your knowledge of it, like what happened to Chogan.

In the words of Nietzsche:

"He who fights with monsters should be careful lest he thereby become a monster. And if thou gaze long into an abyss, the abyss will also gaze into thee."

The tormentor becomes the tormented. People become what they love and hate, because their mind focuses on it, and the hall of mirrors fold in on itself. I also learned now from my experiences with the Dawn's People that they only appear to me in the spiritual world. They manifest themselves as the Chibaiskweda, but I've only been able to see them in the noumena realm. They have shown me the path to reach them. I must view them in a ghost-like medium or spiritual medium, yet remain on the path.

I had traveled freely between both realms since I was a child, but this was different, as I blended them as one. It took me a quite some time to achieve this medium. In the spiritual world time passes at an enormously faster pace, than in the phenomenal world, hours spent in the spiritual world seems like only a few minutes in the phenomenal world. This phenomenon also explains why supernatural beings move so much faster in the phenomenal world.

It was amazing seeing the two realms blended together as an apparition would view it. I thought my experiences in the spiritual world with my spirit guide were amazing, but this was incredible, and when I opened my eyes Ebony was right there by my side. She was experiencing this right along with me. I saw the psychedelic colors of the different energy fields from both realms blending like watching a kaleidoscope or some LSD trip. It was like I was sleepwalking, but being fully aware of what was going on. Now I saw everything as it truly was, including the apparitions.

This moment made me think that all the experiences in my life had a purpose, the sleepwalking and the dreams were preparing me for all of this. I was growing and learning new things about myself each time I interacted with supernaturals, I was evolving.

I kneeled and hugged my panther spirit guide after adjusting to this new state of existence, and then I continued traveling on the right path with my panther guide accompanying me. I didn't have to tell her what to do; we shared a psychic bond. She was guarding my flank, but having fun ridding the tree lines of the nuisance apparitions, as she did previously with the giant-sized raven. She always turns up when I really need her. Until now I had the demons under control, and didn't need her assistance, but she's here now to protect me, even from myself.

When I reached the springs, it was more than what Matunaagd had described. He didn't see the colorful energies of both realms as I saw it. I was evolving, yet something deep inside of me wanted to view the springs just as an ordinary man would see it. I couldn't really share this incredible event with anyone and have them feel what I was witnessing. That was one of the greatest things about being a man, being able to share his emotional experiences, his soul.

I sat in front of the springs for the longest time admiring its beauty, and observing the magnanimous supernatural energy being emitted from the springs. This was the hub of the supernatural energy that shrouded the Abenaki Village and the forest. They didn't communicate with me the entire time I was there. I didn't understand it, they had so much to impart on me while I traveled here, but nothing now. It had been a long day and an even longer journey getting here. I was tired and decided to resume tomorrow, now that I knew how to void all the distractions.

I spent the rest of the night in dreamscape with Asku and my spirit guide. Their advice was to just approach the Dawn's People just as a normal man would. They informed me that I might have scared off the Dawn's People. I didn't know about the later suggestion. I can't conceive such an entity with so much power being afraid of anything.

The next day I had my spirit guide accompany me to the springs, and then I approached by way of only one realm, the realm of mankind. Now I got the chance to experience what Matunaagd and others experienced when they visited the springs. It was just as beautiful, and tranquil, as I watched the cool of the waters splashing against the white rocks of the springs. This was truly a sacred place.

This place felt like it had a soul of its own. It reminded me of what Kateri had told me about the forest being haunted, and you can watch all the seasons move by in minutes. It wasn't quite like that, but it was hard to tell which season you were in, it was as if they were all wrapped up into one. The water wasn't too warm or too cold, it was cool and refreshing. The water gave off the mysterious mist that I've seen countless times before, as it covered the area. The mist seemed to give faces to the rocks that changed randomly, as the mist moved upon them. It was like watching an amphitheater slide show. They were most likely the faces of the Dawn's People.

The mist would indicate that the water was like a hot spring and the surrounding temperatures were cool, but that wasn't the case. The temperature was mild like an autumn day, but there were no leaves falling or any indications of the dying effects of the foliage during autumn. Everything was green like a summer day, and yet when I touched the rocks they were cold like the ice of winter. I've never witness a more utopian climate than this. Now I just had to contact the Dawn's People.

I sat down in front of the springs, as before, in the lotus position, and attempted to summon the Dawn's People. It didn't take long before I received a response. The waters of the spring turned black as tar, as it began to spread over the white rocks, engulfing them, and then on to the ground. I got up quickly watching the thick black tar swallowing the grass, the dirt and everything in sight, as it moved swiftly like the rapids of a raging river.

Then I began to smell this putrid odor. The stench was unbelievable, as it reached down my throat like a hand grasping my gag reflexes. It seemed as if everything inside of me wanted to just rush out. My eyes were watered with tears, as I vomited and fell to my knees. The black tar crawled upon me and began to blanket me in its thick goo. I panicked, struggling to get it off, and free myself, but the thick black resin was too heavy. It clung to me like amber, and slowed down my movements until I couldn't move at all.

It crawled fastidiously upwards to my face, and entered my mouth. I began choking and experiencing extreme convulsions and pain. My veins protruded from the uncovered areas left on my forehead, as I gasped for air until it completely covered me, and I passed out.

I woke up on the ground, once again balled up in a fetal position with watery eyes. There were no signs of the black tar on me or anywhere to be found. Everything in the forest was normal. I would have thought this was a dreamscape implanted in my dreams, but I was wide awake up to the point of the event. Then there was the one undeniable fact of the occurrence which I was covered in, my own vomit. I was dealing with something that I had never faced before and was unprepared. I'm not certain how long I was unconscious, but the sunset was approaching, and I decided to call it day. This was another battle that I had to chalk in the lost column until tomorrow. At least I made a connection. It wasn't the connection that I was looking for, but it was something.

The next day I went at it again. This time when I sat down to communicate with the Dawn's People, hundreds of hands emerged from the ground, attached to nothing but arms, from what I could see. The hands grabbed my legs first, holding me down, as I struggled once more to release myself from their clutches, but I couldn't pull them off, not even with my strength. Before I knew it, there were hands tugging at my shirt and pulling backwards on to the ground. I was pinned to the ground, as the hands held down my head and body. Then they began to strangle me until I passed out.

Again, I woke up hours later, still feeling the effects of being choked out, yet it felt like they were killing me and reviving me each time, instead of being knocked out. I was angry, and tired of this merry go round of horror, and couldn't wait to get back to my hotel suite to have a one on one with Asku and my spirit guide.

Back at the hotel I immediately dreamscaped with Ebony, the black panther. As soon as I arrived in my default realm, the rain forest, all my anxieties and stress faded. This place always seemed to take it all away. When I was here and with my spirit guide I felt secure, as if nothing could defeat me or harm me. Sometimes I wished I could stay within this realm forever, but it was only a place to visit for me. Until death comes for me, my duties lie within the realm of the living.

I sat beside the panther and caressed her soft velvet coat and placed my head upon her back and listened to her purring. I could never get enough of the sedative feeling that it brought to me, clam and relaxing. Then after my short bonding spell I consulted in her. She was my war consigliore. She counseled me in times of battle and confrontation, as well as the spirit world. We communicated through a type of telepathy or bind bonding as I called it. There were never any vocal words passed between us, but I heard her loud and clear, as she heard me.

"I need console on how to communicate with the ancestors of the Abenaki. I believe the lights among the apparitions are the souls of the living, the children of Swanton," I informed her.

"Perhaps you are going about this in the wrong manner. Instead of fighting them maybe you should surrender yourself to them," she replied.

"Surrender myself to them? What good would that do?" I asked disturbed.

"If you can't overpower your enemy with your strength, strike quicker than them with your speed or out think them with your intelligence, you must become one with your enemy," she said.

"But how do I become my enemy or an apparition?" I asked, and then the panther roared so loud in anger I thought she was going to shatter my eardrums.

"You must do as your enemy does, feel what your enemy feels, and think as your enemy thinks. Then you will see clearer," she stated in a flustered tone.

I didn't understand this logic at all, but it was worth a try, and she has never led me astray. After dreamscaping with my spirit guide, I further sought the wisdom of Asku.

My dreamscapes with Asku were always back at the *Wakhan Waki, Mahkah-Odahingum-Mahpee; the* sacred place, where the Earth meets the Water and Sky, high in the Smokey Mountains of North Carolina. It was always beneath a clear night sky with a brilliant low slung full moon, and thousands of pinhole stars in the sky, like many of nights that we've spent there, partaking in a peyote pipe.

"How do I communicate or fight such a thing? When it won't meet me in the spirit realm and constantly tries to kill me in the world of the living? I've seen apparitions before while working on the Coyote case. The Kachinas appeared to me, but they were never this difficult, and they definitely didn't try to harm me," I blustered.

"That's only because they wanted you to see them, as they dispatched justice, also you sat down with them in the spiritual realm and they befriended you," Asku replied.

"So how do you fight such a thing?" I asked.

"What did you spirit guide advise you to do?" he inquired.

"What she said didn't make any sense. She wanted me to become one with the thing that tried to kill me," I replied, harshly.

"You're still alive, aren't you? It sounds like if they wanted you dead, you would be. Didn't they assist you in your time of despair? I believe they are testing you. You must prove yourself to them. Heed your spirit guide's advice. She will never steer you in the wrong direction," he replied.

"S'gi (thank you), Asku, Donadagvhoi (until we meet again).

"Donadagvhoi, Cheveyo" he replied.

I knew I wasn't going to get a straight answer from my spirit guide or Asku. As usual, they provided me with the means or the tools to solve my dilemma without telling me the answer. Asku informed me a long time ago that this was the way of the Shaman and that each shaman must find his own path with guidance, but must chose for himself which direction to go. I might have been gifted in the abilities of the Shaman, but I had to work on my patience with solving these conundrums.

While I was spending my days in the forest at the sacred grounds, the tensions between the town's people and the Abenaki were increasing. There had been numerous outbreaks of violence committed against the Abenaki in Swanton. I did see that I had no choice but to do as my spirit guide had suggested. I wasn't making any headway into finding any other resolutions.

This time when I returned to the sacred springs, I did exactly what my spirit guide suggested. I didn't try to fight the Dawn's People, in fact, I did the exactly the opposite. I jump started the procedures with a risky move. Asku stated that they didn't want to kill me, and each time I've come close to death while around them, only to wake up unharmed. I tested this theory and took off my energy crystal. It was the only thing that kept me alive around them. It was a gesture of sacrifice to show that I come in peace. Without it, I was unprotected to my enemies, and could experience an energy overloading and die.

As soon as I released the glowing crystal, wrapped around my right arm with deer hide bindings, the energy of the Dawn's People immediately rushed in, knocking me backwards to the ground, like being struck by lightning, except the current didn't let go. It held me so tight that I could barely breathe, locked within its grips, paralyzed from head to toe. I thought for sure that I would pass out, again. My heart was beating so fast that the beats felt no longer separated, yet it didn't stop. I felt like I was having a heart attack.

I could feel myself suspended in the air, floating, while the energies of the Dawn's People flowed through me. It was like an electrical current plugging into my nerve center and reacting with every nerve receptor, axiom and fiber within my body, and lighting them up like a Las Vegas Strip! I never felt more alive and energized. It was euphoric, serene, and exhilarating all at once!

Then suddenly it felt as though time had stopped, while I was suspended, and the energy slowly brought me back down to the ground. It felt as if I was in the spirit or dream world, and they had transported me there, but I wasn't. I was still in the forest, but everything within it was motionless in time. They had blended the realms, like I had, but with more precision. I was a novice at it, but they were masters. I was inside the iota of a second, as caught by a camera in still life. It was amazing!

Then the mist slowly creeped in, covering the area, and the Dawn's People appeared. It was just as I had seen them while dreamscaping with Chogan, except now I felt each individual spirit, as they comprised the collective energy. They were separate, yet together, and I was one with the many, merged into the collective. I could feel each one of them, as they could feel me. We shared each other's energies, individually, yet becoming one, the Chibaiskweda; one soul, one spirit, one consciousness with the power and strength of thousands! They could see through my eyes, as I could see myself though theirs.

I was donning a warrior's attire with head gear composed of bones; spiked, jagged and sharp, surrounding my face, like a helmet, and the jagged jawbone of an animal encasing my jawline. I'm uncertain of the animal which composed the bones, it could be from many, but it was beyond the coolest and fiercest thing that I've ever seen!

My attire was striking, but the most phenomenal thing was my face; one third of it displayed my inner panther spirit, and it wasn't paint! It was like I was a hybrid being of some sort! Is this how they view me? I have no idea what this means or the significance, but I've never felt so powerful, and this was only the tip of the iceberg because this was a collective, which means it could integrate and become even more powerful!

I wasn't sure how many of them there were, but it was easily in the hundreds, if not thousands. It explained why collectively they were so strong and has such a magnanimous presence. They were translucent like the mist, yet you could see every detail of them, and in the center of the mist I saw and felt the glowing bright lights of the children's energy again.

Then, one by one, the Dawn's People materialized in front of me, dressed in their ceremonial attire. I couldn't keep up with them; there were so many materializing before my eyes. As the mass grew larger the lights of the children could no longer be seen.

There was no need for us to speak in conventional terms because I had become one with them, like I was one with my spirit guide. They shared their pain and despair with me. It was a saddening pain that I had never experienced before, not even in my long history of nightmares. It was something that they had carried for over hundreds of years. It was beyond unbearable. I felt as if my head was going to explode as I sunk into a depressed state.

I couldn't control my tears, as they flowed freely. I felt a myriad of emotions and all were lugubrious; loneliness, emptiness, barren and broken hearted. I wanted to kill myself and end this insatiable anguish. I couldn't take it any longer, as I dropped to my knees, and yelled at the top of my voice for them to stop, falling face down into the grass. I could still feel the pressure of their energy surging around me and used all the strength I could muster to reach for my energy crystal. I was moving in slow motion against the current and managed to stretch out just enough to place my finger on the crystal. It was all the contact that I needed to break the connection, and end the pain.

After a few minutes the pain had dissipated and the Dawn's People were gone. I was back in the real time at the sacred springs with a splitting headache, and tears in my eyes. I was still saddened by the residual effects of the experience. My spirit guide was correct, becoming one with the Dawn's People enlightened me, and I knew what I had to do. Asku's wisdom prevailed as well. He told me that the power to heal was greater than elemental magic, and he just might be correct. I had to discover the nature of the Dawn's People's pain, the source, and cure them. This was the key to getting the children back.

CHAPTER NINETEEN

THE RAVEN MOCKER

I immediately went back to my hotel suite after making a connection with the Dawn's People. I pulled out my laptop and researched the history of the Abenaki for any transgressions. Kateri mentioned bad blood between the Abenaki and the people of Swanton extending as far back as the French and Indian Wars. I had my work cut out for me, so I had room service bring additional coffee to the room. I searched all night through the Abenaki history until I came upon something worthwhile. It was a catastrophic incident involving the genocide of the Abenaki. The Swanton government sterilized the Abenaki children that eventually led to the deaths of over 50 or more children due to detrimental reactions from the drugs administered, not to mention the genocidal sterilization that wiped out perhaps generations of Abenaki.

I was certain that this was the collective pain that I was feeling when I bonded with the Dawn's People. Their children were taken from them by the people of Swanton, so they took their children to replace their lost. That's what this has been about from the start. The Dawn's People were still longing for their children. I felt the emptiness and pain of their longing for hundreds of years. This also meant that the Abenaki children are separated from them, and in order to solve this, I had to reunite the Dawn's People with their children or at least the souls of their missing children.

I guess it's fair to say that the Dawn's People children aren't buried in the sacred burial grounds of the Sacred Forest, so I needed to do some additional research, which meant enlisted the assistance of Carlyle and Kindle. While I waited for Carlyle to come up with something, I continued on my own. I used the wall of my suite, as a writing board, and wrote everything down that I had on the case. I was hoping to see something that I might have missed. This was a technique I got from working with Steve and the VICAP Unit of the FBI.

I examined what I had on the wall and picked it apart, over and over, but nothing jumped out. The Abenaki Village, Chogan's cabin, the sacred burial site and the sacred springs were all the places where the Dawn's People energy shroud was covering. The more I looked at the wall the more frustrating it became. I checked my cell phone several times to see if I had missed a call from Carlyle. I was like an expecting father waiting to greet his newborn.

Then my thoughts were interrupted by my owl friend tapping on the window. Once again, Mother Earth must have felt my frustration, and sent me a stress relief. I went to the window, opened the curtains, and then the window to greet my friend. This time she didn't have any prey to show off to me. It was sunset and the night's hunt hadn't begun yet. I had worked all day in my room unaware of the time of day. I caressed her feathers and watched her relax her tufts in a sign of appreciation. I was going to miss her when I left Swanton. I thought about taking her with me, but this was her home. She was the queen here and had carved out her domain. These were her hunting grounds, and she knew every inch of it, and where to find a particular type of prey.

After a brief respite with my owl friend, I watched her fly away. The sunset was coming to a close, and giving a final curtain call before the night took over. It was a beautiful sight watching her soar, gracefully and effortless through the amber colored sky. I was captivated, as I watched her b-line from one tree to the next. She was scouting her kingdom with a set goal and purpose, preparing for tonight's hunt.

"Oh, you wonderful and beautiful bird of prey!"

She just gave me an excellent idea, as she scouted her kingdom with precision, from tree to tree, point to point. I went back to the wall of my hotel suite and examined the four points of the Dawn's People activity that I had written down. It was a long shot, but I had nothing else. I examined the distances between them on a map I pulled up on the laptop, and discovered that the estimated distances were even. Then I used the Cartesian Coordinate System to configure where the next axis point would be to close the five-point pentagram.

I did another search on the laptop to see if there was anything of significance in the estimated axis point and discovered that the old factory was in that specific area. I was beyond excited! My days spent as a profiler with the FBI were really paying off with my investigating techniques. I couldn't wait to leave, and then from out of nowhere someone knocked on the door.

I was so excited that I didn't sense her coming in advance. It was Agent Jackson on the other side of the door. She, like Matunaagd, had an uncanny way of showing up at the most inopportune times. This was something that I really didn't need right now. She was here for an update on my progress, which I told her I would do, if she stayed out of my way. I had neglected to keep her in the loop, but up until now there wasn't really anything worth telling her, besides my run-ins with the Dawns' People and that wasn't something she could write on a report.

"Good evening, Carolyn," I said, greeting her at the door. We were on first name bases now.

"Good evening, Chris," she responded, as she moved me aside, and made her way in.

She was determined and wasn't going to let my standing in the doorway deter her from questioning me. She didn't seem to mind that the lights were out in the room, as she entered without a care in the world. She didn't move towards the light switch, like I've seen so many others do, who couldn't see in the dark. She trusted me and felt secure around me, as she stood in the middle of the room, with her arms crossed, and waiting for me to turn on the light before talking.

She knew exactly how to compartmentalize business and pleasure. This was strictly a business visit, judging by her tone and demeanor. Anything shared between us in the past was just that, in the past. I realized that I was in for an ass chewing. She was taking the stance, as a mother would, before scolding her child. I thought it was cute and funny, as I held back my laughter. I had died several times over in the past few days, and dealt with things that could only be imagined in your worst nightmares, yet here she was, not *the least bit afraid to chew me out, and hold me accountable! You got to love it.*

"I haven't heard from you in several days. You haven't answered my calls or returned any of my messages. I thought we had an agreement," she said, in an angry tone with her face squinched up in frustration.

"I'm sorry, but I didn't have anything concrete to share with you," I responded, and asked, *"Would you like something to drink?"*

"No," she quickly snapped back, and said, *"You've been busy doing nothing this whole time, and couldn't return my calls? Come on, Sands, you can do better than that."*

"What I came across isn't anything you can write down on a report," I replied, and handed her a bottle of water from the fridge to calm her down.

"I've seen your world, Chris, and I know what you're dealing with. You can tell me about it," she said, and held my hand.

She had a concerned look on her face, and I could see that she was sincere. Underneath her tough demeanor lies a passionate and softhearted woman. It would be nice to talk to someone besides Asku and my spirit guide. I used to dreamscape with Nina, and tell her everything until this case made communicating with her a little rougher, wedging a gap between us.

"Look, Carolyn, I will tell you everything when I have it all figured out, but right now, you have to trust me. I promise that you will be the first one I brief, on everything, including the parts that you can't mention on a report, but I'm tired now and need to get some rest."

I escorted her to the door and promised her once again that I would call her when I had something concrete. I didn't want to leave out with her still around, and run the risk of having her following me, so I waited impatiently for about 30 minutes, and I no longer sensed her presence. I was so hyped about what I had discovered about the old factory that it was hard to concentrate on her energy signal or anyone else's as far as that goes. I hurried to the vehicle and drove off quickly.

I received a call from Carlyle on the way to the factory. He advised me that the old factory building used to be the Swanton Hospital a hundred years ago, and this is where the sterilization of the Abenaki most likely took place. I'd place my money on the Dawn's People causing the mysterious illnesses at the factory that eventually led to its closing.

It was quiet outside the old abandoned factory when I arrived. The first thing I noticed was the energy field of the Dawn's People present, as my energy crystal glowed indicating the same, but I didn't have to worry about anyone seeing its glow, because there wasn't a soul in sight, not even the ravens, to my surprise; they had been everywhere in Swanton up to this point. The black duster that Kateri gave me provided enough cover to shield the crystal from sight just in case.

This was the first time that I was elated to sense the super- abounding energy field that hovered over this place, just as it did at the other places in my pentagram. Now that I knew it was the Dawn's People, it gave me room for hope. My heart was beating double time, excited about the possibility of resolving the mystery behind the missing children, and about the unknown that I might face inside the factory. I wasn't built like most people to fear the unknown, it only made me eager and curious. It was a way of seeking new knowledge and learning for me.

I was so busy the past couple of days doing research that I forgot about the lunar calendar. This was the night of the full moon. I looked up and observed the mysterious orb hanging low in the sky, and glowed, like an abstract painting, with no definitive edges, as nebulous clouds floated by, and created waves in the dark blue sea of the night sky.

I've learned a few things about the moon, and its phases from my Shaman training, and tonight's full moon is optimum for supernatural activities. The waxing moon is used for gains; like money, love or healing, and the waning moon is used for decreases, but the full moon is the greatest. It is used to cast hexes, curses, and destruction. Most of the powerful rituals take place during the full moon for all supernaturals, witches, Mskagwedemoos, shapeshifters, shamans, druids, etc.

The clouds gave warning that the rain was on its way, and you could feel it in the air, as the winds picked up. Its touch felt good upon my face, as I closed my eyes and took in a deep breath. This was the quiet before the storm. The heavy snowfalls in Vermont gave way to torrential rains when it wasn't cold outside, and this had the appearance of a strong one coming.

The black leaves were falling from the decaying trees, blowing swiftly, yet steadily, in the wind. Swirling and twirling like ballroom dancers, moving tempestuously towards the grand finale. I had grown accustomed to this obsidian scene, and had even found beauty in its charms; from the ravens to the Mskagwedemoos, the leaves and ash. It was the opposite of a glistening snowy mountainside, as seen in the Smokies, but come to an end it must.

I had run out of time, and all hell was about to break out in Swanton. I don't think I can control the Malsum with their size, speed and agility. I'd have my hands filled with just one or two, but several in a pack; that's a challenging task for any supernatural being. I wished the Padogiyik Seven were still here with me, but this is a path I must take alone. Perhaps I can finally put this entire ordeal behind me, I thought.

I made my way through the stygian blizzard of leaves, and came upon the rusted chain- linked fence surrounding the factory. No one had been inside this place in years, judging by the unkempt grounds. Some of the weeds were as tall as me. I quickly leaped across the 8 feet high fence with the ease and agility of a pole vaulter, and made a perfect cat-like landing into the weeds. I was exhilarated by the leap, but didn't break a sweat. I felt like any athlete or well-tuned engine warming up for more. It was my panther imprinting kicking in the adrenaline.

I could have just knocked the rusted relic down, but why destroy property when you didn't have to, even dilapidated property. I made my way through the tall brush, and then I was completed shocked by what I witnessed next. It was the old creepy building from Tahki's painting! It looked like she set up her easel in the field, and just started painting everything in sight.

It's one of the creepiest buildings that I've ever seen. Its appearance alone would give credence to the rumors of it being cursed. The building was covered in a web of brown, decayed-looking tree-like vines which appeared to be strangling it. I've seen happier places with majestic ivy covering it, instead of these eerie looking vines, but I guess it was fitting for what had occurred here in the past. The paint on the building was faded with chips falling off and giving it a two-tone, diseased look, as if it was sick.

There appeared to be a permanent shadow cast upon the structure, even in the light of the full moon. It had a ghastly aura that screamed bad news, and warning potential trespassers to stay out. Everything appeared dead or decaying around the dilapidated structure. The trees were a rotten mosaic of gray mold and black fungus. There was no grass, just the anemic looking brown weeds, and the black leaves that covered the ground.

As I approached the building, I felt a deep sadness emanating from the structure. It was like I could feel all the hopes, and dreams of the town's people sunk into the factory and destroyed. Now only empathy remained. There was an elaborate matrix of funnel webs from a spider, with eggs, food source, and grime covering the outer door of the factory. Unfortunately, I had to disrupt their intricate haven, as they scurried back and forth in a protective mode when I pulled it down. Now they would have to start all over again, and most of the eggs and food source would be lost to other predators, if there were any.

When I opened the door to the factory, I felt a rush of air exiting the enclosed structure, like a caged animal escaping its prison. It had been a long time since these doors opened and exchanged air. The musty smell inside the dark building was horrendous. The murky dust in the air was a condensed soup mixture of mold, mildew, and the pungent acrid odor of bat excrement. It hit the back of your throat, as you breathed, and caused your gag reflexes to kick in. It was so thick you could taste it on your tongue.

I placed the hood of the coat Kateri had given me, over my head, and covered my face with the bandana she gave me as well. She was right when she stated I would need these items in and around rural Swanton. It was as if she had foresight or something.

It took a while to get used to the air inside, like entering a room filled with cigarette smoke. The bat excrement was the worst of all, and had my eyes watering. I saw and smelt the remnants of other animals, besides the bats that were flying near the ceiling. There were rats and snakes among other smaller animals that made their way inside and contributed to this ecosystem that I thought was dead.

The walls were covered in grime, and slimy fungus-like mushrooms that I've never seen before; growing over the street- Picasso's artwork, and picturesque signatures, like Barnacles on the hull of a ship. I also observed runes deceptively hidden near the graffiti, and the inalienable paintings of blackbirds, which confirmed that I was in the right place.

I searched the building for a little while, and then I heard a blast of thunder outside, like the crash of cymbals, signally the rain to begin. I heard the droplets beating, like drums, on the huge skylights that covered the ceiling, as the movement went on. The lightning lit up the sky, and temporarily illuminated the dark building, with a thunderous boom here, and there, climaxing the score like a well-trained orchestra that I longed to conduct. My aspirations of being a maestro or even a music professor were nothing but a forgotten memory from where I was in this moment in time.

I continued searching the building, and with another loud burst of thunder, they appeared within the flash of lightning. I had reached some sort of staging area for the factory. I didn't detect their energy signatures, and my energy crystal was not illuminating, as usual. I didn't know how the Mskagwedemoos were masking themselves, but I believe it was the Dawns' People energy field preventing me from sensing them.

They weren't hiding behind human slaves this time. The red-eyed demonic witches moved steadily towards me, in an erratic synchronized motion, like they were jolting time, and causing it to pause randomly. They were chanting some ancient Aramaic song, as they moved closer and closer, dressed as they were in the forest, adorned with the mesh of black leaves and vines. This same piceous matrix began to cover the floor which they were standing on, and spreading like a virus. It grew larger, and larger, engulfing the interior walls and floors of the building, as any infection would. Now my energy crystal lit up! The Mskagwedemoos could mask themselves, but they couldn't mask their black magic.

I'm perplexed by the way I viewed these creatures, because they still seemed sexy as hell to me. I considered it a shame to kill such beauty, even dark beauty. Was it my shaman compassion towards all things of nature or was I being bewitched or mystified in some way by their charms? It didn't matter because it was a minor thing, and I knew what I had to do this night.

They didn't have any weapons, as their human slaves carried; they didn't feel the need for such trinkets. They relied upon their black magic; twisting their way into the minds of others, and using them to do their bidding. When their charms didn't work; they used other means of deceit, like corrupting nature with their black touch, and using it for malefic purposes. Their last defense was to get physical, and even then, they were still worthy adversaries. They had supernatural speed, although not as fast as mine, and razor-sharp claws on each finger.

With each strike of lightning the insidious matrix grew, until it encapsulated us. It was already dark inside of the abandoned building, but they suffocated it even more. Now you couldn't even see the lightning strikes random illumination, as the Mskagwedemoos continued to sing their ancient Aramaic song. This had no effect on me what so ever. If it was a scare tactic, I wasn't impressed, and if used to blind me, it didn't work. I could already see in the dark. This black web continued to move about, as if it was alive, twisting, shifting and crawling on the walls, and below my feet. I already knew what was coming next. It would attempt to engulf me as well. Did that, done that with the Dawn's People.

I didn't wait for it to entomb me. I raised my right arm, which contained the energy crystal, spread my fingers outward and absorbed its energy. I heard the deafening screams of the Mskagwedemoos, in one last desperate effort to harm me, as they and the obsidian growth around me, crumbled, and turned to ash. Damn! There was another horde of Mskagwedemoos waiting for me in the shadows, when the ash cleared. I'd hope they would have given up by now. I was really getting tired of all the killings, and just wanted to find the children, and put an end to this madness. They didn't approach me this time, as they stood at attention, watching me with those fire red eyes.

"What is this, a staring contest? I don't get a song, and dance this time; where's your manners? I really enjoyed the first act, not too fond of the second, but I'm certain we can make this closing act well worth it," I boasted.

Then another siren walked forward, through the standing mob. She was wearing a red hooded robe, and a Victorian style mask, like the siren that appeared at the hotel. The mask was different than before, this time it was crimson colored, matching her robe, and adorned with black rubies, onyx perhaps, and the scarlet eyes of a demon glaring through the mask.

"You didn't think it would be that easy, did you, Agent Sands?" I thought I recognized the voice but it couldn't be!

The horde spread out as she made her way towards the front. Several of the Mskagwedemoos surrounded me, constantly circling me, like a merry-go-round. It was a clever tactic. They weren't giving me a stationary point of attack. The hooded one walked slowly through the horde, stopped inside the circle.

"You've been a lot of trouble Agent Sands or do you prefer Cheveyo; Spirit Warrior? You are one hell of an anomaly, aren't you? I've made slaves out of too many shamans to count, but you're different," she said and stopped in front of me.

She was the least bit afraid of me, as if she knew something that I didn't, because I was running out of time, and patience with them.

"Look, I'd love to continue with this chit-chat, but there's something I need to do before it gets any later, so I'll ask you bone question. If I like the answer I'll let you live, if not, well…"

Then she took off her mask, before I could continue. I was astonished and heartbroken by what I saw next. I thought I'd recognize the voice, but I wouldn't have predicted this coming in a million years. Those beautiful brown eyes were now blood red. It was Tahki, to my surprise! She smiled at me, as I looked at her with contempt.

"It was you all along. I should have known. You were with Chogan when this whole thing started. You probably vexed or charmed him into agreeing with your plans from the start, but you needed to keep him in check, didn't you? Your own uncle, how could you?" I asked, shaking my head in disappointment.

"He was fine, until you started poking your nose where it didn't belong. Even he tried to warn you, shaman, but you just kept right on pushing. You're the blame for his demise, and no one else," she said, with a smirk, and taking a defensive stand in front of the horde.

"His blood is on your hands alone. You probably put him in that wheelchair, and took away his faculties. His warnings to me were a plea for help. He was going to confess until you killed him," I replied, waiting for the attack.

I scrutinized the horde, and my surroundings, like a chess master concentrating on the board, strategizing my moves ahead of time, but I knew sooner than later, I would be winging it, due to their numbers. She had killed her own uncle, and I couldn't wait to return the favor.

"It seems almost a shame to kill such a worthy opponent. You destroyed the Gici Awas, and everything we've sent your way, but it's too late. The wheels are already in motion. Everything we've planned for is coming to fruition tonight, shaman." She pontificated with a smile, *"Kill him,"* she ordered the horde, and stepped outside of the circle.

This time they caught me by surprise, I was still in awe with discovering Tahki's true nature. They screeched, all at once, and their deafening sound shattered several of the remaining windows in the abandoned building. There was glass flying everywhere. It showered from above; where there were skylights in the ceiling, and exploded from the left and right; where the perimeter windows and doors were located. I fell to my knees, cringing, and holding my hands to my ears. I could feel the blood seeping through my hands, from my damaged eardrums. This must have been how Chogan died.

"Ayv wiwadvhv nvgi Ganolvvsgv, hnadvga gadousdi ayv adanetsedi"

I quickly created a wind tunnel around my circumference to attenuate their murdering sound. Then I expanded it outwards, flinging them from their feet, and fiercely sending them hurdling backwards, crashing to the floor, and walls of the building. Then I drained them of energy life source, but Tahki wasn't present. She had escaped my wrath. Therefore, I ventured further into the depths of the abandoned factory and came to the assembly area. Everything in here was rusted, and enveloped in the slimy fungus covering the walls.

Then suddenly, all the machinery came on in the assembly line area, but the lights remained off. I was caught off guard by the plethora of sounds emanating from the machines; from high powered water hoses, to the sounds of crashing waves against the rocks of a jagged coast line. Some sounds were repetitive, like a car crossing over expansion joints on the highway, and the sound of a washing machine during its wash cycle.

I heard a loud sprinkler on the lawn of a sweltering summer day, and then I heard the pounding of a bulldozer stumping the ground, with the subtle clanking of dishes being clean by a dishwasher. The oddest sound resonating through all this clamorous chaos was the sound of an old freight train whistle blowing steadily, off and on. These Mskagwedemoos were clever to turn on the machinery because I couldn't use my panther imprinting to locate them over the loud and distracting sounds of the machinery.

Then I saw them, there were ghosts running the machines. These are the lost souls that are trapped here on earth, and can't find their way. They continued to work and haunt the place where they spent most of their time or perhaps even died here, due to the curse. I've come across a few of these apparitions in the past, and they can be quite nasty when provoked. I don't have the time or the patience to deal with them currently. These lost souls are just more pawns being manipulated, as others by the Mskagwedemoos, in their line of defense. I must be getting close to ending this, once and for all. They didn't bother me nor seemed concerned with my presence. These ghosts appeared to be content, and I'd like to keep them that way.

Therefore, I quietly made my way through the apparitions, only to be attacked by the Mskagwedemoos, waiting in the shadows. They rushed in and out, using the machines for cover, as they attacked me in the dark and disharmonic machinery area. They were emulating what the Gici Awas did in their underwater caverns, using stealth guerilla tactics. I'm not certain if they taught this technique to the Gici Awas or if it was the other way around, but one by one, they swooped in on me, quickly slashing me with their razor-sharp claws, and vanishing into the darkness. I was a sitting duck.

Nothing would have given me more pleasure than to rip the life out of these Mskagwedemoos at this point, and drain their energy, but I've already taken too many risks in here. I wasn't certain where the Abenaki children rest and I couldn't risk accidentally transferring their paranormal energy. I've already observed the presence of apparitions; therefore, I must do this the hard way, and fight my way out of this. I fell back on my b-plan again, and manipulated the wind. I wasn't certain how the apparitions would react to this, but I had no choice, I was running out of time.

"Ayv wiwadvhv nvgi Ganolvvsgv, ale atsilv, hnadvga gadousdi ayv adanetsedi"

I used turbulent gale winds; streaming them in different directions, as I turned in a circle, destroying everything within reach. When I finished, there was nothing left but remnants of the machinery. It looked like a scrapyard for metal parts. If there were any Mskagwedemoos in the area, they were buried under the ruins. I don't think I killed them, but I temporarily eliminated the distraction. *You have to take their heads,* Eirik advised me.

Then the strangest thing occurred, the lights began to flicker. How in the hell would there be any electricity on in this place, especially after the destruction that just occurred? Damn! I must have awakened the lost souls. These apparitions are basically composed of energy, which means I can absorb it, but I can't disperse it from my energy crystal in this realm.

They attacked like a swarm of angry wasp, hitting and knocking me down in a furious raid. I had to continue with my defense strategy, and remain mindful of the Abenaki children, as we fought amongst the ruins. I'm not certain where all these lost souls came from, but they were proving to be formidable opponents. I was getting the mess beat out of me, as they flung all sorts of projectiles from the ruins at me through psychokinesis. I did my best to duck and move while absorbing their energies when I could.

After being beaten like a ragdoll, I finally made my way out of the assembly area. The apparitions didn't follow me. I'm guessing one of the many runes I observed amongst the multifarious graffiti images was a containment spell. I paused for a moment, and went down on one knee to catch my breath. I was exhausted after my encounter with the lost souls, and needed to heal, and reenergize. Then Tahki appeared out of the darkness, and one by one, several Mskagwedemoos appeared. They were fewer in numbers this time, as I listened to their lamented whispers which sounded like a soulful song.

"You promised us his blood, where is it. We want his sacrifice."

Apparently the Mskagwedemoos had ulterior plans for me; a nefarious purpose that I was unaware of or perhaps that was just their way of saying they wanted me dead. It doesn't really matter either way this didn't sound appealing in the least bit, as they continued their woeful song.

My time was being cut drastically by the supernatural sentries in this place. They had me spinning the wheel; therefore, I decided to strike while they were in bickering. I rushed Tahki without notice, but she was quick, and leaped upward onto the side of the wall. She was suspended there like a fly or any other pest without knowledge of gravity. She smiled looking down at me, as I jumped towards her, but she quickly leaped to a different corner of the room, and suspended herself on the wall, as before. I've seen demons and the possessed suspend themselves on walls and ceilings, but she had perfected it into a formidable tactic.

I landed near the Mskagwedemoos, who glared at me with hell stricken eyes from the shadows, moving back and forth, like caged lioness preparing to attack, but they didn't. They remained in the shadows, glaring at me with hell stricken eyes. They were either smarter than the others or very disobedient. They were afraid and didn't want to die. I was equally tired of killing them. I took a defensive stance in preparation, but they retreated into the shadows.

This is the first time I've witnessed evil back down. In retrospect, I guess I had acquired quite a kill record up to this point. This would have pleased the Padogiyik. I then turned my attention back towards Tahki, but she was no longer there. Once again, she decided to run, instead of fight. She was a nuisance, just like a fly, but her plan to hinder my progress was literally working like a charm. As much as I wanted to end her annoyance, I need to *move on*, I didn't have the time.

The thunder returned, after I departed the assembly area. I could see the lightning, and the rain beating against the skylights once again, as I ventured down the dark corridors of the demon infested building. A mural of shadows and careless whispers coursed the walls, teasing and coercing me with temptations of sex, power, and wealth. All the sinful desires of man, displayed like a buffet, ready to serve. These were the mind games of the Mskagwedemoos, to feed upon the desires of lesser men with treasures of this phenomenal realm, but I'm a dream walker, and I've seen scores of other realms. I know better than to put faith in such animate things.

I continued down the hallway, instead of deterring me, I'd hoped their deceptions would lead me to the source of their wickedness. Just as I suspected, they led me to a receiving area of the factory. The area was filled with Mayan and Aztec artifacts, scattered around, like a museum's warehouse. There were crates everywhere; some still had antiquities inside of them while others were empty.

Then Tahki appeared with several other Mskagwedemoos, as the storm picked up outside, and then another figure appeared next to her. It was the hooded figure dressed in black that possessed the receptionist, and mostly likely everyone else in and around Swanton. Now I was getting somewhere, she was the real leader of this nefarious group. I'm guessing I finally killed my way up to the top dog.

"Good evening, Cheveyo," the hooded figure hissed in a low indistinguishable voice that seemed to resonate through the halls of the building.

I couldn't tell if it was man or woman, but I was more than ready to tangle with it again. It didn't do so well the last time we fought, in fact it fled. I was looking forward to fighting it again.

"So, this is your temple, this little shit hole?" I said, to arouse the mistress, and throw her off.

"That's the problem with your kind; you place too much importance on this realm, like it's the only one that matters." She quipped.

"If it isn't, then why are you and your kind so obsessed with it?" I replied.

"It's because you hairless monkeys are so easy to control, like puppets on a string, slaves to do my bidding." She professed, conceitedly.

"You see, and therein lay the problem with your kind, thinking you are above mankind. This realm was never promised to you, and you have no right to it. Man, isn't the cause for your downfall from grace, you created that through your own decadence. You thought you were his equals, and could rival him. It's not man's fault you fell short and came up with the shit-end of the stick." I smiled, taking pleasure in teasing them.

"I must admit, you truly are a remarkable being, Agent Sands. I've only seen angels do the things you're capable of doing, and you're no angel, are you, Cheveyo? No, there's darkness within you, one that you've been hiding and trying to fight. You have an unexplainable affinity towards the creatures, and things of the night. You feel alive in the darkness, like its home. Your ability to blend into the shadows, and your insatiable rage and ambivalence when it comes to fire, yes, I'd say there's something very dark within you, Cheveyo. They're coming for you, Spirit Warrior. Have you seen them, yet? Don't worry you will soon enough, trust me, you will soon enough."

"What do you want here demon?" I asked, as it laughed.

"You know fully well why I'm here. You do realize how this is going to end. Although, it seems a shame to kill such beauty," it answered, smiling, as it repeated the words I'd said before about killing the Mskagwedemoos.

"I'm not here to be flattered by your threats demon. I'm here to free the souls trapped in here."

"Well of course you are, but you will die trying," it retorted, slithering towards me.

"Who are you demon? Reveal yourself to me, before I kill you!" I threatened.

"I would have thought the ravens would have given you some indication of who I am. I've been known by several names throughout time. Some call me a demon; others call me a siren, a witch, and a goddess. I am Tlazolteotl, but your kind refers to me as Kalona Ayeliski in Cherokee, and Atsolowas in Abenaki, but commonly known as the Raven Mocker." She pulled down her hood and revealed the ornamented Victorian mask that I witnessed during a dreamscape when the witch tried to seduce me.

The mask looked like a relic, and should be in a museum somewhere instead of on the witch's face. It was black with diamonds surrounding its perimeter, hiding her nose and upper facial features, except for those scarlet red eyes, that seemed to glow from beyond this realm.

"So, the legends are true about the demon witch, but why did you kill Chogan?"

"Well technically it was Tahki who killed him, but it was on my orders. He was going to tell you everything we had planned here, and I couldn't let that happen," she answered.

"So, you were working together?" I asked, in a surprised tone.

"The Nixkamich was desperate, when the factory poisoned the waters, and caused the deaths of his people. The local government and the Federal Government washed their hands of the situation, and covered it up. Winchester's money and the Mayor had a lot to do with that. Therefore, the Nixkamich made a deal with me..." she said, before I interrupted.

"So, let me guess, the both of you cursed the factory, but he went back on his word somewhere along the line he reneged on the deal," I pondered.

"Yes, he became soft. He didn't agree with me summoning the Gici Awas, the beasts of the lake. He was supposed to summon his ancestors to protect the village against Winchester and others who would try to harm the Abenaki, but soon found out that they had their own agenda, and he had no control over them. They protected the village alright, but they had a reckoning of their own to settle."

"So, taking the children wasn't enough. You wanted more blood to spill, so you summoned the beasts of the lake." I bellowed.

"The missing children were Chogan and the People of the Dawn's mess, but I did see opportunity in it. Summoning the Gici Awas only provided a catalyst for the events to come, the real show. Too bad you won't be here to see it unfold. If wasn't for the People of the Dawn protecting you, I would have just killed you alongside Chogan, but they wanted you alive. I guess for this purpose."

"And what is your grand scheme for being here?" I inquired.

"You're slipping Shaman, you don't hear that? That's the sounds of sweet success and the Dawn's People will kill them all. After they rip each other apart, the Dawn's People will go into the town, and claim the rest," she said, grinning from ear to ear.

"A win, win situation for you, huh?"

"Well it isn't exactly as I planned it, but yes, it will suffice," she said gloating.

Winchester and the mob from town were assembling outside of the factory to march on the Abenaki Village. Their intent was to burn down the village, and killing the Abenaki that opposed them. The witch was pleased with herself. She had set all the events in motion leading to this one finale. She wanted to get as many of the town's people to attack the Abenaki Village, so the Dawn's People would destroy them and everyone in Swanton. That is why she had the Gici Awas, the monsters of Lake Champlain, kill so many in the forest, with the intent on stirring up civil unrest. If no Abenaki were attacked in the forest it rightfully placed suspicion on them, even I was suspicious.

When the Dawn's People took the children, it was all the ammunition that she needed to tip the scale to this moment. The people of Swanton had no idea what horrors waited for them. I've been killed over and over by the Dawn's People and each time was as horrible as the next. They also had to deal with the shifters who protected the village. This would be an all-out war with the town of Swanton caught in the crossfire. There wouldn't be a soul left alive in Swanton after this night. Kalona Ayeliski (Raven Mocker) had wormed her way into the minds of the entire town and village.

I saw the Sheriff peeping far in the background before I responded. He watched quietly like a mouse in the corner of the room. He must have followed me here from the hotel. In my zealousness to leave the hotel, I didn't sense his presence. Lucky for him the Mskagwedemoos couldn't sense him or he'd be dead. I had to buy myself some time. I needed the sheriff out of here, and out there with the mob.

"But why, what have these people done to you. You clearly aren't concerned with the souls of the Abenaki children?"

Then it hit me, as I was looking at the archaic symbols, and the many different elaborate ravens tattooed on the Mskagwedemoos, and on the walls. I remembered where I had seen the archaic symbols "CRO". I saw it on the hanging tree, in the Lost Colony of Roanoke. Everyone thought it was short for Croatan, but they were trying to warn of the crows, and the Raven Mocker!

"I see you understand and know who I am now," she said, with a heinous grin.

"CRO is a symbol for the Raven in Mesopotamia cuneiform. The Raven was considered a bird of deity in the Mesopotamian civilization. You have been destroying towns like Roanoke for centuries. The ghost towns that I visited in the spirit realm; the Anjikuni Inuit Village, and the

Kanawha River Village, were all destroyed by you, and now you're trying to do it here." I retorted.

"I was hoping you were smarter than you look half-breed. I thought the tattoos of the ravens would have been a sure hint for a shaman with your abilities, but I guess I was wrong," she replied.

"And the energy masking is that written within the design of the tattoos also?" I inquired.

"You're just a little too late to be getting smart, shaman. There's nothing you can do to prevent this from happening. By now the Abenaki warriors are heading here also. I made sure that they were made aware of this meeting of the town's people and their plans to attack the village." She hissed.

She was the queen trickster and masterfully planned the destruction and death of the town of Swanton and the Abenaki Village. She ensured that death would come tonight and covered all angles, including showing up here and stopping me. She had a thrones chair to witness it all going down right outside of the factory. I must admit it was an ingenious plan with no rhyme or reason except for carnage and evil intent

I had to act now! I needed to lead them away from this location and hopefully give the sheriff time to escape and assist on the outside. I summons the wind, and manipulated it into knocking down the entire front row of the Mskagwedemoos, and then I ran to lead them away. The Mskagwedemoos chased me with almost matching supernatural speeds, as I anticipated. All of them didn't follow me. The Raven Mocker was smart not to send them all, but divide and conquer worked for me. When I was far enough away I stopped running and waited for them. Before they could advance, I immediately drained them of their energy, and turned them into black ash.

Upon seeing this in the distance, the Raven Mocker screeched like a banshee, and then a loud thunderous boom came from the ceiling. I thought the roof was coming down, as flocks of ravens came crashing through the skylight and bringing the tempest force of the storm with them. It looked and sounded like heaven had exploded, as glass mixed with the wind and rain rushed in with the black mass, like an oil rig bursting open! It was quite a sight to see, if it wasn't for their malefic intent, as they poured into the building.

The red eyed possessed birds were back, enraged, and flying at a remarkable speed, faster than my previous encounters with them. They had been a constant nuisance since I arrived in Swanton and tried to kill me on several occasions in one way or another. I would have loved to set this whole place on fire and kill them all, but the collateral damage would be too high. The sheriff was still hiding in the building, and this is the home of innocent animals, not to mention the imminent threat to the town's people on the perimeter. I had to proceed with control in this fight, so I did what came as natural to me as any of my abilities, I shadowed myself.

The ravens aren't nocturnal like owls, nor do they possess the keen senses of wolves to determine my location when I shadowed myself. They were completely in the dark, but it didn't discourage them from causing havoc in the air. The term ravenous is aptly applied here, because the mass of black birds quickly attacked and devoured the bats and anything else living near the ceiling. I watched them tearing bats apart in midair. There was no escaping this black mass of death, as blood fell from above with the rain. Personally, I'm not a fan of the hairy flying vermin, but I felt sorry for them this night, as I listened to their squeals from being eaten alive. I would have suffered the same fate if I didn't shadow myself, so I took my frustration out on the Mskagwedemoos. The squeals of the bats were quickly replaced by the screams of Mskagwedemoos, as I made my move on them.

I stealthily went through the band of Mskagwedemoos like the angel of death, ripping off their limbs like a surgeon. I was enraged by all the destruction and evil caused by these witches, and wanted them to suffer. Then the blackbirds did what they are programed to do, they turned on the bleeding Mskagwedemoos. I saved Tahki and the Raven Mocker for last. I wanted them to hear the screams of others in the dark, as the ravens picked them apart, one by one. It was something I learned from my panther guide, as she would taunt and tease her prey before killing it. Perhaps it was imprinting on me also.

The fear tactics were working on the Mskagwedemoos and Tahki, as they began to panic. They swung their deadly claws wildly in the air at nothing, and turned frantically in all directions, in a desperate attempt. They slipped in the blood of their fallen sisters, as they watched the mob of carnivorous ravens gathered on the dark floor, fighting over the carrion. I just moved through the remainder with patience and precision, relieving them of their heads, as they turned to black ash. Now only Tahki and Atsolowas were left standing in a pool of blood and black ash.

I continued with my stealth tactics, appearing and reappearing and throwing my voice until I separated Tahki and the Raven Mocker, and placed a good amount of distance between them. I snuck up on Tahki and plunged my fist into her chest, and with all my strength and speed, I pulled out her cold black heart. Now she truly was heartless. The last expression on her face was priceless. It was the face of shock and terror, as I ripped off her head! Her eyes remained wide open and her mouth the same. Then I whispered in her ear, "That's for your uncle," as I dropped her head, before she turned into ash.

I was drenched in the blood, guts and the black ash of the Mskagwedemoos, from head to toe, like a Chicago slaughter house worker. I've been fighting and killing my way through a labyrinth of demons, guzzling time, and preventing me from sensing them. I was tired, and it was time to put a swift end to this.

I was a fast learner, and evolving more than even I could imagine. Everything I experienced, I picked up quickly, like a Rhodes Scholar, especially supernatural abilities. It was time to end the fighting, and give the Raven Mocker a taste of her own medicine. I was going to possess her, just like I entered those demons at the tree. It would be risky, and uncontrollable, but I was running out of time, and this had to end.

I quickly reappeared in front of the Raven Mocker, submerged in blood and guts, and providing a target for the ravens to attack. Just as they began their descent upon me, I merged with her, like the Dawn's People taught me. I didn't know if the ravens would fallback or still attack, they weren't very intelligent creatures, but their appetite was unmatched.

I was giving the Raven Mocker a dose of her own medicine, she was now the one being possessed, as the ravens continued their attack, but on the both of us. Their sharp claws and talons cut quickly and sharply as they knocked us both to the floor. She could call them off, but there would be no helping her, now that I was inside her psyche. I took the fight to the spiritual realm to eliminate the collateral damage.

CHAPTER TWENTY
THE AZTEC TEMPLE

I woke up groggy, lying on the ground at the base of the steps to the Aztec Temple. This was the realm of the masked figure known as the Raven Mocker. I was so weak; I couldn't stand up, like something had completely drained me. It seemed hotter here than the last time I visited to free the receptionist from her possession. If only I had known then, what I know now. It was still dark with an overcast sky and no sun. This might well be hell for all I know.

The few trees outside of the temple all looked dead, like everything else in this place. There was no green grass, just brown weeds that seemed to move like snakes on the ground. This place was beyond gloomy, it was depressing. I heard the slight beating of drums coming from inside of the temple, and then from out of nowhere, she appeared standing over me.

"My, my, now I didn't see that one coming. You would sacrifice yourself for them, just like he did. They named you appropriately, Christian, of Christ. I'm sure your father had something to do with that one. Now let's see if you can live up to your shamanic given name, Cheveyo, Spirit Warrior," she said, and then grabbed my arm and dragged me effortlessly, as if she was sliding a laundry bag across the floor, as my head hit each and every step before passing out!

This time, I woke up tied to a totem pole inside the Temple, still weak, and unable to free myself from the bonds. I was adjacent to a magnificent throne which overlooked the rest of the temple. I was shocked and amazed at what I observed inside. The outside of the temple might have been unkempt, but the inside was exquisite. It looked like an oasis compared to the outside. The floors were marble and the ceiling was hundreds of feet high with palm trees and totems reaching up towards it. Standing inside the entrance of the temple were two giant-sized, black totem statues that depictured ravens and several other golden totems towering over everything with torches lighting the surroundings.

In the center of the temple was a huge open fire hearth made of gold with a magnificent fire blazing upward towards a huge golden ornamented circular portal that resembled a skylight with ancient symbols surrounding it. I've never seen a fire burning so high and under control.

There were hundreds of Mskagwedemoos on the east and west sides of the great hall, dressed in the attire of female Aztec Warriors, and ravens swarming in the air above, and resting high on the huge surrounding totems of Ravens. There were other Mskagwedemoos dancing and mingling to the festive music of the drums, flutes, rattles and string instruments. These were dressed in white linen attire, nothing like the black assassin's attire they adorned in the old factory.

It appeared like a ceremonial celebration that I've seen throughout my travels in Native America, but on a smaller scale. At the north end of the temple was the Raven Mocker or Tlazolteotl, as she referred to herself, sitting on a throne behind an altar. She looked like an Aztec queen. As I walked down the stairs to meet my host, cocky and unafraid, all eyes were on me, including the red eyed ravens, as I walked towards the altar.

She wore a black and gold mask that covered her eyes and nose, and gold in color plumage covered her head. She had a skirt made of gold with black trimmings and her breasts were covered with matching gold fabric which crossed over her chest and went around the back of her neck and tied behind her upper back. Her attire left her shoulders, stomach, back and arms exposed. Her entire left shoulder bared the tattoo of a raven whose wings spread out covering the left portion of her chest and back shoulder blade. Her right arm bared the tattoo of a black snake, wrapping around it, and ending at the shoulder with the snake's head. She was deadly gorgeous.

"Welcome back, Cheveyo," she grinned, insidiously.

"So, this is where you're originally from?" I asked.

"I've been here before your kind learned how to walk up straight; when you were merely grunting, and making feeble undiscernible sounds. I assisted in cultivating Mesopotamia, Samaria, and Babylon to name a few. They worshipped me as the Aztecs and Mayans; I was their mother, queen and goddess. I can be this, and so much more for you, Cheveyo," she replied.

"You're no goddess, witch! You're just a soulless demon who's about to say goodnight," I threatened.

"You've been trying to find a place where you belong, and fit in, since you can remember, a tribe, a family, a race. You've struggled with identity issues your entire life. You can have all you've ever wanted here with me," she said, holding out her hands at the surroundings.

"And end up a lap dog or footstool for you?" I retorted.

"No, you are like none other, Cheveyo, just like me. I want you to take your rightful place next to me, as it should be," she replied.

"Enslaving the living, against their will, on a throne of death and destruction? I think I'll pass on that," I said rejecting her offer, and looking at her with disgust.

"I bet you don't even know who your father is half-breed" she snapped back, infuriated by my rejection.

"Really, is that the best you can do? I see why you are the goddess of mindless puppets now. There's not an ounce of intelligent imagination in this place, is there?" I quipped.

Then her eyes turned amber in color, as she peered intensely at me. It took all the strength I had left not to scream out loud from the excruciating pain, as I clenched my fist and grinded my teeth! It felt like I was lying in a tub of acid and my flesh was melting away from skeleton. Then her eyes turned back to their original color, black as coal, and I let out a sigh in relief, as the pain subsided.

I didn't expect anything less, judging by my predicament, but I can't believe she actually went there with the insults. I've been called a half-breed for most of my life, in one way or another, to the point that I've become immune to them. Her petty insult rolled off me like water on a duck's bill. I felt it was beneath her, since she claimed to be a goddess. She was in my head and extracting everything she could find, as a weakness. I was even weaker now than before, but I couldn't show defeat.

"Finished so soon? I've had nightmares with more intensity than that, witch, let's get on with it," I insisted with a shallow voice.

"Did you really think you could defeat me, half-breed? I've seen empires, and dynasties rise and fall; the Babylonians, Hittites, Israelites, Persians, Greeks, Egyptians, Aztecs, Mayans, Mongols, Ming, Romans, Ottomans, Qing, Byzantine, Russians, British; are you keeping up? And now the USA! Stay with me, now half breed! I was there when Sampson fell under the spell of Delilah, and when the Great Solomon, and King David gave into the flesh, just as you have." Then she shapeshifted into Dianna.

"Why did you leave me, Christian? I waited for you, but you never came back to me, why?" She asked, in Dianna's voice.

"I know you're not Dianna, witch, you're wasting your time." I said, angrily, and then she morphed into Nina.

"How could you do this to us, Chris? You said, you'd be faithful, you promised. I thought you loved me," she replied, in Nina's voice.

"You're the mother of tricksters, siren, these games won't help you," I said, a little rattled by the personal merry-go-round.

"It's not a trick or an illusion, Christian, it was me, all this time; in D.C. (she shapeshifts into Dianna), and in Arizona (she shapeshifts into Nina).

The trickster was ripping my deepest and innermost secrets from my mind, and there was nothing I could do. Then in one quick procession, her face rapidly changed into numerous women of my past, when I was young and promiscuous. It was a time that I would like to forget, when I was just learning how to manipulate dreams during dreamscaping. It was a time when I didn't care about the repercussions of whom I hurt, married or single didn't matter to me. She was getting to me, and I needed her to stop.

"These are the same games Tahki tried, now look at her," I grunted in desperate attempt to cease her attack on my emotional baggage. Then she shapeshifted into Kateri.

"Will you rip out my heart and take my head too, Christian?" She asked, solemnly, in Kateri's voice.

"You're not them, and you never will be! You're just a leach that lives off others. No matter how many souls you possess or enslave, you'll always be nothing but a virus upon mankind, and nothing more, than a soulless witch!" I yelled, flustered, as her eyes turned colors again, and she tortured me.

"You either join me or perish!" She exclaimed, as she stopped.

I was out of breath, and ready to fold. I could see the pleasure that she as getting out of torturing me, but I still wouldn't give her the satisfaction of surrendering. Then, before I could say another word, the witch reached out her hand, and ripped off my shirt from several yards away. It was only then that I recognized that my energy was black as the leaves I witness in the forest. It was like some sort of black tar or soot had encased it.

"Don't look so surprise, Spirit Warrior, yes, I subdued your energy crystal. That's why you're so weak. The Bow and Arrow People have always been very clever spiritualists. It's a shame you aren't as clever, as your ancestors, but then again, you are a half-breed in their eyes also, aren't you? I wanted to see if you were worthy to be at my side, but I see now that you're not! I'm a goddess, the Sun, and you are but a flicker of light. How silly of you to try and merge with me. But don't worry, if you were trying to sacrifice yourself, I will surely make that happen for you," she grinned.

"Do your best witch, but you better make it permanent, because there won't be a realm that you can hide in, if you don't!" I warned her with a weakened, non-threatening voice, as she laughed.

"You're the least of my worries. I would have killed you long time ago, if it wasn't for those meddlesome Dawn's People. Now I'm going to give you a taste of what real power is before you die. The power that only Gods and Goddesses can wield and control, and wannabe half-breeds, like you, only fall to its strength!"

Then she reached out her hand, once again. This time, the rope tying the blacken energy crystal around my neck snapped, and the crystal went flying into her hands.

The hot rush of burning energy revitalized me, and sent me, and the totem hurdling backwards to the floor. I imagine this is how it feels to truck by lightning or electrocuted. I was freed from the totem, but the surge of energy kept me pinned to the floor, and held me there. I was paralyzed, as a wave of her slaves fell immediately into black ash, while she stood tall on the throne. I uncontrollably absorbed their energy life source. They were sacrifices. I guess even demons could be benevolent in the proliferation of evil. I had made a grave error in judgment and underestimated my enemy.

The Raven Mocker had tricked me into believing that I had the upper hand, once again, and was superior to her. She played on my hubris, thinking I couldn't be defeated in the spiritual realm, and I fell right into her trap. The trickster was a step ahead of me all the time.

After killings scores of demon slaves by absorbing their energy, I became weakened, like a glutton stuffing himself to the point where I couldn't move. Then her slaves moved in closer. A few continued to turn to ash, as I continued absorbing their energy, but there were enough to pick me up from the floor, and chain me to another totem pole adjacent to the sacrificial hearth. There was nothing I could do, languid, and helpless, as an invalid. I was dying from the energy absorption. The crystal is what held it at bay, and with it no longer there, the dam had burst, and I was drowning in this tsunami tide.

They let the ravens pick at me while they prepared what was next to come. Now I know what the pre-celebration was about. It was in preparation of my arrival. They were going to sacrifice me. The ceremonial hearth was lit just for my occasion. Then the Raven Mocker approached me to gloat further, in front of the horde of demons waiting for their sacrifice.

"Here stands the Spirit Warrior, the Rider and Prince of Dreams, defender of the earth realm against all the evil that exists. Well, I have existed for thousands of years, hunting the dreams of men half-breed, and now I will hunt them while they're awake," she smugly boasted, and immediately began working on my psyche, again.

I thought I could defeat her like I had before in dreamscape, but she had suckered me in. She was more powerful than I thought. Her manipulations were far superior to mine, as she controlled my every thought. I was helpless, as she tortured me over and over in the blink of an eye, which seemed like an eternity. I had endured unspeakable things until they came to the final preparation ritual. In Aztec rituals, the human sacrifice is skinned alive before they toss you into the open flames. They were going to let the ravens slowly do this task for them.

I was prepared to give up at this point; I was weak and ready to pass out. I could feel my soul leaving me for its eternal journey when she appeared. My spirit guide jumped from out of nowhere. She had been blocked out of this realm by the Raven Mocker, but found her way to me. She began ripping through the demon horde, mangling them, and turning them into black ash. She had killed scores of them until they surrounded her with swords in hand. Then I surprisingly witnessed her do something that I had never seen before. I thought it was an illusion, and I was seeing things before I died. She had morphed into a beautiful hybrid; half-woman, and half-leopard. I've never seen anything like it or more beautiful.

Her head displayed the features of both woman and panther. The top portion of her head and face displayed all the features of a panther. She had the ears and green ovular eyes of a panther, even the roundness of her head. The lower portion of her head and face from the ears and eyes down was that of a woman. She displayed the slender nose of a woman, perfectly shaped lips of a woman and the fine jaw line and chin of a woman. The rest of her body was a very well-shaped woman with chiseled facial features, and a tail protruding from the rear of her exquisitely beautiful naked body. She was black all over and like a gorgeous work of art.

"You're not alone, Cheveyo," she said to me.

The demons hesitated too long, dumbfounded like I, as they watched her change. She immediately leaped on the nearest demon slave with the agility and quickness of a panther, took its sword and sent it to ash. She continued moving through the horde, gracefully, yet deadly, cutting them down like a snow plow, as black ashes filled the air. She was a fierce warrior, but unfortunately it wasn't enough. There were just too many of them, the witch queen had an army of slaves. I could feel death approaching for both of us, struggling on my last breaths, as I watched them close in on her. They were slashing her left and right, and then the cuts came from all around, as she spoke to me without saying a word. It was the same thing she said before.

"You're not alone, Cheveyo. There are still others who will fight with you."

Then I heard Asku's voice resonating inside my head.

"One should never measure a man by his strength alone, for he carries the will and the strength of his family, friends and people."

It was what he told me before I left Cherokee, North Carolina, and what my spirit guide told me, that echoed throughout the chambers of my mind. Everything Asku had prophesized was holding true. This time their advice wasn't in riddles, I understood it clearly. They reminded me of my bond with the Dawn's People. They were the ones that protected me from her killing me before, as she bragged to me. They were the only ones that could absorb all the energy that she was bombarding me with. It was a mistake giving me that information because the Dawn's People were now a part of my family and friends. I called upon them with what little energy I had left.

The Dawn's People appeared, as an ominous mist in the temple, scaring everything within it, just by its presence. It surrounded me and my spirit guide, like a beacon of light in the darkness, thousands of souls were ready to battle, and Chogan appeared as one of the hundreds. They had a score to settle with the Raven Mocker, as well.

They released me from the totem, and merged my spirit energy with theirs, as we became one again. Then the mist spread outward throughout the temple, killing Mskagwedemoos, ravens and everything else in its path. It was like the plague of death during the Hebrew Passover, as it cut down the Egyptians, promising death. I could feel it strangle the life out of the demons and apparitions, as we absorbed their energies, the sum greater than the one.

This time the screams of the Mskagwedemoos was from fear, as they tried to escape the mist, to no avail. The Raven Mocker attempted to flee also, but I still had a connection with her, and held her at bay, clutching her black soul. She struggled and fought to the very end to hold on to her energy, sinking into the collective like quick sand. I watched her spirit drown, as we ripped it apart, absorbed her energy, and extracted the Life Source from her. The tables had been turned now, and I was the one with the power, as the temple came crumbling down. Afterwards, Chogan appeared to me, and apologized for being weak and losing his way. Then he left me with these parting words.

"Now the rest is up to you, Cheveyo. You must find the children, and release them all. Only then will you release us, and end this."

When it was all over, I woke up on the blood-filled floor of the old factory across from the Raven Mocker. She was motionless and holding my energy crystal languidly in her hand. I assumed she was dead. She had a dark almost black-like blood oozing from her ears. This was the same way Chogan was found in his cabin, justice had been served.

All the carnage, blood, and headless bodies were still scattered on the floor, as the ravens ate the carrion feast of Mskagwedemoos that I had left them. I was lucky the ravens were preoccupied with the dead or I would have been on the menu also. They were no longer under the influence of the Raven Mocker. Their eyes were no longer red, but black as the night, and doing what ravens naturally do, eating carrion.

I felt charged with new life from the energy I absorbed from the Dawn's People collective, as we absorbed all the energies of the Mskagwedemoos and the Raven Mocker, but it was dispersed over hundreds instead of just one. I got up and retrieved my protection crystal and place it back where it belonged, around my arm. It was shining, like a star, and lit up the entire building from the burst of energy I received from the collective. There was nothing I could do to contain it. I just had to wait until it subsided.

I took this time to finally see who or what was under the mask of the Raven Mocker. She was just barely hanging on to life or at least what she called life. I sat on the floor next to her and placed her head in my lap, as her breaths became faint, and she struggled to breathe. Death would be coming soon, as I removed the mask. My jaw dropped, as my heart sunk to an all-time low. I couldn't believe what I was witnessing. It must be the last of the trickster's disguises; I was praying that it was.

"Please, show me your real face, there's nothing left to hide, I know this isn't you, I beg you, please show me what you really look like," I pleaded, with her, as my eyes welled up, because in the back of my mind something told me that it wasn't an illusion.

"The gift and the curse, huh?" She faintly whispered, still trying to read my mind. It was exactly what I was thinking.

"Do you know what the real curse is for those like you and me?" She struggled to say, as I slowly shook my head in response.

"Being alone, and dying alone. Thank you, for not letting me die alone, Christian."

This was the first time the Raven Mocker called me, Christian. Then she gathered the last bit of strength that she had, and touched the side of my face, like Kateri always did, smiled, and slowly exhaled for the last time. I was speechless, as a plethora of mixed emotions flooded my senses, and a dam of tears began to fall.

I continued holding her in my arms, now rocking, back and forth in anguish. Then I was finally able to utter the word, *"Why?"* She smiled, as

I watched the last fading light of energy leave her. I watched the energy caress the cloak that she gave me, and then it began to glow with different archaic symbols that weren't present before, or at least that I could see. I have no idea what they mean, but it didn't seem to be harming or affecting me in anyway.

I watched her quickly begin to age, hundreds of years, withering before my eyes, until she dwindled into black ash that slipped through my fingers, like dust in the wind. I stayed there on the floor staring at the debris until my last tear fell upon it. I looked up and saw the cowardly sheriff still peeping from the hole he was hiding in, as he quickly jerked back behind the wall. I'm surprised he's still alive. He witnessed the whole event.

"You can come out now sheriff." I informed him, wiping the remaining tears from my face.

He slowly emerged from behind the wall with his gun pulled out. His hands were shaking tremendously. I tried in earnest not to laugh, but couldn't help smiling. After all he just witnessed, did he really think his gun would be any type of defense? He didn't know what to make of what he saw. It was all too surreal and unbelievable for him. He was understandably scared. Who wouldn't be?

"I'm not going to harm you, sheriff. You can put the gun away."

"I don't know exactly what you are, but you're coming with me," his voice trembled, as he continued to shake while I walked towards him.

"Stop, don't take another step," he insisted, and then I disappeared into the shadows.

"I told you that I'm not here to hurt you sheriff," I said, from the shadows of the factory, as he hysterically turned in all direction, terrified of what I might do to him. He was feeling guilty about what he did.

He had no idea where my voice was coming from, as it ricocheted off walls of the barren and macabre filled factory. Each time the voice seemed to be in another direction. He quickly twisted and turned, shooting several times into empty space until I was right behind him. I grabbed his arm with the strength of a panther, took his weapon, and pushed him to the floor with a gust of wind.

"I told you I wasn't going to hurt you, but don't push me. It's been a long night, and we still have work to do." I extended my hand to help him up from the ground, and that was all I needed to confirm my suspicions of him.

I held on to his hand, tightly, as he struggled to free it. He could feel the energy surge in the form of heat, as I locked in on his dreams, and quickly picked apart what I needed from the day in question.

"I knew it was you, sheriff, I've known it was you for quite some time, but I just needed to confirm it with that handshake. No police responded for the shooting, just one FBI agent. The others came, but remained outside the door and turned around once they discovered who was involved. It was something that you were counting on; with a mob of FBI Agents in the hotel not one would lift a finger to investigate my murder after those agents died. It was the opportune moment for you to do Winchester's dirty work."

"It's nothing you can prove," he barked, and attempted to wipe the filth from the floor off his clothes.

"That's blood and guts, sheriff; it doesn't come off so easily. You have blood on your hands also, but why don't you do something good for a change, and really help a town you swore an oath to defend." I told him, and handed him back his weapon.

"You are under ..." he said, still shaking, before I quickly, yet temperately, cut him off!

"Shut up! You hear that mob outside. I need you to do your damn job! Now go out there and calm down that mob before they kill each other! I think I have a way of resolving this, but I need you to go outside and deal with that!" I demanded, angrily.

He could see the anger on my face, and had a front row seat on witnessing what I can do. Therefore, he departed without any further questions. I didn't have time for his bullshit, and needed him to buy me time.

I had to find the souls of the Dawn's People children in this factory which was once a hospital. I was certain I could find them, but I needed the sheriff to give me time. I couldn't rely on my supernatural senses or my energy crystal; it came down to me using my good old fashion human instinct, investigative techniques, and a little assistance from my panther imprinting.

My instincts led me to a creepy, decrepit set of stairs that twisted downward towards the basement. Most of the morgues and crematories were in the basements of old hospitals. I hoped that this thing was coming to an end, but this stairwell really creeped me out! I moved fastidiously down the winding stairs that never seemed to end, until I reached the bottom. It was cold and dark down here with water everywhere, and it wasn't just from the torrential storms outside. This place had been waterlogged for quite some time, judging by the water damaged walls and markings.

There was moss, several types of fungi, and slime covering the walls. There were bats hanging from poles in the ceiling, screeching, and flapping their wings upon my intrusion. There were huge sized rats that joined the hanging audible pests with squeals of their own, as they crawled on a matrix of fallen ceiling, beams, poles, and debris that wasn't submerged. A few snakes darted through the water, as I wadded through, and who knows what else lived in this cavernous dungeon ecosystem. The stringent aroma of urea was so intense that I had to tie a bandana over my nose and mouth. Once again, the clothing Kateri provided to me was useful, as she predicted.

I'm uncertain now if it was Kateri, the Aztec Goddess Tlazolteotl, Kalona Ayeliski, and Atsolowas or formerly known as the Raven Mocker that befriended me. She was as complex, and ambivalent, as I am; constantly struggling between dual personas. Asku told me it would be hard to distinguish friend from foe, but he never mentioned that it could be both. Then again, maybe that's exactly what he was trying to convey in his puzzling way.

The area beneath the hospital reminded me of the small waterways that run beneath Rome that I once visited in college. I jumped into the water, which rose to my knees in depth, and continued my search, wading through the murky waters of the cold, dark, and forsaken basement. Then I arrived at a location that was different than the others. A normal person in touch with his or her senses could tell that this place was different. My panther instinct told me that death was once present here.

It felt colder here, although it wasn't. It was just the slight supernatural energy reacting kinetically with the cilia on my body and opening my pores wider. This reaction causes it to feel colder. This is the real reason behind the myth of the air turning colder around the undead. When most people feel this sensation, they dismiss it, and label what they don't understand as being creepy. Then saw it, on the slimy, moss filled walls of the decrepit structure. There were several archaic runes written in the like the ones I saw previously throughout the factory. They were containment runes, written in ancient Sumerian cuneiform. This was most likely the place that once held the crematoria or morgue.

I searched the water filled area for something to sketch on the walls with, but couldn't find anything. Then I reflected upon the markings that revealed themselves on the coat Kateri, the Raven Mocker, gave me. It was worth a try. I recited the words of a conjuring spell, and the ancient signs and symbols reappeared and began to glow! I summoned the spirits of the dead Abenaki children.

The water began to glisten with multifarious tiny beads of bright lights, shimmering like the Sun reflecting upon the water, except there was no sunlight in this dark, cold chasm. I could feel their warm energy, as the lights rose closer to the surface, and brighten this dismal abyss.

The lights rose from the water, and filled the room like a galaxy of stars. I could feel every one of the individual souls, as their energies surrounded me, and flowed through me. It felt just like my merging with the Dawn's People, except a bit more euphoric, because all these souls were young and vibrant! I can see the attraction, and lust for such energy, and power, as my energy crystal glowed like a lighthouse beacon welcoming the arrival of the lost souls. They were finally free.

They continued their dance about the room, and embracing me, for several minutes. They were elated to be released from their prison, and showing their thanks before they gradually dissipated from the area, and once again, I was alone in the dark, cold, water filled chasm below the factory. I'm not certain where they went, but I needed to get topside, and check on the mob scene brewing outside.

As I made my way out of the dark watery tomb below, I could hear and smell the Sheriff's sinister handiwork, the singe and crackle of combustion, and the scent of smoke. Then, I could feel the heat and see the smoke, as I grew closer. The place was engulfed in flames! I guess the sheriff's fear of going to jail outweighed his civic duties to save the town or perhaps he just wanted to finally finish what he started, killing me for Boss Winchester.

I didn't have a problem with the flames; I could walk right through them, and not be scathed; naked, but unharmed. Unfortunately, my emergence would set off a plethora questions and attention that I didn't need at this point.

While I walked through the burning factory searching for an inconspicuous way out, I witnessed the debris from Kateri's corpse began to gather in a pile and mix with the ash and kindling on the floor. Then the ashes and fire particles rose into the air, suspending itself, and hovering above me. I reached out to touch the suspended debris, when suddenly it was sucked upwardly towards the burning ceiling, which consumed the surrounding air, and dispersing it until it vanished. I got the strangest feeling that this wasn't the last that I would see of the Raven Mocker.

I finally found a way out of the burning factory in the rear of the building, and made my way around to the front. The tension outside was just as heated as the flames inside. I thought the fire would help subside the conflict, but it seemed to ignite the hatred even further, seeing the factory burning. It looks like the Raven Mocker may get her wish, posthumously.

Matunaagd and the Malsum, the Abenaki men that comprised the wolf pack, were on one side, and the town's people on the other with Sheriff Meehan and Boos Winchester in the middle, inciting the mob. Then there was Agent Jackson on the side searching for a voice to be heard amongst the chaos. She spotted me before anyone else took notice and approached me.

"My God, Chris, it looks like a mediaeval witch hunt here. Are you alright?" She inquired looking at the smut on my face from the fire.

"Yes, everything is going to be fine now," I replied, in a low melancholy voice.

"Well, tell that to this mob, because World War III is about to erupt out there and back up is delayed due to flash flooding in the area. I sure could use your help," she said, anxiously.

"Well, I've done all I can do on the other side. I'm not certain what I can do with this mob, but I'll try," I replied. My opinion and voice meant even less to both sides, a biracial Native/ Black American, who didn't fit in with any of the conflicting parties, including law enforcement!

The sheriff was standing next to Boss Winchester when he gazed upon me in the distance. He looked like he'd seen a ghost. The fear in his cagey eyes was priceless, as I watched him tremble. It was a characteristic that I had seen countless times. He was experiencing what we call, Fight or Flight Syndrome, and wavering between running or pulling his gun. Then, I observed an insidious grin curl upon Boss Winchester's face. He'd intimidated enough men to know the look, as well. The puppet master was pleased with himself, and the turn of events, as the crowd turned into a raging mob! I'm certain he doesn't know it was Sheriff Meehan who set fire to his factory?

The sheriff was shaken to the point beyond reasoning. I couldn't risk his unpredictability, and killing innocents in the crossfire, therefore I shook my head to warn him, in the same manner as I did previously, when he fired at me. I could see him ruminating on what he witnessed in the factory, and his next move. He looked at Boss Winchester, and slowly shook his head, as a submission of defeat.

The grin that was pleasantly curled upon Boss Winchester's face was ironed straight by Meehan's resolve, and his appeasement was replaced with rage! Then Boss Winchester raised his weapon, but only to hear the clicking of Agent Jackson cocking her weapon directly behind him.

"I wouldn't do that if I were you," she warned Boss Winchester, as Sheriff Meehan lowered his head in shame.

The mob became further infuriated now that their leader was about to get arrested. Things just escalated to the point of being violently out of hand, as the armed crowd began threatening Agent Jackson. I sensed it wouldn't be long before the Malsum morphed, and all out carnage ensued or the Dawn's People emerge and wipe out the whole town. Perhaps, that's just what I need to happen, not the destruction of the town, but to merge with the Dawn's People one last time.

I was apprehensive about summoning them, because I didn't know what they would do. They were originally summoned to protect the Abenaki village by Chogan, so I could be calling for the immediate death of everyone in Swanton. All of this would have been for nothing if the Dawn's People slaughter the town and the Raven Mocker wins, but if I let this play out, it'll be the same result in the end. The attack on the Abenaki is an attack on Swanton. The Malsum or the Dawn's People would slaughter them all. The people of Swanton have more armed people gathered, but the odds are truly stacked against them.

I lowered my head and closed my eyes, amidst the raging crowd, and called upon the Dawn's People in a faint voice. Only Agent Jackson could hear me, besides the mob was too engaged to pay any attention to me. I could sense their energies now that the Dawn's People lifted their energy field. I was hoping that my bond with the Dawn's People would assist me in seeing the children returned and ending this fight before it started

The Chibaiskweda quickly ascended upon the rival mobs, covering the area, and taking them by surprise. The people of Swanton had no idea what was occurring. They had never seen the fog move so quickly, like it was driven with purpose. I yelled through the mist, and asked everyone to remain calm, and lower their weapons, as the town's people became edgy. I could feel the energy of the Dawn's People within the mist and quickly merged with them again and shared my thoughts. Agent Jackson quickly grabbed my hand, as she watched me go into a trance like state.

I urged the Dawn's People to release the children of Swanton, now that I had returned their children. There was some opposition in the collective, because some of the spirits had become attached to the light, as most apparition do in the darkness, but the majority agreed to allow them to depart. They knew that the children didn't belong with them.

In the thick mist, small pin sized lights appeared that grew to the size of golf balls. It kept growing throughout the mist, one by one, until they became translucent figures of bright light energy, in the size and shape of children. The mob became silent, and the people of Swanton were paralyzed with astonishment by what they were witnessing. This was nothing new for the Abenaki shape shifters, but they too admired the beauty of the soft bright lights of energy.

Everyone's weapon was lowered and no one thought of firing a shot. I was one with the Dawn's People again. I felt the children reaching out to their parents, and the parents felt their energy, as they got closer. They became more visible, and distinguishable, until all the lights had disappeared, and only the children remained standing in the middle of the road, amongst the mist, and between the rival mobs. The children were still in their pajamas, and whatever else they had on when they were abducted. The parents rushed through the mist to get their children, elated to have them safely back.

The mysterious and thick Chibaiskweda moved towards the Abenaki men, as their ancestors appeared to them. They passed through them and around them while mingling with their energies. I felt the whole thing, as a part of the collective. The town's people held on to their children tight, as we watched hundreds of apparitions, the ghosts of the Abenaki, dissipate, and the Abenaki tribes disappear with the Chibaiskweda. The town's people remained in the middle of the road in shock for several minutes hugging and questioning their children.

Everyone had tears of joy including Agent Jackson, who was hugging me, when I came out of my trance, and didn't let go. She stated that my energy crystal began shining through my coat, so she hugged me to shield it. She also stated that she felt this incredible euphoric feeling when she held me. She was feeling the residual energies I was absorbing in the crystal. It's the same euphoric energy felt during dreamscape. It made her horny in short terms. I also imparted knowledge to her about who shot me.

"Wow, that was remarkable, I see how your skills could make one a hell of an agent," she smiled.

About an hour later the FBI and the sheriff's department arrived on the scene. They were mystified at the sight of the children, and interested in the details. The Abenaki had departed by the time the FBI arrived, and Agent Jackson had already worked out the details of the case. Then just when I thought it was over, I heard the weirdest sound. It was the sound of a freight train's whistle blowing again from inside of the factory. I paused for a few seconds to see if I'd hear it again when Carolyn interrupted.

"Hey, you alright?" She asked, gently squeezing my hand.

"Yeah, I'm alright, I just thought I heard something."

"What is it?" She replied, curiously.

"Oh, it was just something I thought I heard in the factory earlier."

"You sure everything is finished in there?" She retorted with concern.

"Everything we need to be concerned about. There are still some ghosts in there, but I'll try to assist them in finding their way before I depart. Are there any trains running near here?"

"No, not for at least 20 miles. There is the old freight train that used to run to Winchester's factory, and connect with the main tracks, but that hasn't been used since the factory closed," she informed me.

"Thanks," I retorted, in a subdued tone.

"So, tell me, why is it that you're the only face here that doesn't seem happy?" She asked.

"Oh, I'm fine, I just can't believe it's over. I lost a lot on this one," I solemnly replied.

"But you also gained a lot more. You've solved the unsolvable," she said with a warm accompanying smile.

"Yeah, I guess," I retorted.

"Well, at least we have a plausible excuse for the missing women this time. We can say they were a part of a cult that abducted the missing children, and they burned in the fire," Agent Jackson suggested.

"You're getting good at this Carolyn, except no one will be looking for them. There isn't a missing persons registry for Native American Women. There has been over 500 First Nations and Metis Women that have gone missing in the past 30 years in the New England area and neighboring Canada, and no one seems to care."

"The gift and the curse, huh?" She interjected.

"Funny, but I was just thinking about someone else telling me that, not along ago," I replied with a slight smile, as she peered at me with scrutinizing eyes, and then Sheriff Meehan approached me.

After all that's taken place, it still didn't stop him from attempting to arrest me. All we could do was laugh, as he pulled out his cuffs, and began reading me the Miranda Act. Agent Jackson denied him custody over me, and arrested him on suspicions of attempted murder of a Federal Agent. She would also be opening an investigation into the sheriff's department for wrongful doings against the Abenaki and obstruction of justice charges.

Our story was that the children were kidnapped by a cult. I with the assistance of Agent Jackson infiltrated the cult at the Dame's Dance Club and tracked them to the old factory, where they were holding the children. Things got a little messy with the beheading, but no one questioned how the heads were ripped off, because the bigger and better story was the return of the mysteriously missing children, who hadn't aged. The mystery of how they were abducted remains. The cult was also blamed for the gruesome murders in the forest and for the deaths of the federal agents, and Chogan. No one wanted to keep the books open on this one and was happy to file it under the cult.

Kateri and Tahki were believed to have been abducted by the cult, but neither they nor their bodies were ever found. That remains an open cold case. I convinced Agent Jackson to back me with that story. If the town's people discovered that Kateri and Tahki were involved in any way with this investigation it would only continue the bad blood between them and the Abenaki.

Once again, I was branded a hero, and credited for finding the missing children of Swanton in the old factory, although it was the Dawn's People children that I really found there. The case was messy, like the Coyote case, and a lot of good people had died, civilians and agents. Once again, no one was banging down the door to offer me a job, but I was good with it. I had already decided that this was absolutely going to be my last job, before I returned to Cherokee, North Carolina and the Smokey Mountains Range.

There were still a lot of questions to be answered, but this time I learned from my past to keep my mouth shut, as to what really occurred. People don't really want to know the truth. They want to remain safe and feel secluded from the unknown, from what their rational minds can't explain, like the children appearing unharmed and haven't aged. That's why they look for people like me to deal with it, so they can sleep at night.

The people of Swanton now know what the Abenaki and other Native Americans have known for thousands of years; that the supernatural world does exist. My last act before leaving Swanton was to visit Mr. Winchester. I couldn't dreamscape with him because now he had placed dream catchers and other totems around his house. He was a true believer now, but I had to make sure he stayed on the right track, so shadowed myself and paid him a personal visit.

As I drove from Swanton, I was filled with a plethora of emotions. I didn't feel the energy sphere that I have grown to fear and revere, but I was satisfied in knowing that I'm taking a part of it with me. Then I observed the blackbirds, perched on a telephone line, scrutinizing my departure with those beady insidious eyes. I hoped that it was the last of my contact with them, but I knew that I would see them again, in this realm or the next.

I took pleasure in viewing the different colored leaves on the trees, signaling that autumn had arrived, but saddened by the absence of black leaves. I had developed an attraction for them, like the rare black roses of Halfeti, which reminded me of Kateri and the beautiful Mskagwedemoos. Yes, I think what I'll miss most of all, are the black leaves falling.

THE END.

THE PATHS OF VR McCOY
BY JACQUELINE TRESCOTT

We, as American readers, have enjoyed a long line of gifted writers who find new directions. What is exciting is when a writer examines old genres and takes the reader on unexpected journeys.

. As a reader who searches for new voices, especially those that take the African American experience and give you fictional wallops that you hadn't read, or thought about, I am always wishing for something more. You can settle down with a lauded writer, like Toni Morrison and Walter Mosley, and look for the literary superlatives and character surprises. But discovery of a writer who dares to try unusual storylines and presents a literary package that sings is rare indeed.

Let me introduce you to VR McCoy, who is presenting supernatural thrillers and crime thrillers, with twists that are not only the plot but the cultural innards of his work. McCoy grew up in Washington, D.C., which has been home, sometimes temporarily, to many superb authors. He attended Archbishop Carroll High School, the school of the highly popular Alex Cross/ James Patterson novels. Lastly, McCoy attended Howard University, the famed college where many of the leaders of Black Literature studied and taught. Just a few included novelist Zora Neale Hurston, poet Paul Laurence Dunbar, poet May Miller, novelist Toni Morrison, writer Amiri Baraka, poet Sterling Brown, poet Lucille Clifton, author and playwright Pearl Cleage, playwright and actor Ossie Davis and novelist Valerie Wilson Wesley. Their strong tradition of placing African American characters in central roles certainly influenced his decision to put a complex black man at the center of his work. But he has gone further blending cultural identity, history, science fiction.

This literary gumbo is sometimes called speculative fiction and is at the heart of a movement labeled and praised as Black Speculative Arts. Nothing is simplistic about the current school of black writers.

It's important to mention his literary forefathers and foremothers, those pioneers in science fiction and mystery. McCoy is heir to the work of Samuel R. Delany, Octavia Butler, Walter Mosley, and a lively group of younger voices, N.K. Jemisin and Nalo Hopkinson. Their work has gone way beyond dedicated African American readers to be acknowledged as must-read among mystery and science fiction devotees. McCoy counts himself among the readers who look for broad and excellent action, including Tom Clancy, Stephen King, as well as Patterson and Mosley.

In a tumultuous time in publishing, McCoy definitely deserves a space in the conversation about writing as social media takes over the promotion machines of legacy publishers and the methods of publishing change almost weekly. So he not only writes and thinks differently but has presented his own work through newer channels.

For the public, McCoy has created the Native Knights Collection. The first was "Shaman-The Awakening," which was a domestic and international best-seller. Here McCoy Christian Sands, an FBI agent. Naturally Sands is introduced us to tracking down a serial killer but his thought process is enabled by his ability to dreamscape. Is there truth in his dreams? Deep into this story rest the values of Native American culture. That understanding in the hands of McCoy enriches the story's action. Are those the answers in the beliefs of the Navajo Nation?

The second was "The Merchant," another domestic bestseller, set in New Orleans. The location is enough to reflect comfortably McCoy's love of history and the spirits even more interesting than the cast of characters. But J. Icarus is one to remember, as he has lived several lives and comes back in the 1920s to witness the city's growth and the development of jazz.

McCoy knows how to mix up the supernatural, the unique population and the fun always present in New Orleans.

The latest is "Shaman-The Dawn's People," now on many bookselling platforms. McCoy brings back Christian Sands, the FBI agent trying to put his life together but called back to solve another mystery. Sands, and McCoy, take a real sensibility about Native American beliefs into another compact detective story. What McCoy is saying is "let's think and write differently," and we should all be grateful he has a prime imagination and skill to take a chance and bring us along on a daring journey.

ACKNOWLEDGEMENTS

I would like to thank God (The Great Spirit) for blessing me with the opportunity to bring Christian Sands, and his world alive again. Thank you to all the fans for their love and support of the Shaman series and Native Knights Collection.

*A special thank you to **Dr. Gregory Banks, VanDaBry Lit and VanDaBry Entertainment Media** for their unending support, faith, and patience in publishing this novel. None of this could have happened without you. "I know it was like prying teeth at times, but thanks, Nupe."*

Thank you to my VanDaBry Posse: John Townsend, Kai Shanklin, Donna McGregor-Hall, Tommy Taylor Jr. and Fatina Smith

*Special Thank you to **Ms. Jacqueline Trescott** ~ I appreciate your patience, arduous work, diligence, and professionalism. Your input was invaluable to the completion of this project. I look forward to working with you in the future, my friend.*

*Thank you to **Debbie and Lauren at The Cover Collection** for providing the beautiful covers for my novels and putting up with all my *&%#. Thanks for your patience and ability to transfer my visions into art. http://www.thecovercollection.com*

*Thank you to **Evander Banks** "Ecko" for providing the exquisite artwork for the VanDayBry Lit Brand and artistic contributions.*

Thank you to my family for always giving me 100 percent in my dreams and efforts, no matter where they may lead me.

Shout out to my number one fan, **Talayah C. McCoy.** *Luv ya.*

Thank you to the **First Nations of North America** *and special shout out to the* **Black Cherokee Freedmen, Cherokee and Abenaki People.**

Shout out to the following organizations:

VanDaBry Entertainment and Media LLC., Kappa Alpha Psi Fraternity, Prince Hall Free Masons, Reading Is Fundamental, Black Lives Matter, Freedman Rights Association, Descendants of Freedmen Association, African Indian Foundation and Native American Rights Foundation.

Ms. Dimplezz at Nappy Roots Studio *in Union City, Georgia.*

VANDABRY MEDIA

Facebook: https://www.facebook.com/vandabry
Twitter: https://twitter.com/Vandabry
Instagram: https://www.instagram.com/vandabry
Website: VanDaBry, LLC VanDaBry.com

VR McCOY

Twitter: https://twitter.com/VRMcCoy
Facebook: https://www.facebook.com/vrmccoy
and https://www.facebook.com/reggie.mccoy.79
Instagram: https://www.instagram.com/VR_McCoy
Amazon Author Page: ViewAuthor.at/VRMcCoyBooks
LinkedIn: https://www.linkedin.com/in/vr-mccoy-0a606a74
Website: http://vrmccoy.wixsite.com/author
Google Plus: https://plus.google.com/+VRMcCoy
Google Plus: https://plus.google.com/communities/113020098479460168874
Goodreads: http://www.goodreads.com/author/show/7102759.V_R_McCoy

DEDICATION

I would like to dedicate this novel to all those who stand up against tyranny, prejudice, racism, and indifferences in the world.

The Cherokee Freedmen, *and other numerous Freedmen Tribes, who are still fighting to be acknowledged by the Dawes Rolls Act (List), continue the good fight!*

Ms. Natosha Tonya Mahoney (R.I.P) *~ I will always love you.*

Until we, as a people, realize that the word "RACE" itself denotes a competition; in this case; the immoral pitting and demarcation of two or more people against each other, because they don't share similar phenotype traits; we cannot truly place ourselves above the apes or other simple-minded animals fighting for scraps in the jungle. Why must I identify my skin color on forms and applications for housing, jobs, schools, loans etc...? I will not identify or dignify this madness any longer. I'm proud of my heritage, but when asked what Race I belong, I will simply state; the human race, and anything else should fall short of that, feel me? Peace

NOTE FROM THE AUTHOR

*Chapter 18 contains several **bold italicized words.** These words are a montage of songs by George Michaels. It was kind of wild, but I was listening to his Christmas song when I heard the news of his passing. I was a fan and listened to his music regularly. His music was soulful, and helped me greatly. Thank you and Rest in Peace.*

MY GEORGE MICHAELS SONG LIST:

Jesus to a Child, To be Forgiven, Move On, Fast love, Round Here, Moment with You, Like a Baby, The Strangest Thing, Though, Older, Free, Spinning the Wheel, You have been loved, It doesn't really Matter, A Different Corner, Father Figure, and Careless Whispers

VR McCOY